KU-524-591

PATRICK GALE

FACING

THE

TANK

TINDER
PRESS

First published in Great Britain by Hutchinson in 1988.

First published in this paperback edition in 2018 by Tinder Press
An imprint of HEADLINE PUBLISHING GROUP

1

Cataloguing in Publication Data is available from the British Library

ISBN 978 1 4722 5554 9

Typeset in Sabon 10.5/14.55 pt by Jouve (UK), Milton Keynes

Printed and bound in Great Britain by Clays Ltd, Elcograf S.p.A.

HEADLINE PUBLISHING GROUP
An Hachette UK Company
Carmelite House
50 Victoria Embankment
London EC4Y 0DZ

www.tinderpress.co.uk
www.headline.co.uk
www.hachette.co.uk

Patrick Gale was born on the Isle of Wight. He spent his infancy at Wandsworth Prison, which his father governed, then grew up in Winchester before going to Oxford University. He now lives on a farm near Land's End. One of this country's best-loved novelists, his most recent works are *A Perfectly Good Man,* the Richard and Judy bestseller *Notes from an Exhibition,* and the bestselling *A Place Called Winter.*

Praise for *Facing the Tank*:

'Gale is intoxicated with words and feeds upon them with a kind of manic relish . . . The sheer funniness of *Facing the Tank* made me laugh out loud. Its optimism delighted me' *Sunday Times*

'Gale speedily unleashes his merrily black mischief. The uncovering of the sadness behind the doilies and twinsets is in the best tradition of black humour' *Observer*

'A commendably intelligent, entertaining and moving novel' *TLS*

'Original and amusing. An elegant, witty writer with an engagingly bizarre imagination. Patrick Gale writes with great zest. I kept on reading because I was perpetually astonished to find what Mr Gale had thought up next' *Sunday Telegraph*

'The first thing that catches the attention about Patrick Gale is a sardonic eye, an engagingly leery way of looking at life, or the half-life he has chosen as his base in *Facing the Tank*. It's as though *Cold Comfort Farm* had called in the interior decorators' *Guardian*

'Gale has a fondness for his characters and a deep tolerance of their foibles which shines through his writing. *Facing the Tank* is a potent brew . . . Assured and immensely enjoyable' *Gay Times*

'If you can imagine a cross of *Barchester Towers* and *Rosemary's Baby* as written by Muriel Spark, you may have some idea of what you'll be

527 833 46 8

By Patrick Gale and available from Tinder Press

For two very dear, long-suffering parents

And I saw a new Heaven and a new Earth, for the first Heaven and the first Earth were passed away; and there was no more sea ... And God shall wipe away all tears from their eyes; and there shall be no more death, neither sorrow, nor crying, neither shall there be any more pain: for the former things are passed away.

Revelations XXI

Blessed are they that do his commandments, that they may have right to the tree of life, and may enter in through the gates into the city. For without are dogs, and sorcerers, and whoremongers, and murderers, and idolaters, and whosoever loveth and maketh a lie.

Revelations XXII

Evan was working at seat G16 at one of the long desks that radiated from the heart of the reading room. Before him was a pile of books, to one side a copy of *The New Yorker*, a packet of Winstons and a sheaf of book demand slips blank save for the boxes already filled with 'G16' and 'Evan J. Kirby'. The J stood for Joseph, his father's name. He always took G16 because G15 was always taken by a woman with astonishing hair that fell in sheeny black waves to the small of her back. She called herself, 'Cooper, Prof. C.J.' and she had spent the past two months reading up on ancient death cults of the Middle East and the Nile Delta. They had never spoken. She did not smoke so it was impossible to follow her to the portico for nicotine breaks and she never seemed to take lunch. Evan arrived minutes before opening time so was always sure of securing G16. Cooper, Prof. C.J. arrived at about ten and always stayed on past Evan's breaking point. Even if she drifted in towards eleven, G15 remained uncannily vacant for her. They would never speak and he rarely saw her face (which, indeed, was less exciting than her hair) but he sensed that if some M.A. upstart or theological harridan were to approach G15 before her arrival he would feel compelled to apologize and say that it was already taken. He might even say it was taken by his wife.

He still wore a wedding ring; a plain band of gold whose

inside surface was filled with 'Evan and Miriam and' to ghastly perpetuity.

Cooper, Prof. C.J. sat in G15 now. When he had returned from his elevenses, which had turned into lunch because of *The New Yorker*, she had been there poring over a small pigskin-bound volume that looked as though its pages would smell bad, and she had not moved for three and a half hours. Unless, that was, she leaped from her seat whenever he left for a smoke. But no, that thought smacked of the obsessive and he was not the obsessive type.

Without taking his eye from the page, he reached a hand into a jacket pocket and brought out a mint imperial which he slid furtively to his mouth. Mints were meant to take his mind off smoking and cut down the tobacco breaks to once an hour, only he was not sure whether they counted as 'food' and were therefore illicit in the reading room. Sometimes they worked wonders. Sometimes they only caused a dull ache in his more receded gums.

He took up his pen now and copied a passage from the book before him, checking the spine for the date and volume number.

'*Psychic Journal* 1921,' he wrote. 'Vol. 15. Letter from Mrs Vaux of Wilton, Wilts. "In November 1908 I was staying with my cousin the Bishop of Barrowcester. I was sleeping with Miss V. S. when I suddenly saw a tall white figure sweep through the bedroom from the door to the open casement. It was only hazy in outline and was gone in a second or two. I was beside myself with terror and called out at once, 'Did you see that?' and at the exact same moment my companion, Miss V. S. exclaimed, 'Did you hear that?' Then I declared, 'I saw an Angel sweeping through the air,' and she replied, 'I heard an Angel's song.' We were both much afraid but said nothing of this matter to anyone. Miss V. S. has now passed over to the other side to join my late husband." '

Finishing, Evan set down his pen, flipped to the next page and cracked his knuckles. He glanced at Cooper, Prof. C.J. She was so intent that she had let her hair slip round into a curtain across her forehead. He wondered how she could see to read. Perhaps she was dozing; the library was dotted with people who had acquired the skill of dozing in a studious position. His eyes roamed up to the dome and across to the clock. It was nearly time for his teatime Winston. He watched as a young librarian emerged on to the upper gallery from a door that was disguised as a bookcase. He watched him walk half way round the circle of wall then, with two books under one arm, stretch on a stool to push a third book into a high shelf. He was pushing from too low a point on its spine and Evan was not suprised to see it topple back out of his grip. The librarian looked young enough to forget where he was and swear loudly, but if he did so his voice was swallowed by the dome. The book struck him a glancing blow on the shoulder, bounced off the gallery railing and flew out into the abyss, scattering pages in its wake. The librarian fled blame through another secret door. One reader jumped up to avoid being hit but most continued their work undisturbed. A few then reacted in slow motion, dulled by hours of rustling papers, distant gurney wheels and dully echoed thuds of giant indices. When the book crashed innocently on an empty desk, these stared first in the direction of the noise then peered up at the flock of sheets making a slower descent on the currents of body heat and yawn. Somebody chuckled and was silenced by shushing.

Evan rose, scooping up his cigarettes. The mint imperial had worn off and the room had begun to feel submarinely quiet and slow. He changed his mind five yards from G16 and returned to pick up his books and file. Cooper, Prof. C.J. did not look up. Perhaps she was asleep. Perhaps she was dead. Evan waited for the man at the desk for surnames G to M to check that he had handed in everything he had taken out. It had not been a productive day. The bulk of his text was ready but, while waiting for his agent to fix up a trip to some ancient libraries in the Midlands, he was meant to be checking through the bibliography and quotations. The latter tended to be such fun that he kept being sidetracked and would spend half an hour or more dipping into irrelevant correspondence or journalism. An hour after lunch had been squandered on a romance called *Wings of Flame* by 'A Member of His Majesty's Armed Forces' that was sent to his desk because of a misread catalogue number. It had turned out to be the story of a nurse who fell in love with an RAF pilot after he lost his sight and could not see that she wore a built-up shoe. The thought of disability made Evan queasy and it was only this that had caused him to toss the novel aside in embarrassed disgust rather than relish it to the end.

He strode out via the readers-only Gents, throwing a twinkle to his favourite black security guard whose elaborate coiffure lifted her uniform cap two inches off her forehead. Out in the fresher air he smoked two Winstons in quick succession with the other reading-room refugees then, packet in hand, he left the striped sunshine of the portico and headed after the first of the two buses that would take him back to the Booths's flat in Notting Hill.

Will Booth was an historian friend from Evan's doctorate days in Boston who had married a British girl, taken a job at London University and settled off Ladbroke Grove. Evan had given them the keys to his cottage in Vermont in exchange for the use of their flat so that he might spend the spring in England finishing his new book. This was a study of Paradise legends that would provide a companion piece to his surprisingly successful investigation of the concept of Hell. It was also a good excuse to stay away from America, which he was coming to mistrust, and out of the territories of his estranged wife, Miriam, whose influence he was trying to slough off. It was thanks to Miriam that he now had great difficulty in smoking or eating in the street or in putting more than one artificial sweetener in his coffee.

Rocking in the top of a number 12 from Oxford Circus, he lit another Winston then waved his travel pass at the conductor. The photograph was far from flattering. It had been said that his looks faintly echoed Gary Cooper but photo booths made him look more like a tired, cocaine-blasted airline pilot.

As the man beside him rose to leave, Evan had to rise slightly too because he was sitting on the man's coat, then he felt in his breast pocket for the letter from his lawyers in Boston. He had read the front and the back of the envelope several times since breakfast, he had even begun to open it with a knife in the greasy spoon where he had spent the elevenses that had turned into lunch. Now however he had read *The New Yorker* from cover to cover and had twenty minutes on a bus with nothing to do but take out the letter and, as the Brits said, face the music.

They met at one of his mother's interminable bridge evenings when he was thirty-five and Miriam was thirty. He rented a flat on the other side of Boston but six times a month he put on a tie, splashed on whatever aftershave Mother had given him that Christmas and rode a bus out to her fat house in Back Bay. Four times out of six this was for Sunday lunch where he would meet his younger sister, smug brother-in-law and brutal nephews and would eat enough to keep him going on Graham crackers and peanut butter for the next six days. The other two times, in part payment for the Sunday lunches, were to put in a welcome bachelor appearance at Mother's bridge evenings. There was never more than one game in evidence and that was invariably played by Mother, a fourth-generation rag-trade widow from next door, a distinguished but silent man they called the Commander and pallid young Mr Trudeau who did not seem to work and, like Evan, was a bachelor.

'With Evan,' Mother would say, 'it's just a matter of time. With young Mr Trudeau' (it had always been *young* Mr Trudeau – it probably still was) 'with young Mr Trudeau,' she would say, 'I think it's sort of a confirmed thing.'

Mother thought bridge conferred a gracious status on her evenings but she was forever interrupting the game to yell a greeting at a new arrival or to hiss polite requests to Mona Mae, the coloured maid she hired for the occasions and instructed to act 'in residence'.

There were usually ten or so guests besides the three bridge players and these quickly learned to fend for themselves without the manipulation of an active hostess. Evan's sister rarely came. The unspoken understanding was that it was Evan's duty to do so to 'keep up his side' in the struggle to find him a wife. Being thoroughly uninterested, Evan allowed it to be assumed that he was a bachelor of the helpless variety, although he was quite content with Graham crackers, peanut butter and the occasional invitation to dinner from a fellow academic's wife. He had been known to spread the peanut butter with jam or to scatter it with chopped tomato and once in a while he bought a family-size pizza which would lie conveniently to hand on a bookshelf and be eaten in slow, cold slices. The faculty women were either old enough to play bridge with Mother or, if single, loud and intimidating. There was rarely more temptation on offer at the fat house in Back Bay. Then he met Miriam. She was out on the porch sipping her mint julep (it was heat-hazy July) and being talked at by a woman in huge round tortoiseshell spectacles. He remembered the detail about the spectacles because two years after their marriage she had insisted on buying some like them. He had crept out hoping for a little peace and had forgotten he was still obediently clutching a plate of stuffed eggs.

'Gee thanks,' Miriam said and took one.

She was five foot five with a heart-shaped face, honey-blonde hair and the kind of thinness that screamed nerves at anyone within a four-yard radius. A titless rake. She had smiled full in his face and everything had changed. After what in retrospect was an astonishingly naive courtship, though with little more than the usual diplomatic deceit on the woman's part and an immoderate element of belated adolescence on the man's, they had a curt white wedding in the university chapel followed by a fairly delirious fortnight in Paris. Miriam had never been to Europe and Evan had never gone accompanied to bed, hence the measure of delirium. Then they moved into his flat and everything changed again. Miriam had not been to college and grew quickly impatient with the fact that Evan still had not left his at thirty-five. However hard he tried to explain that research with a little teaching could be a profitable end in itself, she persisted in the belief that he had somehow failed his first degree or had been left behind to iron out some minor problems so that he could 'leave school' like everybody else. She had moved straight from high school to work in a real estate business which, by the time she took a stuffed egg off Evan, she was almost running single-handed. As she set about trying to tidy Evan's work into the corner behind the new Regency television one week and the next throwing awesomely engineered dinner parties for faculty members in an effort to help him to 'get on', he realized that he did not know why she had married him. He had only found the courage to put to her this question ten or fifteen years later, by which time she had set up her own real estate firm using his money, had enjoyed several flagrant affairs and had started hiring a coloured maid for dinner parties.

'Well, I didn't take you on to have kids, honey,' she replied, ''cause it didn't take long to find out you were *incapable* in that department. I guess it was because you were a pushover. A rich, virgin pushover.'

To the relief of the faculty wives, among whom Miriam had rarely deigned to mix, Evan left her. To their chagrin he also resigned all but his honorary post and left with his books for his cottage in picturesque Nowhere, Vermont. Here he started writing a book about eternal punishment. There was a general store in Nowhere, Vermont which gladly delivered cigarettes, Graham crackers, peanut butter and deep-frozen pizza. There Evan led a pleasant existence, broken pleasantly by trips to New York, where he revived old friendships and then increasingly to London, where he made new ones. With the help of agents in each capital he began to do comfortable, tasteful things like give lecture series and speak on the radio. After keeping blissfully silent for months, with the help of hard work and one Huby Stokes traced by Evan's mother, Miriam sued for divorce. Ever since the launch of the book on Hell she had been muddying his complacent pool with questions of money and maintenance. His mother had begged him to sue her at the outset of their separation on grounds of infidelities and (Mother being ignorant of her son's incapacity) her refusal to start a family, however he still bore his wife an ounce or two of misplaced sympathy and ten years of her shrill get-up-and-go dogmatism had brainwashed him into feeling the guilty party. Now she had taken the initiative on grounds of desertion and irreparable breakdown of marriage. She had founded most of her real estate firm in her simple sister's name, blinding Evan with jabber of tax evasion. Only now, with a lawyer's help, had he come to see that this had been insurance against the day when one of them chose to bolt.

As the bus lurched towards Notting Hill Gate, Evan clutched the letter and pulled out his glasses so that he could read it without holding it at arm's length. He forgot to light another Winston and he almost smiled. Everything was settled. Miriam was going to rob him of only half what he thought she thought she could get. As of Tuesday week he would be a free man. Sweet L.I.B.E.R.T.Y. was his. As if carried away by sympathetic excitement, Evan's lawyer polished off the letter with an unprofessional flourish of news about his wife and family. Marni was well, Sal came tenth in the junior marathon and little Kim had just had the braces taken off her teeth.

'God bless them all,' thought Evan, bounding down the stairs as the bus stopped by the Coronet cinema, 'and I bet Kim looks swell.'

He dived into a cake shop and emerged with a bag of chocolate fudge brownies. Heading down Kensington Park Gardens he bought a *Standard* and two bunches of anemones. He liked anemones because they looked dead until one gave them something to drink. He liked the deep colours as they revived. Miriam had liked dried flowers, often spraying them with gold or silver paint. She had liked the way they lasted. The flat, and then the house where she had insisted they move, had crackled with their spidery shapes. They would catch on his cardigan sleeves as he passed by and he would relax on a sofa only to have them rustle in his ear.

Two little girls slid past on roller skates, attached by headphones to the same Walkman. A woman who had to jump out of the way with her shopping bags appealed for support in her wrath but he was smiling and eating chocolate fudge brownies in the street so she turned elsewhere, doubly indignant.

The Booths's flat lay on the first floor of one of the high

white terraces that swing out on either side of Ladbroke Grove. It faced south over an attractively undercultivated park that one could reach from a spiral staircase off the living room balcony. Evan threw open the balcony windows as he came in, letting in new-mown grass to fight with last night's tobacco smoke. He flung himself full length on the sofa – he was very tall, so this involved resting his feet on an adjacent table – and stared up into the sunshot greens of the chestnut trees. He had eaten one brownie too many and was dizzied with sweetness. Euphoria had evaporated with his hunger.

Freedom. As Miriam would have said, whoopee shit. He was in his middling forties and he had never had an affair. He couldn't drive and tried to avoid air travel. Try as he might he could not grow a paunch and he remained firmly what his English agent, Jeremy called 'coincé heterosexual'. What price freedom? Evan picked up the *Standard* to ogle a spread of skinny models flaunting 'this summer's look', but it was hard to read it lying down so he soon let it fall. The telephone rang. It was Jeremy.

Though arguably *coincé*, Jeremy was no longer heterosexual. Following certain discoveries regarding the frequency of his trips to the family's vet, his wife had divorced him. She had kept the children. The dog and Jeremy now lived with said vet in a state of seamless domesticity that varied only from his former married bliss in its higher joint income and more fashionable cookery. For all the disparity in their ages, Jeremy contrived to treat Evan as a kind aunt might an eccentric child.

'Evan, I've fixed up Brooster for you.'

'Where?'

'Barrowcester to you but it's pronounced like rooster with a b on the front. The inhabitants are called Barrowers though which you pronounce as spelt.'

'How do I get there?'

'Express-ish train from King's Cross and it takes two hours plus. Now let me check that I've got this right. You wanted to use both the cathedral and the school libraries, yes?'

'That's right.'

'Super. Well I've spoken to the Dean who says you'll have the run of the library and can photograph anything you like as long as they get an acknowledgement – we'd send them a signed copy obviously – and I've been on to the headmaster of Tatham's – only they call him the Lord – and he says that's fine there too only you had better talk to the librarian about photographs. Have I done well?'

'You have, Jerry.'

'Now I must hurry but I want to take you out to lunch tomorrow. How about Manzi's at quarter to?'

'Great.'

'Now Deb's made arrangements for where you can stay so can I hand you over to her?'

'By all means.'

'Such a shame she's not available. We *must* find you someone else and have you and whoever to supper soon.'

'See you at Manzi's, Jerry.'

'Bye.'

There was a pause as Jeremy pressed buttons then Deborah came on the line. Of his team of beautiful assistants, Deborah was Evan's favourite because she had wavy raven hair and was extraordinarily capable. She also had the kind of husky telephone manner that could dissolve tiresome contracts and double advances.

As she said 'Hi,' Evan could picture the loose cream cotton and the pearls at her throat and forgot about brownie sickness. 'How's Notting Hill?' she asked.

'Full of rotting fruit skins and old Colonel Sanders boxes. How's Bloomsbury?'

'Sticky. Now look.'

'I love it when you're masterful.'

'Don't be playful, Evan, I'm holding the fort and I haven't got time.'

'Sorry.'

'Not at all.' She chuckled slowly and he crossed his legs. 'I've found you lovely lodgings in Barrowcester.'

'Is it really pronounced like that?'

'Yes.'

'Why?'

'This is England. There's a very motherly landlady who'll do you a power of good and cook for you and the house is pretty and old. It's right in the thick of things so you won't have far to walk.'

'I think I love you, Deborah.'

'Do you want to go tomorrow evening or have you still got work at the B.L.?'

'Sod the B.L. Sorry.'

'That's quite all right.'

'No. I've finished there, but I've got to do dull things like wait for dry cleaning and hand over keys to the girl who'll feed the parrot. I'll catch the train on Sunday afternoon.'

'Well, make sure you're at the station on time. I know how unpunctual you are. There's a train on Sunday at five.'

'Yes sir.'

'Ssh. And I'll give names and addresses to Jeremy to hand over to you at lunch tomorrow.'

'Good thinking, Batman.'

'Now I must go. Have a good trip. It's a beautiful place. Very quiet. Jeremy has a cousin there so you must be sure to ask him for her address.'

'Will do.'

'Goodbye.'

'Bye Debs, and thank you.'

'Not at all.'

Without leaving the sofa Evan replaced the receiver and stretched up to the bookcase for a copy of *English Cathedral Towns*. So far Barrowcester had only been a name on library catalogues and bibliographical cross references. He reached behind him to switch on a light and settled down with an ill-advised third brownie to read about the place.

2

Emma glanced at her watch. It was twelve-fifteen. The room before her was full of small boys drawing. She had cheated this morning. She had meant to quiz them on the journeys of Saint Paul but one sight of their unscored little faces had changed her mind. They wanted nothing to do with the ceaseless meanderings of that crazed bigot and she had no desire to force him on them.

'Do you want to hear a *really* bloodthirsty story?' she had asked.

'Yes please, Miss.'

'Excuse me, Miss?'

'Yes, James?'

'I thought we were going to do Saint Paul.'

'Ssh!' said one boy.

'Sneak!' snapped a second.

'Do you like Saint Paul, James?' she asked.

'Well . . .' James looked uncomfortable. 'Not much.'

There was laughter at which she smiled.

'You'll have to know all about him one day,' she said, 'but today it's Saturday and it's so sunny and the birds are singing and the flowers are out so I thought . . .' She paused in her walking to pick up a small boy's rude drawing, which she frowned at and crumpled in her palm. 'I thought we should listen to a *really* bloodthirsty story.'

There was more laughter. Blue eyes shining, cheeks

radiating health, Emma sat on the front of her desk and read them the story of Jael, Sisera and the tent-peg. Their delight at the description of supper in a lordly dish and brains spilt on sand was her delight and she capped it by letting them spend the last half of the lesson drawing an illustration to the grisly tale.

'Right,' she now said, 'time for your lunch.' There was a wild opening and slamming shut of desk-lids and a buzz of released conversation. 'Wait a minute, wait a minute.' Loving her, they were still at once. 'Put your nasty drawings on my desk and I'll put the best, nastiest ones on the wall for everyone to laugh at.' They hurried forward and slammed gory picture after gory picture beside her. 'And next time,' she shouted over the hubbub, 'it'll *have* to be Saint Paul.'

There were groans and they were gone. She gathered the drawings into a pile which she locked in her desk. As she walked down the battered parquet corridor to the playground and freedom, she could hear the dim murmur of,

'Oh Lord, the Giver of Bounty, bless this food for ourselves and ourselves for Thy service. Amen,' and the appalling clatter of benches being clambered over and plates being slung along tables as Junior Lunch started.

The choir school was little, fleshing out its income and classes by taking in a few day boys as well as the twenty-six choristers. The standard of everything except music was cheerfully low, but the cachet of the place as an accepted springboard into Tatham's was such that parents of unmusical sons continued to fork out inflated sums to send their children there. Emma's qualification for teaching Divinity was less her history degree than the fact that her late father used to be Dean. The head of English had come there to teach the 'cello once and had somehow taken over the English department during an epidemic of gastric flu. The French master was distinctly Dutch, although no one but Emma seemed impolite enough to have noticed. Anyone in the area with a Latin degree had been lured away by the house that came, along with better pay, with a job at Tatham's, so what Classics the little boys gleaned had been gathered in a team effort from the staff's school-day memories. A well-thumbed copy of Kennedy's *Latin Primer* was kept on a string by the kettle in the common room, the idea being to stay one lesson ahead of one's class. Emma heard James Rees (Forestry degree) leading a senior class in their declension of an irregular verb as she mounted her bicycle and rode out into the Close. The lawns were covered with families in their Sunday best because the city schools' confirmation service had just finished.

Her father's house stood on the corner of Dimity and Tatham Streets in an overstocked, walled garden. He had died five years ago leaving a twenty-two-year-old Emma sole heir, but it was still very much his house. He had retired there from the Deanery when Emma was just start-ing at Tatham's. An historian who was also a priest, the ex-Dean had brought his history to the fore once more. He dedicated the eight years he spent in the house before his death to writing a double biography of Thomas More and Cardinal Wolsey. The book, *Disparate Men*, had been a posthumous steady seller, not least in Barrowcester where Dyce-Hamilton's discovery of an unlikely friendship between Tatham and Wolsey was a matter for some concern.

The late Dean was regarded as having been a fair and

noble one, not only in his policy of non-interference but also in his adoption of the baby Emma. He had married late, to general rejoicing and, his wife being well past a safe child-bearing age, they filed for adoption and were granted a baby girl. Mrs Dyce-Hamilton died of cancer all too soon after Emma's arrival, to general despair, and although a nanny had to be found, the care of the child was taken on whenever possible by her late-middle-aged father. As soon as she was old enough to sit still and silent on a grown-up chair, she was led by him to services in the Cathedral – hence her dispassionate but extensive knowledge of the Scriptures. The sight of him walking patiently slowly with her hand in his and, later, of them walking arm in arm, she now patiently slow, was one dear to the hearts of the diocese. She attended a local day school, but it was his careful coaching that had seen her through the Tatham's entrance exam at thirteen. Once he had retired and begun work in earnest on *Disparate Men* she repaid the favour by devoting many of her weekends to helping him track down passages and, as the work grew, to typing up finished chapters. Then as now, Emma felt herself marked out by the other Barrowers as A Faithful Daughter Old Before Her Time.

Dyce-Hamilton smoked to jubilant excess and had received several cautions from Dr Morton so the news that he was dying of lung cancer had caused his daughter little shock. Hurrying home from Edinburgh, Emma saw him through the last disgusting stages of his affliction, seeing the good doctor to and from the front door via the occasional glass of sherry, and dodging downstairs to the telephone each evening to receive chatty and irrelevant messages from university friends. She had brought her work home with her and studied at his bedside, sometimes holding one-way conversations on her topics. He was forbidden to talk much, was indeed incapable of doing so without inducing violent coughing fits, but he could scribble on a pad and would insist on interrupting from time to time to correct or expand a point or to direct her to a source she had perhaps ignored.

He died, not peacefully but fast, one morning after breakfast, while she was reading him the morning's news. It was a characteristically considerate time to die. She returned to Edinburgh to sit her finals in a numb fog, seeing few and speaking to less, then slipped back to Barrowcester so as to be about her father's posthumous business. She was awarded a respectable two-one in one city and a rush of love and support in the other.

Five years had passed but Emma could not leave. She had tried. She had taken weekends off to visit friends in their unappetizing bedsits in London. Said friends had descended on her or bombarded her with letters, demanding her immediate removal to the capital and even offering to find her somewhere to live. He had not left her badly off, and since new fast trains drawing it into the commuter town bracket had sent Barrowcester's property prices soaring, she could have bought a two-bedroom flat in Clapham on the proceeds of her father's house. But she couldn't leave, and Barrowcester was not going to let her go. In letters to supportive friends she made lists that set the reasons for her leaving against those for her staying put. She was attached to the house. She loved the garden. She liked Barrowcester well enough – certainly more than filthy London – but found it painfully small. Most of the time she wanted to hate the Barrowers, but this was rarely as easy as it sounded. They were civilized, kind, amusing and often intelligent. Her spurts of rage against their frequent narrowness of outlook were extinguished by her depressing realization that they were as incapable of broadening their horizons as she of leaving. Sometimes she would weep, get drunk on sherry, break something beautiful and storm around the house, furious at the futile job she had drifted into, loathing the gardening she had started to enjoy so much, determined not to be branded as yet another Barrower maiden of certain age. Then she would flop exhausted on a sofa and see two thrushes or a chaffinch in the garden, or hear kind laughter from the street, or a splash of harpsichord music from Dr Feltram's house next door, and she would moan as the sedation of place soothed her pumping thoughts.

Emma paused on her way through the garden to wind some trailing wisteria back into its wire arch, then left her bicycle by the porch. The telephone was ringing as she let herself in. It was Lydia Hart.

'Lydia. How lovely,' Emma said. 'How are you? Were you at the eight o'clock, this morning?'

'No. I overslept.'

'I couldn't make it either. Some days it's so hard to get up. How's Clive?'

'Fine.'

'And Tobit?'

'Fine too. Working hard as ever. His dresses are a great success. There was something in the *Standard* yesterday; you know the sort of thing – models showing them off – this summer's look. Very good publicity.'

'Good for him,' said Emma, who had sat down and was holding the receiver under her chin while she used her hands to pull off her sensible shoes and massage an ache in her feet. 'When's he coming home again?'

'God knows. I try not to ask. Being a mother gets awfully hard when they've just left home.'

'I wouldn't know.'

Lydia laughed politely at the other end.

'That reminds me,' she went on, 'can you manage supper one night soon?'

'What fun. Yes. Every night but tonight.' Emma was doing nothing tonight either, but there was a serial she wanted to watch. Keeping up to date with serials, along with enjoying the garden, was one of the activities whose increasing importance in her life was so abhorred.

'Do you know Fergus Gibson? I thought I might ask him?'

'Which is he?'

'The rather nice Scotsman who lives in the big house at our end of Tracer Lane.'

'No. I don't think we've met. What's he do?'

'You've probably seen him around. Awfully handsome. He runs an interiors firm. He's just redone a manor house out towards Clough – it was in *The Barrower* last Friday – and he completely redid Mrs Chattock's flat at the Palace. He prettied up our extension for me, too.'

'Oh. I remember something . . . yes.'

'And I'm feeling rather sorry for him because his business partner died last year, which must mean an awful lot more work and, as if that wasn't enough, his elderly mother has become bedridden and he refuses to let anyone . . .' Here Lydia's voice trailed off slightly. 'Help him with her.'

'Maybe I can persuade him to redecorate here,' said Emma, helping her out.

'What a *marvellous* idea! Not that it needs it exactly but, well ... You must suggest it when you both meet,' Lydia enthused. 'Now I must dash up and see how the girls are getting on. There are two new Saturday ones in the shop and they're little more than children.'

'Oh dear,' said Emma, trying to put back on a shoe and dropping it. 'About supper; when shall I come?'

'Oh!' Lydia laughed. 'Silly me. Yes. How about next Friday?'

'That would be fine. Eightish?'

'Perfect.'

'How nice. Bye Lydia.'

'Bye.'

Emma hung up the receiver, scribbled 'Harts, supper' in her diary on Friday next then stood, shoes in hand. She wandered in stockinged feet across the hall and into the sitting room. She stood on the threshold and gazed about her. The ceiling had been white once, but was yellowed like most of them with her father's tobacco smoke. The walls were painted a toneless caramel and the curtains were drab old things that had come from many years' service at the Deanery. There were a few good rugs, but the carpet was stained and threadbare. She suspected there were boards underneath that could be cleaned and polished. It would do no harm to try. She had no idea how much such services cost but, if she were ever to sell the house it would raise the value considerably if it could be advertised as an 'interior designed' one.

She sat down in the hall again and took up the telephone

directory. She turned to G for Gibson and found several which looked like private people then saw,

'GIBSON, Drinkwater &, Dsgn Cnsltnts, 3 Tracer Lane, Bwstr.'

She dialled the number given, waited and got an answering machine. This panicked her so she replaced the receiver, scribbled her message on a notepad then rang back. To her surprise someone picked up the receiver at the other end half way through the machine's recital and a soft Scots voice said,

'Good morning?'

'Oh. Is that . . .' Emma glanced towards the phone book but it had slipped shut.

'Drinkwater and Gibson Consultants?' There was a chuckle in his voice.

'Er. Yes.'

''Tis they speaking. How can I help?'

'My name's Emma Hamilton. I was wondering about doing up my house. What normally happens? Do you come round for a look or do I come round to you?'

'I come round for a look.'

'Sorry. Is that Mr Gibson?'

'Yes.'

'Ah. I think we've been invited to the same dinner party on Friday.'

'So you're Emma *Dyce*-Hamilton.'

'That's right. As opposed to Nelson's bit of fluff.'

He laughed.

'Well Friday's some way off. Shall I come round this afternoon?'

'No. Better not. I've got to go out.' She had to do some housework.

'How about Monday. After lunch?'

'Two-thirty?'

'Lovely.'

'I'll see you then, then.'

'Yes.'

'Goodbye, Miss Hamilton.'

'Bye.'

She replaced the receiver. Dr Feltram was playing the harpsichord next door. Emma slid the directory back into the hall bookcase and walked, whistling, to the cupboard under the stairs to find the Hoover. She would start at the bottom and work up.

3

They had left his trunk and strong box by the mountain of luggage that the porters were slowly dismantling, then they had taken a quick, discouraging glance at his dormitory and a slightly more cheering tour of the sitting room that was to be his *burrow*. A cup of stewed tea and a fondant fancy had followed with the *Lord*, the Master of Scholars and two keen, unmotherly wives. Crispin was the only new scholar this term. The others who had passed the fiendish entrance exam that spring would not arrive until September. Crispin's mother had told him that Tatham's wanted him earlier because he was so clever, but he had recently taken to sitting on the stairs when his parents thought he was in bed and so knew otherwise. The Governing Body were making an exception in his case because his father used to be a Tathamite (a fee-paying one) and because he could no longer afford to keep Crispin at his nearly-local day school, Drummond Lodge.

Crispin's mother hated farewells and was keen to have this one over with as soon as possible.

'Now darling, I must get back before the rush hour starts,' she said, opening the car door. She stopped to fiddle with her purse and pull out a bank note. 'Get yourself that book on dog breeding we saw,' she said and pecked him briskly on the cheek. She had overpowdered and some of it fell off on to his shoulder. She giggled and brushed it off him then sat behind the wheel and shut the door. She looked a frump. He felt people watching. Crispin moved a little closer as she wound down the window. 'Oh don't look so *glum*, Crisp!' she exclaimed, trying to cheer herself up. 'Remember what Dad said last night. He was miserable for about a day and a half, then had the best five years of his whole life. Not very flattering for those who came later, hmm?'

He wouldn't smile. He *would* not.

'Say hello to him for me,' he said, 'and thank Sarah for the cake.'

'I will.' She started the engine but was forced to stay put by an enormous Jaguar which was reversing across her path.

'She's wishing she'd given the car a wash,' thought Crispin.

'Now we aren't allowed to have you home for a Sunday for three weeks.'

'It's called an *exeat*,' said Crispin. 'Dad told me.'

'Yes. But your godmother Emma lives just around the corner and I'm sure she'll be allowed to smuggle you out for tea now and then. Ah. We're off.' Her relief was such that she had to bite on a smile.

'You won't forget, will you?'

'No. I won't,' she called, wheeling out over the cobbles. 'As soon as the puppies are born, I'll let you know. Bye.' She waved.

'See you,' he said, not waving back. Hers was the only old car in sight. Not vintage old, just fifteen years, dented-door old. The carpet was covered with torn maps and toffee wrappers and there were always empty fertilizer bags on the back seat in case she passed a good spot for firewood. The aerial had been snapped off and replaced with an unwound coathanger.

Crispin turned away from the gatehouse and crossed the cobbled quadrangle to his *burrow*. His trunk had been carried up to the dormitory, he saw. It would take hours to unpack. He had spent bad-tempered hours touring seedy 'gentlemen's outfitters' in Leeds with his eldest sister Sarah in search of awkward items on the clothes list like galoshes and navy blue cotton-drill football shorts. Most of the football shorts were in brightly coloured imitation satin and they had to explain to several shop assistants what exactly galoshes were. Overtried tempers had frayed further at list-ticking time this morning when it was seen that they had failed to buy garters ('two pairs – charcoal grey'). Crispin's mother had hastily run up two rather messy pairs with white knicker elastic.

'And if they tell you they're the wrong colour they can bloody well dye them for you,' she had snarled, chafing his calves as she tried one on him for size.

Third Burrow was a broad, oak-ceilinged room with windows on to the cobbles at one side and a dank walled garden on the other. There were a grafitti-trimmed fireplace, several tired and unclean sofas, ten desks ranged around the walls and a bookcase with half the longer Oxford dictionary and a London telephone directory for S to Z. A note, evidently the work of a pupil, was pinned to one shelf. 'The other half of this dictionary is in *Fourth Burrow* because there weren't enough to go round. Remember we are grateful recipients of charity.' Someone had added a comment after this in Greek which Crispin failed to understand. He had only been studying Greek a year and wanted to give it up in favour of more maths.

'Is there a "Clay, Crispin of Runnymede Farm, Totley-St-Martha" in here?' A boy with lank black hair and dark glasses was advancing, a thin white plastic walking stick in his hand.

'Yes.'

'I'm David Speake. I'm your *magister* and you're my *oik*. Hello.' He smiled the too-sharp smile of the blind and they shook hands.

'Hello,' said Crispin.

'If we're still speaking after your *Lingua* exam you can call me David or Speake but till then it's *magister* from you and *oik* from me, I'm afraid. Actually it's quite smart to pronounce it *meister* and to leave the *k* off the *oik* but I leave that up to your taste and discretion. Have you *sacked* your *womb*?'

'Sorry?'

'Has your mother left?'

'Oh. Yes.'

'Very good-looking in a *distraite* sort of way, I gather. Jermyn quite fancied her. Is there a small, thin girl sitting cross legged, intent on a book?'

'Yes.'

'That'll be her. Jermyn's having a brief crisis about her sexuality. She's the only girl – sorry, Jermyn, woman – in this burrow. But next door there are eight to be reckoned with. You've got desk four.' He tapped rapidly along the desks, counting. 'That's this one, and this' – he tapped the shelf above – 'is your shelf and no one's allowed to touch either on pain of severe rejection. Sorry I'm talking so

28

much so fast, but I've got to go and play the organ for a bit.'

'That's all right,' said Crispin.

'Glad you approve. Now this,' said David, producing a battered, pink-bound notebook, 'is the key to our relationship. It's the *Lingua* – well it's a sort of *Reader's Digest* version for beginners – and you've got to learn it all in three weeks. You'll pick up quite a lot by necessity because everyone'll be speaking it at you, but some of the rare stuff's a bit harder. The house rules are in there too. Scholars have different ones from everyone else because we're so special. If you fail the exam I don't get let out on the first *exeat* and if you pass – when you pass, rather – you can buy me a box of after-dinner mints. Now I must fly. Have I forgotten anything?'

'Gowns,' said Jermyn, nose still in her book.

'God yes. Thanks, Jermyn dear. Gowns. There's a gown parade in the *piggery* – that's the dining hall – at six. As you're new you just stand to one side. An old sweetie called Dr Feltram inspects all our gowns for wear and tear and then he'll notice you and issue you with yours. It's on the house but you pay for repairs and you give it back when you leave. There's a dinky little eighteenth-century waistcoat too, but that's only for the winter months. I'll be back before six to make sure you don't get lost. Bye.'

'Goodbye.'

His *magister* left in a wild flap of braille organ scores and Crispin noticed that his strong box had materialized by some unseen agency. It felt odd having grown men doing things for one. As the munificence of his scholarship had been explained to him in strictly historical terms using phrases like 'sons of the indigent worthy' and 'episcopal patronage' he had visualized his new life at Tatham's as that of some put-upon waif or poor relation. Perhaps Tatham's would prove to be like Drummond Lodge where hordes of servants appeared only hours before any massed parental occasion and vanished, pay packets in hand, in the wake of the last departing Volvo.

Crispin sat at his desk and opened the little pink book. '*LINGUA*' it said over the school crest and a Latin motto which seemed to mean power through stealth, which couldn't be right, 'Being the Language and Principle Customs of Tatham's School, Barrowcester (Revised 1946).' He turned a page and read,

'Never run when you could walk.

Never hum when you could talk.

Never talk when you could read.'

Someone had scribbled below this, 'Never read when you could run' and someone else below that,

'Any man who runs when he could be eating is an idiot and a fresh-air prude.'

Crispin turned another page and found list upon list of seemingly pointless alternative vocabulary. A few words with bracketed references to dots on a small map of the school and surrounding streets were clearly proper nouns and excusable, but the bulk seemed to be childish, snide or nonsensical replacements of everyday words such as water, chair or blotting paper. Blotting paper was *parch* and water was *hoo*. For chair there were specifics:

'Straight-backed dining chair – *sedan*

Upholstered armchair – *bulldog*'

The generic term seemed to be *bench*. He turned more

pages. There was a great deal to memorize in three weeks. He had been well trained in blind obedience. It was the one subject Drummond Lodge could be said to have taught thoroughly, being a preparatory school that compensated for the brevity of its history with disciplinary and power structures that provided a striking object lesson in the feudal system.

'You can stick pictures up if you like,' said Jermyn, who had finished her book. 'I always do.' She tossed her book on to her desk and left the room.

Crispin was alone. In the days that followed he was to discover what a rare luxury solitude could be. Although the general underpopulation of the school was a kind of privilege, it only served to accentuate the fact that one was hardly ever alone. After three or four minutes of peace, someone always walked in. They might ignore one and sit silently on the other side of the room but they were there. Only the girls, who lived with teacher's families and in lodgings around town, had their own bedrooms. Boys slept twelve to a room and even had to use a vast Seventeenth-Century communal bath house called *jugs*. Crispin came to see the faintly Roman enjoyment that could be had from chatting and washing at the same time but he often longed for a small bathroom all to himself instead of *jugs*'s great arched chambers with their sluices and steam.

'If you want to be alone,' David would advise him the next morning, 'you have to take a good book and lock yourself in the loo. It's either that or take up the organ. Have you thought of the alto viol?'

Alone briefly on this first evening as a boarder, Crispin

started to unpack his strong box. He put paper and pencil case in the desk and ranged his new dictionaries and battered Bible on his shelf. The only novels he had brought with him were *Call of the Wild*, a favourite he was rereading with deliberate nostalgia, and *Barchester Towers*. This looked dull but it was a present from his other sister, Polly.

'It might help you understand where they're sending you to live for the next five years,' she had said darkly. 'Forewarned is forearmed.'

He would have liked to stick up pictures as Jermyn had suggested, but he had brought none with him. Perhaps on his first *exeat* he could pull a poster off his bedroom wall and bring that. He had brought one picture but it wasn't one he would care to hang. He opened the crisp front cover of *Barchester Towers* to check that it was still there. Then felt a familiar prickling in his stomach and wished he hadn't.

It was a photograph of Lottie, his dog. She was an extremely pretty mongrel. She was white with a brown splash on her back, fluffy ears and a tail like a squirrel's. Crispin had been allowed to choose her from a litter born in a neighbouring farm a few days before his eleventh birthday. As she had grown his mother had said she looked like a Cavalier King Charles 'gone wrong'. She was called Lottie after the assistant matron at Drummond Lodge with whom Crispin was madly in love at the time. The photograph was not an expert one, being ill-lit and lopsided, but it was typical in that Lottie had her head quizzically to one side and had been interrupted in dancing on Crispin's bed. Looking at it, the gnawing sick worry of the past weeks – the melancholia his mother had mistaken for impending homesickness – came seeping back. The business of getting packed and saying goodbye to everyone had chased it briefly away but now he was alone, a naked prey.

Crispin had only recently started to masturbate. A friend had taught him as a kind of leaving present at Drummond Lodge. He kept up the practice religiously, not out of any great enjoyment, for he had scant material and insufficient knowledge for a vigorous fantasy life, but from a firm belief that it was not like riding a bicycle; that if he stopped for long he would forget how it was done. One evening several weeks back he had only just finished a strictly medicinal session before his bath when Lottie came pounding in through the door, leaped on the bed and licked him with wild excitement and not on the nose. He had suppressed the memory of this little incident, not least because of the guilty pleasure it had given him. When however his mother announced more recently that Lottie was unquestionably pregnant it came back to him and a terrible connection was made. He had sat at one end of the table while his mother teased Lottie at the other, saying,

'Yes you are. You *are*! And you're going to have babies. Yes! Lots and lots. And I wonder who the father is.'

As has been said, Drummond Lodge was weak on most subjects other than discipline. Human biology was to be dealt with this term and Crispin was having to miss it to spare his father's bank balance. In any event this was probably too specialized a case to be dealt with in the parameters of a Common Entrance paper. At every opportunity since hearing the news, he had taken Lottie for walks past local houses in the hope that her mate would run out with a

friendly yap and make himself known. He had made her
jump back and forth over ditches, made her climb stiles,
even, when left alone one afternoon, exhausted himself
running her up and down stairs. He had sat her down in
pride of place on his quilt and begged her, in their secret
whispered language, to show that he was blameless in this
affair, but she had only gazed devotedly back and raised a
reassuring paw which made the outlook blacker still. His
imagination, which proved so feeble at conjuring up shades
of fantasy lovers, tortured him now with nightmare scenes
of his mother shrieking as puppy after glistening puppy
emerged with the family nose, or human hands instead of
paws or maybe just one baby would be born, nearly human,
marred only by a squirrel tail and a tendency to yap at the
postman. Yet again Crispin stared hard at the dog's image
and thought, 'Please no.'

A boy came silently in, then two, then a whole gang.
Boxes were opened, old friends greeted, books and insults
hurled. Crispin slipped the photograph back inside Trol-
lope and sat on his desk facing the room and shyly answered
the exaggeratedly grown-up questions that were occasionally put to him. After a few minutes, Jermyn came back in.
She sat on the desk beside his in a faintly protective way
and together they watched the *burrow* come to life.

4

In the bedroom of number five, Bross Gardens, her alarm clock woke Dawn Harper at ten to midnight. Dawn stretched out an arm and silenced it. Without even a frown, she threw off her duvet, walked to the bathroom and brushed her teeth. She took a hairbrush and ran it several times through her hair, which was shoulder-length and straw-coloured. Then she crossed her arms and pulled her nightdress over her head. The bedroom window was open and a breeze from off the Bross caused the gingham curtains to stir slightly. Dawn walked down the stairs of her cottage in the dark. Everything was in a familiar place, their order remaining unchanged since she lived alone and received no guests, so she had no need of light. In the kitchen she opened the drawer of the table and took out a black candle in a dark wooden candlestick and an atomizer. She sprayed herself all over with the latter and the night air was touched with citronella. Then she lit the candle with a lighter from the drawer before opening the kitchen door into her back garden.

Bross Gardens was a row of Victorian labourers' cottages, so called because their gardens ran down to the River Bross at the foot of Barrowcester Hill. The cottages were cheap because poky, damp and awkwardly situated. To reach them by car, one had to take a lengthy route around the entire hill. There was a long flight of steps up the bank behind the cottages which led to an unmade-up lane off Station Approach. Dawn went everywhere on foot and used this route for her daily trips into town. Dawn was no beauty – her late mother nicknamed her Old Father Time – but through the ceaseless exercise she received up and down the hill, she was as lean as a gazelle. Had anyone ever been in a position to see them, they would have found that she was possessed of exquisite legs.

She reached out to the right of the back door and found her plastic deck chair leaning where she had left it in the small hours of yesterday. She set the candlestick down on the grass and walked to the part of her little garden where a cherry tree was in flower. There she set up the chair and returned for the candle.

'Damn,' said Dawn, for the breeze had blown it out. She returned for the lighter, lit the candle again and walked with it to the deck chair, shielding it with a hand. She sat in the chair, the blossoms framing her naked form, the light flickering up on her hereditary double chin, down on to her granite breasts and throwing into dancing contrast the features of her sombre face. 'Nema,' she began, 'Reve dna reve rof yrolg eht dna rewop.' She paused for breath. Her speech had the local vowel sounds but was peculiarly toneless, lacking the singsong patter that greeted the visiting ear in Barrowcester market. 'Eht modgnik eht si eniht rof noitatpmet otni ton su dael dna.'

'Temptation' was one of the hardest words to say backwards along with 'kingdom' and 'against'. 'Against' backwards sounded like something in a kung-fu film. Dawn had been reciting the Lord's Prayer back to front every night for several months. It had taken effect once, it would do so again. She had given up the Cathedral long ago, and it was far too long now for her to own up her problem to the police. This way was discreet and enjoyable. She liked the stroke of the night air on her skin and the scents of the river blending with her own. The last pleasure was marred by the necessity, now that the mosquitoes were here, of using citronella every night.

She had gleaned the fundamentals of her new religion from a book called *Visions of Torment; a Study of Ideas of Hell* by an American. She had read it several times in the public library, then embarked on her new philosophy by stealing it. A list of further reading had guided her to more detailed sources but *Visions of Torment* remained her bible; she kept it by her bed.

It was amusing to see how easily one could perform this ritual on a nightly basis and yet walk amongst one's fellows without let or hindrance. When people suggested she join them for a Christian service – strictly forbidden now, if she was to have her heart's desire – she would simply mutter,

'It's not really my scene, I'm afraid,' or 'I think I'm a little bit too cynical for that myself,' or even 'I think my beliefs lie in quite another direction,' and that would be that. Very civilized. She had once tried the bald truth. When Mrs Delaney-Siedentrop had said, in that wheedling voice of hers,

'Oh Dawn dear, why is it we so rarely see *you* inside the sacred precincts?'

Dawn had answered flatly,

'I'm a Satanist.'

Mrs Delaney-Siedentrop had only stared a moment,

then roared with laughter, within the limits of her gentility. Dawn thought it might be disrespectful to continue to make people laugh in this way at her practices, so she had contented herself with half-truths. Since her new Lord was father of lies there was no occasion for guilt. The only other time she had come close to telling the truth about this business had been when Fergus, her only friend, had asked her what she had been up to and she had replied,

'Oh, nothing much. Sitting naked on a deck chair at midnight; that sort of thing.'

He had found this so funny that it had entered the idiom of their friendship and had become a way of saying goodbye.

Something stirred in the bushes to her right. Dawn paused in her incantation.

'Sasha?' she called. There was no reply and no further noise, so she assumed it had been the wind. She brought the prayer to an end. 'Nevaeh ni tra ohw rehtaf ruo,' she declared, furrowing her brow over 'ruo' as she had trouble saying her Rs. Then, alone with her black candle and the pitchy billows of the Bross, she sat and waited for her heart's desire.

5

Evan had shared his corner of the carriage with three aunty women in hats, and a fox terrier. His attempts to read his colleague Sukie Lark Rosen's *Towards a New Mythology* which he was meant to be reviewing for the *Observer* were thwarted by the impossibility of not eavesdropping on his first three Barrowers. He had taken a look at them as they boarded at King's Cross and asked him whether it was the Barrowcester train. Finding him to be American, they had thanked him warmly for his confirmation then the short, neat one with the fox terrier had proceeded to put the same question to an English couple in the seat across the aisle. Amused rather than offended, Evan had buried his smile in Sukie's new book but gradually found his attention poached by their interminable conversation. They were not maiden sisters as he had at first supposed, but three friends who had come 'to Town' in a pack for security. The one with the dog had been to stay Saturday night with her sister and regaled the others with every detail concerning the latter's lighthouse-keeper husband and children. The others were bored with this pathetic display of total recall, as they showed by their aggressively irrelevant interruptions concerning litter, cinema posters and scandal concerning a recent sermon of their Bishop's. They had spent their weekend together. They had passed the weekend in a 'small hotel', had today visited a Cecil Beaton exhibition in the Barbican Centre, where they had got lost, and had spent Saturday evening watching a Frederick Lonsdale revival which they had found 'silly and dated but rather fun'.

'A bit like us, really,' had chipped in the one with the fox terrier and they had all laughed.

Evan had taken this opportunity to look up from his book to take a better look at them but the dog, which was too close for comfort, had caught his eye and bared its yellow teeth in a quietly gargling growl and driven him back to his work. When he had lit up the first of several cigarettes there had been an outbreak of gentle coughing until, with a further bout of hilarity, they had seen that they had settled inadvertently in 'a smoker'. This had led the conversation, via an atoning hymn to their pipe-smoking fathers, to a less tactful discussion of cancer and so to the fluting round of reminiscence, acrimony and lurid horrors with which they whiled away the remaining miles. The only interruptions had been the visit of the ticket inspector (leading to a brief chat about the Colonies), the punctual six o'clock feed of the dog from an array of miniature plastic cartons and Evan's escape with his case when they were within fifteen minutes of arrival for a restorative vodka tonic.

There were three taxis on the station forecourt. The fox terrier woman claimed the first, her companions fairly ran to the second and the one behind was taken, with an apologetic chuckle, by an elegant undertaker Evan had engaged in desultory conversation in the buffet car. Other passengers melted into the car park while a few headed into the station approach at the spruce pace of those who choose to walk whenever possible. Evan cast an appraising eye over the steep hill ahead of them and lit a Winston. His head inches from one of the hanging baskets that adorned the entrance arcade, he waited for another taxi and admired the view.

Allowing for the inevitable spread, the place echoed Cordes or Mont-St-Michel. A hundred or so years ago it must have been the stereotypical hill town of illuminated margins; a bustle of houses on a hill, bounded by a river and a wall, dwarfed by a heaven-pointing church in its midst. If Barrowcester Cathedral pointed heavenward it did so with two fingers; a victory V, naturally.

Once one of the original taxis had returned and was bearing him up past the shopfronts of the principal streets, Evan turned briefly to peer down the hill towards the railway viaduct and the pink-fluffed evening sky. The station site could have been chosen with a view to royal visits. An important limousine could sweep in a straight line from the station door up the High Street and on to the pompous, slightly Bavarian building Evan took to be the town hall. He chatted to the driver with half an ear, feasting his eyes as they left the High Street and were suddenly steering along a road of perfect Early Georgian. Then they swung under an impressive arch into the Close.

'Cathedral,' announced the driver and fell silent, used to the awe of new arrivals.

Evan saw, framed by soaring lime trees, a colossal buttressed T of silver stone which threw up two filigreed spires from its centre. He was suitably awestruck. Even in the softening glow of a sinking sun it was a brutal, proud structure demanding nothing so banal as a tourist's admiration. The Close road formed a crescent from one transept to the other, via the high west end. Evan was staring so intently over his shoulder that their arrival, passing out by another fortified arch and stopping almost at once, took him by surprise.

'Tracer Lane, Professor,' announced the taxi driver, who had gleaned something of Evan's work from their brief chat, and he named the price of the ride. He was so sedulous in carrying the Professor's suitcase up the steps to the front door that Evan assumed he had overtipped as usual.

It was the only house in the row that failed to harmonize. Where the others were balanced, two-and-a-half-storey Georgian (or earlier), painted various but not warring shades of cream, blue and pale pink, 8 Tracer Lane was a piece of exotic-bricked Victoriana. It was one room wide, as if it had elbowed its way into the row and been forced to stand sideways and was now craning its neck over four storeys so as to enjoy a view of the Close at the cost of any indignity. The white front door opened before Evan had time to reach its knocker.

'Professor Kirby?'

'Yes.'

'Mercedes Merluza, but everyone calls me Mercy. How *do* you do? We've been expecting you. Come in.'

He wondered why she had used the plural. Perhaps she spoke on behalf of the community. She was not English. She pronounced these few short phrases with the exaggerated precision of one who has learnt her lesson but remains nervous of failure. He followed her into the hall which was furnished to extend the exotica of the exterior. A wide arch of gilt-edged mirror was framed by two Egyptian-looking vases from which rose high fronds of pampas grass.

'That nice girl from your literary agency rang up on

Friday night to say you would be coming on the five o'clock train,' she said. 'I would have come to pick you up but I don't drive.'

The attempt to say literary had given her away.

'*Es española, Usted?*' he had to ask.

'Yes, but it's a long story which can wait,' she said in Spanish, then went on in English with the same brittle smile. 'I put my lodgers in here in the granny flat.'

She ran pointed fingers through her hair as she spoke. Surmounting nails and lips in traffic-light red, eyebrows plucked into constant shock and a tan fudge foundation, this full mane of black resembled a superior wig. Evan wondered if this were an habitual gesture to scotch rumours.

She led the way up two steps immediately to the right of the front door into a set of rooms carved from little space with cunning and much chipboard. The 'kitchenette' came first with a net-curtained view of the pavements of Tracer Lane, then a noisily sliding door let one into a windowless bathroom with no lavatory or shower from which a second sliding door led on to the bedroom. This was delightful, having French windows on to one of the overgrown gardens that seemed to be the fashion in Barrowcester and a desk by a second window where Evan could work. Evan slung his suitcase on to the bed. He could tell from the way it bounced that the mattress was too soft and would give him backache but there was room for him to drag the mattress on to the floor if things got really bad. Mrs Merluza showed him how the key to the French windows dangled from a nail elsewhere to deter burglars and demonstrated with a flush of pride the string that drew the plum-coloured curtains.

'Now I'm afraid the little boys' room is out in the hall,'

she said, 'but you'll need to come there now anyway as that's where we hang our coats.'

He followed her to the hall. A small passage led into the kitchen and beside it a door opened out into a lavatory like a bowling alley where he duly hung up his coat.

'Now what about food?' she asked.

'Well ... I thought I'd take myself off on an explore tonight and maybe eat out.'

'Lovely. I'll get your breakfast in the morning. Is eight-fifteen all right?'

'Sounds great.'

'I'm afraid I may have to leave it on a hot plate for you as I tend to go to the early Communion across the way.'

'Of course. My agent recommended I try eating at Le Tarte Tartin. Is it good?'

'Oh yes,' she said, 'very good. Very good indeed.' Then she added, 'I gather,' and he knew that she could not afford to eat there. He sensed that she had spent her all on buying the house and been forced to furnish it with atmospheric junk and to take in lodgers. In answer to his smile of sympathy, she asked him up to her sitting room for a quick sherry before he went out. They sat across from each other on sofas whose age she had masked with shawls, and drank two glasses each of Amontillado – one quick, one slow. With the minimum of prompting he confessed to being on the brink of divorce and then, while he studied her curiously, she told him in hushed tones of her family's tragedy involving a large house on the outskirts of Barcelona and a small but efficacious incendiary bomb.

Evan accepted a third 'small' glass. He was going to enjoy himself in Barrowcester.

6

Mr Gavin Tree, socialist thinker, author of *More by Less* and Bishop of the diocese of Barrowcester, let himself into the Cathedral through a small door in the south transept soon after six-thirty on Monday morning. He was not officiating this morning so wore a plain suit over his purple shirt front but even had he been, his principles would have forced him to leave his mitre, crook and title at home. Even now that the full flush of spring was here, the floors of the building exuded ancient chill. Mr Tree had taken the popular, but inadmissible, precaution of sneaking on a pair of pyjama bottoms beneath his trousers. He walked slowly, hands in the pockets of his anorak, towards the Patron's chapel where the morning's ceremony was to take place. He had come an hour early; he needed to think.

He did not come here often unless forced to by an official invitation from the Dean. The chapel at the Bishop's Palace was more intimate. Being only eighteenth century it posed less of a threat. There had been revolutions in the eighteenth century. Unlike the Cathedral, the Bishop's private chapel didn't keep interrupting with boasts of how long it had stood there. Usually, when a crisis struck, Gavin would slip quietly in there for a while. The Classical lines were unadorned; there were no memorials and no flowers.

The Bishop had nothing against flowers in a garden, but he had always thought it tyrannical to make a practice of cutting them. What appalled him in Barrowcester was their inextricable association with the diocesan women. Here, where every venerable tomb, every altar and, outside the coffer-draining annual fortnight when the heating *had* to be turned on, every dustbin-shaped Victorian radiator was garnished with the blooms in season, he could feel them watching him.

'I may be tucked up in bed,' whispered Miss McCreery's narcissi, 'but I'm here in spirit.'

'Never fear,' sighed an alarming spray of things with salmon-pink tongues a little further on, 'Mrs Delaney-Siedentrop is here.'

There had been flowers everywhere when disaster had struck on Saturday. He had been here (officially invited) to confirm the latest batch of boys and girls from the town's grammar school and high school. He had sat on his lesser, portable throne (the lurid gargantua full of lights being mercifully stuck in an impractical corner of the quire) and a nave-long column of boys and girls had come to kneel in pairs before him. Their uniforms were picturesque affairs in pea green and sky blue. Mrs Delaney-Siedentrop, in her role as Captain of the flower arrangers, had achieved the coup of using only those blooms that would match the uniforms. It was a pretty sight. (The Captain being there in person there had been no need for her flowers to keep an eye on the Bishop.)

Each child held before them a card with their Christian name printed so that as they knelt in pairs Gavin could lay his hands on their well-brushed heads and announce,

'I confirm thee ...' glance at the card and continue, 'Jemima in the knowledge and love et cetera.' All went well until he was dealing with the fifteenth pair when suddenly his words seemed so much gibberish to him. It was all he could do to keep them coming out in the right order. He took a mouthful of cool water from the glass held by a server at his elbow and continued. His panic abated, the words fell back into place, the recital of unfair Christian names continued, but the business had lost all importance.

Gavin had suffered attacks of doubt before and gladly so; they were part of a healthy spiritual life. With the death of questioning came too much certainty and an excess of certainty was a moral blindfold. This was different. It seemed less an attack than an unexpected retreat. Meandering through his incantations, patting youthful scalps, he felt the last collapse of mystery and was left, Father Christmas in an overcrowded Norman grotto.

He had always been a man of iron principle. He had threatened to resign his Oxford fellowship when he took exception to his warden's support of a certain African charity. During his recent post at York he had sprung into limelight for criticizing the government both from the pulpit and from a small piece in the *Guardian*. It was chiefly because of the latter that he was so keenly watched over by the more powerful diocesan matrons. By the time he was laying hands on the last pair of heads and preparing to rise and bless the newly confirmed, his mind was made up to flex his principle anew.

After a hymn to relax everyone and a jolly bit of Gibbons from the choir to put them in the mood for an anodyne chat about growing up, he scaled the pulpit. He had prepared a sermon about duty, an uncomfortable topic at the best of times. He condensed this into a brief introductory paragraph then set aside his notes and improvised for the first time in his professional life. The peroration to which he treated an increasingly attentive audience was on doubt. In an unprecedented display of iron principle he went so far as to *share* his doubts with those he was appointed to lead. He cast aspersions on the Virgin Birth; less on whether or not it had happened than on whether this question were remotely important in a world of unemployment, famine, incurable plagues and impending war. There were surprised faces certainly but no one walked out since Barrowcester had long prided itself on its aggressive stance towards the Beast of Rome. What did cause a flurry of walk-outs, including a whole clutch from the Sisters of Bethesda and a shepherded crocodile from Saint Cecilia's High, was his merciless swipe at the angelic host. The cosy cult of these peripheral characters, he declared, as typified by the tasteless Christmas card motifs that even made their way into television commercials as Yuletide market aids, represented a sickness in our spiritual standards and a wilful cold-shouldering of less palatable, more urgent truths. Those who were not already wriggling in their seats did so like singed maggots when he went on to remind them that Barrowcester had the least unemployment, lowest crime rate, fewest council flats and tiniest immigrant population of any English city.

As he warmed to his theme, doubt gave place to rage at the serried ranks of Christian Barrowers before him, at their unthinking coupling of Bible study with share application, of paying for farmyard holidays for inner-city children and taking themselves off to converted farmhouses in Tuscany. He raged and they listened.

One of the golden rules of preaching was that one typed the sermon out in advance, partly to give one's ideas shape and to balance their expression but principally to prevent one's getting carried away. In the cold light of the following dawn, indeed in the cold light in the eyes of his fellow clergy as he stepped from the pulpit, Gavin could see that he had been carried far far away. A kind of madness had come over him more suited, some would say, to newer religions than Barrowcester's. He refrained from foaming at the mouth, which was perhaps a blessing, but he did see a vision.

As he wound up his attack, he saw a small, furred creature staring up at him from behind one of Mrs Delaney-Siedentrop's grosser arrangements. So absorbed was he in its wild yet child-like frame, so startled at the speed with which it darted from sight with a flash of red hair, that he regained his full concentration only in time to hear himself declaim, in a most unepiscopal tone, something about the softness of a cherubic bum. Having had what sounded so very like the last word, he threw out a deeply felt blessing with an extra line in it to show them who was still a step ahead, then retreated to his painfully visible throne for the final hymn.

There had still been a cheery queue at the west door waiting to shake his hand after the service, but certain key faces had been missing and he had walked home with a heavy heart. The next day, predictably perhaps given the number of quondam shorthand typists that had been present, he was quoted word perfect in *The Sunday Times*. *The Times* carried a similarly scandalized piece on Monday as did the *Daily Mail*. The *Guardian* put the same quotations to opposite ends. Rather than write the replies and explanations demanded by each paper, he had agreed to air his views on a television debate later in the week.

Gavin took a short cut across the quire to the Patron's chapel. Saint Boniface of Barrow (pron. *Brew*) was reputedly a Viking who, while leading a raid on the original

Saxon abbey of *Barr*, on the hill where Barrowcester now stood, had been enveloped in a dazzling light. From the middle of said light he launched, on divine prompting say some, not surprisingly say others, into the Lord's Prayer. This rousing combination of fireworks and linguistic virtuosity (for notwithstanding the date he had, of course, prayed in English) converted his hordes to Christianity on the spot. When the light dissolved, their leader had lost his sight. Legend further had it that he became Abbot. Depending on how far the pillaging had gone before the intervention of the light, he would either have done this straight away or nearer his well-behaved dotage, when he died a saintly death amid angelic clamour having swallowed a quantity of water when rescuing a child from the Bross. Under the Normans the abbey had become a moderately fine cathedral and under their descendants Barrowcester had grown into a sizeable market town and thence to a city, gaining the curious pronunciation of its name along the way. In the late 1960s an unpleasant French historian had been allowed the freedom of the Cathedral's superb library for an entire summer, only to emerge declaring that the 'cester' bit was the result of a typographical error in the early seventeenth century. He left in a hurry and was not greatly missed. Tradition also had it that the original Viking settlement was responsible for a smattering of curious local surnames and for a local Scandinavian colouring known as 'Barrowcester blond'.

No one was certain when he had been canonized, but the reformed Viking butcher had been the city's patron since at least the eleventh century, for the rood screen and the tympanum bore carvings of his good deeds. He was traditionally portayed as a giant of a man with a ball of fire

in one hand. An illumination in a fifteenth-century chronicle of Barrowcester embellished the image with an equally
fiery shock of blond hair. His final resting place was a stark
box of rough-hewn local stone in one of the few sections of
the Saxon abbey untouched by the Normans. Whatever
their master builder's plans, it was plain that his workmen
had a profound reverence for the tomb's totemic force.

Boniface had worked no miracles since his death apart
from an incident in 1908 when a small boy fell into a city
cesspit and was saved from an unsavoury death by a pair of
hands that hoisted him back to safety. Said boy swore they
were the hands of a blond giant and went on to become Dean.
Medallions of the saint had since become popular around the
necks of local potholers and sanitation engineers.

Like several of England's greater churches, the Cathedral
was built on unstable ground; a massy challenge in faith to
Nature. Barrowcester's hill was riddled with caves, streams
and uncharted passages that tended to make their presence
known in a dramatic fashion. A cottage would move a foot in
the night, a herbaceous border would fold in on itself. Occasionally whole houses had collapsed. An attempt in the late
nineteenth century to drive a railway through the hillside had
ended in tragedy with many workers buried alive and several
children maimed by a briefly liquefied school. Seismologists
had produced what they swore were accurate maps of the
hill's interior. These were enough to put any fool off digging
a mine but, as far as householders, Dean or Chapter were
concerned, had arrived a little late in the day. Severe accidents
were rare enough to be outweighed by the attractions of the
place, but close enough in public memory for Barrowers to
see themselves as invested with a certain brave, frontier spirit.

Nine centuries on, alas, Nature had begun to tamper where Normandy had held off and the Saxon section was at risk. The first warning came as long ago as 1908 when a new altar was installed in the Patron's chapel and the floor was found to be so out of true that a portion of the new stone had slid forward and smashed against Saint Boniface's tomb. With the more recent appearance of alarming cracks in the outside wall of the chapel and the tumbling, during eight o'clock Communion, of the Patron's crucifix and one of the larger flower arrangements on his tomb, it was decided to declare an emergency and launch an appeal. An expatriate Californian billionaire kindly put up two thirds of the money needed, without even coming to see the damage, and so forced Mrs Delaney-Siedentrop to soften, if not exactly to recant her views on his people.

Work was to begin today, supervised by the family of masons who had arrived from Glasgow between the wars and since secured a monopoly on all work at the Cathedral and Tatham's. Although only the retired patriarch retained his Glaswegian accent, his several sons were still known as 'the Scottish Masons' and it was cause for pride if one could ever secure their time to labour on anything so mundane as a house. Before they could move in, the Patron had to be shifted. A charming service of apology and explanation had been concocted by the Dean and this morning, with the aid of a winch and the attendance of such local archaeologists, well-wishers and press as could not be put off by an ungodly hour, the tomb was to be opened. The sainted contents were eventually to be removed to a cavity before the high altar. The cavity in question was actually something to do with a redundant heating system but, by the tender attentions of the Scottish Masons, had been transformed into a clean and passable tomb. Because the sight of such important bones being slid on to an unpoetic plastic sheet might upset the congregation, no more than the sarcophagus lid was to be moved during the little service. The rest would happen once the crowds had departed and once the area was afforded the discretion of a curtain and no-entry sign.

With the saint safely stowed, the massive task was to begin of dismantling the east end, stone by historied stone, so that the cavity beneath it could be dealt with. William Walker, a fearless diver, had spent months and at last his health, swimming through mud to shore up the sinking mass of Winchester Cathedral earlier in the century, so it was assumed that the brave workers of Glasgow would not be averse to clambering in Barrowcester's primeval potholes to erect similar supports. The whole secure, the east end would be rebuilt. It had occurred to Gavin to suggest that the rain-smoothed gargoyles and carvings be replaced with stone caricatures of modern figures so as to continue the medieval tradition. It was a suggestion which he thought could now wait a little.

He entered the Patron's chapel. The winch that was arranged over the tomb, its chains cunningly attached to the corners and sides of the sarcophagus lid, was entwined with Mrs Delaney-Siedentrop, or at least her watchful flowers. He walked over, not knowing their names, and took a sniff to show he was not afraid. They were white and smelled of honey and dust. He touched the pulley chain and made it and its scented burden swing with a sound like distant mice.

Temptation overcame him. It would be another half hour before the first verger came to open up shop. He pulled hard on the chain, grinding flowers as he did so.

The pulley and gears ground into action and the lid shifted. He pulled more, harder and faster until it was five inches clear of the tomb. He was getting hot. Leaving the lid to swing, he unfastened his anorak, draped it over a nearby chair and returned to pulling the chain. The sound echoed but he had gone too far to stop. He could plead religious fervour or divine prompting. He could say he had had a dream – vergers loved to talk about dreams. As he pulled he realized that more than anything he needed to see for himself that Saint Boniface or at least a body's remains lay within. On top of Saturday's sermon, a vanished patron would be too disastrous. There was no smell. He had expected a smell or at the very least a cloud of ancient dust. Of course; in order to secure the chain, the workmen had already prised the lid clear. There was to be no mystery, no unveiling.

Panting, still curious despite his realization that he was not the first to do so, Gavin crouched to peer inside. While no miraculous preservation of the corpse had occurred, as might have been the case nearer the dread lair of the Beast of Rome, the patronal skeleton was remarkably well kept and had not crumbled to dust. The skull was rolled to one side as in sleep and the hands were unusually draped across the pelvis. No. The hands were grasped in prayer over the ribs so the other hands . . . Gavin Tree frowned. As well as his sainted compliment of skeletal arms and legs, Saint Boniface of Barrow had the remains of a great pair of wings. What had seemed to be hands were in fact the tips of two delicate webs of tiny wing bones which were draped protectively across the saintly shoulders, chest and midriff. Before bursting into wild and rapid action, the Bishop calmly observed that legend was in this case truth in that the body measured at least six and a half feet.

Reaching deep into the sarcophagus, he laid hands on first one wing then the other. Age had been only superficially kind to the bones; as he pulled at the join where the top wing bone entered the back of the massive rib cage, he felt it turn to a sort of crumbled biscuit in his grip. He dislocated both wings then lifted them gingerly through the cavity. He wanted to run because time was short and he still had to lower the lid, yet he was terrified of tripping and landing in a mass of someone else's broken wing cartilage. Also the skeletal wings were too long to carry from his waist, so he had to keep his fists at shoulder height. Thinking quickly, he lurched like a crippled dragonfly to the entrance of the crypt. He took both wings in one hand, turned the doorknob and leaned on the door with his back. As he scrabbled with his free hand for the light switch, Gavin heard something scamper in the dark and splash into the water. Rats. Rats? No time to think. He hurried, bones flailing, to the point where the city's subterranean stream swirled in a black U in and out of one mossy wall. It was difficult to throw the bones any distance but the swift current helped him.

There was a distant sound of an animal gnawing as he closed the door. He didn't look back but hurried to the Patron's chapel where he lowered the lid as fast as he could. Only then, when he was at liberty to fall to his knees and beg forgiveness, did the full enormity of his crime begin to dawn upon him. Quite apart from his proud motives, his act had been one of scientific as well as religious desecration. Wise men would kill to have had even a glimpse of the remains that the rats were now chewing so eagerly.

Perhaps that was a good reason for having destroyed them; a less shamefully selfish one than not wishing to have an overhasty sermon rendered ridiculous by untimely evidence of the miraculous. Gavin chewed on a thumb knuckle and thought hard about humility.

There was a rattling of fat keys in the south transept door before someone found it was already unlocked, then footsteps across the quire. Sam the verger came in, paused to recognize the Bishop and appreciate the importance of what he was at, then came tutting forward and picked up the crushed flowers from around the tomb. Through the cracks in between his raised fingers, Gavin saw him do this and cursed himself for forgetting to gather them before he kneeled. He lowered his head and, sliding back on to a chair, smiled at Sam.

'Morning, my lord,' said Sam, obstinate as his colleagues on the little matter of calling a Bishop plain 'mister'.

'Hello, Sam. A fine day for it.'

'Suppose so,' said Sam, 'though I reckon it's a dangerous thing to do. If a church is going to fall, I say it will. There'll be a war soon, anyway, and all the money will have been wasted.' Before the shepherd of his soul could answer he held out the crumpled petals. 'Least we're not a sinking ship,' he chuckled, 'we've got ourselves a colony of rats still.'

'Really?' asked his lord, relieved.

'They chew flowers, tear surplices; I reckon they'd eat those wafers if they could open the safe.'

He laughed out loud as only vergers seem able to do in a Cathedral and went to throw away the rat-mauled flowers. Gavin sighed, rose and went for a little walk to count his remaining blessings.

7

Strapped into the passenger seat, Clive Hart picked the yellow sleep from behind his glasses. His wife toured the Close in search of a parking space. It was a little after seven o'clock. His wolfed coffee and slab of home-made bread were being ungraciously received by a stomach that was barely awake. Last night he had been all in favour of coming to the service of disinterment. It had been his idea and he had had to ply Lydia with arguments of 'rare opportunity' and 'kick yourself for missing it'. Tables had turned this morning. It was she, the habitual early riser, who had plied him with breakfast and a running shower and he who did the self-kicking.

'Won't that warden nab us here?' he asked as she gave up the search and parked on a yellow line.

'No. I slipped her a cheapo Stilton in the shop when her family came to stay at Easter and she knows our car.'

She was so damned arrogant and she always got away with it. He couldn't bribe a child. People stole his bike lights with heartless regularity.

They shivered because the sun had not yet rounded the east end to dry the dew on the grass or chase the chill off the pavements. They walked around the lawn and entered through the south transept. The Glurry was the only door open at this time of day but *habitués* used it all day long so as to avoid the embarrassment of having to greet an acquaintance on begging box duty in the main entrance at the west end.

Lydia had slipped her arm through his soon after leaving the car. The action was common between them; a thoughtless gesture of affection and territory, a twenty-one-year habit. Today she also did it for comfort. Quite apart from the faintly revolting nature of what they were about to witness, the Cathedral's interior made her feel unimportant, little-wifey and slightly guilty.

Her faith was not especially strong. She loved singing hymns and listening to the choir. Some – by no means all – passages of the Bible and the liturgy made her feel safe and whole. Clive only came here if persuaded and he had very little faith, if any. He shared her love of the music however, never ceased to be inspired by the building and had a wry respect for its importance as a social hub. When he retired from Tatham's she would like him to train to be one of the guides; it would give him something to do when they weren't at the house she intended they buy on the Tarn. She already had the Lady chapel to dust each week and was on a reserve list for the begging boxes.

Lydia led the way up the steps towards the east end, where she had seen a friend. Clive lingered by a noticeboard to see what the choir would be singing at Evensong for the rest of the week. Sometimes it was possible to slip over during a gap in his afternoon's teaching. He didn't always bother to tell Lydia about these trips. In fact it was so long since he had done so that he feared it might look suspicious if he suddenly started telling her again. She seemed to regard church-going as a showy, diplomatic, distinctly *female* affair; certainly not for men of pre-retirement age to 'get into'. When she suggested he accompany her, she expected him to sigh as if he had something more manly and important on his mind, so he did. He followed her more slowly, watching her talk to the unfamiliar friend. She was wearing her new spring coat, a light creamy cashmere which hid her bum but showed off her legs. It looked expensive, but that was usually the desired effect. She made so much more money from her books and shop than he ever could from teaching that she tended to buy him clothes rather than he her.

Like the Bishop, Lydia was a 1970s success story. When they had met, Clive was the ambitious one and she the adoring mouse. He had had his first play accepted by the BBC and had had a second commissioned by the Royal Court. He was a fashionable go-getter with a fashionably seedy address and fashionably black Chelsea boots. She had just finished at secretarial college and was in her first year at cookery school. They got married because simply everybody was living in sin so it seemed more daring to run to a register office then toast their joint future in a Portobello Road pub. Then she had produced a son and everything had changed.

He would say 'went wrong' but it had not been like that. When even the Royal Court regulars were staying away in droves from his third play and when, in the same month, the cookery book she had written on the sly was becoming a bestseller, he had coped remarkably well. By and large he had not had to cope, in fact, because she had *managed* him so cleverly. They became the perfect late-sixties couple; she writing witty guides on how to live cheerfully well on *Nothing At All* (second bestseller) and he, one of those faces which everyone recognized but nobody could quite place. As she made more money and gained more confidence, she found in him the perfect seventies husband; a complaisant drone, hairy and supportive. She persuaded him to grow a beard and take a teaching post in an ancient public school. They were getting tired of living in a gentrified slum and suddenly it was oh so chic to discover the countryside again.

'Welcome to the Earthly Paradise,' their new neighbours had said.

Nothing had gone wrong. When chauvinist friends of either sex sneered that he had opted out and been emasculated by a distaff cash flow, he retorted that they were the ones who had opted out by not daring to bare their innate passivity. Lydia and he had found their levels. He *liked* being underneath. She turned and smiled as he approached. The beard had gone recently; she had said he would look younger without it, and he did. He took her hand discreetly and they found seats in the sixth row.

The Patron's chapel filled fast. People soon forgot that they were light-headed from lack of sleep or breakfast and before long there was much twisting in seats and nodding to friends. It felt more like a fire practice than the preliminary to a service; the occasion was altogether strange. Sam had been joined by another verger, Mrs Moore, who was helping him to lay out extra chairs outside the chapel door to accommodate the overflow. Lydia finished the difficult bit where one had to kneel and compose one's thoughts and sat up in her chair to see who had come.

Mrs Chattock, Gavin Tree's mother (twice widowed, poor woman) drifted to the front where her son would be waiting for her. She had grown increasingly otherworldly since her minor stroke last autumn and was purportedly cultivating a mystic circle. A spectral smile, doubtless learnt in her days as Coward's Elvira in northern rep, conveyed her serene greetings to all as she advanced, but forbade any from being so fleshly as to do more than bow in return. Fergus Gibson had taken a seat in a darkish corner as usual. His partner in the city's only interior design business had died suddenly some months ago and Lydia knew he was having a terrible time with his old mother. The latter had got religion on the death of her husband and rushed off to darkest Africa to become a missionary. Illness had forced her home and into her son's care. It was said that she was quite seriously unhinged. Poor Fergus. Lydia tried to catch his eye but he was looking sad and preoccupied, which was scarcely surprising. Mrs Delaney-Siedentrop had said something awfully tactless to him last week. Lydia made a mental note to buy something special for when he came to supper with darling Emma Dyce-Hamilton. Funny little Emma was just the right age for him. The Delaney-Siedentrop had secured a front seat as usual through the agency of her ex-stockbroker husband St John who was a sidesman and wore his medals rather too often. She was wearing one of her habitual navy blue suits and had just beckoned Mercy Merluza over to join her on a spare seat. Mrs Merluza was a once-luscious Spaniard who would not have looked out of place in an Italian toga epic of the fifties. One of Barrowcester's few exotica, she ran a craft shop, a disappointingly tame occupation given her striking appearance, Lydia and Clive had asked her for drinks occasionally when she first arrived but had found her hopelessly narrow-minded and dull. Clive finished composing his thoughts and sat back in the chair to Lydia's right. She smiled encouragingly at him then looked across to bow to peculiar Dr Morton who had just found a seat.

Early morning sunlight was pointing out the cobwebs on

the eastern windows that were so soon to be dismantled and cleaned. The poplars outside waved, clattering, and caused the light to dance on faces and over stone. Behind the congregation, in the quire, the organ brought whatever it had been playing to an end. There was a pause and then the choristers burst into plainsong somewhere nearby. The combination of the white flower arrangements, the brilliant sunshine and their high voices that scalded the still air and wobbled slightly because they were processing, made Lydia want to cry, so she laid her right hand on the back of Clive's left and squeezed. He caught her eye and smiled. Sweet Clive! Accessible Clive! She wished their son Tobit were here so that she could be the filling in a love sandwich.

Gavin Tree had spoken of love last time she heard him preach. A wise and principled man. Apparently his sermon at Saturday's confirmation service was an outrage to some. She had been working at the time but the reported gist of it struck her as extremely sensible. She was as guilty as the next person of overindulging in prettiness and sentiment – angels, flowers and choristers – but at least she was aware of doing so and felt the shame of it. Someone had given her Gavin's book for Christmas two years ago. She had still to read it.

The choristers drew near. Sam marched in with his staff, leading the Dean and, behind him, Canon Wedlake who had such a noble profile, and behind him the choristers. The Dean and Canon Wedlake took up stations to either side of the Patron's tomb and the choristers passed them in two lines to form a semi-circle that met behind the altar. Sam's arrival in the chapel doorway started a wave of rising congregation so that by the time the choristers were filing round the apse, everyone was on their feet.

'Dearly beloved,' began the Dean, 'welcome.'

The service that followed was remembered by all present as having been pertinent and tasteful but it was so eclipsed by the raising of the sarcophagus lid that the remembrance was hazy at best. After a hymn, a brief address by the Dean reminding the few strangers present of St Boniface's history and a briefer summary by Canon Wedlake of the enormity of the task lying in store for the cathedral masons, there were some prayers and then everyone stood again for the start of the disinterment. The choristers sang a suitably medieval psalm setting and the Dean laid hands on the winch chain and began to pull.

There was an unrestrained craning of necks as the lid rose the first five inches. Several service sheets fluttered irreverently to the flagstones from fingers parted with excitement. Dr Morton stood on his hassock and his peculiar beady-eyed face, which had always reminded Lydia of an ostrich's, rose above the crowd, hungry for view. Clive froze in the middle of unwrapping a throat pastille, apparently aware that he was rustling too loudly, and Lydia felt a sudden extraordinary temptation to climb on to her chair. There was then a slight threat of anti-climax. Everyone realized that from where they were placed it was impossible to see *inside* the tomb and that the prospect of one's Dean hauling a slab of pre-Norman stone into the air on a winch teetered on the dull side of inspiring. Then two things happened extremely fast. Five small birds like canaries, only white, flew at great speed from under the lid and disappeared into the quire. More obviously the Bishop groaned and fell in a dead faint. Gavin Tree was a tall man and his fall put two chairs and the Dean's wife off their balance and gathered a rush of helpful hands and counsel. As Sam, the Dean and a man Lydia did not know helped to carry him out, pursued by a still otherworldly Mrs Chattock and an undisciplined gaggle of choristers, it became clear both that the service was considered thoroughly finished and that not everyone had seen the apparition of the white birds. Clive had not for a start, but he had notoriously slow reactions so he took it on trust from Lydia, who had seen. Mrs Delaney-Siedentrop certainly had not, and was making increasingly unsubtle references to popery and cheap stagecraft. The scene was like a re-enactment of the one at Babel. Those who had seen pointed for the benefit of their less fortunate neighbours and made gliding motions with their hands. Those who had not, scoffed and indicated the weight of the lid while muttering about oxygen. Gradually the crowd dispersed, having waited for the news that the poor Bishop was well on the way to recovery, and the Scottish Masons began to move in. There was a small scuffle amongst the local radio crew when it transpired that their smuggled video camera had jammed at the crucial moment.

Over the days that followed there was a marked increase in the ranks of Those Who Had Seen – the party that was tasting the sweet tang of autobeatification. Soon the less fortunate party came to number only three; Clive, who none the less counted himself as a believer, Mrs Delaney-Siedentrop, who most certainly did not, and Fergus Gibson, who had suddenly had a bad feeling about his mother and had left the service during the Dean's brief address.

8

'Mother?'

Fergus stood in the doorway of Lilias Gibson's room. The old woman was slumped sideways against her pillows. Between her dashingly military wedding photograph and a silver-framed one of her adopted Nigerian chiefling, the early morning tea he had brought her before leaving remained untouched.

'Mother? Are you asleep?'

Fergus advanced to the bedstead. A huge round mirror on the wall to stage left of her bed reflected the touching scene; rapidly greying interior designer peering concerned at snow-white, unconscious ex-missionary.

'Mother?'

Still she lay, her head dangling in mid-air. Her hair, still brushed out for the night, formed a lacquer-stiffened cloud around her tiny skull. The draught through the open door caused it to drift slightly. Its whiteness and that of the pillows made her ancient skin seem a warm, toffee brown.

'Please no. Mother?' He reached out and touched her neck with his fingertips. The skin was still warm. 'Mother!' he shouted. He took her firmly by the shoulders and swung her into a more dignified vertical, pulling the pillows around her to hold her in place. Even with her shoulders upright, her head continued to loll drunkenly. He pressed his ear to where he thought her heart should be. Nothing.

He moved his head. Nothing. He didn't bother with a pulse. He could never find those anyway. 'Oh Ma,' he said quietly and sat on the side of the bed.

He wondered what he should do now. Dr Morton had been in the Patron's chapel so it was pointless to call him out yet. There was no hurry now. What did one *do* with a dead mother? What did one do with a dead anybody? He had been so firm about politely refusing offers of help from Mrs Moore, Lydia Hart and co. that he could hardly call them in now, at the grisly last. It was difficult to picture Lydia having anything to do with a corpse.

Oh Mother. You've become a corpse.

Fergus's eye turned across the room he had prepared for her before he met her flight from Lagos in November. Her photographs, some on the table, some on the mantelshelf. Her Bible, of course, sun-baked from the new widow's proselytizing trips into the African bush. The wardrobe full of long-outdated winter clothes he had had sent down from Inverness for her. He had unpacked them so carefully and she had never been well enough to get up and wear them again. The mirror and the bed, placed so that she could see the Cathedral, in reflection, from her pillows. In her brief hours of sanity she had lain there identifying the silhouettes of birds flying around its twin towers. Her *Guide to British Birds*, signed by her friend the author, lay on the carpet beside her brown corduroy slippers and the WI Book.

Brightening, Fergus bent down and took up the latter. Ever since she married his father at eighteen and left her native Dundee for his family's farm near Inverness, she had made a collection of recipes, advice pages, natural remedies and nursing hints and glued them into this great black volume. She called it the W I Book because the original idea, and many of the pamphlets, came from the Women's Institute to which the young and inexperienced Mrs Gibson was introduced by dour Mrs Gibson senior. Over the years, for son as much as mother, the black tome had come to represent security in crisis. When he had a toothache or had cut his knee or was simply feeling low, he had only to reach for the W I Book. It had helped when Granny Gibson was bitten by an adder, it would help now.

Fergus opened the book on his lap and turned to the back pages where, in her flawless antiquated copperplate, his mother had kept an index of everything she pasted in. He turned to D for death and O for old, without success. Then his eye landed on L and found an entry under Last Offices – page 75. Seventy-five was early on in the collection. The black-bordered pamphlet must have been given to her when her father-in-law died of a heart attack. Fergus read.

'The first action should be to remove any hot-water bottles from the bed and all pillows bar one.' He pulled her hot-water bottle out and emptied the tepid water into her bedroom basin. Then, holding her shrunken shoulders out of the way, he removed all pillows bar one and laid her gently back on that. Her mouth fell open and he tried in vain to close it. Clicking his tongue he returned to the book and read on, hoping for advice about mouths. 'Close the eyelids with wet cotton wool if possible and straighten the limbs. Clean and replace any dentures, tucking a pillow firmly under the lower jaw until mouth can remain closed of its own accord.' So. Her false teeth were still soaking by the sink. He had had plenty of practice at taking those in and out for her over the last months, and was no longer squeamish. Fergus took a pillow from the floor, after dealing with the teeth, and tucked it firmly under the jaw. The corpse was less alarming with a shut mouth. 'Cover the face with the sheet,' the sage wives advised none the less, 'and prepare all requirements for the final laying-out. While doing this it is advisable to find out the relatives' wishes regarding any personal jewellery such as the wedding ring.' There was a list of 'requirements' such as towels, soap and hot water, all of which were to hand. Jewellery, he assumed, had all been left to her fertile Scottish nieces. 'Remove remaining bedclothes leaving top sheet to cover.'

He pulled off the quilt and draped it over the landing banisters to air before starting to untuck the blankets. God bless the W I. It was like having a capable nurse in the room; starchy but comforting because her knowledge was absolute and so bore one up.

Her body beneath the lone white sheet was slight as an old cat's. He had grown used to it after countless bed baths but, suddenly so still, it seemed frailer than ever. He was not going to cry. She had been dying too long. She had been so unlike herself for so long that the corpse before him was not her. She had been mercifully removed from all these indignities some time before she left Lagos.

Christmas had been when the lavatorial obsession had set in. No sooner did Dr Morton declare her physically well at Easter than she started her refusal to leave the bed even to hobble on his arm to the bathroom. Easter also saw her lapse into a hateful second infancy. She must have been a *horrible* baby. It was only when Lydia had kindly had

words with Dr Morton behind Fergus's back that the latter
had discreetly delivered a large box of disposable nappies
for the elderly and infirm.

No. He was not going to cry. He did need to blow his
nose, however. His hands shook and he dropped the handkerchief. As he stooped to pick it up, his head level with the
mattress, Mrs Gibson let fly a long and expressive fart and
proceeded to laugh uproariously from under her white
sheet. Fergus watched her mouth opening and closing on
the cotton, then pulled back her shroud and saw the monstrous glee in her eyes.

'Devil!' he shouted, pulling the pillow from under her
jaw and preparing to hit her with it. She only laughed the
louder, dribbling and farting some more, so instead he
tucked it back behind her shoulders and unrolled the blankets over her again. With her giggling in his ears, he worked
his way along both sides of the mattress, tucking the bedding back in and making perfect hospital corners, then
walked out and shut the door. Slumped on the landing
floor and pulling her quilt off the banisters and over his
head, he tried to cry.

9

'Faster!' yelled Gloire. The air poured over the windscreen and into her artfully straightened mane. 'Faster for Chrissakes!' Tobit Hart flattened the accelerator as her brown hand clamped harder on his inner thigh. 'Faster. Oh. Oh God! Yes. Please. *Now!*' As the engine neared apoplexy Tobit blared the horn for a full eight seconds as his fiancée subsided in vanilla-scented ecstasy beside him. 'I love you when you drive,' she confessed at last.

'I love you back,' he returned and pressed his lips to the pale inside of her nearest wrist.

'Child of nature, huh?'

'More. Much more,' he said and smiled at himself in the mirror. She took his left hand from the wheel and bit lightly at the fleshy part of its thumb.

'My candy-coated conversion,' she said and nibbled. 'What have you told Lydia and Clive about their future in-laws?'

'Not a lot,' he replied. There was a pause before a grin laid bare his teeth. 'They don't even know about you.'

'Oh Jesus,' she murmured.

'This is a surprise visit,' he went on.

Gloire laughed, then threw back her head and yelled into the motorway wind.

She had strolled into his shop in Marylebone two months ago and ordered a white evening dress.

'I trust the design entirely to you,' she said, leaning an elbow on the anatomy textbook she had been clutching, 'but it has to be easy to pee in.'

She left her improbably Hollywood name and a Chelsea phone number then walked out. Somehow she had found out his home number and rang him there the following night at eleven.

'Good evening to you too,' she said. 'Tell me about my new dress.' Her voice was softly American.

'I think it should have a slit in it to show off your spine,' he said, lolling on the carpet and remembering her languid good looks.

'When can I have a fitting?'

'I'll ring you.'

'When can I have a fitting, Tobit?'

'Tuesday at five-thirty, Gloire.'

'Perfect.'

'Is that really your name?'

She arrived on Tuesday at five-thirty and stripped to ivory bra and panties as soon as they were in the fitting room. He stood her on a footstool and sheathed her in white silk and net.

'This isn't a ball gown,' she complained.

'It's better. There are pins,' he threatened her, 'so don't move or you'll bleed and wreck it.'

It clung to her almost immodestly low then flung out a skirt that would lift out at the slightest turn of her hips. He walked slowly round her, scowling with concentration and making adjustments with a needle and thread while she gazed angelic into the middle distance. As he worked his way down the back, arranging the fabric window so that her vertebrae were teasingly framed, he found 'kiss me here' and an X written small with eye pencil on her skin. He stooped and kissed the X where a light down marked the descent to her buttocks, then crouched to pin up the hem.

'How does it look?' she asked.

'Perfect,' he said. 'Come by tomorrow at six and it'll be ready.'

'Do you take American Express?'

'No. But it's yours if you'll buy me dinner and meet my parents.'

'I bet you say that to all the broads.' She twitched her narrow shoulders and sent the half-made garment rustling around the stool at her feet.

'Funnily enough,' he said, handing her down, 'you'd be the first.'

She kicked the fitting-room door shut, he pulled down the blind, and they got to know each other at length on a mound of taffeta.

Tobit was officially gay, insofar as that is what his parents, friends, acquaintance and colleagues assumed him to be. As far as he was concerned, his sex life had bordered on the non-existent for so long that he was not anything. His friend, Seth, could argue till his head fell off that sexuality was defined by desire and not its fulfilment, Tobit remained unconvinced.

He had first fallen in lust with the carpentry master at school. As part of a last-year project, a group of pupils, Tobit included, had built a pavilion. Tim Tunning had supervised them and on the first day of work, when Tim was correcting the angle of his saw, Tobit's humdrum adolescent vision focused itself in an unexpected direction. Encouraged by the school philosophy of free thinking and open discussion, he had run around telling everyone of his new discovery, delighted at last to have found something interesting about himself. Word reached Tim Tunning in no time and he invited Tobit to his cottage for a glass of home-brewed beer and had explained that, while he was just an ordinary heterosexual carpenter with a wife and two kids, he really appreciated Tobit's affection and hoped they could be friends. Tobit was overjoyed at this paltry reciprocation but, as intended, the earnest pursuit of friendship stifled physical desire. By the end of the year, his interest in the carpentry teacher was several degrees cooler than the carpentry teacher's growing, confused interest in him.

At art school he had shared a bed with his flatmate. They were too poor to afford the rent on a two-bedroom flat, they were good friends and it was pleasant to share a bed because they could talk for hours without either of them freezing his feet or having to say goodnight. When his parents came to visit and had overinterpreted the situation, Tobit did not disillusion them. He assumed he would have a lover sooner or later and it was convenient to get the parental enlightenment ordeal over and done with. Five or so years later, however, a lover had not yet come his way. Several had tried to, but they had proved so unsatisfactory, had come and gone so rapidly that none of them had counted. With each man who was rejected as too insipid, dull, pig-headed or highbrow, Tobit's romantic standards became more difficult to satisfy and the intervals between disappointments grew increasingly lengthy. By the time that the first AIDS tremors were hitting London, bringing with them the much-vaunted death of promiscuity and *soi-disant* return of drawing-room introductions and old-fashioned courtship, Tobit was joking with a trace of rancour that he was a founder member of the swelling league of Born-again Virgins. Thanks to his mother's loan and the contacts she pushed his way, celibacy was easy. The more he stayed in the more he earned, and the more he earned the easier it was to entertain at home and so avoid the nightclub snare.

Then came Gloire. The extraordinary resurgence of lust that came in her wake could hardly be explained away by the purity of the months preceding her arrival since what she offered was so far removed from the objects of his abstention. As she teased, he had not had biblical knowledge of what he was missing. From what he had overheard and from what he had seen in films (for Tobit never read) the essential quality of the female body was softness and this had always repelled him as carrying distastefully maternal overtones. Gloire's body was firm to the point of rigidity. She was a keen athlete and the only thing in her bedroom besides her bed was a sleekly challenging rowing machine. Even her buttocks were hard. Tobit swam in the summer and occasionally played tennis, but he felt flabby by comparison. Since he had read little, he assumed that this was how most heterosexual men must feel all the time. The first thing he had seen as they left his shop to go back to her flat and try it again was an attractive man so, however loudly bells had rung, he had no illusions about being converted. While Gloire was the exception that proved the rule, she was yet sufficiently exceptional for the rule to be waived indefinitely.

74

After the second, even more bell-ridden round of love-making, she had gazed at him as he lay slowly panting and laughed.

'You could grow to like this, huh?' and he thought he had detected a tone of pride and was glad to be as exceptional for her as she for him. Then she had peeled them a post-coital orange because neither of them smoked. 'Jesus, I'm foolish,' she had sighed.

'What?'

'I'm gonna have to do better than this.'

'What? Tell me.' He grinned then saw that she was serious.

'When did you last ... like ... lay a *guy*?' she asked.

'God. I don't know.'

'Think, Tobit.'

'Er ...' He had no idea. Yes he had. Four or five months ago there had been that dreary model from Los Angeles. Not a very wise choice. Oh God. Suddenly he saw what she was driving at and lied. 'If you're worrying about that, don't. I had the test three months ago and the results were negative.'

'Where did you go?' she pursued, still serious, and he was reminded that she was a professional. He thought fast.

'That clap clinic off Charlotte Street.'

'Thank Christ for that,' she said, relieved. 'Am I dumb or am I dumb? But that's a great relief.'

'Why?'

She popped the last segment of orange into his mouth and tweaked the end of his nose.

'Because the lady is *not* partial to latex.'

He had dumbly sworn then and there to hasten to said

75

clinic the next morning to make a half-truth of his lie. He had put off having the AIDS test ever since his friends had started to take it. The more he had heard them bragging that they had been proved 'safe' the more likely it had seemed that he would be the one person they all knew who won the booby prize. Every day for a week after his test he came to Gloire or she came to him and they made extensive love. They hardly talked but when they did he found that she was far, far brighter than he and this seemed to please them both. He was also disturbed to find that the result of his lie – that he seemed a little more her murderer every time he entered her – seemed to lend a sharper edge to his pleasure. Then he opened a plain brown envelope one morning that requested he return to the clinic as soon as possible.

Tobit was not courageous. He had given the clinic a false name and told them he had lost his medical card. He had known as soon as he opened the envelope that he would not be going back there. Why bother? They would sit him in a little room with a cactus on the table, and a well-trained social worker would say that his blood showed signs of contamination by the HTLVIII virus and would he please stay calm and give them his complete sex history so that they could call in the relevant people for tests.

'I'll tell Gloire when I see her tonight,' he thought, but it took courage to tell someone you think you are beginning to love and who you hope is beginning to love you that you are almost certain to develop symptoms of an almost certainly fatal disease and that, thanks to your cowardice so, almost certainly, are they. That night she drove round to his flat. He kissed her. She kissed him. They fell on to his bed chewing at each other's lips and tearing off each other's clothes; he was now not surprised to find the experience even more pleasurable. 'Maybe I'll tell her tomorrow,' he thought but tomorrow she had spoken first.

'You know I said I was worried about us and AIDS,' she murmured and for a moment he thought she was going to say she had had the test too. She would be the first woman to announce that she had AIDS-infected blood and be greeted by cheers.

'Yes?' he said.

'Well I was reading a report today and it was even more depressing than most. It said that they weren't sure now how accurate the blood tests are. It said that a researcher in London had taken eight different tests in two weeks and come out negative in six and positive in two.'

'No!' exclaimed Tobit, not understanding.

'That means,' she continued, seeing that he didn't, 'that your test could well have been wrong and that we're both infected.' He understood now and said nothing. 'Curiously,' she said and played with one of his hands, 'I'm not all that sure that I care any more. I mean, it's too late. If we die now we die; as long as we don't fool around, we can't load the dice against us any more than they already are.'

'We could always . . . er.'

'No,' she said. 'No latex. That risk I'm prepared to take.'

And they laughed because they might be going to die and began to make love again because they were both so glad that she hated latex.

'Would you marry me?' she asked suddenly, pulling back from him. 'If I asked you, that is.'

'Why?' he demanded, running a finger up and down one of her collar bones.

'That's not a very flattering reaction.'

'No. But why?'

'Well,' she grabbed his hand to stop him tickling her and started to play with it again. It reminded him of being small and having his fingernails cut; the only action of hers that recalled his mother. Possibly this was because his mother was not black. 'Well to be honest it's partly because I'd like to marry someone over here because I'd like to become a UK citizen for work.'

'I thought you said there was more money for research over there.'

'There is but I don't want to research; I want to be a doctor. I'm just a nurse at heart, with an extra qualification or two to cover up.' She paused. 'And the other reason is altogether less straightforward.'

'What?'

'What what what,' she mimicked, giggling.

'What?' he pursued, serious in his turn.

'I'd like it to be you I marry.'

'But I'm gay.'

'Not any more, you're not.'

'Yes I am. At least, I'm fairly sure.'

'Not with me you're not and if you laid a finger on anyone else, man or woman, once we were married, I'd inject you with something lethal.'

'Ah.'

'Besides, I hate categories. We're not gay or straight; we're just Tobit and Gloire who fancy each other.'

'Clever Dick.'

'I know,' she said. He kissed her ear. She held him away. 'Well?' she asked.

'Yes.'

'You'll marry me?'

'Yes. And soon.'

'How about this month. Flowers are cheap and my parents are in Europe.'

Her parents had been telephoned over champagne within an hour of his acceptance. As they sped on to break the glad news to his, Tobit swung sickened between wild delight at having a perfect, loving creature beside him and blank-eyed panic at what he was doing. He had become a much faster driver since he met Gloire. Sometimes, when she urged him on and he slammed down the accelerator, he was tempted, with one easy swing of the steering wheel, to destroy them both. They would be torn, crushed, possibly burned beyond recognition, but at least it would be quick. At least it would be now.

10

It was barely seven-thirty on his first morning in Barrow-cester when Evan was roused by the growls of crawling cars and an ensemble clicking of well-heeled feet. He pulled on his dressing gown and bleary-eyed his way through both the sliding doors to the kitchenette. He tweaked aside the net curtain to find both pavements full of Barrowers in their Sunday best heading towards the Close, and dropped it in a hurry when he caught the giggling eye of some behatted females passing three abreast. He was on the point of returning to check that his alarm clock had not stopped when there was a knock at the granny-flat door and Mrs Merluza called out,

'Professor?'

'Good morning.'

'How did you sleep?'

'Very well, thanks. How about you?'

She opened the door a crack but kept her face turned firmly away, twisted by modesty. She had on a small, pearly-pink hat that matched her jacket.

'I quite forgot that there's an earlier service today,' she said, raising her voice to compensate for having her back turned to him. 'They're digging up Saint Boniface, but there's fresh coffee on the stove and I've just made you breakfast which is keeping hot on the hot plate.'

'Fantastic. What was that you said?'

'Are you out straight away?'

Evan rubbed at his white hair, which was still wild from sleep. He frowned from the effort of forming words so early.

'Ah. Yes. I aim to be at the cathedral library at nine.'

'Well I'll see you this evening then.'

She closed the door. He heard a sudden rise and fall in the sound of excited chatter and feet as she let herself out of the house, then he set a bath running and left the granny flat to totter to what he had already rechristened The Little Boys' Bowling Alley.

Bathed, shaved and discreetly scented, he came in search of breakfast half an hour later, an unaccustomed tie wrenching at his Adam's apple. A slight, thin woman was polishing the hall mirror. As far as he could see, she had nothing on but a sea-green nylon housecoat thing. Her extraordinarily good legs ended in the sheepskin slippers that he could have sworn he saw Mrs Merluza wearing the night before.

'Hello,' said Evan. She stared at him in the mirror from a face like Old Father Time.

'You must be her new lodger,' she said and continued to polish.

'Yes. I'm here for a couple of weeks, maybe less. To do some research in the libraries.'

'I'm the slave. Two mornings' cleaning a week and occasional gardening. Dawn Harper.'

'Hello.'

'You've said that once. She's left breakfast on the hot plate for you.'

'Smells . . . er . . . great.'

81

'She makes the fried bread with olive oil. You do that in America?'

'Er . . . no.'

He walked past her into the kitchen, where the air was already thick with the scents of frying. On the hot plate, under a Pyrex cover, lay a plate bearing fried bread, glistening pink bacon, a halved, blackened tomato and a fried egg whose yolk looked firm to dryness.

'I'm not sure I can, first thing.'

'Chuck it,' she said, standing in the doorway to watch him.

'Could I?'

'I won't tell. Here, let me.'

She scooped up the plate, using her duster as protection from its heat, and sloshed his breakfast into the pedal bin.

'I'll have this emptied before she gets back,' she said, and watched him as he filled a mug with coffee. His hand shook slightly.

'What did you say your name was?' she asked.

'I didn't,' he said, setting down his mug and spooning in several sugars, and saw that he had left his wedding ring in the bathroom. 'It's Evan. Evan Kirby.'

'I thought you looked familiar,' she said. 'Can I have one of those?'

'Be my guest.'

'Thanks.' She poured herself a coffee and stood sipping it, staring at him. He smiled briefly up at her, unnerved, and cast a glance around for a newspaper. There was a *Telegraph* but he would have had to get up and pass close by her to fetch it so he stayed put. 'I've read your book,' she said at last.

'Really?' He tried not to sound surprised. There had been a television documentary, after all; she might have read the picture-book spin-off.

'Yes. I read it a few times in the library, but it was too long to read comfortably in one go, and besides I wanted a copy of my own, so I stole it.'

'You don't say.'

'I keep it by my bed.'

She examined him with the blank stare of a psychopath, or was it the guileless gaze of a rustic innocent? Not altogether rustic, evidently; she had read and clearly enjoyed the full version of *Visions of Hell*, much of which was meaty stuff.

'Sit down.' He waved a cigarette at the spare chair on the other side of the table.

'No,' she said. 'You should be having breakfast.'

'Go on,' he said.

She sat.

'I'm after something big,' she said. 'The police couldn't help and the Cathedral lot's too feeble. You could tell me, I know you could.'

'What?'

'What's the strongest invocation for finding a missing person?'

He played for time.

'Sorry.' He laughed. 'I don't quite . . . er. Invocation to whom, exactly?'

She fixed him with her small eyes.

'You know,' she said, and smiled. Her teeth were clean and even, but looked unnaturally wide – like a horse's. He knew.

'You mean, the Devil?' he asked.

'Well, in your words, Professor, "he wears many faces". My manual suggested I aim high and try for Belial.'

'Which manual are you using?'

'*Bugwash and Stavey*, seventh edition.'

'Reputable enough,' he said, seeing a way, albeit a rash one, of losing this rather frightening woman's attentions. 'But I think you could do better.'

'Tell me.'

He saw her tough hands tighten their grip on her mug.

'How badly do you need this . . . This person?' He was putting it on, now, fobbing her off. She had probably fallen for some local swain beyond her reach; an estate agent, perhaps, or simply a plasterer bound round with wife and clinging children.

'More than life,' she said. She said it almost airily. Was he doing the right thing? His interest was purely academic. He didn't believe, but there were plenty of unpleasant stories of those who did.

'I've a better book,' he said. 'I'll lend it to you to copy the relevant sections.'

'Thank you,' she said. 'Thanks.' He rose. 'Finish your coffee, first,' she said. 'It can wait.'

But he knew it couldn't. She might only be after a local swain, but he sensed that if he didn't find her the book now, she would gladly turn his room upside down in order to steal it.

'It's OK,' he said. 'I'd finished.'

It was a valuable book, rarer than she could know, which was why he was carrying it with him rather than leaving it behind at the Booths's. An early eighteenth-century demonic lexicon. He had found it cunningly sewn into the middle of the books of Isaiah in a later family Bible, and he had cut it out and had it rebound. The Bible had cost a small fortune, but the lexicon was worth more and the bookseller had given the Bible no more than a cursory glance front and back and knew nothing of the nasty little secret it held. Little more than thirty pages, but something Satanists would kill to possess. He had quoted it in *Visions of Hell* but a passing fear, doubtless irrational, had led him to lie about the source. Why then was he lending it to his landlady's cleaning woman?

'Because she needs it more than I do,' he thought as he slid the little book from the lining of his suitcase, 'and maybe because she can lose it for me.'

She said nothing when he passed it to her but opened it at once and began to read, scowling at the crabbed print and blotchy vellum.

'I'll be here for at least a week,' he told the top of her head. 'Drop it back when you've finished. I'll ... er ... I'll be off to the library now, then.' And he left her to read and set out along the gleaming pavements, a cigarette defiantly in hand and a queasy uncertainty as to the wisdom of facing the day with an empty stomach, olive oil or no.

The well-dressed crowd was coming back from the Cathedral but in a state of overexcitement out of all proportion to what they had just been through. From what he could remember from the compulsory church-going of his Boston childhood, freshly emerged congregations rewarded their virtue and patience with a spirited round of greetings and, possibly, gossip. But that was on a Sunday, after a sermon and in most cases a week of unsociable labour; these people had emerged from what Evan took to be a sermon-free Holy Communion, a service to which he assumed they were inured. As he walked through to the Close, it became almost embarrassing to meet the directionless sparkle of so many happy faces. Their elation rested uneasily on these types of prosperous conformity as it had on the mundane forms of the worshippers he used to watch leaving the Chapel of Charismatics in his street in Nowhere, Vermont. He kept his eyes firmly on the Cathedral and cut an easy swathe through the beaming, mostly skirted, pedestrians. Then, nearing the foot of the south transept he had to ask the way to the library. He accosted a round, amiable creature in powder blue.

'Carry on from here,' she directed, 'then turn right through that passage – we call it the Glurry – and on the other side you'll see a lovely round building. That's the Chapter House and the library is on the first floor.'

'Thank you,' he said.

'But I think I should warn you that there's no visiting until ten-thirty.'

'Can't you see he's doing research?' clucked her companion, who wore navy and a less approachable aspect.

'Actually yes, I am,' confessed Evan.

'Silly me,' laughed the first woman, pointing with a gloved hand to his briefcase.

'Tell me,' he asked, feeling sorry for her as her navy companion clicked her tongue and stared, impatient, at the passers-by. 'Why all the excitement? What have I missed? My landlady said something about a saint.'

'Oh a miracle!' gushed the first woman. 'You missed a real *miracle*. And we saw it *all*, didn't we, Marge?'

'Popish tripe,' snarled Marge. 'So nice talking to you,' she said to Evan and steered her companion away.

Evan watched them pass, bickering, round the corner of the transept then followed the path through the Glurry to find a chapter house every bit as fine as its equivalents in Salisbury and Wells. A short, neat, grey-haired woman was waiting for him at the door. He recognized her at once as the one with the fox terrier on the train from London.

'Professor Kirby?'

'Yes?'

'How do you do. Petra Dixon.' She shook his hand and her reading spectacles bounced on their chain against her small, no-nonsense bosom.

'I should have introduced myself on the train,' he said.

'But you didn't know me from Adam and I certainly had no idea who you were, so I would have found it rather odd,' she replied simply. 'I ran into Mrs Merluza in the Close just now and she told me you'd be on your way so I thought I'd wait outside in case you got lost,' she went on, unlocking the door on to a short spiral staircase. As he followed her, Evan noticed that her hair was not cut short as he had at first supposed, but grown long then brushed back tightly off her head and swept up in an unexpectedly baroque chignon with a black velvet bow.

'I trust *you* didn't miss the miracle,' he ventured.

'I jolly well did,' she said, pausing to open a second door into the high, vaulted chamber above. 'My temper gets filthy if I don't have seven hours' sleep and I never turn in until I've heard the shipping forecast.'

'Oh,' he said, nonplussed. 'I see.'

'My brother-in-law's a lighthouse keeper,' she explained,

reading his expression. 'It helps me feel in touch. Had you not seen photographs?' she continued.

'No,' said Evan who was involuntarily gazing up at the ceiling. 'It's incredible.'

'Mmh,' said Miss Dixon, sitting sidesaddle at her desk to change into her comfortable shoes before opening the mail she had brought up with her from downstairs. 'Thirteenth-century. The shelves are much later of course. Downstairs is much the same only without the view and with stone thrones in place of books.'

The central single pillar seemed far too delicate to support such a massive structure. A maze of tracery radiated from it. The effect was like a magnification of the underside of a beech leaf. Though the Chapter House seemed round on the outside, within it was octagonal. The staircase and door took up one of the eight sides, high oak bookcases laden with riches took up four and the remaining three held leaded windows with views across the Close and on to the nearby windows of the Cathedral's quire and south transept. The higher glass was clear though pleasantly uneven with age. The lower five inches of each window had been stained with a stylized design of running water with, here and there, a darting fish.

'What exactly were you hoping to read?' Miss Dixon's tone brought him back to earth.

'Pardon me,' he laughed, 'but I'm sure you're used to people gaping.' She said nothing so he dug in his briefcase and brought out an index card. 'Right,' he said, '*Barrow 341* to start with then Memling's *Gravitas* and *Barrow 22* – that's *On the Nature of Briddes*.'

'Very *à propos*,' Petra Dixon commented as she left her

desk to find *Barrow 341*, a twelfth-century compilation of miracles, fables and saintly legends.

'How so?' asked Evan. 'May I sit here?'

'Yes do. It seems you'd be interested in this morning's little phenomenon.'

'Tell me more.'

'Well, because we need to carry out drastic building works in the east end, the patron saint is having to be moved.' She pulled over a set of rolling steps, flipped down the brake shoe with her foot and began to climb them.

'Saint Boniface of Barrow?'

'Yes. You've done your homework, only it's pronounced "Brew".'

'Sorry. He's the tall one with the sparkler, yes?'

'That's right. Anyway there was a service this morning for the opening of his tomb and a flock of doves shot from inside.'

'My word.'

'At least, I say doves but I wasn't there and my inform-ant owned to having been between long-range and reading specs at the time. But they were certainly white.' Miss Dixon grunted slightly as she tugged a large, vellum-bound volume from the shelf.

'Here. Let me,' said Evan, bounding forward, and he took it from her so that she had both hands free to climb with. 'Fascinating,' he went on. 'You don't think it was a put-up job?'

'We're not in Ireland, Professor.'

'No. Of course not. But I was thinking of Augustan Rome and those funerals they still have in Japan sometimes, where they let out a flight of birds to represent the departed soul.'

'Possibly. It's not very us but then the Bishop is still very new here. I was thinking more of Claudia of Knightcote.' She wheeled the steps back to their place and returned to her desk.

'You've got me there.'

'Marvellous story. Hang on.' She twisted to a small shelf beside her. '*Keller and Baynton* vol. three,' she said, thawing as she pulled out the book. 'My favourite.' And she read him the story of how Claudia of Knightcote's corpse was replaced in the turning of a handmaid's back, into a bedful of fluttering doves. She then shamed his ignorance further, but with charm, by pointing out a reference in his own early work, *The Visionary Tradition*, to St Marty of Rabastens who drove pillaging soldiers off his tomb in the guise of three enraged cob swans. Evan didn't remember that bit and thought he must have plagiarized it.

Miss Dixon proved herself the soul of discreet helpfulness and her library was indeed breathtaking. Evan was already familiar with its contents, having pored over the catalogue often enough in the British Library and back in Harvard, but there was nothing to compare with the happy sensation of feeling the precious manuscripts on a desk before him. He frittered away much of the morning devouring *Barrow 341* for no better reason than the perfection of its illumination. When the huge bells in the spires behind her sounded the lunch hour, Miss Dixon apologized that she had to turn him out for forty minutes while she went home to walk her terrier. Out in the Close again, she directed him to the Tracer's Arms in Tower Place. He enjoyed an excellent lunch of the local herb-flecked sausages and an incautious pint of Old Stoat, the local bitter, before he was led further astray by the siren lure of the Cathedral where he wandered happily for half an hour or more. It had one of those cunning roofs which seem so much higher on the inside than they appear to be from without, but for him the chief attraction was the scattering of fine memorials, whose epitaphs it had long been his bad habit to study. Already there were hordes of tourists searching for small white birds and bothering the Scottish Masons for photographs. The west end tympanum bore a crude representation of the Last Judgement watched over by various saints including a towering Saint Boniface of Barrow, carrying a lantern whose spiky beams represented the ball of fire that had converted him. Tourists were lining up to take photographs of each other in front of him. The rising souls of the blessed on whom he cast his approving, if sightless, gaze seemed to be paddling through water. Ambrosia perhaps, or badly carved clouds.

Evan's afternoon was spent in genuine work, translating the relevant chunks of Memling's *Gravitas* and taking notes for the photograph collectors. As she shut the doors again at five o'clock, Miss Dixon warned him that Tuesdays always saw the place overrun with school parties and a lecture on bookbinding. On her advice, he telephoned Dr Cresswell – the *Lord* of Tatham's – and arranged to spend Tuesday there instead.

11

'No. Don't jump on there. *No!* You'll leave pawprints. Beast! Go on. Pssh. Get *down!*' Emma shouted.

The cat, an immensely fat ginger tom, regarded her with his habitual expression which could convey either hauteur or cretinism, depending on Emma's mood. A damp cloth in hand, to wipe away the pawprints he had indeed left on the kitchen table, she scooped him gently up and carried him out to the stairs. He sat where she left him, sending a gooseberry glare through the banisters as she returned to tidying the kitchen. As well as the house, she had inherited its two cats, Rousillou (said to be Occitan for 'small red thing') and his mother, Blanquette. Blanquette was a smoke-tinted Abyssinian of whom so few traces were imprinted on her son that she was assumed to have married down. Both cats were extremely loquacious, mewing as often from a wish to be sociable as from hunger or irritation. Emma tried not to talk to them too much. It was an easy habit into which to slip, however, so her self-discipline in this quarter tended to stretch only as far as not talking to her cats in front of other people.

Since her telephone conversation with Fergus Gibson yesterday, her house had received a major spring cleaning. Emma's original intention had been merely to run around with a Hoover, to do a little dusting and conceivably, to clean the wash basins. In the event, she had started to enjoy herself so much that she had been quite carried away and had hauled rugs out to the washing line for beating, had turned mattresses, washed windows and even lifted pot plants off the windowsills so as to wipe away the brown rings left underneath. She had retrieved stale copies of Sunday papers (she saved money on weekdays by reading papers in the staff common room), *The Times Literary Supplement*, *History Today* and *The Church Times* from points of accumulation around the house and had tied them up in neat bundles in the woodshed. Her father had taken out a life subscription to *The Church Times* and the paper continued to arrive regardless of his decease. Emma had intended to write them a cancellation letter long ago, but had become a quiet fan of the quirky journal and continued to read it, cherishing the hope that the subscription department would now never notice their oversight.

She had taken everything out of the larder, washed the shelves and even wiped the dust off storage jars and the stickiness off jam pots before she set them neatly back. She had sorted through the bathroom cupboard and thrown out old pills and several tubes of her late father's pile ointment which she had been keeping on the rather depressing offchance that they might come in useful some day. In a final blast of enthusiasm last night, she had taken all her late father's suits, shirts, shoes and ties and piled them into bin liners, along with some clothes she had not donned since the Indian cotton summer of 1977. She had telephoned the Spastics Shop before setting out for this morning's school, and a whinnying sort of woman had just come round to take it all away in her Morris Oxford. The house now had a clean, expectant feel to it.

Emma sat with her post-lunch coffee in the sitting room and waited. Blanquette emerged from under the sofa, jumped with a mew to her lap, sniffed the coffee and, rejecting it, lay down. Mr Gibson had said 'after lunch' but that could be now, which was one-thirty, or in two hours' time. She hoped he would not expect her to harbour any strong tastes of her own. She judged houses on the air they conveyed and was not wont to think in terms of wallpaper or painting effects. On her way home to her rendezvous with the whinnying Spastics envoy, she had bought a copy of *House and Garden* and found it deeply disturbing. Certainly she possessed the initiative to march into town, pore over colour cards and do the place up herself over a score of weekends and long afternoons, but the transformation – exorcism almost – which she had in mind was so momentous that she had a horror of making a mistake. Renovating a late father's house was not so different from building a chapel in which to house his corpse; a task best left to other, impersonal hands.

The garden gate clanged. Emma jumped up and stood peering from the gloom at the back of the room. She barely glimpsed six feet worth of brown tweed striding past the window towards the porch. The knocker was struck. Her coffee was too hot to drink. She hurried into the downstairs lavatory to tip it into the sink, checked her face in the newly polished hall mirror and let him in.

'Miss Dyce-Hamilton?'

'Hello. You must be Mr Gibson. Come in.'

'Thanks. What a garden you have there. I've often admired it on my way past in the car.'

'Isn't it. All my father's work. All I have to do is prune and weed.'

'I'm sure it takes a lot more work than that,' he started, but she was already walking into the sitting room.

He had cast her into confusion. He was not exactly handsome; not her idea of handsome. He had greying sandy hair (which she had never much liked) that appeared to be thinning, and his nose looked as if it had once been broken. He smelled of peppermints and she liked her men to smell of leather and pipe smoke. His eyes were brown and liquid, however, like a spaniel's and one of their brows had a quizzical tuft in it. She was confused. She had no idea how interior designers should look, but she had not been expecting him to look like this and she was confused.

'No!' he shouted involuntarily on seeing the disagreement between curtains and chair covers.

'What is it?' she asked in alarm, visualizing a brutalized mouse or worse underfoot.

'Oh, sorry. It's probably all your mother's . . .'

'No. I quite agree,' she piped up. 'The whole place is quite revolting. Do sit. Please.'

He sat on the sofa opposite her chair. Blanquette, who usually fled from male strangers in a huff, wandered over to sniff his suit trousers then jumped on to his lap and settled immediately into her contented chicken posture.

'Hello,' he said softly.

As he stroked the cat, Emma saw the flash of a signet ring and a strong wrist. She had seen him before. He had once stood immediately in front of her in the queue for Eucharist and she remembered glancing at his hands as he raised them for a wafer.

'Oh. I'm sorry. Do you hate cats?' she asked. 'Just push her off if you like.'

'No. She's lovely. What's her name?'

'Blanquette.'

'As in *veau*?'

'What?'

'*Veau*.'

'Er. Probably. I've seen you before, you know.'

'Really? Well I only live a few streets away.'

'No. It wasn't in the street.' She tried to laugh. 'I was kneeling next to you for Communion. I shouldn't have been looking, I suppose, but . . . sometimes it's hard.'

'Isn't it.'

Should she ask after his mother? Lydia had said he had mother trouble. Perhaps that was too personal.

'I should explain,' she said. 'I'm not certain that I want to stay here but if I decide I do, I shall want the place tidied up and if I decide to sell I think I'll get a better price if I've done some titivating.'

'I see. How much were you thinking of having done?'

'How do you mean?'

'Well, anything structural, for instance? Do you want walls knocking down or windows moving?'

'Goodness no – unless, of course, you think it vital. Just walls and carpets and' – here she grimaced at the sofa – 'I suppose these ghastly old chair covers. Well, I say just, but I expect that costs the earth.'

'It wouldn't be cheap, no, but as you so rightly say, it would help you get a better price. Can I look round?'

'Yes. Of course.' Emma would have preferred to sit here at a safe distance rather than walk side by side. 'Would you like a cup of coffee first?' she added. Once moving, one's limbs were so much freer to move further. He emanated so;

it was insidious, like a sexual equivalent of bad breath only far from repulsive.

'Thank you, but no,' he answered. 'I had some just before I came out.'

So she apologized for the house being in such a terrible mess and they walked round it. He wrote things in a pocket book as they went.

'What are you writing?'

'Extremely rude things about the decor of your lovely house,' he said with his soft Scots accent. She laughed then fell behind for a second to pick a piece of apple peel from between her teeth, cursing herself for not having grinned as well as pouted in the hall mirror before she let him in. It had occurred to her that he could have been taking notes for a burglar friend. It had also occurred to her, as their arms brushed yet again on the stairs, to lock him in the spare room and keep him all to herself.

'I would feed you well,' her mind's voice wheedled, 'and my requirements would be few. No visitors, of course, but I would let you have a sewing machine and a television.'

He seemed delighted. He admired the good state of preservation of the cornices and mouldings, was happy to see that none of the original sash windows had been touched and suggested that she apply for planning permission to replace the one bricked up during the imposition of Window Tax. He tugged, with her permission, at some skirting around the bath and was pleased to find that the bath had lion's feet. As he admired she felt a glow of pride. She had always liked the house because her father had chosen it and she had lived there. Now, through Fergus Gibson's spaniel eyes, she perceived its finer points.

As they returned, at the end of his tour, from a quick trip to the cellar, she snatched a white handkerchief that was riding up out of his pocket and stuffed it up the sleeve of her dress.

They re-entered the sitting room, where Rousillou, who was now sunning himself, took up an enviable position on Fergus Gibson's knees.

'There remains the sticky question of money. Obviously I can't give you an estimate until we've chosen colours and materials but, roughly, what would your budget be?'

'A few thousand,' she suggested, wondering how far her nest egg would stretch. 'How are you paid?'

'Well I charge a set fee for my suggested scheme and then, if you decide to go ahead, I'll provide the workforce and materials then charge you ten per cent on top of their cost.'

'Lovely,' she said, oblivious.

He raised that eyebrow again as he stood.

'Right then, I'll give you a ring when the plans are ready and once I've got the samples together. Probably in two or three days. Wednesday, I expect. Can I call you here during the day?'

'I teach at the Choir School most mornings but, yes, afternoons are fine,' she said. 'Or evenings,' she added.

'You're in the phone book, aren't you?'

Had he already looked her up?

'Yes,' she said, walking him to the front door. He slid his hands into his pockets and paused, frowning. 'Have you lost something?' she asked.

'Nothing really. I think I might have dropped a hand-kerchief somewhere, that's all.'

'I'll keep a look-out for it.'

'Thank you. Goodbye, then.'

'Goodbye. And thank *you.*'

Rousillou followed him down the garden path to the gate then, belly swinging, bounded back asking for a hug. She shut the front door then pulled the stolen handkerchief from her sleeve. There was an F embroidered in one corner, in red with a little toy soldier standing to attention against the upright of the letter. It was exquisitely done, obviously not bought in a shop. Mother trouble. His mother had worked it for him when he was little and before she had become any trouble. F for Fergus. Nothing really, he had said. She sniffed it. It smelled of peppermints too. She would wash and iron it for him. He would be touched. She would be pleased to touch him.

While the cats were eating their supper, Emma sat at her desk and chose a postcard to send to her godson, Crispin, who was thirteen and had just arrived for his first term at Tatham's. His mother had telephoned the other day asking if Emma could invite him round. He was bound to be homesick. She sent him a picture of an elephant from a Bodleian manuscript.

'Dear Crispin,' she wrote. 'Welcome to your "Big" school! I hope everything is well. Your mother rang me the other day and gave me all the family news. How *lovely* about your Lottie going to have puppies. I'll bet you'll find they keep one just for you. Can you come to tea tomorrow at four? (Tuesday is still a half day, isn't it?) If you can't, ask Mr Henryson to let you ring me – otherwise I'll assume it's OK. Lots of love. Emma (D-H). p.s. It's number 8 Tatham Street. p.p.s. Will make a chocolate biscuit cake especially!'

12

Later on Monday afternoon Mrs Merluza, whose husband no one had ever met, left Evan Kirby's room where she had been having a quiet snoop and dialled the Bishop's Palace number.

'Deirdre, *c'est moi*,' she said when someone answered. 'No, I am coming but I'm running rather late. I'll be there in ten minutes . . . Yes. So sorry. Are they all there? . . . Oh Lord. I'll set off now. Bye, dear.'

She kept up a muttered commentary as she hurried, hair-patting, to the kitchen. When alone she no longer spoke Spanish, but worked unconsciously at her English vowels.

'Now. Harrods bag. Bag. Bag. Ah there you are. Harrods bag into which we put one candle.' She pulled a candle from a candlestick. 'One candle yes and one piece of perfect fruit.' She gave the fruit bowl a tentative shake which released a shimmer of fruit fly. 'No,' said Mrs Merluza. 'Not really. Try the fridge.' She tried the fridge and found a cellophane-wrapped bunch of grapes. 'One perfect grape,' she announced, tugging one off and tossing it into her bag. Then she opened the bottom drawer of the dresser and took out a carefully folded square yard of deep blue cloth. 'And one meditation mat,' she declared, folding the mat one more time so as to fit it into the carefully preserved carrier bag. 'Now, what else?' she asked, moving to the hall and pulling a cotton cardigan about her shoulders. '*Ah, si,*' she answered with a frown. Leaving the bag on a chair in the hall she went to open the door of the downstairs lavatory.

The Victorians showed a cavalier attitude towards many of their downstairs lavatories, contorting their importance into whatever awkward space remained on an architect's plan; curious behaviour given their delight in a well-proportioned bathroom. Though half-redeemed by a stained-glass window, Mrs Merluza's was no exception. It stood a little over four feet wide, ten feet deep and twelve feet high. When she emerged a few minutes later her breathing was wild and a faint smile pulled at her lips at every breath. She returned to the kitchen telephone and called the Bishop's Palace again.

'Deirdre? . . . Yes, *c'est moi encore.* Look, you'll have to do without me this evening . . . Yes, you see my little girl's coming home . . . No, I've just found out.' There was a pause for Deirdre Chattock's conjectures then Mrs Merluza (whose name she allowed to be pronounced to rhyme with 'medusa' as in raft of, as opposed to 'marelootha' as in Spanish for hake) explained in the tone of one who knows she will be understood, 'No Deirdre, she hasn't. I just *know.*'

She left her meditation-class paraphernalia on the table beside her then walked to the hall and stood before its mirror a while to calm herself. She ran her pointed fingers through her full black hair. Its deep raven hue was the only part of her colouring which was wholly natural but, Marge Delaney-Siedentrop had recently confided, as only an intimate could, that there were those who took it for a superior wig. She had since taken to braving high winds without a headscarf and had even been seen to comb her hair in public.

Mrs Merluza did not only visit the Palace for meditation classes. In private sessions Deirdre Chattock was helping her to unravel her past. She could remember nothing of her parents, though she liked to think that her mother had possessed the same black hair until her deathday. The story she had allowed to be passed around was that she came of a good Barcelona family and that home and relatives had been destroyed by a Basque separatist incendiary bomb while she was picking her daughter up from a party. Looked on therefore as a sweet refugee, she had let only Mrs Chattock into the secret that she was actually orphaned by amnesia. Try as she might, she could reach back no further than a Barcelona nightclub where she had danced as a child or, more precisely, a *jeune fille* and where Jésus had danced with her and shown her things . . .

Her reverie was interrupted by the opening of the front door. It was her Professor Kirby, who had arrived yesterday. She had been taking lodgers ever since her Madeleine left for university. She missed her daughter's presence – company was not the *mot juste* for that brooding creature's social contribution – and it pleased her to cook the occasional breakfast and to feel that there was someone else under her roof.

Professor Kirby was the first lodger to whom she had entrusted a latchkey. So far they had all been foreign students (Barrowcester was a perennial favourite with the Germans), visitors from further north or shifty little organists who had come to give recitals. He was how she would imagine an eagle might look if turned into a man. He was at once broad-shouldered and thin so that he seemed to stoop, although his posture was perfect. He had a great beak of a nose which made the pale blue of his eyes piercing rather than babyish. His manner towards her was so polite and distinguished that they had been talking for some minutes before she remembered that he was American and that she should say how she had always wanted to see Maine. One of his huge, clever hands was forever teasing at a packet of cigarettes and his lighter was never in the pocket he tried first.

'*Buona sera*, Mrs Merluza.'

'Hello there, Professor,' she tinkled at him from the corridor. 'A productive day, I hope.'

'Very productive, thank you.' He had been shopping and bore a carrier bag of food. She hoped he would not burn anything. 'Yours is a beautiful city,' he said.

'Isn't it, though,' she agreed.

'I went to the Cathedral library and Miss Dixon told me about the happening there this morning. Were you at the service?'

'Yes. It was a beautiful' – she sought momentarily for a word – 'stunt.'

'A stunt? So you don't think it was miraculous?'

He came closer in the hall. She could smell the mixture of his cigarettes and cologne. His hair had streaks of grey in it and there was a curl which refused to lie down and was a terrible temptation to touch.

'No,' she said. 'They need money to pay for the building works. This will bring crowds and crowds mean money.'

'Ah, but might not Saint Boniface have had such a worthy cause in mind?'

'Ouph!' she scoffed with a flap of the hand, and he laughed at her, opening the door to the granny flat.

She returned to the kitchen and opened the fridge to look for food. There was veal and she could make a sauce with tomatoes and basil from the pot outside the French windows. The telephone rang. It was a call-box. After the pips Madeleine's voice said,

'Mum?' in a strained, rushed way.

'*Cariño!*' They always spoke Spanish when alone or on the telephone, it created instant intimacy. When the subject was an awkward one however, or when either mother or daughter lost her temper, they used English. 'Where are you?'

'I'm at King's Cross. Can I come and stay for a bit?'

'But of course!' Mercy Merluza laughed and, kissing her thumb, crossed herself. 'Is everything all right?'

'Sort of. I'll tell you tonight. Be with you in two hours.'

'I'll make up a bed.'

'No. Let me.'

'Ssh. Go catch your train.'

'See you.'

Mercy unhooked an apron from the back of the kitchen door and, tying it around herself, went to knock on the granny-flat door.

'Professor Kirby?'

'Come in.'

She opened the door. Steam was coming from the bathroom. He emerged from it in a long silk dressing gown.

'Oh. Forgive me for disturbing you.'

'Not at all. Forgive my state of half-dress.'

'It was only that my daughter has just rung to say she is coming home and I wondered whether you'd care to join us for dinner.'

'That's very kind but I'm sure she'd rather see you alone.'

'No. Please. Please.' There was almost panic in her voice. 'It's more fun with three and I'm sure she'd like to meet you – she too is an academic.'

'How can I refuse?' He chuckled. 'I'd be delighted. Thank you.'

'About eight? Come up for a sherry in the sitting room first. Now I'll leave you to your, er . . .' She waved a bird claw at the steam.

'Oh. Thank you very much.'

He was an attractive man for a bookworm, she reflected as she climbed the worn stairs. He had a vest under his dressing gown, which she found faintly moving.

Her daughter's room was at the front of the house and looked over a pattern of grey and brown-red roofs to the Cathedral. Mercy preferred to sleep at the back. She loved her view down over the garden and, from her bed, into the great copper beech at the garden's end. She found that the Cathedral loomed quite enough over all their lives, without her having to greet it every morning on waking. Besides, the sight of it at night, spotlit, like some gargantuan Marie Celestial aircraft carrier was unsettling. Far from filling her with a warm sense of Divine protection, it encouraged morbid fantasies. More than once she had dreamt of opening her eyes in the dead of night to find herself transported, mattress, cotton gloves, nightcream and all, to a precarious position on its kestrel-haunted roof

105

with churning flood water glinting all around in bright moonlight.

On leaving home, Madeleine had commanded Mercy to turn her bedroom into a spare room.

'Left to your own devices you'd go and turn it into a horrid shrine,' she had said.

Mercy had complied although her only guests were paying ones and although there was more relief than sadness at seeing Madeleine off for life. She had set about taking down the posters and scratching the stickers off the windows with a heart unmaternally light.

Madeleine had not been an easy daughter. A child of accident, born under trying circumstances, the little burden was not even graced with a lightening beauty. Lumpish and wooden, with muddy skin and curly brown hair, she bore all too strong a likeness to Abi Merluza, Jésus' mother, a cruel, unleavened woman who owned the nightclub and who died soon after his arrest and just before Mercy's slow flight to England. Undemonstrative as she was unlovely, little Madeleine's saving grace was a grim sense of humour far beyond her years. She was an early developer, like her mother; unlike her mother she was fiercely intelligent. Always a good girl on the surface, her sharpness could bring an obstinate set to her public jaw and a needle's point to her private temper.

Soon after their arrival in Bayswater, Mercy had tried to prettify her child, dressing her in frills and sending her to dance classes. She did not do this without a vengeful glint in her eye for the child was so much the reincarnation of Jésus' mother. Then the girl's brain began to frighten her so she left her alone to her dungarees and her books.

They had enough money to live in some comfort. Madeleine had always been told that this was 'family' money and life insurance for her late father, because its actual source pained Mrs Merluza. Jésus died resisting arrest for molesting some schoolgirls and his mother, Abi, died shortly afterwards, rotten with the twin moulds of spite and grief. Nervous and pregnant, Mercy had sat up all night with the smitten corpse then rung the doctor and notary in the morning. She had sold the nightclub and adjoining flat for a handsome price before any relations stepped forward. Quickly ransacking her 'mother-in-law's' boudoir before she left for France, she found a stash of jewellery hidden in the hem of an ugly fur coat which she had intended to take with her to sell when times were hard again. A few quick scratches on the bathroom mirror proved the stones to be better than paste. Abi had never worn or displayed them so, assuming them to be stolen, but thinking of the future of her unborn child, Mercy had sewn some into the linings of her own scant wardrobe and hidden the rest in the hollowed-out heels of some boots. Sweating like a fever victim, she wore the boots and the three most loaded of the dresses all the way to Paris where she quickly sought out a hungry jeweller. She opened a bank account to earn interest on the money from the nightclub and, as soon as she could walk after Madeleine's birth, spent some of the jewellery earnings on a nanny, a smart new outfit and a session in a beautician's sufficiently intensive to secure her work as an assistant in a dress shop. She worked there until Madeleine was old enough to attend school, then upped roots again, moved to London and sold the rest of the jewels. In Paris as a sales assistant and in

London as a dressmaker, she worked so hard that she had never needed to touch the ever swelling money from the sale of her former lover's property.

In the late 1960s, however, London was becoming expensive, so when, on a teacher's advice, Madeleine was entered for and won a full scholarship to Tatham's, her mother had leapt at the opportunity to settle in Barrowcester. In those days the city was several hours from London and still ludicrously cheap. Girls had been admitted to the school for only three years and Madeleine had been the first to win one of the ten annual scholarships. Mercy at last felt a shifting of pride, even if the sight of her fast-growing girl in a scholar's black gown and eighteenth-century waistcoat was something nightmarish.

While Madeleine enjoyed a bargain education (free except for books, which she found or ordered at the city library, and 'extras', for which she never asked) Mercy took over a small curio shop in Tower Place. She changed the name from The Treasure Trove to Boniface Crafts and, although the place only opened between eleven and four each day, did a thriving trade selling overpriced jerseys and unpleasant local pottery. Her taking in lodgers had started with a kind offer made to some enquiring tourists who had just relieved her of an especially difficult coffee pot.

Madeleine was an 'academic in the arts' and underpaid; thus far Mercy could comprehend. The details of her daughter's curious employment bored, when they did not escape her. Madeleine shared a sour-smelling flat in Earls Court with an African dispatch-rider called Georgene. Mercy went to stay the night there when she visited

London for the January sales. Madeleine came home for a fortnight over her birthday in July and for a week at Christmas. She rang once every ten or eleven days to say hello. A spontaneous visit however, like the impending one, was unheard of and alarming. As she made up her daughter's bed, Mercy sorted out the possible explanations. Pregnancy was hardly likely and, if that were the case, London was surely a safer spot to deal with such things than the watchful confines of Barrowcester. Affection, then? Mercy rejected this as being out of character and more frightening than pregnancy. By the time that the bed was made, clean towels hung out and she was on her way to cut some flowers for her daughter's dressing table, the reluctant mother had settled for nervous breakdown. Madeleine had gone into a neurotic decline, as was the wont of plain intellectuals, and had come home to collapse; she was in a crisis and needed her mother.

Trying not to peer too obviously into the granny flat bedroom as she pulled a little strip of variegated ivy off the wall to trail from one side of the vase, Mercy felt a slight ache in her ample bosom. The sensation was unfamiliar but even a vague acquaintance, such as that know-it-all Lydia Hart, could have diagnosed an onset of motherly love.

13

In the kitchen that sprawled through the lower half of the extension designed for her by Fergus Gibson, Lydia Hart was busy chopping onions. Clive was arranging some flowers for the table. They were to eat in the kitchen as this was to be a family occasion. Lydia sniffed loudly.

'Well for pity's sake,' Clive muttered, 'there's no need to cry about it.'

'I'm not. It's the onions,' she snapped, tipping the chopped onions into a heavy sauté pan which she rattled with feeling over a flame.

Hot olive oil spat through the silence. Clive centred the flowers to his satisfaction, swept a heap of discarded leaves on to his hand and into the bin, then pulled open the cutlery drawer and began to count out four of everything. There was an awkward moment as they met, she on her way to the fridge to find mince, he on his way to the table to lay it. He gestured nervously to let her pass. He set out the cutlery as she crushed a pound of mince into the frying onion to brown it.

'It's only that I'm all overexcited and sort of *moved*,' she said. 'This doesn't happen to us every week. I'm just very happy, really,' she continued bitterly as she poured boiling water over a bowl of tomatoes.

'That makes two of us,' he lied, feeling nothing, as he kissed her cheek, but relief at an opening for such an overture.

He held an arm across her shoulders – which always cut her pleasantly down to size – and watched with her as the skin began to break in the heat and slide off the tomatoes.

'Why do you always make lasagna when he comes home?' he asked her.

'Why? Don't you like it?'

'No, I like it a lot. It's just that we never have it when he's not here.'

'Tobit's favourite,' she said with a sniff.

So it wasn't the onions.

'Oh,' said Clive, and leaving her side he took four place mats from another drawer and laid them on the table. 'I mean to say, the way you were going on before you told me, I thought she was in a wheelchair or blind or something.'

'Hateful comparisons.'

'I'm not comparing. I'm just illustrating the effects of your overreaction on my imagination. Of course her being what she is isn't a disability. It used to be *treated* as one but now it's, well, if anything it can be an advantage. Positive discrimination and all that.' He opened two bottles of the Riecine they had brought back with them from Saiole last autumn. Tobit gulped wine as if it were air and Clive suspected that, even after champagne, they'd all need a little extra tonight. There was an ominous silence coming from Lydia's back. 'Tell me about her,' he said.

'There's not much to tell,' said Lydia, turning, 'as I saw her so briefly. She's incredibly attractive. You'll fancy the skin-tight pants off her.'

'Hardly likely.'

'Just try not to show it, that's all I ask.'

'For Christ's sake, I don't go for her type. Never have.'

Lydia raised her eyebrows and turned back with a sigh to her cookery.

'It's such a pity that . . .'

'What?'

Sometimes she detested Clive's habit of chipping in with a 'What?' whenever she was simply reaching for a word or pausing for effect. She detested it this evening. She wished he would leave her to brood. She wanted him to go upstairs and finish in the bathroom so that they wouldn't both have to use it in a rush.

'Him being the way he was though,' she started afresh, pointedly, 'I suppose if he was going to surprise us all by getting married it would *have* to be someone different.'

'Do you think she knows about him?'

'That he's – that he used to be gay?'

'Yes, of course.'

'Oh, bound to have done. A lot of girls like the challenge. He makes a point of telling people. Well, he did. Don't you remember, he told Emma Dyce-Hamilton once? God only knows why because he's far too young to have been her type and poor Emma's scarcely the sort of girl who needs fending off.' Lydia snorted then turned her amusement into a sigh. 'Oh Clive, it's going to be so odd having to reshuffle the way we think of him. I mean, we won't have to make little explanations and excuses any more.'

'Oh I don't know about that,' said her husband. 'Barrowcester isn't exactly Brixton. I'll go and finish in the bathroom.' He walked slowly upstairs, leaving her to make a béchamel sauce and to grate Parmesan.

The bombshell had been dropped this afternoon. At her

feet. She had arrived to find Hart's, her delicatessen, in chaos. Beth, her manageress, had had to go home with flu and three pretty but motiveless assistants had been trying to do the Monday stock-take and serve customers at the same time. At around three, by which hour Lydia had calmed everyone down, tidied up Beth's slatternly office and finished the stock-taking herself, her son Tobit had drifted in from the spring sunshine, dapper in crumpled linen.

'Tobit! What a lovely surprise,' she called out, startled.

'Bigger surprise than you think, Ma,' he said, with the sheepish grin he had inherited from Clive and which went so well with his lively green eyes, which were hers.

Sensing danger, Lydia had tried to gesture him into Beth's office for tea. He had stayed put however, under the decorative gaze of the shop girls. When he had said,

'I've got engaged,' she had therefore been forced to react as a mother should; no glimmer of doubt in her radiant smile.

'Oh Tobit, how perfectly *lovely!* Gilly, this is a celebration. Put up the closed sign and get a bottle of Dom Perignon from Truskers. Half-holiday!' In the instant bustle of girls lowering blinds and draping cheeses, she snatched a few seconds' privacy. 'Tobe darling,' she said and hugged him properly. 'Who is it? I had no idea that . . .'

'Sorry. It's a bit mean to spring it on you like this.' He caught her eye and they both giggled. At least he had giggled and she had sort of gasped. 'It rather took me by surprise too,' he added and glanced over his shoulder at the door.

'Is she up here with you?'

'Yes. It's her day off so I shut up shop and we both escaped. She'd never seen the place before and I thought, as it was such a lovely day . . .'

113

'Can you both come to supper?'

'I was hoping you'd ask that. Yes please. Ah, there she is.' He darted out of the door and brought his fiancée across into his mother's shop.

'Ma, this is Gloire. Gloire, meet my ma.'

Smiling harder than ever as her girls seemed to freeze around her, Lydia held out a hand. The immediate impression of her prospective daughter-in-law was one of height, restrained glamour, poise and intelligence. Gloire was perfection as only Tobit could have found for himself. Gloire was also black as the. Well. Very *very* black.

They had drunk Dom Perignon and the girls had made suitably congratulatory noises and gone on irritatingly about how the bubbles were going up their several noses. Lydia had done her best to charm. Gloire had smiled rather too candidly. Lydia had hugged Tobit again. Tobit had laughed at her. Finally, unable to bear any more, she had kissed Gloire on the cheek and banished them to go sightseeing until sevenish.

Clive and she had spent the last hour simpering liberal platitudes across the kitchen at each other, but she disapproved and knew that he did too, in his way. It upset her that in such a crisis they had been unable to be truthful with each other. She assumed that mixed marriages were common enough in Tobit's trend-setting circles. It would be harder to carry the alliance off in Barrowcester, but that was her problem, not her son's. Lydia's main worry was children. One read of half-caste children having crises through belonging neither to one race nor another. While there was no doubt that any grandchildren produced by Tobit and Gloire would be attractive, intelligent and so forth, she should hate them to be treated as fashion accessories; walking exempla of designer-tag liberalism.

If she was hard on herself, Lydia also dared admit that with him the way he had been, only death could have deprived her of her son. With none of the usual early warnings indulged in by the burgeoning hetero male, he was knocking down the snug exclusivity of their former relationship like so many nursery bricks.

Lydia assembled a faultless dish of lasagna and set it to bake. It was always so much better when cooked in advance and then heated through again. She tidied utensils away into the dishwasher and returned milk to the fridge and Parmesan to the cheese box, cutting off a finger of the cheese to nibble. Clive's bathwater gurgled in the pipe outside the kitchen door. Lydia glanced at her watch and saw that there was not time for her to bathe.

'Bugger the Pope,' she swore and hurried upstairs to give her hair a good brush and to change into something befitting a celebration.

When Tobit sounded the doorbell in ten minutes, she sent Clive down to let him and Gloire in. She flung up her bedroom window, hugging a dressing gown about herself.

'Welcome!' she called down. It is hard to talk loudly when one's head is thrown back, so they did no more than grin shyly up at her. 'Your father's on his way down,' Lydia shouted and realized that she was saying that to both of them. 'Love that dress, Gloire,' she added, recognizing one of Tobit's creations and already beginning to veer out of control. She pictured the girl laughing as she changed in the scant shelter of Tobit's sports car.

14

Madeleine Merluza held her ticket up for inspection then lit her last cigarette. When she realized that she did not want it, she stubbed it out on the sole of her shoe and returned the thing to its packet for later use.

'The demon weed, eh?' piped up the young, ginger-haired commuter on the opposite seat. 'Gets you in the end, you know. You heard of Buerger's Disease?'

'Bugger off,' said Madeleine.

'No offence, I'm sure.'

He returned to the perusal of his evening paper and she to that of her novel.

She had been pretending to read ever since they left King's Cross. Acutely aware, of a sudden, that he had been watching her, she turned several pages with inauthentic rapidity and adjusted the scarlet fabric of her dress over her knees. She then caught sight of her reflection in the window, glared and wondered, as she had done several grim times a day since her spectacularly hormonal thirteenth birthday, why she bothered. She let her mud-brown eyes drift back to staring at the 'scalpel-sharp exposé of soured marriage' in her lap and thought again about flinging wide the door and launching her waistless form off the Barrowcester viaduct when the time came to cross it.

Her fear of annihilation was only marginally greater than her dread of public exposure. Her mother had once forced her into a leotard and dumped her, shivering and fat, in a ballet class. Six inches taller than the nymphs around her, she had also been the only one with braces top and bottom and pigeon toes verging on the deformed. Having heard how her daughter had been shunned at her London school for her warts, Mrs Merluza had not thought to have the growths cut out until the last day of the summer holidays. Madeleine arrived for her first day at Tatham's bandaged like a junior leper. After both these and other, similar occasions she had paced feverishly from river to oven door to bathroom cabinet, only to baulk at the thought of the combined spiritual question mark and physical indignity that would follow hard on the heels of her doing anything 'silly'. No. Shame was deadly, but death was worse. Marginally.

The news would break out tomorrow, which was why she was fleeing to Barrowcester tonight. Even as she and the gingery commuter were borne north-west through cattle-laden fields and minor dormitory towns, computer-assisted typesetters were laying out her doom. The train clattered over some points, past some children waving from the bottom of a lurid cottage garden, and Madeleine pictured the headlines that her travelling companion might be reading this time tomorrow in a recollective flush. CARDINAL IN PREGNANCY SHOCK! ROMAN SCANDALS! MARRY OR BURN? HIGH CHURCH DISGRACE! A red and blue waiter came by and she spurned his teetotal advances.

The clinic had telephoned with her test results during her mid-morning Mars bar and she had telephoned Edmund. He had said,

'Oh God,'

a lot which, given his elevated status in the Roman ecclesiastical hierarchy, took remarkably little effect. He had also sounded a mite disappointed that she was still undecided about whether to go through with the pregnancy, which was unorthodox if human. Evidently his bitch of a bog-Irish housekeeper had been listening in and had bought herself return trips to both Lourdes and Connemara on the proceeds, for Madeleine had returned to find her Earls Court flat besieged by reporters. As she climbed out of her Mini a total stranger came up and said,

'Congratulations, Miss Merluza. What does Cardinal Kilpatrick think of the good news?'

'It's Dr Merluza, actually,' she said, 'and I think you've got the wrong address.'

Another stranger took several photographs of unwed mother-to-be saying bugger off bastard hack as she dug in her briefcase for keys.

Hiding amidst the commuters at the bar, Madeleine bit savagely on a pork pie and took a swig from her can of Newcastle Brown. What had possessed her to catch a train home? Even now she could hear her mother's neighbours – one hesitated to call them friends:

'And she was always such a *quiet* girl.'

They were right. She had always been quiet. Ugly and quiet. Some of course would now nod sagely and call it furtive.

After ballet and warts had bitten the dust, her mother had left her beautifully alone. Well, alone. Studious, in her angry fashion, Madeleine had wound her furtive way through Tatham's, via a degree in Fine Arts and Italian at

Bristol, to the Warburg Institute on whose margins for the past six years she had pursued a devotion to the minute dissection of this thing called beauty. Her doctoral thesis, written with the collaboration of a geneticist friend called Madge and published to discreet notices last year, had provided biological and historical evidence that an obsessive appetite for aesthetic pleasure was a genetic trait and invariably accompanied reduced sexual security.

Madeleine's flatmate, Georgene, had cleverly smuggled her out of the flat through the basement and a back entrance. Georgene's nimble handling of her Harley-Davidson in rush-hour traffic would have shaken off any intrepid reporters who had tried to follow in taxis. Georgene worked as a dispatch rider and was out all day and some nights. She had been left with strict instructions that if anyone, including Edmund, bothered her for Madeleine's whereabouts, she was to say she had left to do some research in Freyburg.

Madeleine finished her beer, crushed the can, gaining less satisfaction from this than usual, then returned to her seat with another pork pie and a reserve packet of cigarettes. The gingery commuter was leaving as she sat down.

'Only forty-five per cent pork in those things, you know,' he chirruped.

She leered back with her mouth full. He had abandoned his newspaper. She snatched it, burrowed in her bag for a pen and set about finishing his crossword. He had only filled in two answers. She replaced his 'paternitty' with 'fatherhood'.

'Hi, Mum. I've met this man . . .'

'How'd you like to be a glamorous granny, Mum?'

'How many Barrowers read the *Sun*, Mum?'

'Hi, Mum. Long time no see. I've just got myself knocked up by a Cardinal.'

To mull over various ways of breaking the news had almost become a game. She was not absolutely certain that she wanted to have the baby. In fact, she was fairly certain that she did not. It would be kinder to Mum, therefore, to keep quiet about the pregnancy and see just how big a splash the papers made of it tomorrow. The 'Mother, he done me wrong' sketch, though corny, was fairly plausible. In terms of gritty experience, Madeleine had embarked on what Georgene called her Beretta Caper as a novice; untried and mildly curious. Sadly she had also been the kind of virgin whose erudition annulled the purity generally accorded those of untouched state.

It was all Madge's fault. Madge managed to lead a double life as a full-time geneticist and a part-time good Catholic girl. The part-time role was mainly for her mother's benefit and involved a quantity of good Catholic socializing. The latter brought her up against the personal secretary to a prominent Cardinal. Even the geneticist side of Madge had fancied this man, one Thurston. She had therefore seen rather more of him than was permitted under good Catholic auspices. His 'boss', it transpired, had recently been left a large library of eighteenth-century erotic prints by his father, a good Catholic blessed, plainly, with a wicked sense of humour. The Cardinal was a broad-minded man, as Cardinals go, and understanding that the collection was unique and unpublished, was seeking a good Catholic art historian for professional advice. Never one to leave a friend's talents to languish under a bushel,

Madge had passed Dr Merluza's credentials and telephone number on to Thurston who, grateful, passed it on to the Cardinal who, delighted, rang Madeleine up and invited her to a good Catholic tea.

Madeleine had never looked at erotica over tea with a cardinal before. It might have proved the substance of a very witty article for a feminist review, only Edmund Kilpatrick had been more handsome and less typically ecclesiastical than she had pictured him as being.

'I never wear my soutane for tea,' he assured her.

In the course of two centuries the Cardinal's late father's collection of erotica had lost none of its powers to excite. Add to these factors the deadly hour of the encounter and one could see the conclusion as thoroughly foregone.

As Madge had often warned her, teatime in England was *the* great erotic hour. This was a fact foolishly ignored by many and exploited by only a churlish few. According to Madge's theory, five to four found the intellect in the twenty-four-hourly doldrums when it could only be raised by a cupful of tannin followed two hours later by a shot of something stronger. The bodily resources were also low. One's blood sugar level had sunk and the working beast had to muster all her remaining strength to stagger on until five-thirty. Five to four was the time of day when, if one stopped for a foolish second to analyze the lie of one's thoughts, there could be nothing dearer to the human frame than to curl up somewhere warm, preferably not alone. When the French began to mock our habit of *le five o'clock* they little appreciated that the institution of teatime from the nursery onwards was a national fortification against lust. Sharp, overbrewed tea brought one back to

121

one's senses. Weaker mortals, more prone to the satyr's influence, backed up the tannic defence with biscuits and cake. Cake, in anything but ungenerous proportions, was death to lust. A swiftly eaten slab of teashop gâteau was guaranteed to floor the most predatory bacchante.

Surrounded, in the Cardinal's well-appointed sitting room, by inviting cushions and rugs, as well as his stimulating inheritance, Madeleine and Edmund foolishly left their macaroons untouched until it was all too late. Then a fanciful illustration to Boccaccio inspired them to put the cakes to a less fattening, rather ticklish use. And it was only four thirty-five.

At around six-thirty she was having great fun discovering the sluice system in his antiquated bathroom and Edmund, dressed again, was sitting on the stairs outside with a whisky beside him. His head in his hands, he was getting ready to admit that this must never happen again. Four days later he was in the same pose, in another part of the house, the same thoughts churning in his mind. And three days after that and two days after that. Edmund was a clever man but a weak one and Madeleine, while both clever and no doubt capable of immense feats of will, was having far too good a time preparing his erotica for publication – not in his name, of course – to think of anything but how to be a Scarlet Woman.

'You're savage,' he told her, taking a mouthful of her hair and pulling.

'Ouch!' She laughed, and moved her face back towards his own. He murmured something and hid his face in her breasts.

'What was that?' she asked, leaning away slightly. 'I hate it when I can't hear what you're saying.'

'I said I can hardly bear it.'

'Bear what?'

'You. Your beauty.'

'Oh come on. You'll have to try harder than than. Go on. Convince me.'

'Your eyes,' he said, deadly serious. 'And your strong round arms and . . .'

'Yes?'

'You have quite extraordinary teeth.'

Exchanges like this were frequent. Their frequency weakened her cynical barricades and afforded Madeleine a glimpse of herself as something other than a waistless lump. Fleeing now to Barrowcester, she was unsure whether this should earn Edmund her graditude or deathless malediction.

Georgene steered her in the direction of a family planning clinic to get her fixed up, unbeknownst to Edmund, with the Pill. Madeleine thought this was great fun too, and immensely clever, but soon became bored and forgetful of her daily dose. Recently she had forgotten to take it for three days and a week before that, she had accidentally knocked the foil packet down the back of a chest of drawers and got bored of trying to tease it out with a coathanger. On both occasions she had, in all innocence, tried to make up for her lapse by wolfing three or four pills at once. The consequence would not be visible for months, but it had made its presence felt. She had alerted Edmund and it seemed unlikely that they would ever meet again. It was only in their final interview, over the telephone, when she laughed at his explanation of the rhythm method, that he had realized that Madge had passed her off as a good

Catholic under false pretences. Conducted entirely in his flat during daylight hours, their affair had been archly indulgent on her part, archly tortured on his, and wholly lacking in any emotional engagement from either party. Confronting the rude comeuppance of this hasty liaison of loin and cerebellum, it had not crossed her mind to be hurt that he had not mentioned marriage, even to explain its impossibility.

They were hurtling over the viaduct. She had left it too late to hurl herself to an easy death. She pulled her case down from the rack, finished her second can of beer and relit a protective cigarette. If things were really bad she could always come down here on foot to put an end to it all. This being Barrowcester, someone would be certain to waylay her however, trying to dissuade her with arguments of eternal love, temporal duty, or at least an invitation to sherry. Madeleine hated Barrowcester. The emotion smote her in the spleen as they pulled into the station and a porter opened her door for her with a smile. She loathed the place. Why was she here? It was too pretty and the people were unnaturally caring and nice and it was all too damned un-her. She handed in her ticket and dawdled out on to Station Approach to begin the long climb up the High Street, along Tower Place, past Boniface Crafts and through the Close to Tracer Lane and home. Home, whose vowel moaned with animal discontent. She kept her head down, ignoring the blandishments of window boxes and kind, open faces. She was not ready to meet anyone and tomorrow, after reading their cleaning ladies' papers, they would be all too ready to avoid her. Oh *why* had she come and why oh why was she in a red dress?

Red in Barrowcester adorned only post boxes, telephone kiosks and the fire engine. The Barrowcester female wore calm browns and greens, tasteful blues and various exclusive shades of cobweb or limestone. Summer brought a brief crisis of pastels and florals but they were few who made brief erroneous ventures into geranium or tiger lily; it was all forget-me-not and jasmine with the occasional blown rose – always prickly old-fashioned, never some easy-care hybrid tea. Within two months of their arrival here from her childhood in florid Bayswater, Madeleine had seen her mother licked into semi-respectable shape. The old glamorous clothes with their poison greens and blood reds had been passed on to that Hades of fashion, the Tatham theatre wardrobe, and been replaced twin-set by twin-set with a uniform that sat awkwardly on a woman with a bosom and a past. Even her mother's past had evaporated. She had never been exactly open about it with her daughter, but now, from what she could glean from conversations on her rare trips home, Madeleine found that most Barrowers had pieced out the outlines of some outrage involving a vast house on the outskirts of Barcelona and a terrorist bomb. She chose not to interfere; Mum had her reasons, not the least of which was that she had to live here.

When the impulse to run home had first entered her mind as she watched a poster curl in the kettle steam and heard Georgene's whooping reports of the swelling crowd of journalists below their windows, Madeleine had pursued a fantasy of being the whore returned from Babylon, striding the cobbled streets, behind her a trail of corrupted youth and lingering pagan odour, before her a confusion of children snatched into safety and door bolts drawn in haste. The reality was a sad affair. As she slid cowering over the junction of the High Street and Tower Place, past her mother's shop and one of the city's few pubs, she sensed that the Barrowers held and would retain the upper hand. She had done the running. They would receive her, smug on their sheltered hill, and get on very nicely thank you without her when she ran away again, as she undoubtedly would in a few days. Earthly Paradise was strictly for pure and undemanding hearts. Madeleine invariably reached breaking point and fled with an inward scream in less than a week. She lit a last cigarette tucking the empty packet into a passing window box, and wondered whether the crisis baying at her heels might keep her there longer than usual.

She passed under an arch into the Close. The Cathedral's twin towers glowed in the last of the evening sun. Before her and slightly to the right she could just make out the spikey roof of the chapel quadrangle at Tatham's. Her pock-marked teens reached out at her from each lengthening shadow and she felt every lumpen pound the returning prodigal. Dining with swine had been a rare treat while it lasted.

15

As he soaked in the shoe box of a bathroom with four crackers spread with peanut butter and sliced banana lined up on the soap rack before him, Evan studied his distant toes and wondered about Mrs Merluza's daughter. Placing the mother's age at fiftyish and assuming her, from her glamour, to be the kind of woman who has her babies early and by mistake, if at all, he would gauge her daughter to be around thirty. Evan munched a cracker, brushing the crumbs off his chest. Since the bomb tragedy that deprived her of her father had occurred in the girl's infancy, she would have been reared wholly under the mother's influence and was probably a creature of no ambition and affected dress, the lamb within turning to premature mutton.

When, spruce a couple of hours later, he climbed the stairs, following voices to the sitting room, he found that he was gravely mistaken. As he knocked at the door a woman's voice, deeper than Mrs Merluza's, muttered something angry in Spanish (possibly Catalan, as he didn't catch it) and he entered. The air was heavy with stifled scene. His landlady was cowering in an armchair and a waistless woman in a red dress was staring away from him into the night beyond.

'Ah, Professor,' chimed up Mrs Merluza, able to rise now that she was not alone, 'this is my dear daughter, Madeleine.'

The woman turned.

'Hello,' she said, not offering to shake hands. 'You'll make a change from all those creepy organists. Mum never invites them to supper.'

'I'm honoured,' Evan muttered.

'Indeed you are. Sit down. What would you like to drink?'

'Scotch?'

'I'll get it,' said Mrs Merluza and fairly ran to rattle ice cubes at a table behind where he was sitting. Madeleine drew the curtains and flopped into an armchair. She was twenty-six or seven. Not conventionally pretty, but then, Evan reflected, neither was he. A big girl, she should not by rights have been wearing scarlet. Were one to drape her statuesqueness in black instead, or darkest purple, she would make an electric Norma or Ariadne. The red, however, showed spirit, as did she in the course of the evening. Her conversation was keen, not to say erudite – he discovered that she specialized in the history of erotica and concepts of visual sensuality – but Evan gained the impression that she was performing. He might have been her supervisor or an attentive brick wall. What fascinated him as they drank together then went down to eat was that she exerted some hold over her parent. It was as if she had a secret that her mother was terrified she might blurt out and her every utterance was followed by appeasement on the older woman's part.

'Delicious, Mrs Merluza. Really delicious,' he said.

'Thank you.'

'Yes, Mum. It's great.'

'Why thank you, darling. Thank you. It's only veal and a little . . .'

'But Evan,' Madeleine interrupted. 'I can call you that, can't I? Good – Evan, don't you find his style apallingly dated? Honours aside, he writes like Castaneda, or even Dylan if you put on the right voice.'

Her English was effortless, even slapdash, compared to her mother's. The only trace of Spanish was a marked softening of her Ss on the rare occasions when she spoke fast. She managed to combine the stolid, contained simmering of an Electra with a corrosive vein of Wickedest Girl in Class. Her hair. Evan wanted to reach out and rub its coarse thickness on his cheek. A luxuriant, coffin-dark mass, it matched her bovine eyes and made her mother's black look navy blue. She had the heavy eyebrows and bangle-jangling, furred forearms of a Costa Brava waitress and the sharpness of Dorothy Parker with a stubbed toe.

'Can I offer you a brandy, Professor?'

'No thanks, Mrs M. I must stay up and work.'

'More coffee then?' Madeleine suggested.

'Please.'

Mrs Merluza made to move but her daughter rose and waved her back.

'Stay put,' she told her. 'I'll get it.'

Evan watched her mother play with a cheese rind.

'They grow up so fast,' she simpered with a sigh and he smiled back to help her relax.

It could not be easy having such a daughter turn up to frighten one. Madeleine was the kind of girl medieval parents would have handed over to the strong arm of the church at the first decent opportunity. It was only when he felt a tumultuous relief on tearing himself away on the pretext of 'important reading' that he realized that even his customary state of amiable self-possession had been upset. He was in awe of someone.

He made another attempt at reading Sukie Lark Rosen's *New Mythology* – an attempt so feeble, even he was not fooled – then sat at the table in his bedroom and took out his diary. He had never kept a daily journal, as he suspected these soon became a litany of self-accusation, drab encounter and supper menu. Instead he kept a book for the recording of states, crises and anecdotes. Its chief purpose was as a safety valve to lower the frequency of shamefully revelatory letters to friends of questionable fidelity.

'Madeleine Merluza is fat and late twenties and I am thin and middle forties,' he wrote. 'I don't like big girls. I have never liked big girls. I was wild about Miriam when first I met her and she was queen of the titless rakes. Maybe that was what was wrong with our marriage, and not babies or Thomas Aquinas? Can one go for forty years of one's life under the misapprehension that one likes titless rakes before making the discovery that their polar opposite is one's true lodestone? Come to think of it, Ma says that Huby Stokes, who Miriam is dating, is built like a lorry driver.'

He shut the book without reading the entry, pulling a large rubber band around it. Then he kicked off his shoes and switched off the light. Lying on his bed in the darkness he heard bells.

16

She had taken Clive's hand and, rather than shake it, only held it in hers and gave it a cool squeeze. Her eyes were almond-shaped. Her nose was long, fine, smooth as wax. Pearl drops kissed the generous lobe of each curiously long ear. She turned smiling to Tobit. Her long hair had been pulled hard away from her face into something midway between a cascade and a bush. She was slightly taller than her fiancé. She was dressed in some kind of delicate, clinging suede whose fawn set off to perfection the richness of her skin. She smelled of vanilla. She was glorious.

'You must be Gloire,' Clive said. 'Welcome to Barrow-cester.'

'It's cute,' she replied. 'Really. We had a lovely walk around by the Cathedral and then along the ramparts over the river.'

He gestured for her to come in and she slid past him so closely that her hair brushed his hand and her scent wafted into his face.

'Hi.'

Tobit was grinning on the steps, car keys in hand. He looked like a poster for driving lessons.

'Tobit. Hello, old man. Congratulations.'

'Thanks.'

Clive's voice always came out wrong when he spoke to

his son. Whereas he sounded like a fairly intelligent school-master when talking to anyone else, he had only to open his mouth to Tobit to sound like a father in a television family; the sort of man who goes jogging with a golden retriever, plays with a train set and spends all weekend in a white tracksuit. A dad rather than a father.

'Come on in,' he said.

'Thanks,' said Tobit, 'Dad.'

As his son passed him, letting slip a waft of what was doubtless some overpriced Italian cologne, Clive found himself patting the boy's back and was disgusted at the image they must be conveying.

'Lovely house,' said Gloire, emerging from the sitting room and peering up the stairs. 'Is it Victorian?'

'A little earlier. You must get Lydia to show you round when she comes down,' said Clive. 'It's more her baby than mine.'

He poured them all champagne which he brought from the kitchen on a tray. As he crossed the hall to the sitting room, Gloire and Tobit started apart from a clinch and giggled. Lydia arrived, adding a third scent to the cocktail that was already thickening the air, and greeted Tobit and Gloire anew. Once she and her future daughter-in-law had stroked, cooing, the tissue of each other's clothes, Gloire asked to be shown around.

'I'm incurably inquisitive, I'm afraid,' she admitted in her faintly American accent and laughed with a cunning approximation of shyness.

'So it's true,' thought Clive. 'They *do* blush.'

Equally appalled at the prospect of being left alone together to make polite conversation, the men of the family followed their women on the tour of the Hart domain, which started in the garden as always.

There had been a time when Clive had worried about his relationship or rather lack of one to his son. If enjoyment of another's company and acceptance of their confidences were the measures of a close relationship, he was closer to most of his male pupils than he was to Tobit. This had not always been the case. When their baby had first arrived, Lydia had suffered an alarming depression and had moaned at the very sight of her creature, which meant that Clive had been thrown into fatherly love at the deep end. He would sit at his typewriter with the cot at his side; the experience was novel and he had enjoyed it. Preconversational infants are little more than helpless animals and as such Tobit had appealed to Clive's charitable impulse. Since his young wife was keen to finish her cookery course, young Clive had delighted in being seen to push a pram around Pimlico. Later he had carried Tobit in an Indian papoose to rehearsals of his ill-fated third play and, on the steps of the Royal Court, had even been interviewed by *Woman's Hour* on the growing importance of paternal involvement. Then, around the time when their fortunes had see-sawed and Lydia had swung into the limelight, she had taken Tobit off Clive's capable hands. She had poached him. Overnight.

'My son is just as important to me as my career,' seemed to be daily on her lips. 'Clive has been a wonderful help and now it's my turn to let him concentrate on *his* work. Share and share alike is the key to our marriage.'

She had poached Tobit and turned him into a pretty, prattling fashion accessory who played sweetly in the background of her *Guardian* column, sat on her lap in her early publicity photograph and who never had anything to say to his father.

Tobit had not been bright but he was clever with a pencil and paintbrush and generally good with his hands, so they had sent him to a new co-educational boarding school in the heart of Devon where design, fine arts and gardening were featured as high on the curriculum as maths or English. Lydia had disliked sending him away to board but felt that he needed to make some friends of his own age – a commodity in which geriatric Barrowcester was sorely lacking. By this time Clive was finding Tobit's combination of feyness and wanton ignorance a depressing contrast to the precocity of the boys and girls in his classes at Tatham's and was secretly glad to have him out of the house. Tobit's bookless approach to the arts was but one of many links slyly forged between him and his mother; Clive had felt himself become jealous of their cherished similarities. The immaculately illustrated, semi-grammatical letters home were addressed firmly to Lydia, although they were meticulous in including 'love' to her husband.

As the boy grew through his teens there was a resounding lack of the adolescent traumas that Clive had been expecting and which might have served to bring them closer together, if only in argument. Too well-behaved by half, the youth left his school, spent two months working behind the counter in Hart's and consorting in a suspiciously matey way with the girls there, then moved to a bedsit in London. He had won a place at St Martin's School of Art to study fashion. He had soon moved into a flat with a fellow student and it had been no surprise to Clive when they had visited him there with flat-warming presents and found that there was only one bed.

Lydia had been as forthright in her 'positive attitude' towards this discovery as she had been earlier this evening on the subject of black fiancées. She had made jokes about how nice it would be to be spared grandparenthood and had been as maternally supportive as ever. Lydia being Lydia this meant a generous allowance. After hearing at first hand how impressed his teachers were with his entries for the finals fashion show, she had set Tobit up with a little business in Marylebone High Street where he ran off extremely popular and staggeringly priced ball gowns and cocktail dresses. What had been jealousy on Clive's part had recently curdled into bored dismissal. Although it was unfashionable to speak of blame in these matters, blame implying that something was *wrong*, the fault was entirely Lydia's. She played Frankenstein to Tobit's monster, and Clive could not but admire the pluck with which she had thrown herself into the role. Today's sudden metamorphosis of monster into conventional handsome prince, however, was going to change matters somewhat.

'So tell me,' asked Lydia, after they had sat down, flushed with champagne, to lasagna and Riecine. 'Have you decided on a date?'

'We thought this Saturday,' said Tobit, who was pouring out wine on his father's behalf.

'Good God!' exclaimed Lydia then softened her tone. 'Darling, isn't that a bit soon?'

'Don't worry, Mrs Hart. He hasn't got me into trouble.'

'Not yet,' said Tobit and the two of them chuckled.

'I didn't mean that,' Lydia hurried on. 'Of course I didn't mean *that*. But, well, guests and things . . .'

'Oh, Ma. Please no,' pleaded Tobit.

'We thought just a quiet family wedding,' added Gloire. 'We're all four of us busy, and weddings on a big scale take so long to fix up.'

'Just we four,' suggested Tobit, 'and Gloire's parents.'

'That's why we want it on Saturday, you see,' said Gloire. 'They'll be in Europe briefly and I know they'd like to be here.'

'Oh but of course they would,' Lydia prattled, artlessly she hoped. 'How lovely. We can have a splendid lunch and lots of flowers and Clive, darling, do you think we could use the Tatham's chantry as you're on the staff?'

Clive had been silent all this time because he was being molested. The moment he had sat down beside her at the table, Gloire had slipped a hand on to his left knee and had begun mercilessly to caress his leg. He was so shocked that he had not yet taken the initiative of moving his leg away. The sensation was also so pleasurable as to have lulled him into silent inactivity. He tried to move his leg now, but her well-honed nails dug into the fabric of his trousers and pulled it back.

'Don't see why not,' he croaked and took a gulp of wine.

'You do want a church service, don't you?' Lydia checked.

'Certainly,' said Tobit. 'Gloire's mother is very devout.'

'Oh,' murmured Lydia.

'Oh, good,' said Clive, uncertainly.

'And where do your family come from?' Lydia pursued.

'Cheltenham,' said Clive.

136

'My father's Jamaican,' said Gloire, 'and my mother's from Martinique.'

'Which makes her a Catholic,' added Tobit.

'Oh,' said Clive, relinquishing the struggle and falling silent.

'More lasagna, Gloire?'

'No thanks. I have to watch my figure. Tobit's made me a very clingy dress.'

'Lucky you,' said Lydia, pouring herself more wine then remembering to pour some out for her guests. 'All he ever made me was a nightie.'

'My stuff's too sexy for you, Ma. You know that.'

'Thanks.'

Gloire leaped in.

'I'm sure Lydia – I may call you that, mayn't I?'

'But of course.'

'I'm sure Lydia would look lovely in that black one you've just finished,' she told her fiancé.

'No. I think Tobe's right,' said Lydia, pushing the lasagna tin towards Clive, partly to make him empty it, partly to rouse him from what looked like near-slumber. 'They aren't terribly – I mean they're *lovely* – but they aren't terribly me.'

Clive tried once more to pull away his leg. Gloire tugged it back and gave it a savage pinch.

'So tell me about your work, Gloire,' he said, rallying, to his wife's relief. 'How much longer before you're set loose on unsuspecting patients?'

'I've been on the wards for nearly two years now,' she said.

'Oh. Forgive me.'

'That's all right,' she said and pinched him again.

The situation was becoming impossible. He waited until she was raising her glass to her full pink lips then stood up sharply. The movement tugged her forward, causing her to drop the glass.

'Oh I'm so sorry,' she exclaimed.

'Clive, you *idiot*! You startled her.'

'No I didn't.'

'I'm not some half-wit antelope,' muttered Gloire.

'Quick. Stand up or it'll go on your dress,' shouted Tobit and he, Lydia and Gloire jumped to their feet as three trickles of wine slid out across the table top from the shattered glass. After a second of staring drunkenly with the rest, Lydia darted into action with a wet cloth.

'Oh dear,' said Gloire. 'No, my dress is fine, Lydia. Honestly. Actually I think a dry cloth might be . . . Oh thanks, Tobit. But your glass, Lydia. Are they special ones?'

'No. Not at all. Clive, I don't see what's so amusing.'

'Nothing,' said Clive. 'Honestly.'

17

Far too full of his landlady's coffee and thoughts of her daughter to think of sleeping yet, Evan took the spare latch key Mrs Merluza had insisted he borrow, and set out for a moonlit walk. He had hoped to see the outside of the Cathedral under floodlights but had forgotten that the Close was locked at ten-thirty. Instead he sought to get as near as he could by turning left out of the front door then swinging right towards the Cathedral along Dimity Street. He was catching his first glimpses of the west end when he was distracted first by voices and then by a sighting of what had to be Barrowcester's token black. After the racial assortment of Notting Hill and, to a more specialized extent, the British Library, he had been disappointed and faintly disturbed by Barrowcester's marked lack of anyone who was not Anglo-Saxon, let alone Third World. There were tourists, of course, but foreign residents seemed to be limited to the families who ran the city's Italian, Chinese and Indian restaurants. Even Le Tarte Tartin was owned, according to his food guide, by one Priscilla Fox and while pretty, its waitresses were far from French.

Light was pouring through an open front door. Someone was evidently leaving a dinner party. A couple emerged on to the doorstep. Evan could not see the faces but from their voices they were roughly his age. The woman hugged a willowy young man, whose face caught the light, while her partner patted him on the back. The youth then clambered into an open-topped car and called out,

'Gloire?'

in the loudest voice Evan had heard since his arrival. While the woman was giggling and telling the youth that he'd wake the neighbours, Evan lingered in the shadows to see who this Gloire was.

'Coming,' called a bright American voice, and he thought he had the answer.

'She's re-doing her hair,' said the man.

'Oh darling, she's so *nice!*' enthused the woman to the youth.

The nubile, unexpectedly black subject of this muttered praise then sailed from the house, swooped with a low murmur on the woman, lingeringly hugged the man, then climbed over the door on the passenger side of the car. There was a roar of high-performance engine, a shout of

'See you Saturday!'

and a waving departure. The couple seemed to sag when left alone. As they returned inside, Evan hurried forward. Their house was extremely large – nearly thrice the width of Chez Merluza – and what little he could make out seemed to be Queen Anne. The front door had a prosperous look to it. Standing still to admire the fanlight, he distinctly heard the woman say,

'I can't bear it. I just *cannot* bear it.'

Intrigued by these bare bones of crisis, he lingered to admire the view of the floodlit Cathedral. Then headed back the way he had come, past the top of Tracer Lane, then down Scholar Street to examine Tatham's by moonlight. He had heard about the school from his agent Jeremy over black buttered skate at Manzi's. It had turned out that Jeremy went there and not to Eton as so many people supposed.

'It should have been abolished long ago,' he declared, trying the Pouilly Fuissé and accepting it after a moue of discerning resignation. 'It's only survived by taking in a bunch of embryo bluestockings and a few thick little rich girls and by letting TV crews inside. The academic record is high but so's the nervous breakdown rate. It used . . . Oh. Thanks.' He paused while their fish arrived. 'It used to be a suspiciously wealthy convent before the Great Divorcer kicked out the sisters and gave it, library, buildings, lock, stock and mead barrel to an upstart pet cleric of his called Tatham. The idea was to churn out a regular supply of Protestant, king-adoring bishops-to-be. Good-looking turbot. How's your skate?'

Madeleine who, Evan gathered, had been Tatham's first female scholar, had told him that the main gates to the old part of the school stayed unlocked until midnight so as to let supervising *gods* out to their families. She said that the place was run like a dictatorial university; with strict regulations but an unusual degree of self-rule and solitary study periods for the pupils. The archway where Evan now arrived would not have looked out of place in Oxford or Cambridge. The porter's lodge was lit but showed no other signs of life, so Evan slipped through the shadows into the chapel quadrangle.

There was a huge moon, now obscured by the gate tower, and the sky was riddled with stars, which made a crenellated silhouette of the four sides. A few windows were still lit, including those to one end of the chapel where

141

someone was quietly practising the organ. There was the occasional shout or rush of stout shoes on old floorboard, but he saw no one. He knew that if he walked along the chapel wall he would find a way through to the cloisters spoken of by Petra Dixon that morning. He walked gingerly across the cobbles and, as his eyes became accustomed to the gloom, saw a black, arch-shaped hole. This led to a passage which duly spilled into a quadrangular colonnade surrounding a tiny chantry. Never frightened by the dark so long as he was alone in it, he began to wander round, piecing out his impression of damp, intricate stonework with remembered photographs and engravings.

Then he got a Bad Feeling. Evan's Washington Aunt Ciboulette used to get Bad Feelings. She said she would walk into a stranger's house sometimes and suddenly feel as if a live catfish had been slipped down the back of her dress.

'And I'd get my Bad Feeling,' she'd say, 'And I'd just *know!*'

Ciboulette had never said what she knew exactly, but his mother had later explained that it must have been something unfitted to tender ears, involving bigamy, lovers in too much riding gear or hatchets buried in the chicken run. Unlike his aunt, Evan hadn't got religion, but he was sensitive to religious atmospheres and suddenly the cloisters did not feel altogether Christian. Besides, it would soon be midnight and he had no wish to spend his night locked in with a crowd of egg-head children when he could be getting his beauty sleep for breakfast with Madeleine.

He was starting rather more quickly out of the cloisters than he had wandered in, therefore, when he saw something move. Because of the obtuse angle of the moon and the few lights from quadrangle buildings, his side of the cloisters was in total darkness. As he turned, something had jumped from within an arch on to the ground about six feet away. He just saw whatever it was slide out of silhouette and he could hear shallow breathing. He had felt countless cigarette butts underfoot so, his shock past, he guessed that this was some boy out for a quick Winston before bedtime.

'It's OK. I'm an addict too, friend,' he said but whoever it was belted like a shocked hare back through the arch and around the other side of the chantry.

Judging from the patter on the stone, he was in bare feet.

Walking briskly out through the passage by the chapel, Evan half slipped on something, only saving himself from a fall by a scrabbling grasp on the uneven wall to his left. Spine unpleasantly jarred, he rubbed his grazed palms on his jacket and cursed. He scraped whatever it was off his shoe and on to the side of the chapel step, supposing the worst. Then he sniffed an unexpected smell of riverbank and stagnant pool.

Returned to the reassuring, electrified gas lamps of Scholar Street, Evan found himself quite seriously jumpy so decided to raid Mrs Merluza's kitchen for cooking brandy to calm his nerves for bed.

18

Dressed in a new pastel cotton from Daniella's, because it was the first day of summer, Mercy Merluza left the kitchen and walked through the hall to the stairs. She frowned at the letter box because her *Daily Telegraph* was inexplicably late, then went upstairs and tapped on her daughter's door.

'*Cariño*?'

'Mmh?'

'I'm just off to have coffee with Mrs Chattock now at the Palace. The Professor doesn't seem to have got up yet. Dawn doesn't come today and I don't want to be late so I wondered . . .'

Madeleine half opened her door, pushing back her unbrushed hair and yawning.

' . . . if I'd make breakfast for him,' she finished.

'Would you?'

'Of course.'

'Bless you.' Disliking to see Madeleine undressed, Mercy turned to go. Remorse tweaked her into pausing on the top of the stairs. 'You are all right, *cariño*, aren't you?'

'Yes, Mum. I'm fine.'

Madeleine shut the door.

'Good,' sighed her mother and walked down to the front door.

Just as Mercy had suspected, Madeleine had come home

because she was in a certain sort of fix. She had started to tell Mercy about an affair she had just finished, then broke down and admitted that she was pregnant and could not decide what to do. Having been through no less than three abortions, Mercy found herself completely unshocked and capable of being extremely sympathetic. She said she knew of a good clinic who would be able to deal with it, as the Stepfords' poor girl had been sent there last year after a problematical French exchange. Madeleine had refused to give her mother the man's name or to explain why he was being so unhelpful. The atmosphere was just starting to feel tense when Professor Kirby had joined them for supper and they were obliged to drop the topic. Mercy hoped that her daughter would not do anything hot-headed such as confide in her lodger. These things left fewest traces when kept under wraps.

As she turned from shutting the front door, she saw that Miss Dyce-Hamilton, who used to be at Tatham's with Madeleine, was approaching on her bicycle. When she was close enough, Mercy gave a little wave she reserved for timid or unmarried women.

'Hello,' she said.

Rather than stop to chat as she normally did, however, Miss Dyce-Hamilton fairly shouted,

'Lovely morning, isn't it? Really lovely!' and shot on.

The look which accompanied this greeting had been so frantic that Mercy glanced at her reflection in the post office window. Her dress was a perfectly innocuous dusky blue, the flowers extremely small, the sleeves long and the hem below the knee. Her hair was fine as ever, her lipstick straight, her shoes tinted the most unpredatory of charcoal greys. Perhaps Miss Dyce-Hamilton had been late for school; they did say she was apt to be scatter-brained.

Mercy continued on her way, enjoying the brilliant blue of the sky and the shrill chatter of the birds in the gardens that backed on to Scholar Walk. A diminished crocodile of eight choristers emerged from the garden gate of the choir school. They raised their caps in unison and the leader said,

'Good morning, Miss.'

Mercy beamed in reply and would have felt better had she not seen Marge Delaney-Siedentrop spring, to the best of a stout woman's ability, through the front door of number thirty-two without so much as a smile. Of all people, Marge had nothing to feel guilty for, and she could not be avoiding Mercy for they had spoken at length in the queue at Hart's yesterday. It was Marge's time of life, Mercy decided; that and her envy of Mercy's friendship with Deirdre Chattock.

Mercy liked to think that this friendship sprang from the fact that both she and Deirdre were wild briar roses ill at ease in Barrowcester's confining borders. When she had arrived, a widow with a foreign surname, a growing girl and the musk of Bayswater on her person, the town had dismayed her. For the first few weeks she was preoccupied with putting her new house in order and with settling Madeleine into Tatham's. Then she grew nervous. She was very much alone, since Madeleine was a scholar and scholars had to board. This was nothing new. She had been almost as alone in London, and prepared to live in Barrowcester in the state of semi-anonymity she had learned to enjoy in the capital. This however proved extremely hard to do in her new surroundings for she was now surrounded by people who knew not only each other, but each other's friends and relations. Barrowers had links. Mercy heard their links jingle into place as they accosted one another in shops or introduced themselves to near strangers climbing out of cars or sweeping front paths.

'Sorry. You probably don't know me but I'm Simon Curlicue and our sisters do begging-box duty together on Tuesdays.'

'Excuse me, but aren't you Mrs Typewriter Hatpin? Yes? What fun! Our littlest are in the same form at Tatham's. Will's enjoying it *so* much.'

Mercy heard them rejoice in their links and felt aware, for the first time in her existence, that she was rootless and, save for Madeleine, denuded of family; a bald log in a buzzing April orchard. She could feel her neighbours, who had barely introduced themselves, sizing her up, looking for links and finding none. Whereas in Bayswater she had been quite content to sit at her sewing machine, watching Australian soap operas in her dressing gown all day while Madeleine was out at school, here she felt guilty for doing so. No one in Barrowcester seemed to watch television unless there was a 'classic' adaptation of Austen, Mrs Gaskell or E.F. Benson. Then they would pull their sets from under wraps and throw 'telly teas', marvelling at the improved standard of television drama since they last watched any and lamenting that their tastes were so old-fashioned as to prevent them from watching more often.

Mercy started to cast her eyes about, to size up her neighbours in return, and she began to notice patterns in their lives. A clutch of them was regularly to be seen walking to the Close at 7.45 in the morning and a far larger group did so, more obviously, on Sunday mornings at 7.45, 10.15 and 11.20. Most intriguing of all, however, were the people that vanished off the face of the hill between 4.45 and 6.00 every day of the week.

Mercy determined to break in on the latter's secret: they displayed an appealing homogeneity lacking in the Sunday group. One Thursday, therefore, she pulled on an uncharacteristic two-piece she had just bought in Daniella's and loitered outside the Close at ten to five. Within five minutes the pavement was dotted with groups of two and four and she could follow the crowd unobserved. They wandered, link-swopping, to the Cathedral, with her in their midst. The first thing she learned was that they used a special entrance. She had been to no services since her arrival in Barrowcester, what little religion ran in her veins being a condensed Roman Catholicism, but she had felt obliged to go with Madeleine on a guided tour of the Cathedral on their first weekend and had returned once on her own. On each occasion she had entered by the huge open door at the west end, where she had been accosted by a woman who lived a few houses away and who was standing in a dark green gown by a giant Perspex moneybox. The woman bade Mercy a hearty welcome without a flicker of recognition then discreetly breathed that the Cathedral needed a fair donation from every visitor if it was to remain standing. As she followed the five o'clock crowd on this Thursday evening, they had led her through a sort of tunnel by the south transept.

'I didn't know we could get in this way,' she admitted to a benign, stork-like man on her right.

'Oh?' he said. 'It's the Glurry. It's really the tradesmen's entrance for the choir and Chapter but it's also handy for those of us in the know as it saves a long walk up a cold nave. They can only afford to heat the quire. After you,' he added and held open a tiny door for her.

'Thank you,' she said with feeling as they walked through a sort of cubby hole into the south transept and on to the quire. As they walked and as Mercy realized that he was quite content to lead a novice to her initiation, she felt a warm sense of arrival seeping through her being to meet the cold that was rising from the floor.

The form of service had been unfamiliar, but there was far less standing and kneeling than in the rather Filipino Carmelite church she had occasionally attended in Kensington. The singing was delightful, the bearing of the clergy was unanimously distinguished and, most importantly, Mercy had enjoyed being surrounded by Barrowers who no longer stared at her or who, if they did, had a kind of tenderness in their curiosity. The hour flew by and as they were going, blessed, on their way and as Mercy was trying to decide whether to be grown up and eat her supper at the table or to damn the consequences and eat it before the television as she normally did, someone laid a hand on her arm. It was an attractive woman with subtle green eyes.

'Hello,' she said. 'You don't know me but I think my husband Clive teaches your daughter Madeleine English. I'm Lydia Hart.'

'Mercy Merluza. How d'you do.'

'Clive and I are having a little drinks party tomorrow and wondered if you'd like to come and meet some of your new neighbours. I'm afraid it's terribly short notice.'

'Oh. How kind.'

'Around seven? Mrs Porter and her husband are coming and as they live just two along from you, Jane said they'd drop by to pick you up and show you the way.'

Links jingled in Mercy's grateful ears.

'How kind of her,' she said.

'Lovely. We'll see you tomorrow then,' said Lydia with a broadish smile.

Of course she and Lydia had never been close since, but Mercy would always be grateful for the forging of that first link. At the drinks party she had made several friends and met the owner of The Treasure Trove who had fallen on hard times and was so keen to make a private sale. From one link grew three, from three grew nine and so the process had continued until it slowed down dramatically to an average gain (balanced by a seasonal pruning) of one link every three months. Along the way, Mercy had felt compelled to fashion herself a new past; amnesia about one's origins was so very suspect and however much Barrowcester prided itself on freedom of outlook, she felt no doubts as to the way her neighbours would look on an ex-cabaret artiste and jewel thief. She began to drop hints about a family and property shattered soon after her marriage by a terrorist attack, adding that her 'little Madeleine' had been spared the details and lived in blissful semi-ignorance of the family tragedy.

As for church-going, Mercy could now be found in the Cathedral every Sunday morning and every evening too except for Monday of course, when the choir had their night off and Mercy might be found, dispossessed and shopping.

Deirdre Chattock had arrived in the wake of her son,

the Bishop, barely eight months ago. Gavin Tree was unmarried, which was a point in his favour in the eyes of Barrowcester, as opposed to his high political colouring, refusal to entertain on an episcopal scale and request that he be addressed as plain mister, which were not. His mother had been married twice, Gavin being an only child, happy fruit of union number one. Granted, she was untainted by divorce, but there was something about a multiple widow which ill accorded with a society where marriage was a duty performed once in a lifetime and where widowhood was mutely regarded as the will of God and therefore beyond the further attentions of man. Before her first marriage, Deirdre had strutted a handful of hours upon various northern stages. More recently she had led a campaign against alcoholism, of an awkwardly revelatory nature. When it suited her son's political credibility, which it did most of the time, she could resuscitate an unmistakable Derbyshire accent. Not a woman likely to find a downy nest in the Barrowcester bosom, she was neither a woman to let Barrowcester snobbery ruffle her plumage. She suffered a mild stroke under anaesthetic for a recent operation and found that it had, as she put it delightedly, 'plugged her into the switchboard of the Spirits'. While she continued to follow her son in orthodox Christian practice, she had instigated a weekly 'at home' meditation group. In the absence of any large-scale entertainment on her son's part, this had proved very popular as a means of regular admission to the Palace.

Mercy had enraged many, however, by bounding into a Palace intimacy long before any stroke had opened doors. Deirdre Chattock had come into Boniface Crafts in her very first week and bought herself a cardigan knitted by a local craftswoman. As she looked around Mercy's shop she had hummed a song to herself. As sometimes happens, the song had penetrated Mercy's unconscious ear and, after selling Deirdre Chattock the cardigan, she had pottered into her store room to put on the kettle for elevenses and had started to sing the song herself.

'Falling in love again,' she sang. 'Never wanted to . . .'

'Pardon me.'

'Yes?'

It was Mrs Chattock, who had not left the shop but was hovering by the counter. Heads turned: Mrs Chattock was a new arrival and therefore subject to scorching local interest.

'That song. I've had it on my brain all morning but can't remember beyond the fourth line,' she said, then sang, 'Da da da *Deedle*-dah, *Deedle* da da *dah*. *Deedle* da da *dah*. Tumtee *tum tum*. I know it does that twice but then I get stuck and I've been going berserk doing the same bit over and over.'

Glad to be of assistance and seeing a chance of forging a twenty-four-carat link, Mercy had continued in her fruity tenor, beating time with her much-jewelled left hand in a slow waltz rhythm.

'Men cluster to me like moths around a flame.'

'Ah-*ha!*' laughed Deirdre, and joined in. 'And if their wings burn I know I'm not to blame!'

While Miss McCreery and the other observers in the shop scurried off to tell their friends (and Marge Delaney-Siedentrop) that they had seen the Bishop's mother purchase the cardigan that no one else could afford and then impersonate Gracie Fields impersonating Marlene Dietrich,

Deirdre Chattock showed her gratitude by inviting Mercy to dinner the following evening.

Dinner had been a great success – they had listened to a stack of old records – and after a prompt reciprocation, gave way to less formal, more intimate lunches and then to downright confidential elevenses and cups of tea. Before Mr Tree had been in office a month, Mrs Merluza was the only woman in Barrowcester on 'popping-in' terms with his mother. Now every Barrowcesterian slight, every ungracious innuendo could be written off by Mercy as mere envy. Whatever sly disapprovals were stretched across her path, she had a friend to help her face them. Needless to say, she was the first after Gavin Tree at Deirdre's sick-bed last year (he had found her a room to herself on the NHS) and had heard long before him of her momentous 'plugging in'. The meditation classes that attracted so many were little more than a smokescreen; Mercy was the only Barrower to have been a party to Mrs Chattock's secret dalliance with powers beyond her control.

Her skin prickling slightly, for despite the sunshine the day was not as warm as she had at first supposed, Mercy turned off Scholar Street into the drive of the Palace. She saw Deirdre at a first-floor window and raised a hand in greeting. Deirdre waved back and slipped from view only to reappear at the front door as Mercy drew near.

'Mercy, Petal, I didn't think you'd come! How are you coping?' She spoke as though Mercy had just tossed away crutches and were inadvisedly walking too far too soon.

'I'm fine thanks. How are . . . ?'

'You're so brave! I said as much to our Gavin over break-fast and he thinks so too.' Mercy was baffled at this sudden solicitous outburst which was quite out of character, but then Deirdre was always slightly larger than life. 'And I'm so touched that you've come despite everything,' her friend continued. They kissed. Although her last husband, the late Mr Chattock had proved a martyr to tobacco, Deirdre remained a compulsive smoker of Players Navy Cut and had a gravelly voice to prove it. 'Come in, Flower,' she said, waving her friend through the porch.

She shut the door and they walked side by side across the huge parqueted hall watched by the portraits of some ten past bishops, and started the slow climb up the stairs to Deirdre's apartment on the first floor. Deirdre had regular visits from a town masseuse to tend her stiff joints, but she was still a painfully stately mover. A typewriter clattered from behind a door on their way.

'Our poor Gavin slaving away,' coughed Deirdre. 'He has to prepare all his arguments for *Faith Forum* on Friday and write a piece on the vision for the *Church Times*, *and* answer any number of cranky letters.'

'Does he get many?' asked Mercy.

'Oh my dear, they arrive by the score. I'd toss them in the Aga if I was him but he insists that every opinion is important and that every voice deserves a hearing and a reply. You thought it all a fake, I gather.'

'Well I wouldn't say that, exactly.'

'No? I heard all about your views from Marge Delaney-Siedentrop who didn't see a thing and is heaping coals on the anti-Roman fire.' Deirdre poked discreet fun by pronouncing Siedentrop with a silent P. 'I can quite see your point of view,' she went on, 'but I can assure you it was the Real Thing.'

'Have you . . . er . . . then?'

'Yes, Petal, I have asked my guides and they all say it was real.'

'Goodness.'

'Quite. And of course it's doing wonders for the appeal fund. I was speaking to the dear Dean yesterday and he's had approaches from two TV channels and all the major papers. People are *pouring* in. There's nothing to see now, mind you – even less than normal in fact because of the builders – but that doesn't seem to stop them.'

She broke down in a fit of coughing at the turn in the stairs. Well-versed, Mercy thumped her vigorously on the bony back to help loosen the phlegm. She was no youthful widow herself, but Deirdre was so much her senior as to make her feel at times agreeably like a young and favoured nurse. When she had recovered, Deirdre continued, leading the way to her sitting room.

'Couldn't do better if we had a wobbly virgin like those pathetic Irish,' she said.

In her sitting room she gestured to Mercy to sit down in her usual chair then took a few deep breaths.

'Do you mind if we skip coffee, Flower, and get straight down to it? I have a strong feeling about this morning and it's getting stronger.'

'But of course. Coffee is so bad for the pancreas, anyway.'

'Poison. Poison,' said Deirdre and, having locked the door, set about drawing the curtains. The room, with its clutter of china figurines, brass candlesticks and clustered photograph frames, with its regulation chintz and early nineteenth-century prints of Durham and Barrowcester, had none of the hackneyed trappings of a traditional medium's parlour, yet it was surprising how effective was the transformation effected by the swish of a curtain and the sparking of a cigarette lighter. As the candle burned more brightly, Deirdre settled back on the sofa, her legs tucked neatly to one side. She nibbled on a biscuit; she always said that a little sugar 'made for a clearer connection'.

Mercy had watched this many times, only recently with a keen personal interest, but had never ceased to be shocked when the vital moment came. She had visited mediums in both Paris and London. They had used incense and atmospheric music, they had paced up and down or sung songs or gargled eau de cologne. Deirdre used no such gimmicks and it was her complete lack of build-up that proved so startling. She sat, quite still, her breathing slowing. Mercy could hear the birds in the garden; a blackbird's alarm call, a woodpigeon's eerie fluting. On account of their tar layer, the motion of Deirdre's lungs was easily audible at a distance of five or six feet. When it stopped, Mercy habitually tensed herself for a new voice. Sitting stock still on her sofa, the Bishop's mother had been the mouthpiece for a small girl, a Cockney barrowboy, an elderly priest from Cardiff and, on one alarming occasion, a woman in labour. There was no question of her faking the voices; it actually sounded as if a differently shaped mouth were speaking. In the case of the small girl, one could hear her juvenile lack of teeth.

Last time, at Mercy's tentative suggestion that they plumb the mystery of her childhood, Deirdre had been inhabited by the soul of Jésus' vile mother. As the bilious, all too familiar phrases spilled forth (it was most unlikely that Deirdre alone could have had such a mastery of vulgar Catalan), it had seemed as if Señora Merluza were sitting on the sofa in all her black-mantled flabbiness and not Deirdre at all. She had spoken of her jealousy of the genderless waif that Jésus had brought into the household, of her impotent fury when the child proved a precociously sensuous dancer and was incorporated into his act, of her rage at the drunken cheering of the crowds for little Mercedes. She had spoken of her spiteful secret pettinesses of revenge. Trapped in her armchair on the other side of the coffee table, Mercy had trembled as if she were a nervy twelve again and had sunk back with exhaustion and relief when Deirdre nodded off and began to snore. Although she burned to learn her orgins, she half hoped that Señora Merluza would not be on call today, whatever she might choose to reveal.

Deirdre stopped breathing. Mercy clutched her hands together with excitement then bit her lip with shock as she heard a long, amorous sigh she still recognized after nearly thirty years.

'Jésus?' she whispered. 'Is that you?' slipping by reflex into Catalan.

'Mercedes,' said Jésus and chuckled. 'My little Mercedes.'

On the sofa in Deirdre's apartment, Jésus hummed softly the song he had always liked to have played at the beginning of the act. Mercy was a girl again, sitting on the edge of her bed in the house over the nightclub. Jésus was kneeling on the floor before her, humming his song and slowly unfastening the buttons on the front of her dance costume. With the undoing of each button he brushed her unbruised skin with his lips. She could smell his sweat and the pomade on his shiny, black hair. An ugly painting of some fishermen mending nets hung on the wall behind him. Gingerly she reached out and laid a hand on his shoulder. His skin felt hot through the cotton and as she touched him he let his tongue flick like a lizard's between her tiny breasts. It felt good. It felt like when another dancer, Julia, stood her naked in the bath backstage and tipped a slow jug of warm water over her back and hair to wash away the sweat of dancing. She leaned forward and pressed a kiss on to the nape of his neck. His head, which seemed so huge, lifted and he stared hard. One of his eyes was blue and seemed to stare harder than its dull, brown partner. She could not stare for long so she arched her spine and threw back her head to watch the ceiling where the flies were circling. She heard him sigh again. Such a sad, burdened sigh.

'Mercedes,' he said, almost in a whisper, 'let's pretend you're my sweet, secret little wife,' and he slipped the costume off her shoulders. Did he sigh or was that the sound of slithering cloth?

On the way home from the Palace, Mercy dropped in at Farquarson's, the newsagents, to ask about their failure to deliver her *Telegraph* that morning. She never registered a complaint however, but simply bought a copy of a tabloid which she sometimes read in secret and which today had no trouble in catching her eye. Madeleine's face was spread over the front page under the headline, 'TOP CARDINAL PREGNANCY SHOCK!'

19

When her alarm woke her soon after seven o'clock on Tuesday morning, Madeleine forced herself to stay awake by sitting bolt upright against her headboard with the bedside light switched on and the latest copy of *Apollo* open in her lap. With her window open, she could hear at last the steady approach of the girl on her paper round. Bicycling, stopping, posting, bicycling, stopping and posting. Bicycling again. When the sounds were only a house away, she snatched about her the dressing gown of her teens, preserved for the homecoming modesty of an habitually naked sleeper, and crept down as quietly as old stairs would permit. No sooner was her mother's *Daily Telegraph* through the door than Madeleine was hurrying back upstairs with it clutched inside her wrap. In the safety of her room, she tossed the dressing gown aside, and clambered back into bed to open out the paper.

She found that she felt nauseous with excitement in the same, not unpleasant way that she had felt when Madge had rung her to say that their collaboration had been reviewed in the *Guardian*. She decided to start on page three and work her way back to the front. There was nothing on page three. A baby had been eaten by greyhounds. The country's oldest postmistress had received a visit from the Queen Mother who had bought a stamp. Nothing. Surely she and Edmund were not a national incident. Were they? She scanned page two. There was a large photograph of the Princess of Wales visiting an innovative, old people's home, a report of industrial action being taken in a Welsh chemicals plant and the details of a large survey on education; nothing about papist illegitimacies. Gingerly Madeleine turned to the front page. Nothing. She whirled the paper over to the back. Nothing. Feverishly she leafed through it page by page, even scanning the foreign news in case their misconduct were thought to pertain more to the Vatican than to Westminster. Her heart leaped at the word 'pregnancy' then she saw that it lay in a generalized piece on schoolgirls and contraception. Nothing. Someone had pulled the plug on the scandal; either that or the *Telegraph* had not thought Edmund newsworthy. Madeleine was almost affronted. She wondered if perhaps Edmund had made a clean breast of things to superior powers and caused some archaic right of veto to be exercised. She tossed the paper to one side and lay back, hands black with newsprint, to think. If by any wonderful chance *The Times* and the *Guardian* had also scorned to cover the story, she could dismiss the tabloid campaign as foundless gossip; she was engaged in legitimate work for Edmund after all. The more she thought about it, the less likely it seemed that they would print anything; it was scarcely a newsworthy event. Edmund was a Cardinal, not a politician and she was just another apolitical, art historical, bachelor girl with an impending baby. Those reporters had panicked her. She would stay in Barrowcester to beat down the scandal for her mother's sake and until she could decide what to do about the baby, then she would take a holiday somewhere wild, woolly and unglamorous where she could rest and maybe do some writing.

There was a knock at the door. It was Mum to say she was on her way out and to ask if she would make Evan Kirby some breakfast when he appeared. She was probably on the sniff for morning sickness too, so Madeleine scared her off by opening the door in the nude, with her hair ruffled up like a witch. As soon as she heard the front door close, she flung back the covers and took a long, thoughtful bath. She dressed in a full brown skirt, white blouse and childish brown sandals. The ensemble, though still gypsyish, was less conspicuous than the scarlet of last night.

She was glad to have Evan Kirby to herself and hoped that the lie-in he had taken meant that he would not be rushing off. He was a tonic, being cynical and avuncular in roughly equal parts. He seemed above any interest in women, which could make him a restful sounding board. She suspected that he found her mother appalling and had only failed to appear for breakfast because he was hiding from her. This seemed to be confirmed when he flung wide the door to the granny flat just as Madeleine had rounded the bottom of the stairs and was heading for the kitchen.

'Hello,' he said. 'I fear I'm too late for your mother's wonderful English breakfast.'

'It's more a *desayuno Catalan* – she uses olive oil.'

'So that's her secret.'

'She asked me to make you some. What do you like? Bacon and eggs? Grilled tomatoes?'

'Couldn't we just have coffee and toast?'

'Good idea.'

He sat at the kitchen table and watched her fill the percolator and slice bread.

'One slice or three?' she asked. 'I have three. It's only white.'

'Two would be fine, unless you'd like me to keep you company. Do you always steal your mother's newspaper before she gets up?'

She paused, her hand on the grill pan, and turned to stare at him.

'Do you always spy on your landladies' daughters?'

'I didn't spy on you – I spied on her. I knew she couldn't have moved up and down stairs so fast and when I next heard steps, I looked through the keyhole to see who was coming down. I saw her fiddling crossly with the letter box.'

'There was an article I wanted to see. I like reading in bed.'

'Oh.'

He sounded unconvinced.

'Where are you working today?' she asked.

'Tatham's. The *Lord* said he'd show me round at twelve then drop me off with the librarian. I suppose I should really ask an Old Girl to give me the tour.'

He grinned up at her.

'I haven't set foot in the place since I left.'

'Unhappy memories?'

'No. I had a nice time there, but I'm just not the Old Girl type,' Madeleine replied, taking out her cigarettes.

'Thank God,' said Evan Kirby. 'And thank God you've taken those out; I thought you never would.' He lit one of his own as he spoke. Madeleine smiled to herself. 'What's funny?' he asked.

'Nothing.'

'No. What?'

'It was just the notion of sending the Old Tathamite magazine a résumé of my most recent employment.'

'Early pornography specialist?'

'That sort of thing. Yes.'

'How often do you come home?' he asked, playing with the butter knife.

'As often as I can bear,' she replied, standing to turn the toast, 'which isn't often enough.'

She disliked talking at breakfast but could cope with being an ear. He seemed keen to talk, so Madeleine ate her toast and drank her coffee while he let his get cold and held forth. He told her about his mother, who was a neurotic hostess type in Boston. He described how she had practised emotional blackmail on him whenever he was away and had made his life impossible whenever he had gone home. This seemed to confirm Madeleine's hopes about his comfortable non-availability. Then he told her about his wife and divorce and she decided it was too late to watch her step. She buttered a slice of toast for him as a reward for not being what she thought she wanted.

'Have you ever wanted to be a mother?' he asked in abrupt return. 'I've often found the motives for becoming a parent so dubious as to be almost uncivilized.'

Madeleine was spared the difficulty of mustering a reply by the doorbell.

'Excuse me,' she said and walked into the hall. As she opened the front door a ring of camera flashes fired, causing her to raise a hand to her eyes. Someone yelled,

'It's her!'

She slammed the door.

'Bugger!' she shouted.

'What's up?' asked Evan who had run into the hall.

'Could you walk into the sitting room and pull the curtains on the windows facing the street?' she asked, beginning to shake. 'Please? Then I'll explain.'

As he walked next door, the doorbell rang again and was backed up by a fist rapping on the wood. Flashes lit up the windows as Evan drew the curtains in the granny flat. He came back to the hall.

'Wow,' he said. 'Are you concubine-in-chief to the IRA or what?'

'Sort of,' she said. 'Let's go back in there and I'll tell you.' As she started to move off, some fingers pushed through the letter box and managed to catch hold of her skirt. She gave a grunt of impatience and, tugging free as the doorbell jangled again, kicked the door as hard as she could. The fingers withdrew but the ringing and knocking continued. Evan pulled a handkerchief from his pocket and, reaching to his considerable height, stuffed it between clapper and bell.

'At least that'll cut the racket down by half,' he said.

'Thanks.' She walked past him to the kitchen. 'Thank God Mum's out.'

'Look. You really don't have to tell me anything,' he said. 'I mean, I'm only the lodger after all.'

'You poor sod,' chuckled Madeleine as if remembering his existence. She lit a cigarette and offered one to him. 'This isn't exactly Mon Repos, Eastbourne.'

He sat across the table from her. They had changed sides. She tipped the percolator over her cup, found it empty and started to make a fresh brew.

'It's a bit Gothic, but the basic situation is very straight-forward,' she said, mumbling because her cigarette was still between her lips so as to give her two spare hands. 'I'm pregnant and the father would seem to be Cardinal Kilpatrick.'

'The old guy with the crinkly white hair and the pink frock?' He laughed.

'He's not *that* old,' she rebuked him. 'He's only just past fifty. And it's called a soutane. He's not much whiter than you, in fact.'

There was a thud on the door. Madeleine scowled, removed her cigarette and shouted,

'Go away!'

'How did the press get to find you?' he asked, accepting the reproof.

'His housekeeper,' she said, thudding the percolator on to the stove. She had a suspicion that she might be about to cry. She cried less often than she threw up, but the warning signs were just as unmistakable. There was another thud on the door. 'I said go *away!*' she yelled along the hall, clenching her fists with frustration.

'It's me!' her mother yelled back.

'Bugger. It's Mum.'

Madeleine hurried to the front door, braced herself with her hands on the knobs, then tried to open it just a fraction. There was a heavy thrust from the other side. Mrs Merluza flew in and fell over, with a muffled whoop. Madeleine was hurled back against the wall and called out in pain as the door struck her left knee. Evan raced forward amid much flashing of bulbs and, kicking various feet and hands out of the way, managed to shut and lock the door again. Madeleine ran to the kitchen, fumbling for a hand-kerchief and not finding one. The Professor helped his landlady to her feet.

'Thank you,' she said, stiffly, then hobbled upstairs fast enough to convey a sense of outrage and was heard slamming the bathroom door behind her.

Slumped against the dresser with a tea towel in her fists, Madeleine had one of the two-minute weeps which had been her speciality since childhood. She was blowing her nose when Evan returned to the kitchen. She heard him pick up the telephone and dial three nines.

'Police, please,' he said. 'Hello? . . . Yes, I'm staying at number eight, Tracer Lane and we're being pestered – terrorized in fact – by a crowd of journalists who are trying to break an entry . . . What's that? . . . Oh. Evan Kirby. K.I.R.B.Y . . . No, I don't live here, I'm just the lodger . . . The Merluzas . . . M.E.R.L.U.Z.A . . . Will you? . . . Thanks.'

'Thank you,' said Madeleine as he hung up, not turning so he was spared her puffed face.

'You're welcome. Ah. Look. I really have to get to work soon. Does that gate at the end of the garden go any place useful?'

'Yes. There's an alley into Scholar Walk. Do you . . .' She inhaled deeply to regain her breathing's balance. 'Do you know the way from there?'

'I reckon so.'

He laid a hand on her shoulder and squeezed slightly, then walked round into the granny flat. She heard him open the French windows in there and saw him walk down the garden, slim briefcase in hand. He dipped his head to avoid the branch of an apple tree and kept it dipped much longer than was necessary.

'Thank you,' she thought, smiling slightly as he sauntered on to the garden gate.

There was a sudden rise in pitch in the noise outside and the beating on the door stopped. Someone shouted,

'Pigs!'

Then there was near-silence. She turned to clear away the breakfast things and saw that Evan had left on the table the copy of the paper which her mother had dropped in her fall. She flattened it out and saw her face growling,

'Bugger off bastard hack,'

from the front page. Under the heading 'TOP CARDINAL PREGNANCY SHOCK!' she read, 'We have exclusive news that sultry brunette Madeleine Merluza, 29, is pregnant by Cardinal Edmund Kilpatrick, 52. Lord have mercy!! The unlikely couple have been indulging in bizarre sex games and most unchristian fun for three months now, says the Cardinal's shocked housekeeper, Maude Gonaghal, 47. "It's a scandal," she added. "They were drawn together by an interest in disgusting old sex books. I used to be forced to dust them." Outside her Earls Court flat, steamy Miss Merluza made no secret of her happy condition. "I'm absolutely delighted," she said. "I'm hoping for a boy." Madeleine has gone to an exclusive clinic in Freyberg, Germany. His Eminence, her lover, was unavailable for comment. Should he make an honest woman of her? Give us your view – see postal vote coupon on page 4. Editorial, page 8.'

Madeleine flicked to page eight where she read that she was a specimen of the New Englishwoman; sexy, 'sparky' and putting experience before outdated morality. Somehow the same paragraph managed to condemn her liaison with Edmund as a symptom of 'a permissive society turned rotten' and compare it unfavourably with the examples set by English royal weddings. She screwed the paper up and tossed it into the bin then walked to the hall.

'Mum?' she called out. There was silence broken only by what sounded like a lecture being delivered by a policeman on the pavement. Madeleine slouched back to the bin, pulled out the paper and cut out the relevant pages with the kitchen scissors. Discarding the rest again, she folded the cuttings neatly and slipped them into the pocket of her skirt. She walked back to the hall and then almost to the top of the stairs. There she sat down, staring reproachfully at the locked bathroom door.

'Mum? Look Mum I'm sorry I didn't tell you.' She heard loo paper being crumpled and a cross sniff. 'I told you most. I only wanted to spare you. Mum? And I'm really sorry about those reporters. I thought I'd got away without them knowing where I'd gone. One of them must have followed me or bribed someone at the Warburg or something. Mum? Anyway, the policemen are here now to keep them away. Oh for God's sake, I can't sit here talking to a bloody bathroom door.'

A tap was turned on in the bathroom basin. In the ceiling overhead there was splashing as the tank was topped up. Then the tap was turned off. Floorboards creaked. Madeleine pictured her mother splashing her eyes to cool them, then patting them dry with a towel. After a pause, in which she assumed her mother was dabbing at her hair and straightening her clothes, the door was unlocked and

Mercy walked straight into her bedroom to sit on her bed. Madeleine followed her and leaned against the brass bedstead, staring at her, scanning her face for a reaction. Her mother gave a shallow sigh then, picking at one of her cuticles, slowly said,

'You stupid, *stupid* girl. What do you think a mother's for? Mmmh?' She looked up at Madeleine. 'You've been crying. Oh, *cariño*.' Changing her tone she stood and took her by the hand. 'Here,' she said, 'come and wash your eyes.'

'There's no need, Mum. I'm fine.'

'You *must* wash them or they'll get old and puffy,' said her mother, and firmly but kindly led her to the sink where she handed her a flannel and made her bathe her eyes. The cool water was beautifully soothing.

'*Gracias*,' said Madeleine, exchanging the flannel for a towel and drying her cheeks. 'Can I have a hug now?'

'Wait while I hang this up to dry,' said her mother, draping the towel on a rail. 'There,' she said, turning, and took Madeleine in her arms.

Hugs had always been rare because they were disarranging to her mother's clothes and hair. The less one hugged someone, the harder it became to find opportunities to do so. As they hugged now in the bathroom, and as Madeleine gazed with the dispassion of the securely held at the reflection of their absurd mismatch in the mirror, it was hard to tell whose clutch was the firmer. Just when Madeleine stopped needing any further hugging and was starting to suspect that her mother's need was greater than her own, they were pulled apart by a rapping on the front door.

169

'Police,' muttered Madeleine and walked downstairs, leaving her mother to rearrange herself. 'Yes?' she called out.

'It's all right, Miss. It's just some letters and things that some friends of yours have brought,' said a policeman through the letter box. She opened the door, leaving the chain on. The journalists had retreated to a pair of cars on the other side of the street. She saw with pride that there were two policemen guarding the door. There was a wild movement in the journalists' car as she took a handful of envelopes and a carrier bag from one of the policemen, but she had shut the door again before anyone had time to climb out and cross the road.

'We're under siege, Mum,' she called up the stairs. 'And it would seem to be Christmas.'

'What do you mean?' asked her mother, coming down.

Together they sat in the kitchen while Madeleine pulled from the bag a small bunch of flowers, their stalks wrapped in damp newspaper and foil, a tin of home-made chocolate biscuits, a bottle of bath oil and a packet of French mandarin-flavoured tea bags. Her mother opened the envelopes and read their contents out loud before passing them over for Madeleine to inspect the pictures.

' "Just some little flowers but they come with a big hug from Emma Dyce-Hamilton." "Big" is underlined. "Have just seen those awful papers and told Farquarson's they should burn the lot. Am so sorry for you both and will pray. Do let me know if I can do any shopping." That's from Marge. The "both" is in brackets.'

'Which is she?'

'Oh you know. Marge. Delaney-Siedentrop. The bossy

one who lets herself in from the alley to cut flowers sometimes.'

'Oh yes,' Madeleine said, not remembering, and taking a squint at the lurid floral motif on the front of the greetings card. Something had been covered over inside with a neat white label. She turned the card over and read the small print on its back.

'The message in this card reads, "My condolences",' it said.

'This one's from the Palace, from Deirdre. She must have rushed out after I left her. "Got together with les girls to show you we think you're wonderful people. Which you are." "Are" underlined. "Polly McCreery wants her biscuit tin back." She would. "But says you're welcome to keep the doily for icing cakes. *A bientôt*. Deirdre." And she sends a kiss.'

There were other messages of support and commiseration, some from people Mercy scarcely knew or whose links she thought she had dropped. There were many from people who knew only of Madeleine by repute. Mother and daughter sighed over some, laughed over others and sniffed a good deal. Mercy bit into a chocolate biscuit and declared it surprisingly delicious considering the state of Polly McCreery's kitchen.

20

There was a large landing on the first floor of the Harts' house. On her 'days' at the house, of which there were two a week plus the occasional night to help with large dinner parties, Dawn Harper did the ironing up there. The ostensible reason was that it was convenient, being the site of the airing cupboard. The actual explanations were that Dawn refused to be banished to the cramped obscurity of the utility room like a maid and that the landing position enabled her to keep an ear and eye on any domestic drama. No Barrower dared have a maid of their own, maids proper being confined to the town's hotels. The acceptable alternatives were visiting 'helps' such as Dawn, or hapless, English-less au pairs from the Continent.

Dawn heard the kitchen door open. She bent to turn down the volume on the radio.

'I don't see why you couldn't buy a dress like anyone else,' she heard Clive Hart complain. 'You earn enough.'

'I felt like making one,' his wife replied with dangerous emphasis. 'It's terribly easy really, and the finished product is so much more special than something from a shop.'

'It took your son Tobit three years to learn, so it can't be that easy.'

'Well Tobit's a man, isn't he? Did I say that?'

'Why hasn't he offered to make you something himself?'

Lydia turned up the stairs to where Dawn appeared to be deep in ironing one of Clive's shirts.

'Dawn?'

'Yes?'

'Could you be a sweetie and get the dressmaker's dummy out of the attic for me? There's a love. Just put it in my bedroom.'

'Of course,' said Dawn, not moving. 'I'll just finish this shirt.'

Lydia flung her a look. Dawn loved answering back.

'I don't *know* why he hasn't offered,' Lydia continued *sotto voce* to Clive, 'but it doesn't matter because his style really isn't suitable. It's all far too young.' Lydia started up the stairs then paused. 'Oh damn,' she said.

'What's up now?' asked Clive.

Dawn glanced up from her ironing. Clive had a brief-case with him and was on the point of leaving for Tatham's.

'Damn,' repeated Lydia.

'What?' Clive asked, exasperated.

'I asked Fergus Gibson and Emma Dyce-Hamilton to dinner on Friday.'

'We can't possibly have them then. You'll be careering around like a drunk wasp getting ready for Saturday.'

'I know,' snapped Lydia. 'I didn't know about Saturday when I invited them, did I?'

'Sor-ree,' sighed Clive. 'I've got to go. See you later.'

'No, Clive. Please.'

'What?'

'Don't shout.'

'I wasn't shouting.'

'You couldn't drop in on Emma and tell her, could you?'

'Can't you ring her?'

'Oh please, darling. You're so much better than I am at being tactful with women and I think I got her all excited about Fergus.'

'Well that was very silly.'

'Why?'

'Fergus is a confirmed bachelor.'

'He's not.'

'Oh of course he is. Who do you think poor Roger Drinkwater was?'

'His business partner,' she replied, already sounding less convinced.

'God!' Clive laughed bitterly at her innocence. 'I *must* go. Bye.' He opened the front door and swung it loudly shut behind him.

'See you,' said Lydia to an empty hall, and came up the stairs. Dawn was ironing the same shirt. 'Fergus Gibson isn't one of those, is he, Dawn?'

'Yes he is,' said Dawn. Lydia had been looking for smiling reassurance, and it pleased her to supply a well-informed contradiction.

'Oh dear. How very embarrassing,' said Lydia. She was always forgetting that Dawn had 'days' at Fergus Gibson's house as well. 'Did you find the dummy all right?'

'Oh, no. Sorry. I'll go now.'

'Thanks.'

Dawn left Lydia to her embarrassment and climbed the next flight of stairs. She took a hooked pole from its resting place in a cupboard and used it to pull at the ring on a trap door in the ceiling. This released a metal ladder which, at a tug from her spatulate hands, slid down to rest on the landing carpet. Climbing with hands as well as feet, Dawn mounted into the gloom. She groped to her right and flicked the light switch. Around her were spread the tenderly guarded unnecessities of over two decades of marriage. Broken anglepoise lamps made drunken gestures towards huge, metal-cornered trunks. A large cardboard box with JIGSAWS ETC marked on its side lay atop a tea chest marked BOOKS – JUMBLE. There was a sky-blue cot and, beside it, a grand old-fashioned pram with suspension straps and luxurious springs. The cot was full of folded curtains in faded or outmoded patterns and sizes that were unlikely to be called for again. The pram held a menagerie of teddies and soft toys. Dawn lifted the plastic sheet that was spread to protect them from the dust. There was a naked doll inside too, incongruously pink and shiny amidst the acetate fur and tear-flattened fluff. Some of the bears were too old to have been bought for Tobit and must have been cherished hand-me-downs from his parents. The doll was ugly and modern. Dawn picked it out by a glossy leg. The head, with its platinum blonde hair, mascara-lengthened eyelashes and cupid's bow mouth rested eerily on the unformed, babyish body below. The ice-blue eyes clicked open and closed at Dawn who, with a snarl, tossed her into a distant corner.

'Dawn? Are you OK?' Lydia called from below.

'Yes. Fine,' Dawn grunted. 'Just banged my shin a bit.'

'Bad luck. I'll be in my bedroom when you want me.'

She had only had time to acquire one teddy before Sasha had gone, and that had disappeared with her. Sasha was the fruit of a drunken lapse on Dawn's eighteenth New Year's Eve. She had gone to the Slug and Lettuce with some girls and met a man called Martin who had bought her several port and lemons and then offered to drive her home. He had had a Ford Escort van with a mattress in the back. He was on his way north to a job on a Scottish oil rig. She remembered nothing else about him. When her mother had caught her, some weeks later, sitting on the edge of the bath untwisting a coathanger, she had locked her in her bedroom.

For the months of Sasha's gestation, Dawn had seen only the four walls of her small pink room and the four, wavy blue ones of the bathroom next door. Her meals had been brought up to her on a tray, though she had had her own kettle for the making of coffee and tea. She had no close friends at the time, and members of the shifting crowd with whom she went out on Saturday nights were told that she had gone on a long stay to her Auntie June's in Leeds. She had slept most of the time and listened to jabbering radio disc jockeys in her waking hours. Her skin acquired a thick, lardy look it had never lost and, after the baby was born, she had been slow to lose weight again. Dawn's father had never been in evidence – she had grown up alone with her mother in the Bross Gardens cottage. Her mother had worked from home, stuffing soft toys. Every week a van came with a bag of white stuffing and a box of empty teddy pelts and took away the animals she had stuffed over the last seven days. The cheques came by post every Tuesday. When Sasha was born her mother had stolen a teddy and given it to her. Four days later, baby and teddy were gone.

Dawn had become hysterical. Throughout her confinement, the child within her had been the focus of her slow, brooding thoughts and by its birthday, bawling baby and young mother were as limbs of one beast. She had tried to tell the police but her mother had held the bread knife to her cheek and said,

'Just you dare!'

Lacking daring, she had told nobody. After a while her mother tried to make her believe that Sasha had been adopted. Dawn had adopted this lie for the sake of peace.

Extra bags of teddy skins were brought so that she too could work to stuff them, and gradually she was allowed out with her crowd again on Saturday nights. She drank brandy sodas now; port and lemon made her sick. Although Dawn looked thirty-five, she was in fact ten years younger, which would make Sasha seven. Her mother was dead now, of some internal growth kept secret too long, but Dawn knew, with a gut-centred, unavowable certainty, that Sasha was still alive. And unadopted.

Alone with the discreet clatters and splashes of her midnight garden last night she had added a terrible invocation from Evan Kirby's book to her usual prayer.

The dressmaker's dummy was shrouded in a pink velour sack. Dawn slipped one arm around its waist and bore it to the trap door. There she took it by the neck and slid it gently down the ladder to the landing. She sealed off the memories of the attic once more and carried the dummy down to the Harts' broad, oatmeal bedroom where Lydia was pinning out the segments of a pattern on a few yards of plum-coloured material.

'Thanks so much,' said Lydia, not looking up.

'If you like,' Dawn said, returning to the ironing to find that the radio channel had been changed to one with talking and no music, 'I could pass on a message to Mr Gibson for you. I'll be seeing him late this afternoon.'

21

Emma opened her fridge and lifted out the chocolate biscuit cake she had made that morning before school. She ran
a knife around its edge then held the tin carefully over a
plate and pressed on its base with her thumbs. The thick
brown blend of biscuit crumbs and chocolate caramel
shifted slightly then slid in a satisfactory block on to the
plate. She had arranged a circle of glacé cherries and walnuts in the bottom of the tin before pouring the mixture in
and, though they had drifted a fraction, these now showed
decoratively through the stickiness of the cake's upper surface. Emma cut two generous slices for Crispin and two
wiser ones for herself. She left the knife on the edge of the
plate to encourage Crispin to accept more, though she suspected that even the iron stomach of a thirteen-year-old
would baulk at a third slice. She would give him the rest to
take back to Tatham's when he left. She had not bothered
with the gesture of a bread and butter introduction. She
plugged in the kettle and spooned tea leaves into a cold pot.
Her hand shook on the third spoonful, scattering leaves
over the kitchen table. Frowning, she swept them into her
hand with a cloth. Rousillou jumped to sniff the cake and
she shouted unnecessarily loudly to chase him off.

A troubled night had left her nervous and sore. She had
been visited by six variations of the same unbridled dream
concerning Fergus Gibson. She invited him home to meet

her parents. Her mother did not appear but was definitely present. Emma's relationship with Mr Gibson was vaguely friendly – they had met at a party in London, apparently – but in each variation of the dream became more specifically so when he opened his bags and drew out a silk dressing gown identical to her father's. With each interruptive awakening had come a fresh stab of irritation at finding herself in Barrowcester with empty arms, and a fresh determination to sleep again in the hope of recapturing her elusive lover. When the sixth reprise was cut short by her alarm clock, she had abandoned bed as smartly as ever but, somewhere between toothbrush and bicycle, a clinging disappointment had descended. It was one of those days when Barrowcester held her too tight. Yet again it was sunny. Yet again birds sang. Yet again new flowers nodded. People smiled and asked her how she was and instead of screaming in their faces, she had smiled back and said she felt fine. Deirdre Chattock had stopped to tell her that Madeleine Merluza, a smug, lumpish girl with whom she had coincided at Tatham's, had been made pregnant by Cardinal Fitzpatrick, and was under siege from the gutter press. Emma went out of her way to pick Madeleine a posy of flowers and to buy her a sort of Get Well Soon card.

The doorbell rang. Emma chased the cats from the kitchen and followed them into the hall. Crispin was no taller. They had made him change from his uniform into his suit for the visit.

'Hello,' she said, sounding as warm as she had done all day. 'Come on in. How smart you look! Is that a new suit?'

'Yes. We bought it in Leeds last week.'

'Very grown up!'

He stooped to pick up Rousillou who was sniffing at his grey flannel turn-ups. The cat seemed bigger than ever in the boy's small, scrabbling grasp. Crispin was a diminutive version of his uncle Jeremy, who was a cousin of Emma's, an eligible London divorcé working as a literary agent. Emma had been best friends with Crispin's eldest sister, following a shared family holiday when they were seventeen. For two years they had gone on trips together, written letters and told each other everything. Then Sarah, amiable but breathtakingly ignorant, had flunked her A-levels. As she drifted into cooking directors' lunches and as Emma passed on to Edinburgh, their lives had painlessly separated. Emma's godmotherhood of Sarah's brother was their only remaining contact.

'Shall we sit in the garden or don't you think it's warm enough yet?' she asked.

'Well, it's not as warm as it looks.'

His voice was half-broken, so it took occasional alarming leaps up an octave or two.

'Let's go into Pa's study then,' she said, 'because it's in the sun at the moment.'

With a ceiling yellowed by tobacco smoke and one wall clouded with grey by an inefficient fireplace, the little study was the room in greatest need of redecoration yet, when it was ablaze with late afternoon sunshine, it was the room she least wanted to alter. It was redolent with tender memories of her father before illness drove him upstairs. She liked to sit there with her marking and a pot of bonfirish, China tea.

'So tell me your news,' she demanded once they were settled. 'You started on Sunday?'

'Saturday. Boarders had to arrive on Saturday afternoon. There was a sort of welcoming tea party.' Crispin pushed back a lock of black hair that was bothering him. It dropped back into his eyes within seconds.

'How grim.'

'Yes. It was. Ma came but she had to leave almost straight away.'

'Have you got a nice study?'

'I haven't got one at all.'

'No?'

'Not a proper one. I share a *burrow* with a nice girl called Jermyn and eight other boys.'

'*Men*,' she corrected him with a smile.

'Blast. Yes, *men*. And I have to sleep in a huge dormitory upstairs.'

'Nice bed?'

'Not very. It sinks in the middle so it's hard to roll over on.'

'Oh dear. Who's your form *god*?'

'We've got two. Officially it's Dr Brightstone.'

'She's nice.'

'Is she? We share her with 5Bii so Mr Hart comes in for English and to set our Saturday essays.'

'*Weekenders*,' she corrected him again.

'Yes.'

'When's your *Lingua* exam?'

'Two weekends away.' Crispin pulled a face. 'I've only got as far as the first two pages of that little guide they hand out. It's all so illogical. Why can't we call a book a book like everyone else? It feels silly calling it a *tablet* and a teacher's a teacher, not a *god*. Didn't you find it hard?'

'Quite. But I'd had a head start by growing up here and hearing *Lingua* all the time. Anyway, as girls had only just been let in, they were too busy building us changing rooms and deciding on our uniform to make sure we learned official slang.'

There was a pause as Crispin stood to peer at a cluster of family photographs on the desk. There were the late Dean and his new bride grinning at the entrance to the Glurry. There was Emma, enchantingly plain and gap-toothed at six, in a bobble hat and pulling a sledge. There was Emma aged seventeen, tanned and smiling in a shape-less cotton jumper amid her equally smiling cousins. Sarah, Crispin's sister number one, then rather stout and a worry to her mother, stood beside Emma with an arm slung round her narrow shoulders. Behind them, Crispin's Uncle Jeremy, ever the exhibitionist, posed with a wreath of bladderwrack on his brow and a long, lean leg protruding from a skimpy white beach wrap. Crispin's parents, Joan and Harry, framed the group. Harry, tubby in a silly hat, held young Crispin on his hairy shoulders. Joan, Jeremy's eldest sister, with the best figure in the group, stood with sun-streaked hair plastered back off her head and grimaced because her batwing sunglasses were less efficient than fashionable. Crispin's other sister, Polly, then a stringy thing of twelve, was adding to her mother's irritation by tugging on one of her arms.

Crispin walked with the photograph back to the sofa. He touched his tongue on his upper lip.

'Your ma sounded so well on the phone,' Emma said. 'She told me all about Sarah getting engaged. What's he like?'

'OK,' said Crispin.

'You don't sound very enthusiastic.'

'He's a bit old.'

'Oh. But he's nice?'

'He's OK. I think Ma finds him rather dull but Sarah's over the moon so she's happy for her sake.'

'Ah.' Emma stood. 'I'll go and make the tea. Is cake all right or do you want bread and butter too?'

'Cake's lovely,' he said. Finally she had made him smile. A watery smile, but a smile none the less.

When she came back with the cake and tea things on a tray, he was crying.

He had dropped the picture on to the sofa beside him, drawn his knees up, and was grinding his fists against wet, scarlet cheeks.

'Crispin, don't. Please don't,' she begged. She set the tray down as fast as she could and hurried over. She sat beside him and laid a hand on his shoulder. He flinched and, trying to stop, slid his feet back to the carpet.

'I'm sorry,' he mumbled, swollen lips groping for the words. 'It's just . . . So sorry.'

'Ssh,' she urged.

He felt roughly in his jacket pockets then stood, lurching, and felt in the pockets of his trousers, sniffing the while. The only handkerchief she had on her was Fergus Gibson's which she had washed and ironed the night before. She had pushed it, like a talisman, into her cardigan pocket as she left the house that morning.

'Here,' she said, passing the pressed white square to Crispin's grasp.

'Danks,' said Crispin in a rush, and hiccoughed. 'Sorry.'

'Ssh. Poor boy. I shouldn't have let you see the photograph. I had no idea.' He sat back and blew his nose hard while she rubbed his back and made sounds of encouragement. When he seemed to be rallying, she left his side to pour their tea and to slide a slice of chocolate biscuit cake on to a plate for him. Rousillou had left the room to watch her collect the tea and so had missed Crispin's tears. He returned now with his mother and jumped on to the sofa. He settled there in a peculiarly canine pose with his chin resting on the boy's nearest thigh. Blanquette watched him from the vantage of Emma's lap.

'It's so silly,' Crispin muttered. 'I'm not homesick, not in the least. It was just being here with carpet and flowers and the photographs. I was starting to forget. I sort of melted.'

'I'm sorry.'

'No. I'm sorry.' The telephone rang on the desk. 'Shall I?' he asked. She nodded, so he answered it. 'Hello? . . . Yes of course. Who's calling? . . . Jeremy, hi! . . . Yes it is. Emma's asked me to tea here . . . Yes. How are you?'

Crispin's face lit up. Jeremy was obviously a favourite uncle. Never exactly a he-man, he was, Emma supposed, still handsome, funny and sophisticated enough to inspire the admiration of an undersized thirteen-year-old. He was precisely the sort of older male relative whose influence, while likely to be bad in large doses, was held to exert a usefully maturing effect on growing sons with no brothers of their own. Emma sipped her tea and watched with Blanquette as the gloom evaporated from Crispin's bright, round face.

'Do you want to speak to Emma now?' Crispin asked finally and she stood to take the receiver from him. 'I'll hand you over.'

'Emma darling,' said Jeremy.

'Jeremy. Hello. How are you?' She could hear a word processor's electronic scything in the background.

'I'm fine. How are . . . Oh, wait a second, Emma.'

He held the receiver away from his face and she heard the languid tones of one of Jeremy's armada of plummy assistants. Emma wondered if he were ringing to ask her to the theatre. He did so sometimes. She would go to his office in Bloomsbury, via a potter in the Hellenic rooms of the British Museum, and a plummy assistant would offer her tea or a glass of delicious, cold wine. Jeremy would emerge, briefly introducing her to the client who was leaving and who was often someone whose name or work she knew, then steer her to a taxi and off to a play or opera. The evening would end with an elegant meal on his company credit card. She entertained no fond illusions about him, sensing that his brand of woman would be at once less earnest and more worldly than she, and that, while their cousinship was distant, it still set a bar on any emotional engagement beyond the familial. Yes, Emma hoped he were ringing to invite her to London.

'Emma.'

'Hello again.'

'Sorry about that.'

'That's OK.'

'I'm fine. Are you?'

'Yes. Perfectly. I've got Crispin here.'

'Yes. Lovely.' She could hear him nodding at an assistant to leave something on his desk or to ask someone else to hold on. 'Emma darling, can you do me a huge favour?'

'Of course,' she said, disappointed, yet curious because the request was so rare. 'What?'

'Well a client of mine is staying in Barrowcester for a week to do some research in the libraries. Evan Kirby.'

'Oh yes. I heard that talk of his on the radio last month.'

'Lovely. Well, could you ask him to tea or something, 'cause he's American and won't know anyone there and he might be feeling a bit low seeing as his divorce has just come through.'

'Of course. Is he at the Gladstone?'

'No. He's staying with . . . Hang on . . . Yup, he's staying at a Mrs Merluza's. I've got the number here.'

'It's OK. I know her. Sort of.' Emma mouthed 'more tea?' at Crispin, who poured them both a second cupful. 'What fun!' she went on. 'I'll drop him a note.'

'You are sweet. He's there for about a week. Emma, I've got to dash as I've got some wretched novelist on the other line, but look, I'm glad you're so well and that young Crispin's keeping an eye on you. And look, you must come up again soon. Maybe *Billy Budd*. Would you like to see *Billy Budd*?'

'Love to.'

'I'll ring you soon then. Bye. And thanks.'

'Bye.' She replaced the receiver. 'What good timing,' she said.

'Yes,' replied Crispin, helping himself to the second large slice of cake. 'I haven't seen Jeremy in ages. Does he ever come down here?'

'No. Not really. He's awfully busy and high-powered nowadays and I think he likes to collapse at weekends.' Jeremy had a house in Camden which Emma had never seen. That, and the fact that he had a lodger who was a vet were all that she knew about his private life. 'Maybe we can coax him down on one of your *exeats*, though.'

'That would be great,' said Crispin, rubbing Rousillou's honey-coloured stomach as the cat stretched languorously and rolled on to his back to give the boy better access. 'It is odd being a a boarder,' he said.

'How do you mean?'

'Well I feel so stupid because all the other new boys, sorry, new *men* in my house have boarded since they were seven and a half or eight. For them, going away to school for twelve weeks at a stretch is like being sent to stay in a rather basic hotel. It's so *hard* getting to sleep in a room full of people muttering and whispering. I've only been to hospital once, when Granny thought I had appendicitis, and it's just like that. It doesn't get quiet until about one in the morning and then I have to get up at six forty-five to wake people.'

'Poor thing! Every morning?'

'Not Sundays. It depends on how early they want waking. I'm a sort of human alarm clock. And the other thing I hate is that it's almost impossible to be alone.'

'But that apart, you're not too miserable?' Emma smiled at him, teasing. 'You're not homesick?'

'Not at *all!*'

The floodgates truly opened now. Emma took a second thin slice of chocolate biscuit cake and decided that the most godmotherly thing was to listen. She sat for half an hour, occasionally clipping off another sliver of cake, and listened to Crispin's heartfelt condemnation of family life. His father was cold and uncommunicative, he said, his mother manipulative and temperamental and his sisters stupid and irritatingly high-spirited. The only thing he seemed to miss about home was cake at teatime and the silent fidelity of his dog, Lottie, who was to have puppies any day now.

Crispin leaped up to go at half past five, realizing that he was going to be late for high tea in school, and thanked Emma profusely for her hospitality. She saw him to the door and pressed on him the remaining half of the cake along with a bag of grapes, because to ply a godson with nothing but chocolate seemed a mite irresponsible. When he had closed the garden gate and she was fluffing out the cushions on the sofa, she remembered that he had left with Fergus Gibson's handkerchief.

She set the tea things back on the kitchen table then took up the cake plate. Bending forward, she licked off the remaining crumbs of chocolate although she was already feeling sick.

She went to sit by the telephone and dialled the number of an old Edinburgh friend who had drifted into corporate finance. She glanced at her watch, though, saw that it was still too early to call at a cheap rate, and hung up before anyone could answer. On the telephone pad she had scribbled,

'Boredom, tedium, melancholy, melancholia, uninterest, flatness, staleness, leadenness, inactivity, repetition, wearisomeness, satiety (12).'

She took up the pencil that lay there, thought for a moment, then added, '*taedium vitae*, insipidity, indifference, irksomeness, disgust, monotony (18).'

22

Fergus was kneeling on a fertilizer bag in a corner of the Gardens of Remembrance. He stretched out to the back of the little rose bed before him and tugged up the last weed. He emptied a bucketful of compost around the bases of the bushes and dug it in with a hand fork. The soil was dry so he walked to a tap hidden along with a wheelbarrow and a dustbin in a spinney of laurels and brought back a bucketful of water which he tipped around the bed. The roses were fleshy pink monsters with a name like Passion Tiger or Lady Jayne. Planted by mistake, or through wilful ignorance on the gardener's part of his request for something old fashioned and white, he had had to leave them there. The prospect of tearing out plants that had fed on one's lover's ashes was abhorrent. As the months passed and the bushes grew sleek and glossy, he had continued to tend them but did so with disgusted resentment, as a child might learn to tolerate a blooming stepmother in lieu of a finer, thinner creature who was no more. He cherished a secret desire that one day he would drive over the Roman Bridge, park the car at the gates and walk the bosky length of these gardens of cypress, rhododendron and mourning laurel to find Roger's roses slashed to death by a vandal's blade and trampled by an unwittingly discerning boot. He had grown half-used to the replacement of Roger with Passion Tiger as he had grown half-used to the substitution of dying lover by all-too-lingering parent.

Roger had been half Barrower. He had grown up in Liverpool where his father was a shipping clerk, but his mother had been a Barrower born. When the two men fell for the place during a day trip one summer then bought a house in Tracer Street it was thus a manner of homecoming. They had met in Liverpool. Fergus had almost finished a half-hearted training in an architect's office and Roger was designing textiles in a cooperative while working as a waiter so as not to starve. They had shared a house in gentrified Toxteth where they ran a 'design' shop, selling wallpapers, fabrics and the occasional obelisk, all-purpose bust or marble-topped table to their largely academic neighbours. The business succeeded after a fashion, eked out by Fergus's freelance architectural work, but after eight or nine years they were both tired of Liverpool. Barrowcester's leafy precincts offered the perfect antidote to the Mersey. The cathedral city was also a perfect site for the interior design consultancy they had always hoped to set up. Since Barrowcester had become a commuter town there was an increasing number of Barrowers blessed with the money to redecorate their houses but neither the time nor the energy to do so themselves. These leaped on Fergus's and Roger's services, chequebooks waving in the wind, as did those keen to decorate themselves but greedy to buy from the more 'exclusive' range of papers and fabrics with which Drinkwater and Gibson Design Consultants could supply them.

They had lived there only two years when Roger fell ill. At first they had assumed it was glandular fever or hepatitis. His glands had swollen and felt sore and he had become listless, no sooner out of bed than ready to collapse again in exhausted sleep. Then he had started to lose weight.

Ever slightly on the plump side, he had been delighted. Rallying from his languor, he had laughed as he pulled on pair after pair of once-outgrown trousers and joked that it was worth being off-colour occasionally if the results were so flattering. But the weight had continued to fall off him. Literally. Flesh dropped where muscle had once held it firm, as if his body were being aged at a supernatural rate. Fergus would wake in the night to find himself drenched in the sweat that was coursing off his lover's limbs, and wake in the morning to see a hollow-cheeked, sunken-eyed face across the pillow that he scarcely recognized.

Roger's fear of death was intense; he was one of those men who swore that they had never had a day's illness in their life, from the superstitious hope that reiteration might assume the power of prophecy. After weeks of hiding behind excuses of a recurrence of glandular fever, he ventured to Saint Boniface's Infirmary. Tests were run and he was found to be half-eaten by a colony of cancers that had mistaken his lymph system for public transport. By the doctor's calculations, the damage had begun at about the time Fergus and Roger came to Barrowcester househunting. Death had been creeping up on them for two years, and they were left like children trying to fight back an insidious high tide with bucket and spade. There was nothing to be done, so Roger came home with jars of drugs, a *House and Garden* he had stolen from the waiting room, and six months to live. The high tide took him into a kind of coma of pain after only two and swept him away a fortnight later.

Barrowcester had a sympathy system that sprang into action on the first sign of suffering, as a concerted campaign of presents and visitations; kindness clustered on

191

kindness around the sufferer like so many stifling antibodies. Anxious to be spared such attentions, Fergus had grieved in near silence and took advantage of the fact that, in their discreet, privet-shaded minds, everyone from Roger's mother to Lydia Hart (whom he had always regarded as a friend) had assumed that he and Roger had been partners only in business, who shared a house for reasons of bachelor economy. To occupy his wheeling mind, Fergus had prepared a vast tea for Roger's family when they descended for the funeral, only to receive 'don't let us keep you' looks when they decided that he had outstayed his welcome on the scene of their mourning.

'There's something you should know,' he had told them. 'Roger and I were lovers and he didn't die of cancer; it was AIDS.'

He still felt guilty about that extra touch. He had felt it was wrong not to let them know that their son had died loving and beloved, but he had found their grim self-satisfaction and hackneyed grief too maddening for tasteful restraint. Inspired by the faces of ogling shock they turned on him and by the thought of how Roger would have laughed, he plied them with detail after gory detail. They had positively fled, leaving home-made cakes uneaten. In seven weeks, the height of their devotion had been a flight of hideous get-well cards and a basket of bruised, mundane fruit. Charged with the confessional spirit, he had thought of enlightening Barrowcester (though without the extra touch), but forbore; a hard, glistening corner of him remained good at business and had doubts about the breadth of the Barrowcesterian mind.

Reasonless guilt at being the partner left behind, led

him to grim fantasies that Roger's cancers were a new variety, somehow contagious, or even that in a retributive masterstroke, the hellish lie told to Roger's family should become fact and AIDS take him in its hydra-handed grip. He began to read obsessively anything with the four beguilingly kind initials in it. Victims lingered month after month, he read, suffering indignities normally spared their fellows; skin infections found on birds and fish, throat infections that barely touched a hamster, attacks on the brain and on the very tissues that made a body look human. Fergus's appetite knew no satisfaction. He read trash. He read inflammatory lies. He read of a man in the South so overrun with sores that, beating down despair with good cheer, the nurses had nicknamed him Mulberry. The man had burst, though, which had spoiled the joke rather.

To be abandoned as caretaker of the relics of so much happiness, condemned by habit to lie to one side of a double bed, to continue to buy the biscuits he had never liked and to watch the programmes he had never found amusing, seemed a far slower ending than any tortures a hellish disease could inflict. Now that the weeks were passing once more at their old fast rate, however, and he found himself still with the bloom of health about him, Fergus had admitted a draught of hope. The remorse swiftly attendant on this obliged him to conduct a merciless daily search for the fatal symptoms. He had begun to weigh himself every day and never soaped himself in the bath without feeling for swollen glands. Since he was condemned either way, to death or to deadly guilt, each slight drop in weight, each bout of flu, each hot, sleepless night charged him with simultaneous thrills of reprieve and death-row despair.

A formerly healthy libido had shrivelled to obsolescence. He masturbated once a week, from a tidy dislike of wet dreams. He found he could do this with a mind clear of fantasy. Indeed, it was less disturbing to concentrate on anything that would not reawaken death-lust associations; a choice of curtain fittings, for instance, or a new stuffing for chicken breasts. He masturbated into clean white handkerchiefs which were then scrupulously boiled and ironed. The only one he never used was the one with an F in the corner, given him by Roger, the one he had lost somewhere.

Fergus's sole confidante and pal, Dawn Harper, was waiting on his doorstep when he parked the car. For want of close, sane relatives, he loved her.

'Hi,' she said with her sympathetic scowl.

'Hello, Harpy,' he said, patting her shoulder and taking out his keys. 'Have you been waiting long?'

'Yes. You stayed to brood, didn't you?'

'No. Honestly. I just weeded then came away.'

'They haven't died, then?'

'No. Worst luck.'

'You should let me go over there one night with a spade to do them in,' she suggested, as he opened the door and waved her past him. 'Still, I suppose I should just do it without telling . . .' Dawn's voice trailed off. Fergus's mother was standing in the hall in her nightdress. Her hair, face, arms and dwindled bosom were smeared with excrement. 'Shit,' Dawn stated.

'Mother,' said Fergus.

'None of you will own up to it but I *know* you all do it differently from me,' said Lilias Gibson and started to cry.

Dawn and Fergus froze, watching the silent oh-oh-oh her mouth was forming. The stench seemed to double as Fergus stared. It was Dawn who started forward first.

'Harpy, you can't,' said Fergus, laying a restraining hand on her arm. She threw him a challenging glance. 'Actually, I'm not sure I could,' he conceded and released her.

'Come along, Mrs Gibson,' she said, steering his mother up the stairs, one hand set firm on her mercifully clean back. 'I think you need a quick shower.'

Fergus stood listening to the sounds of his mother being driven into the bathroom and of the shower being turned on. A chunk of turd caught his eye on the piece of carpet where she had greeted them. Shocked into action, he hurried to the kitchen, donned a pair of rubber gloves, removed the offending object on a coal scuttle then, having searched for more, flung open every available window and squirted the air with some of the *parfum d'ambiance* he always presented to clients at the end of a job. Finally he set to work with a bucket of scalding water, carpet shampoo and an old rag. As he came back from tossing both said rag and the rubber gloves into the dustbin, he found Dawn coming downstairs.

'She's back in bed,' she announced.

'Harpy, you're an angel.'

'I know. Give me a phone book and the usual.'

'Who do you want to phone?'

'Give.'

He found the local directory and left her with it on a sofa while he went to mix her a brandy and soda. He switched on the kettle for a tea for himself then took her the drink.

'Thanks,' she said then held out the directory, a stout forefinger pointing to an entry. 'Ring them,' she added.

' "Brooklea",' he read, ' "Rest home, Brwcstr 657211." Harpy, I can't.'

'You've got to,' she replied, sipping her drink. 'You can't cope.'

'I'll do it later, maybe.'

'Now, Fergus,' she said. 'I'm not doing *that* for you many more times.' On 'that' she jerked her head towards the ceiling. He sighed surrender, walked to the telephone and dialled Barrowcester 657211. He spoke to a nurse who said that yes indeed they did have a vacancy and no there was no waiting list at the moment on account of a long hard winter. She told him that Matron could show him round tomorrow and discuss terms. Did he have power of attorney, she asked him. No? Well they advised all their clients to obtain it so as to facilitate transfer of funds. Fergus arranged to see Matron tomorrow afternoon. He then rang his solicitor and arranged to see her tomorrow morning.

While he was on the telephone, Dawn had been to the kitchen and made him a pot of tea and a plate of Marmite soldiers for two. He lay on the sofa with his head on a cushion in her lap and, while a woman on the television showed them how to make a kite from two bamboo rods and one of father's old shirts, Dawn stroked his thinning hair and fed him.

'What did you do last night, Harpy?' he asked her.

'Sat in the garden in the nuddy and waited for the Devil,' she admitted and he laughed, desperately unhappy.

23

Evan was sitting on the sofa. It was an unpleasantly soft one so his knees were not far from his chin. He was pretending to read Sukie Lark Rosen's *Towards a New Mythology* although there was scarcely any light on his side of the room. Mrs Merluza was sitting in her armchair to his right. Despite the fact that he was apparently absorbed in a book, she had persisted in wittering on about high society in the Barcelona of her youth. He had observed this to be a nervous tic in her, brought on by silence. There was a pile of little presents, all carefully wrapped. Occasionally she would mutter something to herself, reach out to pick one up, finger it curiously then set it back. Madeleine stood glowering in a cloud of smoke. She had changed into a dark red dress. She only joined the others in order to stub out a cigarette and pick up a fresh one.

'Can't I open this tiny one?' asked her mother, fingering another packet.

'No,' Madeleine snapped, swinging back towards the garden window. 'It's probably just another packet of fudge.'

'You used to like fudge,' came the rejoinder after a pause.

'Well only in moderation,' growled Madeleine, 'and not today.' Evan turned a page. 'Besides, they're my presents, not yours.'

'It's very kind of you to sit with us, Professor,' said Mrs

Merluza, seeing that Madeleine had turned her back. 'I do hope you understand.'

'No. No. It's quite all right. A pleasure,' Evan enthused and flicked back a page to trace the beginning of the sentence amidst which he had suddenly found himself.

There was a brief silence punctuated by the occasional clatter and buzz of the policemen's walkie-talkie in the street below and by Madeleine's violent throwing up of the garden window for air. Then the doorbell rang. No one left the room but Madeleine turned to lean against the open window and her mother smoothed out her skirt.

'I wonder who it'll be now,' she said.

The front door was opened and closed, there were footsteps on the stairs and one of the policemen put his head round the sitting-room door.

'A Mr Hart to see you, Mrs Merluza. All right if he comes up?'

'Has he brought fudge?' asked Madeleine.

'Yes, of course, Officer,' said her mother. 'Send him up. And thank you.'

The policeman disappeared and after a while a man Evan thought vaguely familiar took his place. He had hairy hands and was dressed like a schoolmaster.

'Clive, what a lovely surprise,' said Mrs Merluza, rising to take his hand.

'Hello,' the man said and glanced amiably around.

'You know my daughter Madeleine, of course.'

'Actually I don't think we've met since she was a young girl in my Shakespeare class.'

'No. We haven't.'

'How do you do?'

'I won't answer that.'

'Oh,' said Clive and laughed. 'Sorry.'

'And this is Professor Kirby, who is staying with us to do some research for a book on Heaven.'

'Hello. Clive Hart.'

'How d'you do.'

'Heaven. How fascinating.' Evan made deprecating noises and flapped the hand with the book in it. 'I won't keep you,' said Clive. 'Because I'm sure you're about to eat but Lydia rang to ask me to drop in on my way home and bring you this.' He held out a large carrier bag. 'Sorry it's not wrapped up properly.' He glanced at the pile of presents. 'Gosh. It's a bit like Christmas, isn't it?' he said without thinking.

'An amaryllis,' said Mrs Merluza, lifting the plant from its bag. 'How lovely and how kind of you,' she continued as its grossly phallic stem bounced against her cheek. 'And it's going to be a white one. They're our favourites. Look, *cariño*.'

'Lovely,' murmured Madeleine. 'Thank you.'

'Not at all. Just a little nothing, really, but, well, we heard about the fuss in the papers and felt so sorry for you both. People are so insensitive.' He had perched briefly on the arm of a chair and now rose to go. 'Well,' he said. 'Must get back for supper. Bye Madeleine – lovely to see you again. Bye, Professor. Nice meeting you.'

'Oh must you? I'll see you out,' chimed in Mrs M. and followed him out on to the stairs.

'Why's he so familiar?' asked Evan, pushing the door to. 'I'm sure I've seen his face.'

'Redundant sixties playwright-turned-househusband and teacher,' she explained. She had come forward to grab another cigarette, having tossed the last one into the garden. 'I hate amaryllis,' she added.

'They are rather big,' he agreed.

'I suspect it may have had an accident by tomorrow.' She looked up and gave him a tired smile. 'You should escape now before she comes up again. There aren't likely to be any more people tonight.'

'Right. I think I may. Are you sure . . . ?'

'Yes. I'll be fine. I think I'll go to bed in a sec to have some peace. Have you got something for supper?'

'Fish fingers and butterscotch Angel's Delight.'

'Lucky you.' She waited until he was at the door then added, 'Thanks, Evan.'

He glanced back but she was touching her cigarette end on the amaryllis bud and failed to see him. Mrs Merluza was doing something in the kitchen so he hurried into the granny flat and shut the door undetected. He added a pint of milk to the Angel's Delight mix and whipped it up with an egg whisk, working himself into a kind of silent fury as he did so. He set it to thicken in the miniature fridge then arranged the fish fingers in rows in the grill pan. Leaving them to cook, he tugged the curtain across, having realized that he was brightly visible to any journalists who had not yet given up and headed to the Tracer's Arms in search of Old Stoat and local gossip. Then he strode through to the bedroom, causing the sliding doors to rattle as he went. He sat at the table, snatched off the rubber band from his journal and scrawled.

'Why a Cardinal? Cardinals are for weird dames in Webster. I doubt whether even Sukie Lark Rosen would lay a Cardinal. I have to admit, though, that it shows a certain flair. It also confirms my suspicions about her being the wickedest girl in class. Could I keep up? The only time I tried to get kinky for Miriam's sake, I got sick on pineapple chunks and sprained a wrist.'

After the morning's brush with the journalists, he had spent the day feeling like the Invisible Man. It had felt as though his involvement in the talk of the town should show, and it didn't. Not until he came home, that was. To sidestep the besiegers at the front door, he had approached the house from the back, through the passage from Scholar Walk. Finding that the garden gate had been locked, he had started to climb the wall only to be pulled back by a policeman. At Evan's polite insistence, Mrs Merluza's good word had been sent for and he was released, but not before the pressmen had photographed him as a suspect for Scarlet Woman's Beau No. 2.

After what seemed to be a heavily censored tour with the *Lord*, work at Tatham's library had gone well, although Perkin Philby, the fluting, owlish man in charge there, had not been terribly welcoming. He put an old typewriter at Evan's disposal on the bizarre condition that he only use it when it was obvious that no one was 'really trying to read'. Evan suspected that he disliked Americans, so disliked him back.

Compared to the Cathedral's collection, Tatham's library had no views, being housed in a converted stable block and laundry with only a few high windows, and those obscured by rasping shrubs. The most precious manuscripts, which Evan was consulting in the afternoon, were housed in high-security, atmospherically controlled stacks with no windows whatever. Glad of an escape route from thoughts of Madeleine, he had ploughed on with far more perseverance than he had mustered on his first day in Petra

Dixon's company, and kept rigidly to relevant material. Every half hour, however, nature had called him out to smoke a Winston as usual. Under bald sunshine the nearby quadrangle had proved far wider than it had felt by moonlight. A few youths and, here and there, a girl had hauled battle-worn sofas and armchairs on to the cobbles and basked as they read. Back in the library he could hear the occasional complaining of castors as this furniture was tugged around to follow the sun. A blind boy was listening to a tiny one's recitation of some unfamiliar language, giving languid prompts when his flow dried up. There seemed to be an unusual lack of schooltime rush. No handbells rang and no one seemed to be in a hurry for classes. He assumed that this was some scholastic oasis and that the main business of teaching went on elsewhere. He was startled to see Madeleine glaring at him from the front page of the *Sun* as one small boy sat unfurling it as a break from Homer. He bought one of the last copies in a newsagents on his way to the Tracer's Arms for lunch and saw it much bandied about by his drinking companions. As he waited to place his orders the barman even stuck up the offending front page on the mirror between the bottles.

'I love you when you're angry,' he jeered at it, blowing a kiss, and everyone had laughed.

After eating his burnt fish fingers and while waiting for the Angel's Delight to set a little more, Evan had returned to his desk. He had covered four pages of his diary yet if he were to write to even a distant colleague in his present state, he could still be sure of revealing too much. Despite his denial he had spied on her that morning. He had hidden in the kitchenette so as to be sure of having breakfast with her and not her mother. He had seen her rush down-stairs to snatch the newspaper. Her dressing gown had flown out as she turned to run up again. Her thighs were voluptuous rather than athletic, he knew this now. He also knew their shade of pink and the unexpected delight of her tiny feet. It had taken two years for him to persuade Miriam to let him kiss her feet with any seriousness. She had claimed that she was ticklish but when she finally deigned to let him suck at them on a deserted beach one day he had found that she had hard heels and nasty horny bits on the undersides of her toes where her preposterous shoes had squashed and rubbed them. Evan could tell that Madeleine's feet would be soft; not only could one see at a glance that she gave them nothing to do, but she was plainly more an earth child than a stiletto wearer. Forced into high heels, she would be sure to teeter and say 'bugger' a lot. Yes indeed, she was fine when she was angry. He might even say that anger was her element, had he not been struck this morning by her silence. After Mrs Merluza had left, he had crept up to sit on the stairs and listen while Madeleine had her bath. She was a big girl who bumped into things and cast a shadow, but her bathing had been terrifyingly silent. She had not hummed or sighed, talked to herself or made any of the relaxed, splashy noises of most people's bath-times. At least she was a heavy smoker; that made her human. Evan met the stare of his reflection in the dark garden windows and wondered whether she had made a lot of noise in bed with the Cardinal. He smiled at his imaginings then, disgusted with himself, reached for Sukie Lark Rosen and sobriety.

24

It was Wednesday morning and the alarm clock was turning circles on the floor like some poisoned fly. Groaning, Gavin Tree shoved aside the bedding which had twisted itself around him, pulled on his dressing gown and slippers and shuffled to the barn-like episcopal bathroom. He had always groaned on waking. The sound bore no relation to his state of mind but was as purely physiological as a baby's first cry. As he shaved, brushed his thick white hair, gargled with Listerine, replaced his plate and shuffled to his dressing room, the groans gradually modulated to hums and progressed, via snatches of half-remembered melody, to a full-blown pom-pomming rendition of something (usually by Handel or Stanford) as he walked down to his mother's apartment to wake her.

Mrs Chattock had been awake on most mornings, long before his knock on her sitting-room door (the waft of scented bathroom steam betrayed her) but on retiring, one always asked the other when she wished to rise and made a promise to wake her. This was part of the family closeness they had confected since her retirement into her son's pious household from the knocks of an uncaring world.

Gavin liked the effect that his mother and her interior designer friend had created in what used to be a guest flat. The Palace was a minor architectural delight, but less than a joy to inhabit. Successive generations of bishops had worn away any quirks that might serve to make such a building human and left only tide marks of pomp, and memorial encrustations. There were three principle rooms which spanned one side of the building on the ground floor. Neither Gavin, nor his mother, nor his secretary were musically able so the piano which should have been the feature of the music room was draped in a silk shawl and shunted into one corner as a support for photographs and a vase of ever-changing flowers. The dining room was far too large to make dining *à deux* anything but sinister, so all but rare official meals were taken in the backstairs fug of the kitchen. The third main room was the library. The original episcopal collection had long been at the convent for rebinding and the making of copies when the Dissolution arrived. The nuns had locked the books in the cellars for protection but these treasures were then purloined, in a masterly sleight of hand that no one had since dared undo, by Thomas Tatham when he turned the convent into his famous school. The present Palace library contained therefore little beyond an *Encyclopaedia Britannica*, a vast dictionary of Catholic thought ('for mugging up on the Enemy,' Mrs Chattock said), bound copies of all editions of *The Church Times*, *The Barrowcester Chronicle* and minutes of meetings of the General Synod and Lambeth Council. These were fleshed out by a generous and supremely unapproachable collection of ecclesiastical memoirs and biographies (few in one volume) donated by Bishop Herbert Thrush in 1939. The furniture here was slightly more comfortable than that of the music room, there was oak panelling and the blacks and navy blues of the spines were most soothing, so the room made a good setting for the obligatory Christmas punch and pies party. The sprinkling of rugs and the anti-draught sausages by the doors also suited the bodily needs of Mrs Chattock's meditation group. The plasterwork on the ceilings of these great ground-floor spaces was exquisite, especially in early morning when, with the connecting doors thrown open, a whole side of the house was bathed in cool light. However these salons were impossible to heat well and, to fit them for the reception of large numbers, they had acquired a hardwearing industrial carpet and an array of strong, charmless furniture.

While his mother styled herself a homely snug in her flat, whence she descended only for meals, her groups and to walk in the garden, Gavin retreated from the assessing stare of the portraits downstairs into frequent spells in his study. This small, low-ceilinged room was placed off a halfway landing over the front door and so enjoyed a fine view along the plane tree avenue of the drive, and across to Tatham's chapel tower. Gavin had there the desk he had bought off his Oxford landlady and the ragged Turkey carpet which had lain beneath it in every lodging since. Apart from a forbidding copy of *Thring's Uppingham Sermons* that had mysteriously strayed thither from the library and which he had never had the courage to return, he was surrounded by his own books. Bound editions of *The New Statesman* and *New Society* shared a bookcase with his pride and joy; complete first edition sets of Simenon and Dorothy Sayers. On a shelf out of reach in a less important corner, lay the twelve free copies of *Less by More* sent him by his publishers and which he had always lacked the nonchalant poise to give away to friends.

Gavin looked into his study now after 'waking' his mother. He drew the curtains. The Dean had been here for an urgent council last night concerning the ever-swelling publicity for the miracle and how he and the Chapter could best turn this into profits for the cathedral appeal. The Dean chain-smoked on a pipe and the air was rancid with its stale fumes. Gavin threw open both windows and, pom-pomming Britten's *Jubilate* – a new departure, this, inspired by yet another morning of brilliant sunshine – he continued his descent to the kitchen.

Normally a peaceful haven at that time of day, the kitchen had already been invaded by Mrs Jackson. Dispense though he might with the handful of gardeners, maids and cleaners engaged by his higher-living predecessors, it seemed that Gavin had to accept Mrs Jackson the housekeeper and Mr Jakewith the gardener as built-in. Even Bishops with wives were not trusted by the powers that were, it seemed, to keep house, garden and table in good order. Having no female companionship but that of a twice-widowed mother, Gavin was in no position to do anything but waive his principles, it seemed. Mrs Jackson and Mr Jakewith were siblings, cast in the same dourly industrious mould. Like her drear cuisine, Mrs Jackson, who now had one arm up to the elbow in a chicken, was especially lacking in the leaven of joy. Of all his flock, she was possibly the one to whom addressing one's bishop as plain Mr Tree came easiest.

'Good morning, Mrs Jackson. What a pleasant surprise.'

'Morning, Mr Tree. Your breakfast's in the dining room.'

'Really?'

'No room for you both to have it in here. I've got to get ready for that black priest as is coming to lunch.'

'Goodness! Is that today? I believe you're right. Well, thank you, Mrs Jackson.' He turned to go.

'Our Judith's helping out with a spot of cleaning, so don't mind her.'

'How nice,' Gavin said. 'No. I won't.'

He had indeed forgotten that Nigel Okereke, Bishop of Bantawa, an African diocese adopted by Gavin on Barrowcester's behalf, was coming to lunch. Leaving Mrs Jackson to brutalize the chicken, he walked back to the hall and crossed to the dining room. The pom-pomming had regressed to the less confident, fragmentary stage. Judith Jackson, an anaemic teenager as shy as her mother was sullen, scampered, duster in hand, through the doors to the library as he entered. A rack of toast and a coffee pot enfurled in an insulating towel waited at one end of the table, along with two meagre glasses of orange juice and the mail. Already sustained by tea and biscuits, Mrs Chattock would not come down for another fifteen minutes, thus to uphold the charade that her son had woken her. Gavin took a seat and, sipping some juice, picked crestfallen through his letters. He took out the envelopes addressed by hand and opened the unfamiliar one first.

'St Dunstan's Holt
Amberwoods
Clough
Nr. Barrowcester,' he read,

Dear Bishop

I have no hesitation in supplying my name and address since I am quite unabashed of the strength of my feelings.

Your accession to the diocese of Barrowcester, indeed your original entry to the church of Christ, our General and Blessed Sacrifice, and of Elizabeth, our Queen was a blight on our land. You are a curse to the spiritual welfare of many helpless parishioners.

My wife and I have no doubt that you are an emissary of our lionlike enemy the Devil. We are not deceived by the holy robes you wear, knowing you to have obtained them through your evil powers and the deceits of which your chief is father. Your presence in our midst is a lie and a desecration and we abhor the manner in which you seek to infect clean minds with your abominable false doctrines. The Devil has many names with which to lead us astray and communism is one of them.

When you appear on *Faith Forum* later this week we shall foregather with ten other True Christians – thus echoing the number of the blessed disciples of Our Lord Jesus Christ (may his name burn your devilish eyes!!) and we shall conduct a rite of exorcism to rid the diocese of your presence. We pray daily for divine intervention in this matter and know we are not the only ones.

May the pains of Hell be multiplied on your swift return to from whence you came.

I remain in Christ,

Kenneth Kirk (Church Warden)

p.s. We know the so-called miracle was a hellish invention to assist the re-entry of moneychangers into the Temple. The sweet-seeming canary is a well-known posture of Him Whose Name Is Legion.

Gavin pushed the letter over to his mother's plate. Messages of its kind came daily and it amused her to read them. She would perch her reading glasses on her nose, the better to glance up and watch his reactions and, cigarette in hand, she would recite them. Her mimicry of suitable voices was extremely funny. Gavin tried not to be intimidated by his hate mail – it was compensated for by a few letters of support – but it was only human to suspect that his mother's mockery was a temptation to fate. On second thoughts, he took the letter back and thrust it into his jacket pocket.

He heard a familiar smoker's cough and footsteps coming from the hall and poured a cup of coffee for his mother as she came in.

'Morning,' he called out over the tail-end of her bout of coughing. She waved a handkerchief in reply, calmed her raging lungs then came to take her seat before him.

'Very grand this morning, aren't we?'

'Mrs Jackson needs the kitchen to herself so she can do something to a chicken for Nigel Okereke's lunch.'

'Does she, indeed?' She sipped at her coffee and made a face as it scalded her tongue. 'Any letters?'

'Nothing much.' He waited for her to refuse toast then took a piece himself and buttered it. She looked appalling this morning; decades older than her sixty-whatever. She had tried to mask her hangdog pallor with rash dabs of blusher. It looked as though her ancient surface had begun to rust. 'Bad night?' he ventured.

'Christ,' she swore softly and spooned another sugar into her cup.

'Tell me,' he told her. She reached for a piece of toast

after all, but only so as to have something to tear up on her plate.

'I . . .'

'What?'

She looked across at him suddenly. He had never seen such fear in her eyes.

'I know you'll think me a stupid old bat,' she went on cautiously, her own accent surfacing, 'but . . . Petal, do you believe in werewolves?'

'Werewolves? Just misinterpretation of rabies symptoms, weren't they? Hydrophobia; fear of water, walking on all fours, bellowing like a dog.'

'Not werewolves, then, but a kind of possession?'

'That's more serious.' She was beginning to shake. 'Don't have another stroke,' he prayed. 'Don't let her break down on me. Not now.'

'Possession by some kind of beast. Worse than possession; more a sort of opening out – as if there was this ravening beast inside you and it only needed the right words to make it come to the surface and make you sort of lose control.' Her hands shook with sudden violence. One knocked her coffee cup over in its saucer, sending a shock of black across the white linen. Her other hand swept and scrabbled on her plate, scattering torn chunks of toast. Gavin jumped up, helpless, uncertain whether to run to her or run for help. With a visible effort she tugged her hands to her breast, against each other. They quivered still, but their violence was contained. She looked up at him and he knew she saw his fear. 'Gavin.' She had not called him by his name in years; he was always 'Petal' to her, or 'Poppet' or the pleasantly Elizabethan 'Chuck'. 'Gavin, I had a dream,' she said. The hands broke loose again and fluttered under her astonished gaze. For a moment it looked as though she might applaud.

Gavin raced round the ridiculous expanse of the table, feet sliding on the polished wooden floor. He seized her hands and crouched before her. She smiled down at him and her hands, calm now having passed their wildness into him, rose and pressed gently against his cheeks. He smelt gin on her early-morning breath. The door behind her opened and Mrs Jackson's absurd daughter stepped in and paused with a barely audible 'Oh'.

'Poor Gavin,' his mother whispered. 'You're so bloody *pure!*'

25

Brooklea Rest Home nestled in the laburnum heart of Friary Hill, the suburban sprawl beyond the Roman Bridge. This district, which also held the crematorium and Garden of Remembrance, was named after the red-brick mansion built there in 1880 by the Prossers, a family of sanitary porcelain barons who had since moved south. The Prosser estate had been sold to developers after the last war. Its fanciful baronial pile had been converted into flats and now loured from the midst of a tangle of cul-de-sacs strewn with postwar villas, boat trailers and sunset gates. Brooklea was a four down, five up which had put forth bungaloid extensions to its rear and on each side. From the rockery on the front lawn a small motorized stream trickled into a lily pond. There were flowering cherries at war with a laburnum and a forsythia bush. Prison walls of leylandii to the sides and rear protected neighbours and inmates alike from embarrassment. The three steps up to the front door had been half-covered by a wheelchair ramp.

Obeying the polite request mounted above the doorbell, Fergus rang then entered. There were two sets of doors. The first let him into a glass-topped porch housing a rubber plant in rude health and an umbrella stand full of sticks, the second, with a blast of overheated air and disinfectant, let him into the hall. The Matron was waiting for him, a capable, sympathetic-looking woman, her well-coiffed brown hair surmounted by the white crown of her authority.

'Mr Gibson?'

'Yes.'

'Hello. I'm Claire Telcott, the Matron.'

'How do you do?'

Her hand was cold and no doubt often scrubbed. She led him into her study-cum-sitting room which abutted the porch and so had a view like any other house in the road, free of wobbling white heads.

'Now,' she said once they were seated on either side of her desk. 'It's your mother you wish to bring to stay with us?'

'Yes. She's only seventy-two and was perfectly fit and spry. She worked as a missionary in Africa, teaching in a bush school until last autumn. Then she had her first heart attack and had to come back to England. I thought it best to bring her down to live with me rather than let her go back to living alone in her flat in Scotland.' Claire Telcott hummed and made a face to show that she thought this a wise and admirable action. 'Then she had another attack soon after Christmas and her mind seemed to go.'

'It happens.' She sighed. 'Can she walk?'

'Yes, but she's refused to leave her bed for any length of time since I brought her to live with me and frankly, with her . . . well, it's very difficult for me to cope because I have to work and . . .'

'I gather from Dr Morton she's incontinent?'

'Yes. And she's very confused.'

'The poor dear. Does she have many other relatives?'

'Not now. My father died fifteen years ago. There are some cousins in Canada and nieces in Scotland but we've all lost touch.'

'Fine. Did Nurse Drake mention fees?'

'Yes, and I applied to my solicitor for power of attorney this morning.'

'Super. Well what I suggest is that I give you a quick tour and show you the room we'd give Mrs Gibson and then, if you're happy, you can move her in as soon as you like.'

'Perfect.'

Fergus rose, his heart heavy, and tailed her from the room. The lounge, where a circle of old ladies and two old men sat watching *The Ten Commandments* on television, was even hotter than the hall.

'The poor dears suffer terribly from the cold because they get so little exercise,' Claire Telcott explained, 'but we do our best to keep it nice and snug for them. As you see, we've invested in a video for them and Mr Horder from the video shop comes once a week to offer them a new choice – so much nicer than all that sport and violence.'

'Quite.'

'If you'd like to follow me . . .'

Fergus was shown a dining room with a large communal table and several objects like giant high chairs.

'For the naughty ones, bless them,' said his guide. 'Quite like schoolkids they can be. We had trifle on the floor only yesterday.'

He was shown a typical bedroom in one of the bungaloid extensions. It was small and characterless, although it was emphasized that residents were encouraged to bring a few small items of emotional significance 'to make it feel more like a bit of home'. Just a few. His mother was lucky enough to be filling a space in the main body of the house and so to have a slightly larger room with its own bathroom and a bay window.

'Slightly more expensive, but it'll be nice for her to feel a little distinguished, won't it?'

They continued past a sky-blue shoebox of a chapel – 'that nice Canon Wedlake comes in at nine on Sundays and of course he helps out with the sadder moments' – and on to the pride of the institution. This was an old people's gym. All the machines were specially adjusted for the weaker frame and were designed to ease joints and to prevent the ills of too sedentary a life. One of the home's few men was puffing away at a rowing machine as they came in. Matron encouraged him till he was alarmingly red in the face.

'Such a dear,' she said as they headed back to the hall. 'He used to play soccer for Barrowcester Wanderers before the club was amalgamated after the war. Very proud of his fitness, bless him.'

Fergus knew that his mother would take an instant dislike to Claire Telcott. She had always hated women in uniform, nuns included. Luckily the other nurses wore no signs of office other than the watches on their breast pockets.

'We don't want it too like a hospital, after all. And in their own clothes they're just like dutiful daughters, really.'

Back in the study, Fergus filled out a form with his mother's particulars and special needs and/or dislikes. Then he paid the first month's bill in advance, arranged to bring her round on Thursday and left. He had been purposefully unspecific on the subject of her lavatorial obsession, saying only that she was prone to incontinence and confusion.

Since yesterday's disaster, when Harpy had been such a

help, his mother had been calm, reticent almost. The problem of packing her clothes and fetching her with them into the car with the minimum of explanation was one which he had barely faced. Perhaps Harpy could help him. If he could bring his mother down to the sitting room and get her all excited about going on an expensive cure, Harpy could do the packing upstairs. He could not see Mrs Gibson leaving her bed simply at the behest of a nurse, so she was unlikely to need many clothes other than nightdresses and her dressing gown. Seeking to dull his mind to the shame of the treason he was about to perform, he whistled as he strode over the Roman Bridge and back on to the spine of the hill.

He had invited Emma Dyce-Hamilton to tea to show her his plans for renovating her terrible house and dropped in at Hart's on his way up the High Street to buy something to give her. It was very boring of Lydia to invite them to supper on the same night. Quite apart from Lydia's cookery, one of the great pleasures of dining with the Harts was the standard of their gossip. Emma Dyce-Hamilton was sweet enough, but something about the cardigans she wore and the fact that she taught scripture to little boys made Fergus suspect that she would not be a party to malicious chat.

Lydia was not in Hart's – she rarely was. He bought a bag of florentines and asked one of the pretty girls behind the counter how their boss was, and so heard all about Saturday's quiet wedding. Cynically amused at the thought of the notoriously fey Tobit Hart leading such a beauty up the aisle, he must have left the shop with a smile on his lips for a tramp stumbled up to him and said,

'You're a happy man; spare us fifty pee?'

There were always tramps in Barrowcester in the

warmer months. They arrived with the swallows and camped out on a small piece of common at the end of Bross Gardens. They sat drinking around bonfires by night and came up to haunt shoppers and tourists by day. This one stank and the skin of his face was scaly and brown. Fergus always felt that gypsies would curse him if he failed to buy their lucky heather and he harboured a similar superstition about tramps, as if destitution were catching.

'Of course,' he said, feeling in his jacket pockets. He had used most of his change buying the cakes however. What remained was so small that it would certainly enrage the tramp. 'Look, I'm really sorry,' he said. 'I've got nothing but my handkerchief, but why don't you take these?'

He held out the florentines. Emma Dyce-Hamilton would have to make do with whatever remained in the biscuit tin at home.

'Wonderful!' exclaimed the tramp with what might have been a hint of sarcasm. 'You're a real gentleman, Guv'nor!' and he took the cakes and bit into one with a show of relish.

'Hope they won't rot your teeth,' laughed Fergus and continued, relieved, on his way.

However the tramp was not going to let a benefactor go without accepting something in return so he hurried forward into Fergus's path and launched into a wild jig of thanks, waving the bag of cakes in the air and shouting,

'Thank you thank you thank you!'

Because an amused circle of shoppers had formed, Fergus was forced to stay where he was and watch the dance to its hectic close.

'Thank you,' he muttered in return once the tramp had done and he dived into the crowd.

26

A party of pigeons leaped out of Emma's path like so many tossed-up books. She thrust forward the little gear lever and felt the pedals turn with more resistance as the bicycle doubled its speed. As she flew, straight-backed, towards Drinkwater and Gibson Design Consultants, the currents around her played with her newly washed hair and she had to keep patting a hand to her knee to control the flapping of her dress. She had put on an old dress of her mother's. Fifties clothes were meant to be back in fashion now. When Fergus had telephoned to say that his plans were ready and should he drop in on her or, only if it were convenient of course, would she like to drop in on him, her throat had dried with pleasure.

'Oh, it's such a heavenly day, and I'd enjoy the ride,' she had heard herself enthuse. 'Let me come to you.'

So he had invited her to tea. A working tea, he had called it and she had been effortless and laughed. She had started to dry her hair when she had caught sight of her mother's old dress glowing from the wardrobe. It was the only garment of her mother's which she had kept, partly because it was exactly her size and had come from a real Parisian designer, partly because it was the dress her mother wore in the photograph of her holding Emma as a baby. It was in a thick cotton, brilliant white with fat red flowers, somewhere between peonies and poppies. There were no sleeves, the waist was thin as her own and the skirt was flatteringly full. It smelled pleasantly of the pomander which dangled from its coathanger. She could tell from the glances she was getting as she rode through the Close that people thought she had made a mistake, that the dress 'wasn't her', but it was.

'This is me,' she thought as she tossed a radiant smile to Clive Hart. 'This is me and teaching scripture to little boys is not me and neither are pruning roses or camel-coloured cardigans or sensible heels.'

She locked her bicycle to a lamp post. His house was a model of early nineteenth-century delicacy, compensating for its bulk with large, thin-framed windows and a pretty Classical portico. It was a large house for a single man. There was a garden hidden behind a high wall to one side and jasmine had been trained up the bricks from tubs on either side of the entrance. The tubs had been painted dove grey to match the front door, however, which Emma thought a bit much. Like many Barrowcester houses it still had a functioning bell pull. She gave this a gentle tug and heard distant jangling. Mrs Merluza's shop was closed, she noticed, so the poor woman must still be trapped in her house. She wondered whether, although this was a working tea, she should none the less have brought a cake with her.

'Hello, Miss Hamilton.'

'Hello. Please call me Emma. It's less of a mouthful.'

'All right, but only if you call me Fergus.'

'Certainly, Fergus.' She laughed as he stood aside to let her in. She was flirting. She was astonished.

He led her swiftly through a hall where she caught a glimpse of a grandfather clock and prints, to a broad sitting room whose windows gave on to a well-ordered garden centred round a walnut tree.

'How lovely,' she exclaimed. 'Do you get anything off it?'

'Lots, but it's never hot enough to dry them without them turning mouldy. I made the mistake of pickling some the first summer here, though, and there are still jars of the things.'

'Like my green tomato chutney.'

'Really?'

'Yes. I felt I ought to make it because there was so little sun last year and I was left with bowls of green tomatoes, so I made it then realized that I *hate* chutney!'

'I'll swop you some for my walnuts.'

They laughed together. She assumed his offer was not serious, and disliked pickled walnuts, so she made no reply. This seemed to bring things on to a suddenly professional level.

'Now,' he said. 'I've set the samples out for you here where you can see them in the light. I think you're living with far too many colours at the moment, so we should start by calming down the hall and stairs with one of these. You see? The ivory or the slightly creamier one.'

For nearly forty minutes she sat at a table in one of the windows with him standing at her side like a teacher, picking over an assortment of fabric pieces, colour cards and strips of wallpaper that looked almost hand-painted. His eyes lit up as he shared his ideas and his enthusiasm was infectious. He wanted to make her house more feminine, though stopping short at the right side of fussy. At first she was almost scandalized at the boldness of his suggestions – a cerise study, a French pattern of china-blue swallows to replace the fudge-brown curtains in the bathroom,

Provençal tiles in place of the mosaic-pattern lino in the kitchen – then she saw that his proposals were no more outrageous than her mother's old dress. Emma became more and more animated as she envisaged the new setting Fergus had planned for her – for of course he had planned it with precisely her character in mind – and even dared to make a few suggestions of her own. Why not this pattern repeated in the upstairs lavatory, only in a yellow to tone in with the little carved bookcase he had suggested she move to the landing outside? And yes, he thought this a splendid idea.

'At this rate you won't really need me at all,' he said.

'Oh but nonsense,' she gushed. 'I wouldn't know where to begin.' She felt herself redden and dropped her eyes back to a sample of curtain material she was twisting in her hands.

He seemed to have forgotten all about tea when there was a furious beating on the floor over their heads and a hoarse woman's voice called out wildly. Emma heard,

'Leave her to get on with it herself,' but the rest was an angry mumble.

'I'm so sorry,' he said as Emma rose in alarm.

'Your mother . . . ?'

'You've heard. Yes.'

'It's my fault. I've kept you chatting far too long.'

'No. It's only that she . . .'

'Yes I have and I must rush anyway.'

'But I promised to make tea. I am hopeless.'

He wanted her to stay!

'Nonsense.' She took the lead and walked to the hall.

'Stay here,' he told her. 'I won't be a second.'

He ran up the stairs. His hair was thinning but he seemed fit enough. Upstairs Mrs Gibson called again, barking his name as if he were still a child. Emma stood for a moment in the hall then quietly let herself out and unpadlocked her bicycle. She remembered how sometimes she would think to dart up to her father's sickbed for only five minutes then be kept there an hour. Poor Fergus. Perhaps, once work had started on the house and the workmen were able to find coffee and tea for themselves, she could offer to sit with Mrs Gibson in the afternoons. She could take her marking and sit, placid but industrious, in a chair near the bedside. When he came home from visiting clients and checking up on builders she could slip down to greet him and together they would have tea at the table in the sitting-room window. Maybe, when the weather was warmer, they could sit on the bench under the walnut tree.

Then she had to brake suddenly to avoid a car's opening door and she remembered that walnut trees dripped poison or skin irritant or something unpleasant. She rebuked herself for foolish daydreaming and decided to buy the cake she might have taken to Fergus's and call on the poor, besieged Merluzas. If she were nice to Madeleine, something pleasant might happen to her in return. She headed back into town to buy one of Lydia's sinful chestnut and chocolate cakes, reminded herself on the way that she also had to leave a postcard for Evan Kirby inviting him to tea with her before he left and that there was a parents' evening at the choir school that night. Duties in Barrowcester came stuck together like the strands in a monstrous spider's web. For once she found she could scoop them up without repugnance.

27

Evan shut the door of the granny flat, leaning against it a moment to celebrate the first solitude since breakfast with a round of no-hands yawning. Then he slung his briefcase beside the bread bin and yawned again, rubbing his aching scalp. Stooping over the sink, he drank straight from the tap to dilute the taste of Mrs Merluza's sherry. The moment he got in she had lured him upstairs on the pretext that her 'old hands' were having trouble breaking the seal on a new screw-top bottle, only to introduce him to the bishop's mother and force him to stay for a glass. Mrs Chattock was a racy old thing who shook rather and sported an accent even stranger than Mrs Merluza's. It had been amusing enough to chat, but now that the two of them had left for their lecture (with slides) his exhaustion had crept up on him, pounced and hung heavy on his shoulders.

He had worked in the Cathedral library all day, spurred on by the near completion of the book and, although Petra Dixon had closed up shop for an hour as usual to go and walk her terrier, he had been deprived of a lunch break by the necessity of crossing over to Tatham's to talk about illustrations with the officious Perkin Philby. By the time Philby had released him, the Tracer's Arms had shut and the town's food shops had fallen under the dismal pall of something called, with unelucidating frankness, early closing.

As his bath ran, he put some beer in the fridge then drew all the curtains and undressed. Since leaving Miriam, he had begun to dislike his body and had taken to dressing and undressing chastely, like a convent child, with the aid of a silk dressing gown. There was no one to laugh any more, but it felt more comfortable that way. The bath water was too hot but he was too tired to stand around waiting for enough cold water to run in. He felt his face grow scarlet and, ignoring fifteen years of Miriam's habit-weary warning, fell asleep. When he woke, the water was stone cold and the soap had added considerably to his natural wrinkles. He had not drowned because the bath was too short. Though not especially uncomfortable, he knew from the slight blueness in his legs that it might be wiser to get out so, swearing quietly, he tugged out the plug and staggered, dripping to the bedroom where he had left his towel that morning. (Mrs Merluza did not like to tidy too often during a lodger's stay; she felt it to be an intrusion on their privacy.) He glanced at his alarm clock, saw that he had been asleep for an hour and decided not to dress again for dinner. He turned his pyjamas the right way round and put them on, followed by the dressing gown and a pair of clean socks. He had no slippers and there was something of a draught on the kitchenette floor.

He tore open a fresh packet of sliced bread (dyed brown as a sop to Miriam and conscience) and arranged a fistful of slices across the grill pan. While these were grilling, he poured himself a wonderfully cold beer and decided on ravioli. Determined not to go to bed without at least finishing the first chapter of *Towards a New Mythology*, he decided that he might as well read while he ate. He turned the toast, opened the ravioli tin and fetched the neglected book. He had just speared the first pasta envelope when there was a knock on the granny-flat door and Madeleine called,

'Evan? Can I come in?'

'Of course.' He jumped up, licking spicy tomato sauce off his thumb and she came in. She too was in a dressing gown. Her hair seemed to have been brushed the wrong way. According to her mother, she had not left her room all day.

'Hello,' she said. 'Oh. You're eating. I'll go.'

'No. Not at all. Join me, why don't you?'

'You're just saying that.' She was hovering by the door.

'No I'm not. It's too big a tin for one.' That was a lie. 'Here. You sit down and I'll heat it up.'

'Please don't. I prefer it cold. Unless you'd rather . . .' She pulled up the second chair to the tiny table.

'Oh good. So do I.'

'It's got more flavour that way. Your toast's burning.'

He rescued the toast, tipped half the ravioli into a bowl for her and found her a fork.

'Beer?' he said.

'What kind?'

'Heineken.'

'No thanks. Actually, yes I will.' He raked the other can out of the fridge. 'Thank you,' she said as he set it before her. 'Don't bother with a glass.'

He sat opposite her and ate a couple of ravioli.

'You're being very slow reading that book,' she said.

'It's abysmally dull,' he explained. 'How was your day?'

'Confined. I felt sick at first so I spent the morning in bed, then I was stupid and rang Edmund. He told me to bugger off out of his life. Well, more or less. So that put me in such a foul mood that I spent most of the afternoon in bed too. I came down and sat in the kitchen a bit for a change of scene, but Mum got on my nerves wanting to call a doctor, and then a goody-goody girl I was at school with turned up with a chestnut and chocolate gâteau so I escaped back to my room. I've read a very unsuitable novel to pass the time up there.'

'Oh? Which?'

'*Weather in the Streets.*'

'Can't say I know it.'

'Wonderful doomed mid-wars love affair between married man and neglected, would-be authoress. She has an abortion and he falls in love with his wife.'

'Ah. Bad idea.'

They laughed.

'Do you mind my barging in like this?' she asked suddenly. 'I'm sure you do. I know you do, in fact, because you're dying to get on with that bloody book. It's just that, apart from the phone call to Edmund, I've barely said an intelligent word all day and I was starting to argue with the bedside light.' A hot point of red in each of her cheeks lent her a fevered look. Perhaps she had been at her mother's paint-stripper brandy.

'Not at all,' said Evan, scraping absently at the inside of the tin then pushing it aside. 'What do you want to talk about?'

'Well. What would . . . Can I have a cigarette?'

'Sure. Help yourself.'

'Thanks.' She lit up and inhaled briefly before answering. 'What would you do if you were my father?'

'How d'you mean?' he stalled.

'Would you throw me out, make him marry me or fork out for a discreet clinic to tidy things away?'

'Of course not. I mean, neither. I guess I'd let you make your own mind up. If I was your father I assume that all I'd want would be your happiness. But of course, I can't really talk because I've never been one.'

'What?'

'A father.'

'Choice or destiny?'

'Miriam and I couldn't make one.' Light-headed from cold bath and colder beer he added, 'To tell the truth, I think Miriam wanted one as much as I did, at least to start with, but I think there were, er, problems. And they weren't in her department.'

'Oh. I see. But that's only a hunch?'

'Yes.'

'Mmm.' She swigged at her beer as Evan proffered the empty ravioli tin as an ashtray.

'When do you think you'll go back to London?' he asked her.

'Dunno. Not just yet. How about you?'

'The work's almost finished.' He sighed. 'So a couple of days should see me out.'

'The libraries are impressive, aren't they?'

'Out of this world.'

'I think it spoils it, growing up with all that around you. I haven't been around the Cathedral once since I was seventeen and I did a project on illumination. I'd probably be far more astonished now.' Evan offered her a half banana.

'No thanks,' she said, 'Oh all right. Actually, couldn't we have one each?'

'Of course.'

'Got any white sugar to dunk it in? They taste better with sugar.' They dunked their bananas in the sugar basin. She offered to fetch the charity gâteau but he persuaded her to halve a second banana instead.

'Barrowcester continues to disprove my early doubts concerning its lack of an alternative culture,' he said with a chuckle.

'How so?'

'I met a magnificent black Bishop being shown round the Cathedral library this morning.'

'Really?'

'Yes, but his grandeur was a touch diminished after he'd left and the redoutable Petra Dixon explained that he was not resident but was Bishop Okereke of Bantawa.'

'The pet African diocese,' she said. 'It's so touching. Mum and her friends raise all this money to send there without knowing that he's a perfectly wonderful communist.'

Soon after this their conversation died. Evan was trying so hard to find the right moment to ask if they might meet for a drink when they were both back in London that he became tongue-tied. Madeleine began to play with a cigarette stub and a puddle of beer on the tabletop.

'I must go back to bed,' she said eventually. 'I'm slipping into what your Petra Dixon would call a brown study.'

'Oh must you?' said Evan, thinking suddenly of her mother.

'Yes I must. Thanks for the ravioli. It's much better

cold.' She pecked him on the forehead and gave him one of her defeated smiles. 'G'night,' she said and left.

As he had been leaving the Chapter House this evening, Evan had met Bishop Okereke again, who was leaving Evensong. The Bishop broke graciously away from a circle of well-wishers to shake Evan's hand.

'I really must apologize, Professor Kirby,' he had said in his James Mason English, 'for not having said hello properly before. You see, I'd read your excellent books but I failed to recognize you from your flyleaf photograph.'

Had he gone so severely to seed?

28

Lydia was shutting down the Cathedral for the night. She was in there to do her 'holy dusting' and should have had Sam the verger at her elbow waiting to do the locking up himself, but his son was leaving for Northern Ireland soon and it was the last night of his leave. Sam had left her with the keys, therefore, quite unofficially, and sloped off early. This was a frequent enough occurrence. Lydia's place on the dusting rota meant a great deal to her but inevitably she was so busy that she ended up making her contribution minutes before closing time. Sam had long since been bribed to show her the ropes. She would drive over to his dreadful little house on Friary Hill afterwards to post the keys through his letter box. She was able to dust later than usual tonight because it was the occasion of one of Canon de Lisle's candlelit poetry readings in the Lady chapel. The latter was Lydia's particular dusting patch and she had hoped to rush off a quick dust there before anyone arrived, then slip away unnoticed home, but Bernard de Lisle himself had drifted in early, forcing her to stuff her duster out of sight and pretend that she had come expressly for the poetry he selected so beautifully. Sam was delighted to knock off early, so he slipped Lydia the keys, handed out candles then vanished into the gloom, leaving her to sit in the spectral cold for forty minutes listening to various over-emotional types reciting Donne, Blake and Milton.

Sam had already locked the doors to the vestry, treasury and choir room; all Lydia had to do was check for still-lit lights and lock the Glurry door on her way out. A labour-saving device had been installed close to the main fusebox last year. This was a plan of the Cathedral's circuitry with little bulbs that lit up to show at a glance if anything were still switched on and where. For some reason, the lights in the crypt seemed to be on. Irritated at this further delay, she turned on enough lights to find her way without tripping. She climbed the steps up to the quire then descended on the other side and made her way to the north transept. The most thunderous notes of the organ were made here. Great sixty-four-foot black wooden boxes reached up and coiled back on themselves into the darkness. They were linked to the main body of the instrument, the prettier part, by snakes of electric cable sunk beneath the flag-stones. When someone pulled out the *contra bombard* stop, this whole corner of the building throbbed to a sound like an infernal motorbike. The lowest note of all was scarcely recognizable as a note at all; it was more a vibra-tion one felt on the backs of the legs and across one's chest. Sam claimed it made the loose panes of glass rattle. The door to the crypt was set into the wall at the base of these giant pipes. A strip of light showed underneath it.

Lydia was not easily frightened. Clive implied that she lacked imagination to be able to cope with her nocturnal dusting, for he had only to walk past the Close wall and see the Cathedral floodlit to feel a shudder. All the vergers had at least one part of their work that frightened them. Trevor Sly and Mrs Moore shared a horror, bred by old films, of being alone here and hearing the organ play. Sam had an elaborate fantasy in which he would find himself locked in at night and realize that there was a tight, white face watching him from every window. Lydia's one fear was less imaginative, less explicable. She had never liked spaces of enclosed water. From girlhood on, reservoirs, swimming pools and water tanks, however small, had filled her with dread. It had become a secret joke between her and Clive that she panicked at any hint of a problem in a lavatory cistern and would have to leave the room rather than watch him open one up. Barrowcester's subterranean stream terrified her. This rivulet which, strangely in a city of titles, had found no name, bubbled up somewhere under the Close. The builders of the Cathedral had interrupted its flow through the caves and tunnels to the Bross and, for reasons that died with them, diverted it briefly in and out of the crypt. They had contained it in stone, like a sewer, for an inordinate length of its way. Some said it was diverted like this for sanitation while others, scoffing at the idea of pious men building a latrine under their high altar, said that the stream was the site of ancient veneration for a river goddess – one of those rites left half-explained by the departing Romans and half-absorbed into the new religion by their Christian successors. Lydia found neither theory comforting and continued to avoid the crypt as zealously as she steered clear of the public baths in Hanover Street and the reservoir on Friary Hill where Clive liked to walk for the view.

She took a deep breath and approached the crypt door, planning to open it just enough to dart a hand in to click off the light before locking in the underground river and beating a quick retreat. The light would not go off, however. She flicked the switch up and down twice to make sure, then was forced to open the door further to take a look. There was no sign of damage. Presumably something had come loose inside the mechanism. Although she knew she ought to unscrew the light bulb to save the Cathedral money, Lydia decided to leave things as they were, lock the door as usual and tell Sam when she dropped off the keys. She was turning to go when she saw feathers.

They were white ones. Two were sticking to the toe of her shoe with what she saw with disgust was blood. There were several more scattered on the steps where she had been standing. Frowning, her anger at the thought of having to clear something up before heading for home taking brief precedence over her fear of the stream that was swirling in the dark far corner, she walked down. On the last steps she stopped. A small white bird lay below her. Its head had been bitten off then spat out. Its white plumage lay in bloodied disarray. It was the size of a canary but white as a dove.

Lydia raced back to the north transept. There was a broom kept there in the flower arrangers' cupboard. She snatched this, hurried back to the crypt and, her breathing heavy with nerves, swept the feathers off the steps and consigned them, along with the tiny carcass, to the inky waters of the unnamed stream. The bird's remains sank and its feathers, floating, were carried swiftly into the maw of stone in the wall.

Lydia forced herself to stare at her watery enemy. She had not been this close since Sam showed her and Clive around in their first week in Barrowcester. Seen close to like this it was less frightening than when she saw it from the corner of her eye while hovering at the top of the steps. Astonished at her own daring, and dizzy at the thought that she had just saved a saint's miraculous reputation with a few quick strokes of an old broom, she crouched and forced herself to stare into the hole where the waters vanished.

Like a sewer, this tunnel had a narrow ledge at one side just above the lapping of the water. It was easy to imagine monks hiding in there. Perhaps – Lydia shuddered at the thought – one could follow the ledge into a sort of flood-circled underground chapel, deeper even than the crypt. She could only see three or four feet into the hole so she shifted slightly so as to let more light past her shoulders. There was a low growl, as from a cornered cat, and some-thing slid with a flash of brown skin and bright claw into the water.

Lydia had never covered the quarter mile between the Glurry door and her parked car so quickly. On Friary Hill Sam the verger saw her coming and opened his front door to her when she dropped off the keys but she said nothing of what she had seen. She would not even tell Clive, who for some reason was in a filthy temper but, curled beside him in their bed that night, she lay awake and thought of mutant rats and chewed canaries.

29

Dawn was slumped in her deck chair. Her black candle was burnt low. Its guttering light was reflected off the palm of her sheltering hand on to a face heavy with watching. Moths fluttered near this pink-glowing hand, trying to reach the flame. Five had died so far. Their singed corpses had landed on her thighs. She did not brush them off; her flesh was so chilled that she had not felt the tiny pressure of their landing. Occasionally her head would start to bow forwards and, her reflexes sluggish from the moonlit cold, she would summon the strength to jerk it upright once more. Soon she would have to put away deck chair and candle and return to her bed. She could not afford to risk falling asleep where she sat. Quite apart from the likelihood of catching her death, she did not relish the thought of waking to the interested gaze of her neighbours. Mrs Parry at number six was very helpful about passing on details of the various domestic services that Dawn offered – she was a district nurse and so an efficient percolator of local information – but was unlikely to be so diplomatic should she discover that her spinster neighbour was a witch. Unbeknownst to Mrs Parry, a neglected corner of the bottom of her garden, one that could easily be reached through a loose panel in her neighbour's fence, played nutritious host to Dawn's marijuana plants.

The candle had burnt so low that the wick had drifted and was flaming wide and high for the remaining seconds of its life. Dawn blew it out. Drops of hot wax splashed on to her knees as she stood. She swore and tossed the candle stump into the bush behind her. As she folded up the deck chair, uncertain on her numb legs, a twig snapped about four yards away. She froze, leaning on the folded chair. Another twig snapped and she heard the swish of parted branches.

'Sasha?' she whispered. The wooden fence to her left swayed suddenly and there was a sound of scrabbling followed by an unmistakably childish cough. Dawn's heart was racing. She wanted to call out but was terrified of frightening whatever was approaching. The moon had long since vanished but there were stars and these, together with the glow of street lamps up on the hill above Bross Gardens, lent a faint glitter to the black surface of the river. Against this Dawn could just make out a silhouette. The figure seemed naked as herself and would have reached up to her breasts in height.

'Sasha,' she mouthed, clutching the canvas of the chair in her effort to keep perfectly still.

An upstairs window flew open in number six and Mrs Parry called out,

'Hello? Hello? Is somebody down there?' Her tone was imperious. An electric torch was turned on and on the edge of its wandering beam, Dawn barely glimpsed a bone-thin leg streaked with mud and a flash of flaming hair. Then there was a splash as though a small dog had just dived into the river. Dawn dropped her deck chair with a clatter and rushed back to flatten herself against her kitchen door.

The beam of light played back and forth across the garden and Mrs Parry barked, 'I shall call the police, you know.' Dawn stared furiously towards where her lost daughter had vanished back into the night. 'Dawn?' queried Mrs Parry in a softer, more worried tone. 'Dawn?'

30

Evan was crouching at the side of the Patron's tomb. Its lid was raised on a winch by about seven inches and in the brilliant light which flooded the chapel he could make out with ease the body within. This was not Saint Boniface of Barrow however but a pitifully young girl, perhaps seven or eight years old. Dwarfed by her vast resting place, she was wrapped in a pink dressing gown with a blue swallow motif on its pocket, and her hair, whose flame tints were picked out by the light, was brushed in a fan around her sturdy, lifeless face. Deeply moved, he reached out to touch the small corpse's cheek. No sooner did he register that the skin was still warm than the chains of the winch rattled into action and the great lid slammed down over his forearm. He felt no pain, although the bone was certainly shattered, but only faint, pleasurable tingling where the child within was now nibbling at his fingertips.

Struck by the sound of women's voices, Evan craned his neck and peered over the top of the tomb. At the far end of the quire, his mother was advancing, clutching a guidebook and accompanied by her bridge partners, the Commander, the fourth-generation rag-trade widow and young Mr Trudeau. Miriam was coming too, and so was Huby Stokes, who clutched a vase of her dried flowers. Their shoes sounded on the flagstones like a large stable on the move and from the fevered pitch of their voices, he knew that he was their quarry. He scrabbled at the chains in vain; the one he needed to pull had swung out of immediate reach and to lunge any harder towards it would have made the fracture of his arm far worse than it must already be. As the voices grew nearer, he huddled against the side of the tomb, trying to hide some of his length. He shut his eyes tight to await the worst.

There was a kind of warmth on the back of his neck. He looked up and saw a seven-foot man, naked save for a linen suit, whose eyes burned Nordic blue and whose radiant mop of hair was purest Barrowcester blond. Smiling, the man stooped, slipped his great hands under the lid's rim and lifted it like so much sponge. Evan's arm was still whole and the child was wide awake. She jumped free and ran away, bare feet slapping. The man took Evan under the arms. There was a sound of rending linen, then a kind of rhythmic thunder and their feet left the ground. His rescuer had only to flap his broad brownish wings seven or eight times and they were rising with dizzying speed towards the cathedral ceiling. Only instead of the ceiling, they arrived at a kind of mirror image of the floor they had just left.

'Must fix the vertical hold,' Evan murmured.

He was alone again with the Patron's tomb. Its lid was raised on a winch by about seven inches and in the brilliant light which flooded the chapel he could make out with ease the body within. The tall rescuer lay there. His eyes were closed. The wings had vanished. His chest had been torn open from top to bottom however and his rib cage splayed out to either side. Something like an eagle.

31

Madeleine had faced the pressmen and sent them away happy. Free again, Mercy Merluza was parked on Deirdre's sofa in the Palace. They had just drunk coffee and she had eaten a home-made biscuit with a curiously smoky taste that Mercy did not relish. After two days of being under siege, her walk unpursued through sunlit streets had been all too brief. She was in here, with curtains drawn and the candles lit, too soon. The rich perfume of Deirdre's morning bath still hung in the atmosphere, supported by the sweet scent behind Deirdre's ears which clashed with that behind Mercy's own, while both mingled with the sickly vapours of a bunch of freesia on an occasional table to her left. She felt faint at this sensuous assault and, as she listened to Deirdre's slowing breaths, she let herself sink back on the sofa and felt her eyelids grow as heavy as the chesty sighs across the room. Before she could hear her friend's breathing stop, the moment which was normally so thrilling, Mercy perceived that the sofa was executing a slow, stomach-churning somersault beneath her.

'I'm having a stroke,' she thought. 'They'll carry me back to bed and I won't be able to say anything but "water" or "biscuit" in different tones of voice. And the Professor,' she thought, as the rolling stopped and she found herself settling on her back, 'the Professor will have his wicked way with my poor, disgraced Madeleine and I won't be able to lift a finger. I'll simply stare at them and say "Water water water".'

'I'm coming. Sssh,' said a woman's voice somewhere. 'Jesus Maria you do go on so.'

As a candle came close with a glass of water beside it, Mercy realized that her eyes were open and that she was on a bed in a dark room. A young woman was carrying the candle and the glass. She stooped, raised Mercy's head and let her drink.

'Water water water,' echoed the woman, more kindly. 'Soon you'll have to start getting it yourself. I can't always jump up as if you were still a baby.' It was her when young. No. The teeth were wrong. It was a likeness of her when young.

'*Gracias*, Mama,' murmured Mercy and pulled gently back to show that she had drunk enough now. The woman laid her back on the pillow and stroked her forehead.

'Little fool,' she whispered. 'Little Trouble.' There was a tremendous thudding on the stairs outside. The woman cursed and rushed out. Mercy heard a man's voice that she recognized. At first she could not make out their words then she heard him quite distinctly.

'I've come to take her home with me,' he said.

'She's mine,' hissed the woman. 'You left us.'

'She's mine too, remember. I was there. She'd only starve with you. You'll be better off without her. You can work again. Mother and I can give her food and, in time, she can earn her keep and learn a trade off Mother.'

'No!' The woman was almost screaming. 'You'll pervert her. I'd rather hand her over to the nuns. Please no. She's so little. Jésus, please.'

Then there was a clatter and a cry and Mercy knew that her mother had been shoved aside. The man ran up the rest of the stairs and strode into the circle of candlelight. She hid her face and tried to cling to the mattress as he slipped strong hands around her and slung her like a mail bag over one shoulder. The candlelight receded as did the woman's sobbing on the stairs. Mercy had not seen his face but the hands, the pommade on his hair and the faint scent of cloves told her it was Jésus. He slung her down and she was somersaulting slowly with the sofa again. Someone was patting her cheeks.

'Mercy? Mercy, Petal, wake up. Oh heck. *Mercy!*' scolded Deirdre. There was the sound of a striking match, a puff of breath then the acrid smell of smoke just under her nose. Mercy opened her eyes.

'Madeleine is my sister,' she announced flatly. 'I was seduced by my father.'

'What? Nonsense. Don't be a fool, Flower. Now can you stand?'

'No.'

'Yes you can. Come on. Let's get you to the window. You've gone all lardy coloured.' Deirdre slid a surprisingly strong arm round Mercy's back and, wheezing, helped her to a window. A curtain was thrust aside and the window flung open. The shock of fresh air in her face brought to Mercy's notice the fact that she was feeling seriously sick. She raised a hand towards her mouth.

'Deirdre, I think, perhaps . . .'

'Quick, Petal. Through here.'

Deirdre pushed her to the bathroom in the nick of time and shut her in. Mercy vomited the remains of the peculiar

243

smoky biscuit, flushed it away and felt much better. Steady on her legs once more, she rinsed out her mouth and borrowed some of Deirdre's eau de cologne to cool her cheeks which had been slapped so vigorously. She came to her senses. The faintness having passed, she saw that it was just a stupid dream and that they were two foolish old women playing dangerous games.

'No more,' thought Mercy. 'Meditation is good for my posture, Dr Morton said so, but no more curtained rooms and candles.'

She returned to the sitting room. Deirdre had snuffed the candles, drawn the curtains and left the window open. It was as if nothing had happened. She looked up expectantly from her chair.

'Are you better, Flower?'

'Much, thanks. So sorry. Terribly silly of me to faint like that. I'm normally so strong.'

'You didn't faint,' said Deirdre seriously. 'Something happened. You never told me you were sensitive.'

'I'm not. I just fainted.'

'Nonsense. I was just "going under" when it all went blank, as if someone had pulled out a plug on my switchboard. I was back to normal over here and there you were over there muttering in some funny language. I didn't dare move until you keeled over after about three minutes and started breathing properly again.'

'Well, honestly, Deirdre, nothing happened. I just felt a bit faint then sort of passed out. I often talk in my sleep. Madeleine said so when we went on holiday once and had to share a room.' Deirdre was a dear friend and a good friend but there were certain things even she must never know. 'You've changed the biscuits,' Mercy continued, resuming her seat on the sofa and changing the subject. The odd ones had vanished and been replaced by the usual mixture of ginger nuts and *langues de chats*.

'Oh yes,' said Deirdre airily. 'I can't think what those other ones were. They were quite stale. I must have got the tins muddled up. Have another coffee. You're still a bit grey, you know.'

'Yes. Thank you,' Mercy said. 'Then I must go and start work.'

Their eyes met very briefly at the handing over of cups and each smelled duplicity like cordite on the air.

32

'Emma. You're on your way out. I'll come back later.'

'Hello. No honestly, I'm just going to water that tub of fuchsias. Come and talk to me then you can stay for coffee.'

Emma rarely called Clive Hart anything. She knew that he wanted her to call him Clive – she called his wife Lydia, after all – but her impulse was always to call him Mr Hart. She liked Lydia who, with her success and outside contacts, brought a draught of the world beyond to provincial prisoners, and she tried to like Clive as well. The inkling that he was as much a prisoner as she, however, and something hungry and over-eager in his manner towards her repelled her. She knew that other women, Madeleine Merluza for instance, would have no hesitation, if placed in her position, in reaching out and taking what he was so clearly trying to offer. Until faced with the event, Emma could never be sure of escaping Barrowcester and, even had she the stuff of adultery, she lacked the mettle to live brazenly on the scene of such adventure. None of this could negate the fact that Clive's distinctly animal presence attracted and unsettled her. Mr Hart, therefore, or no name at all.

'You do look well,' he said as she showered her pot plants from a watering can filled at the rain butt.

'Thank you,' she replied. Coming from anyone else, this indirect compliment on the resuscitation of her mother's dress might have pleased her but she saw his eyes travelling on her arms and legs and wished she were in gardening slacks and a camel-coloured cardigan. 'How's Lydia?'

'Fairly mad getting ready for Saturday. She's decided to make her own dress, you see.'

'Heavens! What's the special occasion?'

'You haven't heard?' She shook her head. 'Tobit's wedding.'

'How wonderful!'

'It's startled us rather, too.'

'Well it's not that I'm startled. Not really . . .'

'I thought he'd unburdened himself to you once.'

'Yes he did, but I didn't take it very seriously. Come and have some coffee.'

It had been acutely embarrassing. Tobit Hart had volunteered to help her lay a new garden path several summers ago. Emma had assumed he was getting under his parents' feet, it being the end of the long holiday, so she had suggested to Lydia that, should she feel like off-loading her son one day, Emma could always find him something to do. Tobit had rung up and offered his services and Emma had suggested he help her lay a new path. In the event no path was laid; the old one was perfectly serviceable. He had watched her wax the hall floor, watched her buy and cook them lunch then, because she sensed that there was something he wanted to tell her, they had taken a long walk along the banks of the Bross. He had told her he was in love with one of his teachers. Why he had selected her as a confidante remained a mystery – possibly it was because this was the sort of thing brothers confided in older sisters, and she was roughly the right age. He had not seemed to want anything more than a sounding board. He was not worried or unhappy; Tobit had never needed assurance about anything. Emma had listened and said,

'Well, of course I wouldn't know,' a good deal and, though embarrassed, had been none the less touched that he had picked her out. He had told his parents about this confessional much later and Lydia had never stopped apologizing for it, as though it represented some dereliction in her motherly duty.

'Who's the lucky girl?' Emma asked.

'She's a young doctor he's met in London. She's called Gloire DelMonica.'

'Wonderful name. Is she Italian?'

'No. American. Sort of American. But actually, that's why I'm here.'

'Yes please,' thought Emma. 'I'd love to come and I'll buy a new dress especially.'

'What?' she asked, handing him his coffee and sitting at the kitchen table.

'Well, all this has happened terribly quickly and Lydia didn't know about Saturday when she asked you to dinner on Friday. God! Friday's tomorrow. I am sorry.'

'Oh, but of course. She can't possibly cope with a dinner party the night before. She'll be far too busy.' Emma hoped that her tone was reasonable.

'We feel awful. Lydia says maybe the Friday after.'

'I've got an old schoolfriend coming round,' Emma lied, quick as a flash.

'What fun for you. Well, another time, perhaps. I'm sure Lydia'll ring you up for a chat about Saturday anyway, and you can fix up something between you.'

'Who else was coming?'

'Just you and Fergus Gibson. Poor old Fergus. Do you know him?'

'Not really. Lydia said he was a wonderful designer and I'd thought I might get him to come round here and see if he had any ideas for doing the place up. Why do you say "poor"?'

'Well, there's his mother, who I gather is hell on earth at the moment and of course he's still terribly cut up about Roger.'

'That was his partner, wasn't it?'

She wanted to know all she could. The poor man had suffered so much. If she knew more, she could help him through.

'Well yes, but not many people seemed to realize that it wasn't just a business partnership.'

Emma glanced sharply up and saw that Clive was playing studiously with the remainder of his coffee.

'Ohh, of course,' she almost groaned. 'It must have been so hard for him coping with that sort of ignorance.' She wondered how many people Lydia had told about the awkwardness of cancelling the tryst she had arranged between poor Miss Dyce-Hamilton and poor, dear Fergus Gibson. Clive looked up.

'So you did know?' he queried.

'Oh Clive!' She managed both the Christian name and a laugh. 'Of *course* I did. I mean to say, he *is* an interior designer.'

'Thank God for that!' he exclaimed, relief flooding his face in place of the usual blend of pathos and lust it wore for her benefit.

'Why?' she asked, taking a sip of her unwanted coffee.

'Well, you know old Lydia; all very get-up-and-go but

she does have her crises of innocence and it turns out that the latest one was over Fergus. She literally had to wring it out of the man's cleaning lady before she'd believe it. And so I'm afraid this dinner party was ... well ... Oh dear.' He laughed. Loudly.

'She was pairing me off with *Fergus*? Oh really!' Emma tried to join in his laughter but found herself incapable of anything sufficiently convincing. She contented herself with a less than heartfelt simper.

'Ah well.' Clive subsided, glanced at the kitchen clock and rose. 'At least you weren't in the dark too, otherwise it might have been sad as well as funny. Can't wait to see her face when I let her know that you couldn't think what she was up to.'

'Well I wouldn't say that, exactly.'

'Emma, you're sweet to understand about tomorrow.' He patted her shoulder. 'And thanks very much for the coffee. Now I must get my skates on – I've got a class in ten minutes.'

'You've got my godson in one of your classes.'

'Which is he?'

'Crispin Clay.'

'Ah yes. Little chap.'

'That's right.'

'He's very preoccupied. Has he got problems at home or something?'

'No. Just a bit homesick I think.'

'Ah.'

'You must rush,' she reminded him, opening the front door.

'Yes, I must.'

'Goodbye.'

She shut the door before he had reached the gate. Her chequebook lay on her father's desk in the study. She made out a cheque to Drinkwater and Gibson Design Consultants for their initial consultation fee then slipped it into an envelope addressed to Fergus. Then she dialled his number which was already slipping from her memory. As she hoped, she was connected to his answering machine.

'Fergus, hello. It's Emma here. Emma Hamilton. Thanks so much for all your ideas yesterday. I think they're perfect. The trouble is I've just had a word with my bank manager and he doesn't seem to think that things will run that far. I'm furious but there's not much I can do. Anyway, do please hang on to your plans in case I can rustle up some more funds from somewhere, and I'll drop your cheque in after school this morning. We're not meeting tomorrow after all because Lydia's got a wedding on her hands on Saturday, but I'm sure we'll . . . Damn!' The bleeping of an electronic tone announced that she had recorded her fair share. She fairly slammed back the receiver.

Walking to the kitchen, she picked up Clive Hart's empty coffee cup. She opened the door to the basement, walked down a few steps then hurled first cup then saucer hard against the wall before her. Feeling a little better, she returned to the study and lay down on the sofa. She could hear the twittering of Dr Feltram's harpsichord from next door. She would have to leave the house in half an hour to teach. As she spent a few minutes lying on the sofa to trace the nicotine clouds on the ceiling, she decided to postpone St Paul yet again, and tell the little boys about the fury of King Saul.

33

Two greasy youths in grubby black gowns and a most distracting peaches and cream blonde, who could not have been more than sixteen, had been sharing the Tatham's library with Evan most of Thursday morning. Did these children never have lessons? They appeared to be doing nothing more scholastic than using the dank, peaceful room to lay out the copy for a school magazine. There was much wielding of long galley proofs and scissors and a certain amount of fairly heated discussion, so he had felt no qualms about setting up a clatter on the librarian's old Underwood portable.

The Penywern manuscript had occupied him most of the morning. It was a detailed scheme compiled, so Penywern had claimed, by a Portuguese Jesuit in the late seventeenth century, for building a precise earthly replica of the New Jerusalem as depicted in the Book of Revelations. Given no sparing of expense on the part of the laity this, it was claimed, would postpone the coming of the Beast and any number of lesser calamities. The Latin was difficult, being written (as it were) with a Portuguese accent, and much of the text was taken up with a dry debate concerning the choice of hilltop and the meaning of the Divine's words, 'And there was no more sea', but the architectural plans were enthralling. Far from the impracticable sketches of a theorist, they displayed the details of a painstaking neurotic. Evan was reminded of the first, ideal impression gained of Barrowcester as one's train rattled out over the viaduct across the Bross.

The clock in the chapel bell tower rang through the lengthy preamble it gave to every hour, then tolled one o'clock.

'Christ!' shouted one of the greasy youths and the three editors downed tools and raced for the door. The girl's 'sorry' as they ran past Evan's table added to her white ankle socks and hearty flush to lend her a curiously dated air. Evan slipped his reading glasses back in their pouch in his breast pocket and rubbed the strain from his eyes. Leaving his papers on the desk, he closed *Penywern 3*, retied the little leather belts that held it shut and carried it to the glass-fronted cubby hole where Perkin Philby had his lair.

'Lunchtime, already?' said Philby, with a glint of disapproval to his surprise and once again Evan thought of the improbable illustrations one saw of the long-eared owl.

'Yes,' he said. 'I promised I'd drop in at my landlady's shop soon after one.'

'I see.'

'Then I thought I'd go to the Tracer's Arms for some lunch. Care to come along?'

'Thanks awfully,' said Philby, 'but I've got to get this report done for the governing gods by six and I've got lunch here anyway.' He gestured with a wing to the tray behind him where there was a teapot, a kettle, a malt loaf and some rancid-looking butter.

'Fine. Well, I'll leave you this, if I may.'

'*Penywern 3*, isn't it?' asked Philby, who had gone back to his work. 'Still want it this afternoon?'

'Yup, and I could do with a second look at the Bentham collection at around three,' replied Evan, no longer bothering either.

'Leave it there, will you?' Philby asked, looking up briefly and pointing to a filing cabinet just inside the door. 'Help yourself if I'm not here when you get back and give me a shout when you want to be let into the stacks.'

Evan left the library and fumbled for a cigarette.

'Time warp,' he thought and, rare for him, entertained fleeting thoughts of 'come the Revolution'. Then he found himself back in Scholar Street and the sun was glinting on the bay windows. A file of choirboys trotted, brightly uniformed, through an ancient doorway. Evan passed by an old trout perched fearlessly on her kitchen stool to water her hanging baskets and he was soothed back into benignity. Had he seen Barrowcester's sour midwinter face, he told himself as he turned into the Close, his cynicism might have lasted rather longer.

Mrs Merluza found him before he found Boniface Crafts because she came flying from its door and led him in by the forearm. The only people in the shop were some members of an Austrian coach party he had seen wandering into the Tatham's quadrangle during a cigarette break.

'It's so excited, I mean, exciting,' his landlady gushed, her accent broader than usual. 'My Madeleine has faced the press.' One of the Austrians looked up and laughed openly.

'How? What did she tell them?' Evan was one attentive ear.

'Extraordinary! She marched out at about nine-thirty. Of course they started photographing like madmen, but I'd made her do her hair properly for once and she had on a nice, simple, blue woollen dress of mine I'd lent her, so that was all right.'

'Yes?' urged Evan, impatient.

'And she marched out and called them all up to the sitting room. (I'd made her ask for no photographs inside because of burglars, but they were so surprised that they were good as gold) and she sat them all down and said, "Right, gentlemen. Any questions?" No. That's not right. "Fire away!" That's right, she said, "Fire away!" I was so proud.' It would be clear from the papers the next day that Madeleine had gone on to answer every question in barely printable detail. 'And when they asked about the . . . er . . . you know.'

'The baby.'

'Yes. When they ask about that she said she was undecided but that it was her affair, not the Cardinal's and not theirs.'

'And what did she say about the Cardinal?'

'Oh she . . . er,' Mrs Merluza sought a phrase. 'She let him have it. She said he wanted nothing more to do with her and that, now that she had had time to think, she thought she would be happier with it that way. Then she took them down to the garden to photograph her without people gawping and then they left.'

'I should think they rushed.'

'They did quite.' Mrs Merluza laughed and said, in a voice not altogether hers, 'Dreadful little men.'

'Is she celebrating?'

'She's asked herself round to Dr Feltram's – her old Latin teacher – for supper. Forgive me.' She had to leave Evan briefly to take some cash from the Austrians. Evan noted that nothing was priced and assumed that she made a healthy profit; one price for bewildered foreigners, one for friends and one for everybody else. When they were alone, he made carefully diplomatic remarks on the trash she was selling then, none too forcefully, suggested she shut up shop for a while and join him for a drink over the road. 'Too kind,' she said. 'But I can't leave my post. You run along.' And she fairly beamed. 'Oh. While I remember,' she stopped him. 'One of our neighbours came to leave this for you. Emma Dyce-Hamilton. *Such* a dear girl.' Again she was borrowing voices. 'Sometimes we worry that she might be lonely, all alone in that great house, but she has a lovely garden and two cats for company.'

Evan waited until he was sitting on one of the pew-like seats in the pub's dark interior with a round of Stilton sandwiches and a half-pint of Old Stoat before him, then opened the envelope. It was a whimsical detail of an illuminated bestiary in the Bodleian, showing giant rabbits striding on hind legs to hunt tiny men. The writing was unusual; small but legible, dotted with Greek Es.

'Dear Prof. Kirby,' he read. 'Welcome to Heaven on Earth! (I don't think). We have never met, however my late father, the Dean, was a fan of your first book and more importantly, your literary agent is a dear first cousin of mine. I feel this gives grounds enough to invite you to lunch. Would twelve forty-five on Saturday suit you? Very short notice, but I don't know how long you'll be with us. Unless I hear from you, I shall assume you can come. Best wishes. Emma Dyce-Hamilton.'

Given her late father's age at his death, it was to be

assumed that she was considerably older than Jeremy. He had barely discussed her beyond saying that she was a 'sweet old thing' and Mrs Merluza had mentioned that she lived alone so presumably she was a miss or a widow of long standing. Evan took a sip of Old Stoat (he had learnt to drink it in slow, small doses) and made a mental note to remember to keep his tongue padlocked as regarded Jeremy and James, his live-in vet. Jeremy affected abandon but with an acuteness bred of even a brief stay in Barrowcester, Evan doubted that he had enlightened elderly maiden relatives on such matters. Evan chewed on a mouthful of sandwich and gazed peaceably at the crowd around him. Through a brief clearing he saw the photograph of Madeleine still on the wall behind the bar, then his view was blocked again. On his way back to Tatham's he would stop to buy an equally tasteful postcard to say yes please to the invitation. On the day he would take flowers or a packet of home-made fudge from the post office; 'little somethings' seemed to be a deep-rooted local custom.

The Bentham Collection was a typical seventeenth-century miscellany, compiled by some mercantile Croesus with more wealth than scholastic nous. Among the jumble of recipes, incomplete ballads and tracts there were pearls, though, and rooting through it all that afternoon, Evan chanced on a piece that no bibliography had suggested he consult. An Old Norse saga, it told, with the love of violence and non-sequitur that were hallmarks of its provenance, a rambling legend of a Viking saint. Narrated from the pagan viewpoint, it depicted Christianity as a pale, exotic magic. The hero was a Viking captain renowned for his bloodlust and tendency to go *berserkr* at the scent of gore, who sailed to an island wreathed in mist and rain where he fell under the spell of a strange cult of peace and commanded his men to destroy their weapons and carve the new god of love on their ships. The tale had little regard for the unities and there was a crude break in the chronology before the climactic chapter. This told how another fleet of warriors – whose enmity with the hero's line was illustrated at unsavoury length – followed him to the island, slaughtered his unarmed followers and, splitting him open with their axes, skewered him to a church door in the shape of an eagle. There was a miracle, however, and he burst away from the blades that pinned him to the wood and flew into the mists on bloodstained wings. Roughly translated, his Norse name meant 'fair of visage'. Boniface.

34

'Why's Jane coming with us?' Mrs Gibson demanded.

'She's not Jane, she's Dawn,' Fergus corrected, waiting for the lights to change.

'Balls. All maids are called Jane; unless she's a Ruby.' The old woman swung around in her seat to interrogate Dawn who was sitting behind Fergus with Lilias Gibson's suitcase beside her and a spider plant on her lap.

'She's not a maid; she's our friend, Dawn. Miss Harper,' Fergus pursued.

'Are you a Ruby, girl, or a Jane?' continued Mrs Gibson, heedless. Unseen by Fergus, Dawn stuck out her tongue. This had the desired effect of stunning his mother into silence until they reached the Roman Bridge, when she asked, 'Is it very far, this spa we're going to?'

'No,' Fergus said. 'It's just up here on Friary Hill, but I told you, Mother, it's not a spa. It's just a sort of health retreat place.'

'But this is a cemetery,' his mother whimpered.

'Yes,' he countered, 'but Brooklea is further on. Nearly there now.'

It had proved mercifully easy to lure her from the house. The mention of health resorts seemed to trigger off some long-buried yearning for regimented pampering and with it, remembered scenes of expatriate socializing which she had patently concocted from bad novels. Inevitably there was much one-sided discussion about whether there would be a resident bowel specialist, but once Fergus had crossed his fingers and said that he was sure they could find her someone if there was not, she had been a model of cooperation. She had fairly hopped out of bed and, after a brief argument with Dawn as to what she should wear for the trip, she tottered downstairs on Fergus's arm. As they waited in the drawing room for Dawn to gather things into a suitcase, Fergus had encouraged her to select something 'of emotional value' to take with her.

'Whatever should I do that for?'

'Well ... er ... It's all the rage now. People take a picture or a favourite cushion or something, to brighten up their rooms. How about a pot plant? Would you like that fuchsia there? It's not too big and it's going to have lots of flowers.'

'I hate fuchsia. I always have. How about that thing in the bathroom with all the baby bits on stalks?'

'The spider plant. I'll bring it down.'

She had laughed as he left the room.

'Dear me,' he heard her chuckle, 'I've forgotten all my German, but then everybody speaks French in these places as it's altogether more chic.'

'Here we are,' said Fergus as cheerily as he could when the car swung up into the orange-gravelled drive of Brooklea. His nerves seemed to have transferred to his mother whose excitement was now at fever pitch.

'Oh look!' she exclaimed. 'There's Kitty von Hofmansthal and that dreadful goose of a daughter she can't marry off. You didn't say they'd be here. They'll be sure to hound me all weekend.'

A lump in his throat, her son said nothing but walked round the car to open her door.

'Thank you, darling,' she said. She was using a sweetness of tone he had not heard in months, which made things so much worse. He wanted her to snarl and fart and be repellent, if only as a display of evidence for the nurses. Claire Telcott had opened the front door. Beaming, she now advanced and shook Fergus's hand.

'Hello hello,' she said, then put on a nursery teacher voice for his mother, who was hanging on his left arm. 'And is this Mrs Gibson? Hello, dear, how are we feeling?'

'*Bonjour, Madame. Je vais très bien, merci*,' Mrs Gibson enunciated and clutched harder at Fergus's arm for protection. Dawn brought up the rear with the plant and the suitcase. The little procession moved slowly up the stairs to Mrs Gibson's room on the first-floor landing.

'I booked you one of the best rooms, Mother,' Fergus managed to say. Claire Telcott caught his eye and smirked.

'Got your own en suite bathroom, lovey,' she said to the new inmate.

'*Enchantée*,' sang Mrs Gibson then muttered to Fergus, 'Where are you going to sleep?'

'I told you,' he urged, helping her into her armchair as Dawn found a hook for the overcoat that no longer fitted her. 'It's a treat just for you. I'd love to come as well but I've got to work.'

'No. No, please don't leave me,' wailed his mother, clutching at the collar of his jersey with her little, claw-like hands. 'Don't go away. Not yet. Stay to tea. Ruby will start a fire and make us some in the billy, won't you girl?' The lack of luxury in her new surroundings had inspired a rapid slip from Baden-Baden to the African bush.

He had to prise her hands off quite roughly.

'I've got to go,' he said. 'Be good and take the Matron's advice and you'll be strong as an ox in no time. Honest.'

'No. I hate it here. Take me away. It smells and, oh, it's far, far too hot. I can't breathe.'

Claire Telcott clicked her tongue at his elbow.

'Now he doesn't live far away, Mrs Gibson,' she soothed. 'I'm sure he'll come and see you every day.'

'Yes, of course I will,' said Fergus, envisaging a small eternity of daily visits to this infernal place. 'I'll come for tea with you tomorrow and see how things are going.'

Mrs Gibson started to cry. Fergus was going to come forward to comfort her but Dawn laid a hand on his arm.

'I think we should go,' she mouthed and gave a quick squeeze.

'Here I come,' he gulped and followed her from the room without a backward glance. A junior nurse had slipped in to unpack for his mother so the Matron was able to join them briefly in the hall.

'It's always a wee bit hard at first,' she assured them. 'She's really just confused at the change of scenery. It's normally best not to visit for the first couple of days. That way she can get used to our little routine and she'll have things to chat to you about when you come. But do ring up and ask how things are going if you're worried. And by all means send her postcards.'

'Yes, of course. What a good idea. Thank you,' he said.

As Fergus turned the car out of the drive, Claire Telcott hurried back upstairs to see the cause of the small uproar that had broken out. While the junior nurse's back was turned, Lilias Gibson had staked out her new territory on her bedroom carpet in the way that came most naturally.

'I suppose you think that's funny,' the Matron snapped; superfluously, as it happened, because Mrs Gibson was rocking with laughter and waving her soiled skirt up and down with mirth.

35

It was soon after midnight and Crispin was breaking a
school rule for the first time by being away from his bed
after the master switch had been thrown to plunge all the
dormitory block save the prefectural floor into darkness
until soon after dawn. According to a relatively recent
Tathamite custom (dating from the late nineteenth century) the youngest scholar could exempt himself from a
Lingua exam if he could commit an outrage that the head
of house found sufficiently diverting. Jermyn had reminded
Crispin's *magister*, David, of this when the latter was
bemoaning the hopelessness of teaching an *oik* of such
weak memory. Jermyn was proving to be something of a
friend. Crispin had leapt at the idea, less from any hope of
escaping the *Lingua* exam (the head of house was a not-
ably humourless young woman called Marsden-Scott who,
when not writing a book called *Why God Is Not*, played
herself at three-dimensional chess and took notes on her
technique) than from a superstitious belief that a sufficiently daring outrage might spare him and his dog the
wrath of the gods. After an afternoon of mooted plans for
encasing live kittens in a pie crust or painting a giant chess
board on the quadrangle, the three of them had decided on
something simpler. Crispin would creep into chapel late at
night and change all the carefully prepared hymn boards
so that they announced hymn three hundred and one

although there were only three hundred hymns in the book. Feeble though the jest might seem to the average man, this was thought at once sufficiently numerical and untaxing as to appeal even to Marsden-Scott.

Crispin had had to set his alarm to wake him at twelve-fifteen. The prefects were allowed to play rock music until eleven and there were numerous traditional sayings and responses requiring a loud delivery which could be heard being bandied about by those still abroad downstairs. Scholar's House, the dormitory block, had no carpets or curtains so four or five seventeen-year-olds climbing the stairs to their bedsits in the attics was enough to wake even the heaviest-sleeping junior. As on most nights, Crispin had slept for half an hour then been kept wide awake from ten until nearly midnight. The alarm clock was therefore redundant and he had been able to turn it off, slip his scholar's gown over his pyjamas, pull on some gym shoes and creep out of the dormitory disturbing as few people as possible.

The quadrangle was all in darkness save for the great lamp over the dining hall steps. He scurried through the gloom to the main chapel doors then let himself into the organ loft staircase through the second door immediately inside the porch. David was clattering away at the keyboard and pedals, white stick hooked on the rail behind him, practising with the power turned off.

'Who's that?' he asked, hands and feet stopping at the sound of Crispin's gym shoes on the spiral steps.

'Ssh,' said Crispin. 'It's only me. I'm doing my outrage.'

'Splendid,' said David. 'Carry on.' He should not have been there either so returned to his silent voluntary without a further word.

There were two hymn boards dangling by chains, one from the organ loft and one from the gallery, while a third, painted on the wall, faced into the gallery to inform late-comers, and a tiny fourth faced the chaplain and choir. Crispin altered the organ loft one from fifty-two to three hundred and one then bade David goodnight and went to change the choir's board. This was the most important as it ensured that the chaplain, who was tone deaf and never bothered to find his page until midway through the first verse, played his part in the outrage by announcing the non-existent number. Then he left the chapel and made for the cloisters.

Vespers were held every evening in the chapel gallery and this was reached from the cloisters up a narrow side tower. Along with playing human alarm clock, junior scholar had to turn off all the lights after these evening prayers. For once, Crispin was grateful of this; he knew where the switches lay for lighting both cloisters and stair-case and so could dispel with a finger's touch all the unpleasant feeling of the place. He had never been afraid of the dark – well, not for a great many years – but the dark-ness of the cloisters was somehow thicker than everywhere else. He raced up the stairs, already well-versed in their unevenness and occasional small holes. He no longer cared whether his absence was noticed. The all-important thing now was bed; a warm bed in a preciously silent dormitory. He hurried across the gallery, hoisted the hymn board by its chain and changed the numbers then did the same for the board mounted on the gallery wall. At this distance, the gallery light barely reached the organ loft. David and his softly thudding manuals seemed to float in the pitch black. Back in the cloisters, Crispin flicked out the lights, then frowned. The light in the chantry was on. He checked all the switches. They were all in the off position. Candles!

He had heard the rumours about black masses, naturally, but had discounted them as horror stories for new boys – sorry, *men*. He sensed, with the opportunism that became first nature to the smallest, youngest person in a school, that if he could see such a desecration with his own eyes, he would hold something over his seniors. Leaving the lights off in case the Satanists were alarmed, he clambered through one of the cloister arches and padded silently across the grass. The dew splashed up on to his bare ankles and made him shudder. The door was open a crack. He manoeuvred into the right position but could still see nothing. He could hear nothing either. Perhaps someone was at genuine prayer. Feeling awkward and pagan, Crispin turned to go. His gym shoes squeaked on the dewy stone. At once a woman's voice called out,

'Madeleine Merluza, first-generation woman, first female scholar and I'm very very sorry.' Crispin froze. The voice went on in a different tone. 'Well, come in. I'm surprisingly decent.' He pushed open the door and slid round it.

She was lying between the two lit candles on the altar with a half-bottle of whisky open beside her and she was smoking. She sent up a jet of smoke towards the painted ceiling as he came in.

'Sorry,' said Crispin. 'I just wondered what the light was.'

'Hello,' she said, turning her head. She had lots of bushy, blackish-brown hair which she had evidently enjoyed arranging across the stone beneath her. 'You're fearfully young. Is it just you?'

'Yes.'

'You shouldn't be up this late.'

'I know. You see, I left my watch in the gallery after vespers and I needed it to set my alarm clock by,' he lied easily.

'Poor thing. And you didn't dare ask anyone the time in case they gave you the wrong one?'

'No. Are you waiting for a black mass to begin?'

'I'm not a virgin.' She chuckled. 'You have to have a virgin to use as an altar.'

'I'm a virgin,' he confessed. 'I think.' He came a little closer. 'Are you drunk?' he asked.

'Just a little,' she said. 'I went to a *wonderful* dinner with one of your Latin *gods* Dr Feltram. I hadn't seen him since I was your age – well, a bit older than you – and he let me keep the rest of my nightcap for old time's sake. Want some?' she sat up and held out the bottle.

'No thanks. I hate whisky. Could I have a cigarette, though?'

'Be my guest.' She offered the packet. He made no move. She grinned and wiggled the cigarettes. 'Come on,' she said. 'I don't bite. Not often.'

He smiled shyly back and came forward to take a cigarette. She lit it for him then patted the altar stone. He hesitated then jumped up beside her.

'Why do you only *think* you're a virgin?' she asked.

'I can't tell you that, I'm afraid.'

'Secret?'

'Sort of.' He pretended to inhale and saw that she was

smiling. His sisters had made him smoke once and he had been sick. He did not feel sick now. Perhaps this was growing up.

'You can tell me.'

'Why?'

'Because you'll never see me again, because I don't know who you are and because my secrets are far worse and bigger than yours can possibly be.'

'I'm not so sure about that.'

'Try me.'

Could he trust her? Suddenly he felt he could.

'Well . . .' he began. 'Do dogs count?'

When Madeleine had got over her surprise she asked him to explain and he told her everything. She was very kind, not laughing. When she told him that he could have gone 'much further than that' with Lottie without making her pregnant he was so relieved, however, that he laughed and then she joined in.

'Are you *very* relieved?' she asked, but he merely blushed. 'I envy you,' she said, 'my secret isn't half as simple.' Then he recognized her.

'You were in the paper,' he said. 'You're the one that had an affair with the Cardinal in London.'

'Direct little boy, aren't you?' she said.

'I'm fourteen in November.'

'My my.' She sighed and screwed the top back on to the nearly empty bottle. She took a drag on her cigarette and blew a few smoke rings. Crispin was impressed.

'My uncle can do those,' he said.

'I *must* meet him', she replied. 'Is he tall, dark and handsome?'

'Quite.'

'Pity. I seem to prefer them stooped, white and wrinkled.' Crispin swung his legs and coughed. 'Don't cough. You mustn't cough,' she commanded, raising an admonitory finger. 'If you cough you'll cough again. Breathe. That's it. Relax and breathe. Inhale.' He inhaled properly for the first time and the coughing stopped.

'Thanks,' he said, hoping he would not be sick now.

'*Nada*,' she replied.

'Are you going to keep the baby?' he asked.

'What business is it of yours?'

'Well, we're having a debate about you in Deb Soc tomorrow.'

'A debate all about me? I'm honoured.'

'It's not really about you. The motion is, "This House Believes That the Contents of a Mother's Womb Are Her Own Affair", but Jermyn – she's a friend of mine – is proposing and it's fairly obvious that she has you in mind.'

'And you think that it would be impressive if you could stand up and produce evidence from the horse's mouth?'

'Just a bit. Well,' he stubbed out his cigarette on the back of the altar. 'Yes.'

'It's a deal. I'll tell you what I intend to do with my baby if you remind me how to get out of here after lock-up.'

'Done.'

So they swept the cigarette butts under a pew, snuffed the candle and left the chantry. No sooner were they out in the pitch-black cold again than the enormity of his new freedom made him start to shiver. Madeleine sneezed heavily.

'Damn,' she said. 'That's what comes from reclining too long on cold stone. Have you got a hanky?'

'No,' said Crispin. 'Well, yes, actually, but it's not mine and it's not very clean.'

'Never mind,' she replied. 'I'll give it back when I've washed it. Promise.'

After he had fished out his godmother's handkerchief for her and admitted that he had no idea who F stood for, Crispin showed her the way out through the warden's garden. Having tucked three more cigarettes into the breast pocket of his pyjamas and given him the remains of the whisky as a bribe if he ran into a prowling prefect, Madeleine told him what she intended to do with her baby.

36

Endeavouring to ignore the bad way in which Friday morning had found her, Madeleine pulled on a sociable face as she knocked on the granny-flat door.

'Come,' he called, so she came.

'Evan, Mum says you've finished your research.'

'Hi.' He was drying glasses at the sink and waved a tea towel in greeting.

'Hello.'

'Sit,' he told her and she sat. She took a fig roll from a packet on the table.

'Yes I have. No more gaps to fill. But it's so great here and my agent's elderly cousin has invited me to lunch tomorrow so I thought I'd stay on a few more days and do the tidying up on the text here.'

'Who?'

'Emma Dyce-Hamilton.'

'That's the one who brought the charity gâteau. She was at Tatham's with me.'

'Don't tell me any more. I've got to give her a sporting chance.'

'Why?'

'Don't bully me. I'm not your mother.'

'Thank God.' She laughed. 'Have you got all the manuscript with you?'

'Bet your sweet locks I have. I wouldn't sleep a wink if I

left it somewhere else. Some of Jeremy's other clients – sorry, that's Jeremy Barker, my agent – some of them are so nervy that they actually hand over each draft as it's written, for him to put in a safe. He admitted to me, though, that he just shoves them in a file along with everything else. There'd be hell to pay if ever his place burned down – hysterical romance novelists on the warpath.'

He laughed then subsided and stood there cracking his knuckles. Madeleine grinned and offered him a cigarette which he turned down then rapidly accepted. She made him nervous for some reason, which was a shame; he was more attractive when serious. When he was trying to be funny he reminded her of someone anxious for the stability of his toupee, but when he was frowning or deep in thought or, better still, angry – as when he had locked out the bastard hacks the other morning – he looked like an ageing Gary Cooper.

'You see,' she said, 'if you weren't doing anything in particular this morning, I wanted to ask you a favour.'

'Sure,' he said, leaning against the wall in front of her, suddenly the rangy cowboy. 'Anything but put my footnotes in order.'

''Cause I've got to borrow Mum's car and drive out to a clinic a few miles outside town, and I could do with some moral support.'

'Of course. It would be interesting to see something beyond all the quaintness. When do you want to leave?'

'Now-ish?'

'I'll be with you in two minutes.'

'Thanks.'

For the first time since either of them had been in Barrowcester it was not a brilliantly sunny day, indeed the weather showed every sign of turning ugly. There was an unpleasant, skirt-lifting wind from the south, the kind that brought summer colds on its breath, and the sky was oppressive with low clouds. As she left to open her shop, her mother remarked that it was the kind of day on which old people gave up the struggle. The private clinic, where the 'poor Stepfords' girl' had been sent after her disastrous French exchange lay two or three miles to the north of Barrowcester in an undistinguished hamlet. Madeleine took the Clough road as far as the by-pass then turned off that on to a country lane. She heard Evan draw breath as if to speak, so cut in first, in case his chosen topic were gynaecological.

'I had supper with Dr Feltram, one of my old Latin teachers, last night,' she said.

'Yes. Your ma said. How did it go? Was he pleased with how you'd turned out?'

'He was terribly tactful about steering clear of anything to do with Edmund.'

'Who?'

'My Cardinal.'

'Oh. Him.'

'Yes, him. He didn't mention him at all, even though I know that they used to be quite good friends. We just talked about things like work, and people in Barrowcester who had died. He got me terribly drunk because there wasn't much to eat. Since his wife was put away he seems to have been living off crackers and Stilton.'

'Wise man.'

'It palls after an evening of nothing else. Anyway, around eleven o'clock he announced that it was long past his bedtime, but he felt so guilty for turfing me out that he made me take the half-bottle of whisky we were finishing. It's so nice walking in Barrowcester after dark because all the old trouts have gone to bed and the streets are safe. I ended up doing things I'd wanted to do for ages.'

'What?'

'Boozing in the school chantry after lock-up and encouraging a small boy to smoke while telling him the facts of life.'

Evan laughed. She could tell that he did not take this seriously and she was struck again by the New World innocence of the man. Far from closing their age difference this reversed it, making her feel the older by far.

'Did going to Tatham's affect you very much?'

'When I was a pupil, you mean?'

'Yup.'

'I suppose it must have done. I don't see how you can imprison children of that age in buildings of that beauty and spend five and a half years telling them how special they are, and not leave some kind of mark. I've never felt guilty about it, because I did the whole thing as a scholastic free-booter. I was definitely one of the lucky ones, though. I was a fat little thing who enjoyed her work a lot and I've managed to hide away in sunny Academe ever since. But there are plenty who aren't very bright, just disgustingly rich, and who are thrown out into the world at the other end completely unfit for anything except poncing up and down feeling special and wondering why no one will throw a job at them.'

'Will . . . Would you send a child of yours there?'

'No,' she said without hesitation. The amount of smoke they had generated was giving her a headache on top of the one she already had. She opened her window a fraction to suck the cloud away and improve the visibility. 'Would you?'

'I . . . er . . .'

'Oh. I'm sorry. Bugger.' Swallowing this stupid mistake, she fell silent, as did he. They arrived in the clinic's crowded car park after five minutes of brooding. 'It'll only take twenty minutes,' she told him. 'Do you want to come and sit in the waiting room? There's probably a coffee machine. Otherwise you could go for a walk through the village. It's not very thrilling, but the church is quite sweet.'

'I guess I'll come in with you. I'm afraid I haven't given you much in the way of moral support.'

'Yes you have. I needed someone to chat to.'

'What are you coming in for?'

He had been bound to ask in the end. Hating her coyness, she muttered,

'Oh nothing much. Just something sordid and female.'

'Oh,' he said, as they locked up the car. 'Good luck, anyway.' He reddened a little and his hair seemed whiter. They never got as far as the waiting room. They were barely into the anonymous red-brick porch of the building when the glass doors swung open and a horde of journalists and photographers were upon them.

'Oh,' said Evan.

'Run,' said Madeleine.

'What does the Cardinal think about you getting an abortion, Madeleine?' shouted a reporter with a face already familiar.

'Does he even know?' yelled another, as they fled back towards the car.

'Who's your new boyfriend?'

'How long have you been on private medicine?' called a third and a fourth in a cloud of flashing bulbs.

She barely gave Evan time to sit down beside her; he was still struggling to free his seatbelt from the door when she drew away like a maniac and drove, horn blaring, through the wildly scattering crowd. She thudded her clenched fist one more time on the horn button as they swerved out on to the road home. Some of the journalists seemed to be cheering. She let out a grunt of frustration.

'Could you drive just a little slower?' asked Evan.

'Sorry,' she said and slowed to fifty.

'How do you think they found out?'

'I don't know. It's only two hours since I made the appointment and I only gave them my surname. I suppose the receptionist must have made a few calls.'

'No. You misunderstood; I mean, how did they find out you wanted an abortion?'

'They didn't,' she said, accelerating.

'They did. One of them asked what your Cardinal thought about it. I heard.'

'Well I don't know. What business is it of yours anyway?' she snapped. She had been trying to light a cigarette but it slipped out of her fingers on to the floor. She swore, stamping on it briefly with her brake foot so that they lurched going down a hill. She saw Evan's hands whiten as he gripped his knees and that irritated her further.

'Well, none really, I guess,' he said slowly. 'But I just don't think you can have thought about it long enough.'

'I've had nearly a week. Sometimes these decisions are surprisingly straightforward.' She heard her voice take on the high, strange pitch which signified impending loss of temper.

'I just think ... well ... I suppose I wouldn't want you to do anything that might hurt you or that you might regret because . . . well . . . This'll sound stupid but I care about you a good deal, Madeleine.'

Foghorns blared in a headache that was now bordering on white-knuckle migraine.

'OK,' she squeaked, stopping the car. 'That's it. I . . . I . . . That's it.' She could never think of anything to say when she lost her temper so she reached for her cigarettes, her lighter and the door handle. 'Can you drive?' she asked, unable to see his face now that she was outside the car.

'Well, as a matter of fact I can't. But look, I'm . . .'

'There's a bus every half hour or so. I think there's a stop just round this corner.'

She closed the door then pulled out a cigarette, held it in her teeth and strode back to a nearby gate which gave into a broad, boring square of overcropped grass.

'Madeleine,' she heard him call. 'Madeleine?'

She stalked across to a distant hedge, taking fierce deep drags and kicking dried-out cow pats when they came within reach. Once the fresh air started to clear her head and she began to detect an element of pleasure in the scene she was making, she turned and stalked back to the car. Evan had gone. She drove as far as the next bus stop but he was not there either. Cursing him and cursing herself just a little too now, she gritted her teeth and headed for Barrowcester again, and Saint Boniface's Infirmary. An hour and a half later, she was facing a woman doctor who miraculously failed to recognize her or who was too considerate to appear to do so.

'I'm four, maybe five weeks pregnant,' she told her, 'and I haven't had a check-up in ages so I wondered whether you could run some tests to tell me if it's OK to go ahead and become a mother.'

37

The bus dropped its country passengers – two old men in cloth caps, three farmers' wives out for their weekly razzle and Evan – in an anonymous square behind the town hall. It was a part of town he had not seen. He stood by the bus stop and saw a multi-storey car park, a bingo hall, a Methodist chapel and, close by, the Salvation Army building. It was market day. The stalls were ranged along the sides of a gravelled plot in the square's centre. At a loss, he crossed the road and wandered in the crowd. The glare of fruit alternated with the iced sourness of fish barrows and the stench of blood and pine chippings by the butchers' vans. The Salvation Army band was playing 'Abide With Me'. Evan stood to listen but fled when a man wreathed in smiles encouraged him to join in or, at least, give some money to Christ's soldiers.

'Not one, not two, but *three* bottles of real, French perfume for the price of one and I'll throw in a non-stick dry fryer for any lovely lady or gentleman who splashes out and buys a fourth!'

There was a cart laden with garish plastic toys. Dolls dangled by their feet in polythene bags and, in a cage, two wind-up kittens and a Sherman tank gyrated on their backs emitting clockwork mews. A curious stone block like a milestone announced that its observer was now as far from the sea as it was possible to be in the British Isles. The next cart held nothing but brushes, the next, an array of oversize shoes and the next, an assortment of watches, ties and handbags.

'All prices slashed! Real silk! Genuine leather!'

Evan paused to finger an antique, spangled dress on a second-hand clothes stall then moved on to a nightmare array of sweets from which he bought a bag of white chocolate buttons sprinkled with hundreds-and-thousands. Then he saw a place called Kath's Cath Caff and escaped.

The room was redolent of cigarettes, coffee steam and the savoury hiss of frying pork. Evan bought a coffee foaming with hot milk and a doughnut oozing pink jam. The seating was along one wall so that everyone faced the room and one could watch what was going on without seeming obviously rude to one's neighbour, or sit alone with less pathos. Evan sat in a space between a sad young man stirring sugar into his tea and a young couple who were pawing a map. He ate the doughnut quickly because it was more necessary than pleasurable then leaned back to sip coffee and think.

He had wrecked everything and made a fool of himself. Enough. The research was finished. He would lie low tonight then slip away straight after Emma Price-Hamilton's lunch tomorrow.

'Fool,' he thought. 'Goddamned fool,' then 'Why?' then 'Madeleine'. The coffee was too weak and the milk had coated his tongue unpleasantly. Beyond the condensation on the windows the sky was turning darker still.

'OK. Have it your way,' said the map girl and began to pull on a duffle coat. 'But it'll cost us an arm and a leg.'

'Well do you want a bath or don't you?' her companion urged. She sighed impatiently as they rose to leave. Evan was about to follow their example when a pair of deeply tanned middle-aged women in identical mackintoshes arrived to take their place.

'Excuse me. Are these places free?' asked one in broad Texan.

'Indeed they are,' said Evan with an automatic smile and he cleared a space for her friend's tray.

'Oh but you're American!' she exclaimed. 'What a great surprise!'

'Yes,' he said.

'We're just over. This is my sister Amy, and I'm Pam. We're from San Antonio.'

'So I had heard.'

She roared with laughter and dug her sister in the ribs.

'So he had heard. Did you hear that, Amy? So he had heard.' She turned back to Evan with an earnest expression. 'You're very funny. Boy, this is nice.'

'Yes,' said Evan.

'Oh, excuse me?' Pam caught the waitress's attention. 'I think this gentleman would like the same again.'

'What were you wanting?' The waitress stared at Evan, pen poised over pad.

'Oh . . . er . . . a hot chocolate,' said Evan. 'I'm afraid I'm only a Bostonian,' he said to Pam and Amy.

'So *we* had heard,' said Amy and they both roared with laughter this time. Evan watched them laugh.

'This your first day here?' Pam asked him.

'No. I've been working here nearly a week but this is my first day off.'

'We're due on a guided tour at half of eleven. Wanna come?'

'What a perfectly wonderful idea,' he said seriously. 'Watch out for the doughnuts, Amy – they squirt.'

And so he found himself on a guided tour with a pack of trouser-suited Texans. They saw the Cathedral, the Chapter House, Tatham's, the town hall, the Hanover Street baths, the old Guildhall, the Butter Cross and the Hermitage. It was rather fun. The best parts were being shepherded into the Chapter House to see Petra Dixon's face when she caught sight of him in the unlikely crowd and being shown around the Tatham's library by Perkin Philby, whom Evan asked extremely awkward questions and affected not to recognize.

It had been drizzling gently all the while they were looking at the Butter Cross and being told about the Hermitage (now a busy auction house). As they wandered back up the hill, the Texans to go shopping and Evan to go nowhere in particular, a storm broke. He and the sisters managed to lose the others and took shelter in a tea shop where, it being mid-afternoon and dark as a midwinter five o'clock, they felt no guilt about ordering a full cream tea for three. The storm was the most spectacular Evan had ever witnessed outside New England. The rain was so heavy that it became hard to see across the High Street between the white flares of lightning. A wind howled down the chimney beside them and the thunder was so loud that Amy grew quite querulous. Pam, the elder, told her to stop making a fuss and to eat her second scone, which calmed her down. Pam was the older by four years, Evan learned, and married to a man who had perfected a fake fur that sold for half the price of mink and was far more comfortable on sticky summer evenings. Amy had recently lost her husband, a pharmacist. At least, he was not dead but he had become a little too eccentric and had had to be moved to a special place ('very exclusive') and they had come to Europe to help her forget. Evan pictured Amy's husband, scrawny in cord-free pyjamas, talking to thin air and hidden micro-phones about the New Jerusalem, staring at the towering cacti from his padded suite and trailed by discreetly mounted cameras.

The storm blew itself away after half an hour and there was a sudden rush for the sisters to rejoin their coach. Feel-ing sick, Evan insisted on treating them and they left, clutching his ex-wife's address should they ever be up in Massachusetts. He paid the bill, smoked a cigarette then ventured out. A weak sun was creeping through rags of cloud and as he crossed the Close the grass glittered and steamed. The car had not returned and he had to use his key to get in so he knew himself to be alone. There was a note on the hall table.

'Dear Ma and Evan,' it said. 'Have just driven over to Arkfield to cinema. Back 9-ish. Love, M.'

Cheered by the inclusion of his name, though still feel-ing sick from the cream tea, he let himself into the granny flat. He slung his damp coat over a chairback and decided to enjoy a quiet lie-down, possibly with Sukie Lark Rosen.

His first thought as he slid back the second bathroom door was that there had been a burglary. The French win-dows were open, one of the curtains hung free, the other, twisted over the outside of a door, was rain-soaked. His suitcase, which he had never unpacked, seemed to have exploded. His shirts littered the room. The one he picked up as he came in had had its sleeves ripped off. The others were in a similar condition – some almost in rags. There were little muddy trails across the carpet and over the unmade bed. This was the work of an animal, not a burglar. Curiously, considering its importance, it was only when he started forward to pull the sodden curtain back inside that Evan remembered his manuscript.

He tended to work in fountain pen in small, fifty-leaf exercise books which, as they were filled up, became strung across with a weave of directions and cross references that only he could decipher. He always did the typing up himself because it would have taken too long to explain to any typist his system of codes and arrows, also because he relished the days of undemanding drudgery at the typewriter after months of brainwork. There was a simple pleasure in watching the pile of freshly-typed sheets growing from the battered heap of little notebooks. Whoever – whatever – had broken into the bedroom had taken the notebooks and scattered them across Mrs Merluza's garden. A few remained whole, the others had been torn from their staples and been thrown into the wind to flutter on to bush and border. Feeling nothing yet but weakening disbelief, Evan pushed past the ripped curtains and drifted into the garden. Judging from all the mud inside, the visitor had been fairly wet on arrival, but the manuscript would seem to have received the benefit of at least half the storm. He stooped to pick up one of the whole books and it squelched in his grasp. The cover disintegrated as he tried to open it and the precious contents had turned to so much inky porridge. A few pages at the centre were still legible but even as he laid them bare, trickles of blue-black rain slipped across them, slicing angels, obliterating saints. He returned to his room and emerged with a carrier bag from the local stores and began carefully to load it with the sodden text.

'I'm the man collecting tinned peaches for my children

after the blast,' he thought. 'I'm the radio officer tapping out polite requests for information after the power has died. This is a last whimper.'

One of the few typed sheets – those he had produced on the old Underwood at Tatham's – had been speared on a rose bush. Evan teased it off, trying not to tear it further, then stuffed it in the bag. The bag was thick paper, not plastic, and the weight of waterlogged manuscript soon tore through its base. Evan stopped in the act of reaching up to an apple tree and looked down at the heap by his feet. He dropped the remains of the bag, wiped some paper off his shoe and walked back inside. He found a local number under the Pest Control section of the Yellow Pages.

'No, I'm sorry, but you've got to come now,' he said, quite calmly. 'Tomorrow's no good. I leave tomorrow.'

A man came in a little van and left bowls of poisoned nuts around the garden.

'You don't have a dog, do you, sir?' he asked.

'No,' said Evan. 'I live alone,' and he wrote the man a cheque.

Unable to do the professional thing by telephoning Jeremy, he pulled on his damp coat again. He locked the French windows and, with a banana in his pocket, Mrs Merluza's cooking brandy and the white chocolate buttons, he set out to follow Madeleine's example and take refuge in the thoughtless dark of a cinema. He too left her mother a note.

'Dear Mrs M,' he wrote. 'You've got rats. Big ones. Have had poison put in garden. No dogs. Back late. Evan.'

38

'Dawn, my little darling. What weather this afternoon! Come on in.' Having greeted her masseuse, Deirdre Chattock leaned against the Palace door and broke out in a thick cough. Dawn reached out a sure hand and pressed a point below Deirdre's left ear with her forefinger. The coughing stopped at once. Not even breathless, Deirdre exclaimed. 'I wish you'd teach me to do that. Old Merloozy just beats me till my back's blue.'

'You can't do it yourself unless you're completely relaxed,' Dawn told her. 'And you're hardly relaxed if you're coughing your lungs up.'

They made the slow ascent to Deirdre's apartment.

'I suppose I should get you to teach Gavin, in case of emergencies,' said Deirdre.

'If he got the wrong spot, though, he could kill you,' Dawn replied placidly. 'I saw him on *Faith Forum* in the rental shop window on my way up, by the way,' she went on.

'Isn't it exciting! He's almost finished. Do you mind if we watch the last bit, Petal, before we get down to business?'

'Fine by me.'

'Good.'

They walked through to the bedroom which was in darkness except for a television's spectral beam which lit up Deirdre's generous double bed. The two of them climbed on and sat side by side, leaning against the cushioned head-board. By normal light the latter was cerise with grey buttons.

In the past half hour, Mr Gavin Tree had run circles round a panel comprising the Bishop of Bath and Wells, the chairwoman of a morality watchdog group, the MP for Bournemouth West (Con) and a senior committee member of the Mother's Union. Not only had he led them to air the less palatable of their doctrines but he had utterly charmed the studio audience which, as Deirdre rejoined the pro-gramme, was being given the final air time to pose a few questions of its own.

'Do you believe in a female priesthood?' asked a forth-right man in plate-glass spectacles.

'Well, like the Holy Ghost, women priests are seen to be everywhere and are therefore undeniable,' answered Gavin and raised a laugh which he stilled by continuing. 'Yes, of course I do. It's daft in this instance to draw up biblical evidence and say that all the disciples and apostles were male; society has altered far too radically since then, praise be. Despite appearances, we are not, like poor Saint Paul, members of a patriarchal society under military rule. I think there is a place for women on an active level in the church, just as there will always be a place for women doc-tors, lawyers, roadsweepers and fisherpersons.' There was a quiet cheer. The camera cut briefly to the disgusted expression on the face of the Bishop of Bath and Wells and then to the presenter.

'And I'm afraid we've run out of time,' she said, 'though I'm sure that our studio audience will keep the Bishop busy for at least another hour. So thank you to Basil Amiss,

Conservative MP for Bournemouth West, to May Gerard of Parents in Moral Authority, to . . .'

Deirdre pressed a button on her remote control unit and the presenter continued in silence.

'Good old Gav,' she said. 'It was taped an hour or two ago. They daren't do these things live in case some bore in the audience tries to ruin things. He should be home soon. Of course, we'll be flooded with cards and little somethings tomorrow.'

Dawn was taking off her shoes and pop socks.

'Your hour has come, Mrs Chattock,' she said.

'Off we go, then,' said Deirdre. She stood and stripped down to a black bra and discreetly lacy, black panty-girdle. Humming to herself, she tossed a pillow on to the floor and lay down on her front, the pillow under her chin. Dawn turned on a bedside light then switched off the television. She walked through to the sitting room and pushed a cassette into the stereo system that was hidden by the sofa. Peggy Lee began to croon that she was feeling kind of lonesome and hadn't slept a wink. Deirdre gave a contented sigh and hummed along in a lower register. Dawn took a jar of yellowish cream from her bag and slapped three fingersful of it on to Deirdre's well-padded spine and some more onto her legs. It must have been cold, for the Bishop's mother said 'ooh' and chuckled. Then, arms folded in the Oriental fashion, with fingers straight, Dawn began to walk very slowly on her client. For the following ten minutes, as attention was paid in this way to her spine, legs, pelvis and shoulders, Deirdre kept up a throaty monologue along the lines of,

'Oh! Your feet are bloody cold dear why couldn't you

have oh Christ that's good it, hurts but oh oh God yes there that's it buggery hell yes ooh mmm you're incredible Miss Harper ow! steady on mmm yes and in between I drink ooh black coffee mmm yes love's a hand-me-down brew shit Jesus God that's oh oh oh. Thanks.' When Dawn finally stepped off and began to pull on her socks again, Deirdre sighed, 'You always stop too soon.'

'It's better that way. If you go on too long you get bruises. Here. Look.'

'What?' Deirdre sat up and readjusted her bra straps on her shoulders with a gesture young beneath her years.

'I made another batch of dope cakes.'

'Wonderful.'

'Twenty-five for that lot.' Dawn handed over a bag of home-made biscuits.

'My purse is on the desk, Petal. I meant to tell you,' Deirdre laughed. 'Well, perhaps I shouldn't. I'm normally so discreet.'

'Oh go on,' said Dawn, smirking as she returned from the desk, tucking two brown notes and a blue into the back pocket of her jeans. 'I'm quiet as the tomb.'

'Well I gave one to old Merloozy yesterday.'

'You never!'

'I did.' Deirdre laughed and nearly coughed again. 'I put a whole collection out on a plate. I always eat one anyway before she comes, because they help me go under, but she normally gets nothing stronger than ginger nuts.'

'What happened?'

'Bless me if she didn't go into a trance and chatter in Swahili or something. It was quite scary. Sick as a parrot when she woke up; I knew she'd never had the stuff before.'

'Poor old bat. Did she tell you what she saw?'

'No. Mouth tight as a drum. Pretended she'd just fainted but I could see she'd seen something and was nervous as hell about it, whatever it was.'

'Do it for me,' said Dawn after a moment's reflection.

'Do what?'

'Go into a trance. Contact someone.'

Deirdre stopped, half way into a Turkish silk dressing gown. 'Are you serious?' she asked.

'Course.'

'Is there someone you want to hear from, then? Yes, I think there must be,' she teased. 'Your face, my lady, is as a book.'

'Well?'

'Just this once. Because you've got rid of my bloody backache.'

'Fantastic!'

'Come on then.'

Deirdre walked into her sitting room and set about lighting candles.

'Do you want a dope cake?' Dawn asked her.

'Yes, but it's OK. I've still got one of the ones I offered Merloozy in this tin.' Munching, she took her usual seat and told Dawn to turn off the music and bedside light then come to the sofa. Dawn did as she was bidden.

'What now?' she asked. 'Do you need a name or—'

'Ssh!' Deirdre interrupted her. 'Just sit and listen. Sssh!' Slowly her breathing came under such control that Dawn would never have believed she was a smoker. Then it grew slower and slower. And slower still. Tense on the edge of the sofa, Dawn clenched her eyes tight and conjured up a silhouette against the glinting Bross. A bush of red hair. A gleam of muddy thigh. A narrow, childish leg.

'Sasha,' she thought. 'Sashasashasasha.' Deirdre's breathing stopped altogether. 'Christ!' thought Dawn. 'The old bird's heart's stopped.' She opened her eyes and was about to speak when there was a growl from the chair opposite. In the thin wash of light from the candle she could just see Deirdre's lips curled back like a dog's. Her teeth – not her own, Dawn had once seen the Dentufix in her desk – her teeth were just visible. They looked wet and sharp. Dawn could just hear the tobaccoey phlegm flapping in the older woman's throat. Another growl emerged, louder this time. 'Sasha?' Dawn whispered. 'Is that you, Sasha?' the growl lurched into a blood-chilling guttural bark and Deirdre flew forwards out of her chair, knocking out the candle, and tried to bite Dawn's ankles. Dawn swore brutally and, leaping to her feet, pushed her back hard with a foot. The growling continued, enraged. Dawn lost her nerve and ran to flick on the standard lamp. After much groping for the switch, she was successful and span around.

Deirdre was on all fours, her dressing gown hanging open on her unlikely underwear. Her eyes were turned up into her head so that only their blood-laced whites were showing. She was dribbling profusely. She looked far from friendly.

'Sasha?' tried Dawn once more and the beast in Deirdre took another lunge towards her.

Snatching her bag from the bed, Dawn ran from the flat, slamming the door. She ran as fast as her remarkably good legs would carry her, down the great stairs, past the portraits of previous Bishops and out of the front door which took two hands to lug it open. A light rain was falling. She put up her collapsible umbrella and hurried on down the avenue. At the gateway she ducked back into the shadows to watch the Bishop arrive home in a taxi.

39

Faith Forum had been an unmitigated success. It was as if the representatives of his opposition had been selected precisely for their qualities of narrow-mindedness and crass obstinacy. (This was more than likely, on reflection, since the powers that were would do anything for 'good' television, but *tant* piss as mother would say.) They had defeated themselves ignominiously and all he had had to do was charm. There had been several telephone calls to his dressing room from friends wanting to know how things had gone and with each description that he gave, he had felt his awkward public anger being tidied up, painted bright new colours and renamed Growth. He had gone for a celebratory sherry with an important friend in Lambeth then caught the fast train home, basking in the kind of glow he had not felt since his initial appointment. Things went from good to better as he walked to the taxi rank outside Barrowcester station. None less than Mrs Delaney-Siedentrop was lying in wait for him. His look of terror changed to one of bewildered relief as she wrang him warmly by the hand, introduced her husband St John, and congratulated him on his performance.

'So many of us have underestimated you, my lord,' she said and all but curtseyed.

Gavin gave the taxi driver an extra-large tip and strolled, heedless of the rain, to the front door of the Palace. All was dark within. He was on an economy drive to enable the funding of a crèche for working mothers in an empty flat over the garages and Mrs Chattock respected his whims. Having slung his document case and mackintosh on the stairs, he hurried down the passage to the chapel. There he flicked on the small light over the altar painting, a crude but charming, late fourteenth-century nativity with glory of angels. He knelt for a few minutes, saying thank you, then sat back in a seat, watching the painting and listening to his breathing until he knew he was calm.

There was a sudden gust of wind and the door blew open behind him with a bang. Gavin sighed. In his excitement, he must have forgotten to shut the front door. He was very happy sitting where he was, but the rain would be coming in and splashing the hall floor and making more work for poor Mrs Jackson. He observed with curiosity that, while it had been quite cold outside, this draught felt warm. He stood with a quick glance at the altar and walked back along the passage. The draught continued and seemed to become warmer as he neared the hall. He had obviously had one sherry too many with his friend in Lambeth. Hands in pockets, thinking that when he had shut the front door he might nip along to the kitchen to fix himself a little something from the fridge, he turned into the hall and came to a startled halt. He was not alone.

There was an extremely tall man waiting for him at the foot of the stairs. A Barrowcester blond. Perhaps he had the wrong night for the meditation class.

'Hello,' said Gavin. 'Can I help you in some way?' The man, who seemed familiar, said nothing. The warm draught had ceased but the temperature was definitely higher; pleasantly so. There was also a delicious smell which Gavin could not place; somewhere between rosemary and freshly cut lemons. 'Just let me find the . . . oh.' Gavin had reached out towards a light switch but found the power was dead. 'Oh dear,' he murmured. Then the door of the downstairs lavatory flew open. Its light was on, but seemed far stronger than usual. The man smiled kindly at Gavin then walked along the path made by the light in the dark hall. Gavin just had time to see that he wore no shoes on his spotless feet before the door slammed behind his visitor. Then a hot wind blew full in his face, shutting his eyes. There was a sound of rushing waters. When the wind dropped seconds later he found the words 'Borrowed time, I'm afraid' to the forefront of his mind as though they had just been spoken, or he were on the point of voicing them. The light had gone off in the lavatory but Gavin had just had an idea who his visitor was and so did not bother to check as he knew there would no longer be anyone there. He staggered to a hall chair and sat down. He wondered if he were going mad but he feared that what he had just seen and felt was beyond any malfunction of a puny brain. A distant murmur made him look up. Remembering his mother, he climbed the stairs to her rooms, cranefly legs straddling two steps at a time.

He knocked quietly on the door then again, more loudly. 'Hello?' he called and let himself in and switched on the light. At first he saw nothing but the mess where a candle had been knocked in a pool of wax to the carpet. He was on his way to look in her bedroom when another murmur made him turn. Her legs were poking out from the skirts of a long-legged armchair. He stepped round to the other side to find the rest of her. She was dressed only in her underwear – something he had not seen in years – and her dressing gown lay in a heap beside her. She was clutching a great bunch of unseasonal roses to her breast. The thorn of one had pricked her and there was a trickle of brilliant blood from her plump side. The buds were beginning to open, split seams revealing fleshy pink. The leaves were still wet with rain. He knelt down and touched her cheek. She was warm. He sniffed her breath for alcohol but smelled nothing. He lifted one eyelid and saw her eyeballs swerving wildly back and forth, apparently sightless.

'Can you hear me, Mam? It's Gavin, what's been going on?'

'Lovely,' she murmured. 'Lovely.' Her voice was slurred and content as if she were talking from the gaudy midst of a pleasant dream.

'Mam?'

'Lovely.'

He pushed the chair off her and had a difficult time trying to make her decent, for her panty-girdle had slipped and she was no longer a sylph. There was a telephone on her desk. He rang Dr Morton.

'Hello?' said a keen voice on the other end.

'Dr Morton?'

'Speaking.'

'Sorry to bother you so late. It's Gavin Tree.'

'Splendid programme earlier. Brenda and I watched it all.'

'Oh. Thank you. Actually, there's a bit of a problem with my mother.'

'Yes?'

'I think she may have had another stroke.'

'I'll be there in six minutes. Is she in bed?'

'No. She's on the carpet. She seems quite comfortable.'

'Don't move her, just keep her warm.'

'Fine.'

Dr Morton hung up with a professional grunt. Gavin turned back to his mother who was still murmuring lovely from time to time. He freed the mound of roses from her grasp and tossed them miserably into her bathroom wash basin, then he looked for something with which to keep her warm. Picking up her dressing gown he found it torn in strips.

'Mmm. Lovely,' sighed Mrs Chattock and yawned widely.

40

The old prewar cinema had been converted into two smaller ones. In one deserted auditorium Evan wept with an increasing lack of restraint through a re-release of *Mary Poppins*, then sat morosely through the late show of a strangely unerotic piece of soft porn in the more crowded other. He ate the banana during the first film and the white chocolate buttons and two chocolate sundaes during *Oriental Kittens*. The brandy bottle was drained and thrown furiously aside by the start of the 'It's a Jolly Holiday with Mary' sequence but the cinema had a small bar where he slipped out every twenty minutes or so for another double. By the time he lurched into the night his vision was a long way from twenty-twenty.

It had started to rain again, not hard but penetratingly. He had suede brogues on and they were blackened beyond recovery. The steaming streets, dangerously underlit in the name of conservation, were largely empty except for Barrowcester's disaffected youth whom Evan felt he was meeting for the first time. Outside the Gladstone, the town's principal hotel, he stood to applaud as an extremely smart black couple were helped out of their chauffeured Bentley. The doorman asked him to move on.

'Do you know who I am?' Evan asked him.

'Just move on, would you, sir? I don't want to be unpleasant.'

'I am an . . . an eminent angelologist.'

'And I'm a very busy doorman. Goodnight, sir.'

'Bastard.'

'Oi!' The doorman gestured to a policeman but Evan had already moved on.

He found a place rejoicing under the name of the Saucy Kipper where he lingered to eat a piece of tasteless battered dogfish and a bag of chips, most of which ended up on his coat-front. There was a sign above the counter. A kipper grinned and pointed a flipper at the words 'The chippy furthest from the sea'. Stumbling homewards along a back street behind the Gladstone, he passed a familiar limousine. He paused, chuckled back to where it was parked and, his face contorted with spite, dragged Mrs Merluza's latchkey hard along its glossy surfaces. The screeching of metal on metal disturbed him however and he staggered on, pausing only to piss into a prissily painted tub of flowers outside a front door near the Cathedral. In Dimity Street, he stopped to shout up at a lit upper-storey window.

' "For without are dogs and sorcerers and whoremongers and murderers and idolators and whatsoever loveth and maketh a lie!" '

The window flew up and a woman put her head out.

'Do you know what time it is?' she asked him curtly.

'Time for the whoremongers?' he suggested, slightly abashed. He recognized her as the hostess he had overheard saying that she just couldn't bear entertaining black Americans.

'You're drunk,' she snapped. 'Go home or I'll get my husband to call the police.'

She slammed her window down again and drew the curtains. Evan stared up for a moment then felt in his pocket for a pen. On the clean white paintwork of her Queen Anne porch he scribbled:

'Beware the dogs without! A well-wisher.'

He walked for what seemed like hours, round and round the hill, on to the Roman Bridge and down to the Bross. He even spent some time wandering in the cemetery and Gardens of Remembrance but a very large someone else was moving around in the darkness there, which scared him. By the time he let himself in, the sky had begun to turn from navy blue to grey. With the dawn and apprehension that he was both wet and bitterly cold, came the aching return of sobriety and a terrible wakefulness. He sat at his desk, opened his diary and wrote,

'The herbaceous borders of the Earthly Paradise are nothing but a genteel attempt to divert the attention of the uneasy from the gateway to Hell that is set, a brazen trap door, in their midst.'

Then he abandoned the attempt, peeled off his soaking clothes and went to lie like a corpse between the clean sheets which someone had kindly laid on the bed for him.

41

Mrs DelMonica raised a long, chocolate thigh from the oil-skinned water and rubbed the kneecap with a body brush.

'Sweet Jesus, I do not want today,' she whispered, chafing her heel with a pumice stone then sliding the leg back into the soothing waters before repeating the process on the other side. On waking in the bridal suite of the Gladstone, she had telephoned to the next room to wake Mr DelMonica then had called down to defer their breakfast for an hour while she bathed. Breakfast was something she took seriously; her dietician had pronounced it the only useful intake of the day. As she ran her bath, as she poured in Chanel No. 5, as she tossed a knob of cocoa butter with practised accuracy beneath the flow of the hot tap, as she pissed, weighed and sighed, Mrs DelMonica had offered a series of prayers to Saint Rita, reputed to be of great efficacy in the happy salvation of utterly hopeless causes.

'Holy Rita,' she now exclaimed, standing to rub her lathered self all over with a battery-powered massage mitt, 'you know I just adore you, but how can I be sure you're giving me anything in return?'

The bathroom was in that side of the hotel that faced across the roofs of Dean Row to the Close. The sunlight played on the stained-glass saints of the Cathedral's east window. It also played on the declining cheeks of Mrs

DelMonica's biscuit-coloured bottom. Mrs DelMonica patted herself dry.

'Rita. *Lady* Rita. If our baby's doing the right thing, give me a sign,' she begged. 'Right now,' she added, banging herself all over with a talc puff. A fine shower of the scented powder fell around her so that, when she finished the task and returned to her bedroom to choose a dress, she left the outline of two size sevens on the bathroom carpet. 'Rita,' she said, throwing on a little Givenchy frock because she had decided to make up her mind after breakfast had given her strength, 'Rita you're hopeless.'

In her sprawling kitchen in Dimity Street, the mother of the groom stirred two cupfuls of grated sweet potato into the bowl of a rumbling cake-mixer.

'Are you quite sure it says two cupfuls?' she asked, frowning as she wiped her juicy hands on her threadbare kaftan. Dawn was making chicken and sweetcorn patties, dextrously slapping them into shape with two small floured boards.

'Quite sure,' she replied in her peculiar monotone, 'but I'll check.' She rubbed the flour from her hands and picked up a new cookery book that was propped between a chicken carcass and a bunch of small green bananas, delivered at considerable expense from New Covent Garden that morning. 'Yes,' she confirmed, 'page seventy-eight, Trinidad Wedding Cake: two cupfuls grated sweet potato. There's an asterisk, though.'

'What's it say?'

' "Or more, to taste." You'd better bake it quick if you want to ice it.'

'What's the time, then?' Lydia asked, scraping the cake mixture into a carefully lined tin.

'Just past eight.'

'Damn! Dawn, can you be an angel and finish the rest for me? There's not much left to do. I've made the icing but it's not nearly cool yet.'

'D'you think it's going to set with all that molasses in it?'

'Oh God, I don't know. If it's still that consistency around eleven, you'd better knock up something else. What are the other icings they give there?'

Dawn stretched out languorously for the book once more and scanned the index. Her voice was quite uninfected by her employer's nerves.

'Well it says here . . .'

'Yes?'

'Wait for it, wait for it. Icings. Icings. Yeah. I quote. "Icing, Banana Cream. Icing, Jamaican Planter". That's what you've made. Then, "Icing, Pineapple Glacé, Icing, Royal Grenadan and Icing, Rum Butter".'

'What's in Royal Grenadan?'

' "Royal Grenadan – pee one-oh-five".' Dawn flicked to the one hundred and fifth page of *Caribbean Cuisine for You and Me* and stared hard at what she found. Lydia decided that she was being slow to vex her. 'It's a sort of syllabub,' she announced finally. 'Lots of lemon juice, not much sugar and a couple of tablespoons of sherry.'

'Not very Caribbean. OK. If this muck doesn't work, try that and if that doesn't work, just dust it with icing sugar and tie something pretty round the sides. It's revoltingly rich anyway.'

'Right you are, then,' Dawn mumbled, returning to her stack of patties. The telephone rang. Lydia wiped her hands on her kaftan again and answered.

'Hello,' she said, far too brusquely, then melted so audibly that Dawn grinned over her work. 'Oh, Fergus. What a lovely surprise. Look, I'm so sorry we couldn't have you and Emma round last . . . Oh. She did? Well it's sweet of you to say so. Maybe next week . . . Well, yes. It is rather hectic . . . Tell me quickly, then.' There was a longer pause as Fergus told her a story. 'No!' she exclaimed, then 'Oh poor . . .' and let the poor trail off into a moan of sympathy as he continued. 'Is she allowed visitors?' she asked when he had finished. 'Oh, I see . . . Dawn? Yes. She's here. Slaving away . . . Yes I'll tell her . . . Bye, Fergus love.' She hung up. 'That was Fergus,' she said.

'I gathered,' said Dawn.

'He says to tell you he's still expecting you for tea at five.'

'Right.'

'Awful news, though,' Lydia hurried on, unwilling to contemplate the thought that Fergus and Dawn were actually *friends*. 'Poor Mrs Chattock had another stroke last night. The Bishop found her when he got back from the television studios. She can't talk and they don't think there's much chance of her walking again.'

Dawn clicked her tongue in sympathy.

'Fancy,' she said. 'Poor old soul.'

'How many of those things are you making?' enquired Lydia, pointing at the patties and remembering that she was in the thick of a panic.

'Two each, then two pineapple ones each, half a stuffed

christophine each, a couple of fried plantains each and then rice salad. Oh, and there's the turkey too.'

'Lordy.'

'I thought West Indians ate goat.'

'Dawn *really*.' Lydia laughed and went to wake her husband.

Their room was in chaos. She had sat up half Friday night to finish her dress. She had held a secret hope that, too 'young' or no, Tobit might announce that he would give her one of his own to wear, but no offer had been forthcoming. The pink dummy, its dials adjusted so as to make it all too three-dimensional a record of her vital statistics, stood garbed in her handiwork. Clive had pronounced the dress 'charming' but he had no visual sense whatever and had been wanting her to come to bed. Tobit would praise her needlework, but condemn the garment as a 'bit hippyish' and she suspected he would be right. The carpet around it was littered with scraps of velvet and corduroy, swirls of thread, pins, lining and frayed interfacing. Since she had slipped out two hours ago, Clive had rolled over to invade as much bedspace as possible. His face was buried full in the pillows, arms and legs lying starfishwise. He had tried to wake and failed, for one hand lay on a handful of essays, scooped up from the pile he had been cursing over as she sewed last night. She switched on the bedside radio and turned up the volume slightly from its six a.m. level. Then she crawled around the carpet, wastepaper basket under one arm, kaftan riding high, to claw up the rags of material.

It was not meant to happen like this. Long ago – it seemed so very long ago – when Tobit had asked them up to London for the weekend and they had met his rather sweet flatmate and made certain discoveries involving sleeping arrangements, she had resigned herself to the idea that It would never happen at all. Still, she had a fertile imagination and she had decided that It, albeit a strictly hypothetical It, would consist of early summer flowers, frothy white frocks, several handpicked bridesmaids, a page boy or two, a long, silk-lined marquee in the Warden's garden at Tatham's. And lots of friends and ghastly relations in their best clothes, and proper invitations and the choir singing Mozart and maybe even a thirties jazz band in a corner of the garden. That was how, in the realm of Lydia's hypothesis, her son would make his symbolic departure from her life. Not like. Well. At least it was June and they would have early summer flowers.

Clive rolled on to her side of the bed, furling the duvet about him. Soon he would become overheated and get up in a foul mood. His temper had been untrustworthy all week, ever since they had had Tobit and Gloire to supper. When she had ticked off that dreadful American drunk outside the house last night, he had almost rounded on her. She stacked the essays he had marked in one heap and those awaiting his attention in another.

'Clive?'

'Mmh?'

'Clive, darling, it's half past eight. I told Emma you'd pick up the flowers at nine-fifteen.'

'Mmh. Lovely,' he mumbled, groping with a hairy hand for the back of his neck which, finding, he rubbed.

*

Mr DelMonica stared hard at the wilting *croissant*, foil-wrapped butter pats and miniature plastic pots of jam on the linen before him.

'And what,' he asked, 'is this?'

'Breakfast, sir,' said the waiter.

'Take it away, would you, before my wife sees it.'

'Sir?'

'Yes. She'd work up a rage and she's a Big Woman. What fruit do you have?'

'Fruit sir?'

'Yes. Bring us two plates, two knives and a large selection of all the fruit this historic dump can provide.'

'Sir.'

The waiter whisked away the apology for a breakfast and glided across the muffling pile. He returned in a few seconds to ask if Mr DelMonica would mind moving to the table in the alcove.

'Why the Hell?' asked Mr DelMonica, curiosity replacing the storm in his voice.

'Well you see, sir,' hissed the waiter, 'we don't want to upset the other residents. Strictly speaking, fruit other than grapefruit segments, isn't on the menu until lunchtime.'

'You don't say!' laughed Mr DelMonica, adding in a mutter, 'Sick country she's marrying into.' He moved however, and soon got down to the more serious business of slicing a pineapple and musing on the paragon that was his wife.

On finishing his economics studies at Yale, he had found a strong sleeping partner in one of his white fellow graduates and, with the latter's aid, had set up his inordinately successful firm importing Japanese technology to the West

Indies and West Indian rum to Japan. Josephine had walked, impeccably uniformed, up the aisle on one of his island-hopping flights and had arranged his blanket in so accommodating a manner that he had bought her a flat in a comfortable suburb of his native Kingston. Whenever their visits there coincided, and their mutual obsession ensured that this was more often than not, he would crawl over the mattress towards her and lay a fat pearl on her belly button. Before long they had made a necklace. By the time they had made a double rope, she was demanding a ring to match. She announced her intention to fly in the face of her fellow Martiniquaises and be the first of her family's women not to give birth out of wedlock.

A staunch believer in the dignity of labour, he had waited until their daughter, Gloire, could safely be left in the hands of an imported Scottish nanny, then made his wife the senior shareholder in a firm importing high French fashion to all parts of the Caribbean. Josephine's business sense was as keen as her piety and by now she had paid him back in full and made herself a discreet tycoon. Gloire, to whom they had never ceased to be grateful for bringing them together in such a substantial state of bliss, demanded rather more of life than hard cash. Fiercely independent, she had made a moderate success of her years at Vassar then had come to London to study medicine at a place she called Barts. All of which made the sudden announcement of her intention to marry a white, English dress designer all the more surprising.

'Hello,' said Clive.

'Mr Hart,' said Emma. 'You've come for the flowers.'

'Yes.'

'Let's go and see what I can find you. I told Lydia, you should have mentioned the other day that you'd be needing some. I could have brought them round and spared you the time.'

'Well actually at that stage I didn't know we were going to be doing flowers at all.'

'But you can't have a wedding without flowers,' she protested, picking up a basket and her secateurs from the porch. 'Even a little one.' The sun was warm above another sagging grey sky. Bees hummed dangerously beneath an apple tree. Tiny beads of sweat stood above Emma's unkissed lips and broke out beneath Clive's thick but receded hairline. 'Shame it isn't sunnier for it,' she went on, gathering some greenery.

'Well, you never know,' he replied.

'How about some of this greenhouse jasmine? It arranges so well and smells so good.'

'Lovely.'

'I don't know what they put in our water but Barrowers always seem to get flowers earlier and longer than anyone else. Now what else? Some lilac, of course, and I've loads of alchemilla.'

She was too young to be doing this, Clive thought. The long tweed skirt, the sensible gardening shoes, the way she kept her hair back with practical pins and kept to surname terms with every man she knew; none of these could disguise her neglected youth. She had come straight back from Durham or Edinburgh, he forgot which, to nurse her father through his last illness and had never seemed to want to move on. She lived in his old house with his old books and his old cats. The old smells of tobacco and sickness had long been expunged with pots of jasmine and bowls of dried flowers, but she wore his old gardening hat if the sun were out. The easy speed she attained on his old bicycle (the late Dean had always ridden his late wife's) and the brilliance of her occasional smile, however, betrayed her cruel lack of years. She seemed to be losing touch with all the spheres of reference for one of her age. When he had found her so unexpectedly dressed up the other day it had been in the elegance of some three decades ago.

'You're too young to be doing this.'

'What?' She was stretching up for some sprays of philadelphus.

'So kind of you to be doing this.'

'Nonsense. It's a special occasion.' She draped the philadelphus across a now full basket. 'It would be silly if Lydia spent a fortune in a florist's when these are going to waste here.'

'All the same . . . It's . . .' He took the basket from her. 'Oh. Thanks. I'll bring it straight back. I only wish we could invite you but, you see, Tobit doesn't want any fuss.'

'Of course he doesn't. Do give him my love, though.'

'No,' Clive thought. 'Anyone but him. Give it to me. Run into the streets and give it. Give it all out.'

'If he remembers me, that is,' she continued. 'Time stands so still here. It's quite a shock to have him grow up all of a sudden and she . . . I . . . Sorry, I can't remember her name.'

'Gloire.'

'Yes, Gloire. Lovely name. There are no coloured people here, so I think it's a good thing.' She licked the sweat off her lips with a little darting movement of her tongue and pushed a pin more firmly into her hair. 'So lovely.'

Clive was uncertain what to say next so he left and hurried to the Tatham's chantry. Twelfth-century, set amid cloisters of distinction, the interior of the little building had been wrecked by the agents of the Gothic Revival. The effect of sitting on the bottom of an unwashed fishtank was made doubly eerie by clamorous rumours that a School of Night among Tathamites held regular black masses in the place. The sunnier main chapel however was too large for a quiet wedding and, as Lydia had implied, the use of the chantry was a rare privilege worthy of abject gratitude.

With two Victorian columns and a quantity of Oasis, brought in the back of the car, Clive did his skilful utmost to make the chantry festive but only succeeded in elevating it from Satanic crypt to Los Angelic funeral parlour. He stood back, scowled and set about rearranging. A small scholar walked in who, on second glance, proved to be female.

'Sorry, sir,' she said. 'Is it all right if I have my piano practice?'

'Fine, er . . .' He remembered her name. 'Fine, Jermyn. Go ahead.'

'Thank you, sir.'

The diminutive creature, typically spidery and repressed, carefully took off her gown then clambered on to the piano stool and launched unexpectedly into a furious Scarlatti sonata. Clive wound flowers around a column and thought of the son he was not to lose and the daughter he was rather going to gain.

He had been surprised at the news of the impending marriage but not shocked as Lydia had been, just as he had been surprised but not shocked when Tobit had embarked on simultaneous careers of uranism and *haute couture*. The boy had always faintly bored him, however, and this he did find shocking. A child who shone could stir one's pride. A child who rebelled could be fought with. A child born crippled could be loved. A child born plain could be sent to expensive schools. But a child who bored one? The thought was appalling, the prospect of this day on which a father must show pride, love and interest in generous quantities, not less so.

Gloire. He must concentrate on Gloire. Her febrile charms and subsequent sly behaviour had captivated him. Were their lives differently placed, her warmth and intelligence might have held him in thrall. Were it not unutterably bourgeois, were it not perilously close to a demonstration of paternal interest, he would say that Tobit had managed to arouse his passionate envy.

After slicing off its skin with her knife, Josephine bore the last morsel of peach to her mouth on her fork. She patted her chin with the corner of a napkin then gently scraped Mr DelMonica's calf with a crocodile toe.

'What you say we skip the big Norman church and go back upstairs to change?' she said.

A stray drop of juice glistened on one of her plumper pearls.

'If it's a choice between some old building and my wife,' he replied, meeting her stare, 'I'll go settle up then see her in her room.'

42

Soon after noon, Madeleine slunk down from her bedroom where she had been lurking with old magazines all morning and with a portable television most of last night. Mum had left for work soon after breakfast so that she could drop in at the hospital to see a friend of hers who had just had a stroke. She had told Madeleine that Evan was out to lunch with Goody Goody Hamilton and leaving either tonight or first thing tomorrow morning. Last night she had also told her about his professional tragedy and it was this which had scared her away rather than any embarrassment over her loss of temper in the car. What did one say to someone whose worst nightmare had just come true? While writing her thesis she had shut each page in a drawer as she finished it in case she dropped a mug of coffee or spilled a glass of wine. Madeleine sympathized, therefore, but found the victim of such a crisis none the less unapproachable. At school she had choked a beautiful friendship by refusing to talk about a friend's bereavement. It was not that she was selfish, only that she was easily awed.

And yes she did feel a mite foolish after her little display yesterday. She could so easily have explained that he had misunderstood and that it was not an abortion she sought but professional reassurance as an unfit chainsmoker on the brink of maternity. Instead she had chosen to take umbrage at his 'typically male' attitude to the sanctity of the womb. It was only when she had been half way back to Barrowcester that she had replayed their exchange in her mind and found traces of his having said that he cared for her. She had singled out this portion and re-run it in her head several times both last night and this morning and had now dismissed it as being pseudo-paternal, protective posturing of a piece with his attitude towards whatever she was incubating.

She was ready to be on her way. The trouble was that there was nowhere to go but back to London and, as always after a few days of pretty, peaceful, loathsome Barrowcester, it required a good deal of auto-hypnosis to convince herself that Earls Court was a more desirable residence than her mother's. Lying in a pleasant stupor in the bath just now, she had brewed up a delightful scenario in which one of her colleagues at the Warburg, or some beneficent old Barrowcester trout telephoned to offer her the use of an isolated cottage near the sea for the duration of her pregnancy. She would recklessly give up her room in the flat in Earls Court, pack a case full of books, divert her magazine subscriptions and retire to the sea to knit baby clothes and write a book about eroticism, shamelessly cashing in on her recent ordeal. Sadly, most of her colleagues were as unlikely as she to own cottages by the sea, and the beneficence of old trouts in Barrowcester never stretched beyond their infernal 'little somethings' which conveyed so much and cost so little. Also she had never learned to knit. The book, however, was not a bad idea. There had already been two telephone calls from high priests of trash offering obscene sums for the exclusive rights to her story. She had turned these all down since her animosity towards Edmund was tempered with affectionate memories of a scandalous good time. A certain wily foresight, which she was quite content to have misread as high-minded restraint, told her that her notoriety, however bankable, would feed her longer if she invested it steadily and in small portions.

Perhaps she would remain in Barrowcester for a time and write the book here. She could pay her mother rent and possibly move into the granny flat to give the two of them a modicum of independence. The thought was thrilling in a way, because so dangerous. She might be a far cry from a Goody Goody Hamilton now, but what if she were still here in a year's time? Earls Court, while the respirational equivalent of thirty a day for her growing baby, was at least safer from her own point of view. So, she would do her packing (throw things into a holdall), take her mother out for lunch then catch an evening train back to London. She would be brave and return to a flat full of fading yuccas, curling Venice carnival posters and Georgene's motorbike gear. But first she meant to leave Evan a propitiatory note.

She pushed open the door to the granny flat. He had splashed himself with aftershave before keeping his appointment with Goody Goody Hamilton; its tang still hung on the air. She cast around in the mess for some paper and a pen and saw his paperwork – or what remained of it – on the desk by the garden window of the bedroom. She strolled over, with a frown at the savaged curtains, and took a seat. There was a pad of file paper in his briefcase. She pulled it out and started to write on the top sheet.

'Dear Evan,

'Mum has just told me about yesterday's horror. There's not a great deal one can say, but I exclaim in sympathy and . . .'

No. That was altogether too facetious. She tore off the first sheet and started afresh.

'Dear Evan,

'I'm so very sorry. I had been going to apologize for my ridiculous rudeness to you yesterday – you were only trying to help, I know – when Mum told me about your manuscript. Suddenly I realize that I must be the last thing on your mind. At least when someone dies, one can share their memories; with a "dead" book that no one else has read, you are so alone. I hope you managed to salvage something, and have no doubt that, with your brain, it will be more an irritation than a labour to rewrite the thing. I shall be in London most of the summer. Will leave you my numbers and address in hope that you'll get in touch when you're back there. It would be good to meet for a . . .'

Madeleine stopped writing as her eyes caught sight of her name written several times over in his shrunken, academic hand on a scrap of paper that seemed to serve as a bookmark in a small hardback exercise book. Naturally she had no hesitation in pulling the rubber band off the book, just to see if the inscriptions of her name continued all the way up. It was a diary of sorts. Her first, weak, noble impulse was to shut it at once and finish her message. Her second, stronger, base one was to flip back a few pages and see if her name were mentioned.

Not only was she mentioned by name, she was examined, eulogized even, at great length and the text was illustrated here and there with a clever cartoon of what she realized must be her in a dressing gown in a high wind. The cartoon was repeated over and over and was evidently a stereotype which he sought to perfect. The most recent one was marred by a pair of horns and a pointed tail.

For ten minutes the flat was utterly silent except for the hum of the fridge, Madeleine's occasional deep intakes of breath and the rustle when she turned a page forward or back. The silence was broken by her oath when the cigarette burning uninhaled in her hand singed her fingers. Then she stubbed it out, closed the diary and stuffed both her notes into her dressing gown pocket. She emptied the ashtray into the waste bin in the kitchenette then slipped upstairs to find some clothes.

43

'Clive?'

'Mmh?'

'I can't bear it.'

Lydia and Clive had arrived early, as she wanted to inspect his flower arrangements in the chantry and felt that if she stayed any longer in the house the temptation to change out of the frock she had made into an old one that she knew to be flattering, might have proved unendurable. They were now pacing anxiously in the entrance to the cloisters. A small black cloud bank was drifting across the sun.

'I just know Dawn's going to spill paint,' she said.

'What paint? What would she want with paint? She's cooking.'

'White paint. That revolting American drunk last night put grafitti on our porch. Didn't you see it when you left?'

'No,' said Clive. 'There's going to be another storm,' he went on.

'Shut up.'

'Don't be so bloody tense. In three hours it'll all be over.'

'Three hours can be a very long time.'

'Well what's the worst that could happen?' he asked as she tidied his hair with her comb.

'They might be shocked. They *will* be.'

'What at?'

'For pity's sake, Clive, they're West Indian. Oh, it's just that I feel so,' Lydia pulled off her gloves and stuffed them into her handbag, 'so very . . .'

'What?'

'*Will* you let me finish?'

'OK. OK. So very what?'

'Rich.'

'Rich?'

'Yes. Rich and comfortable and smug and, well, white.'

'If they could afford the flight to Europe, I scarcely think they'll have come from a shanty town.' Clive lit a cigarette and thought of Gloire washing pans in a river, wearing nothing but a long, wet, muslin shift.

'They've probably had to sell all their goats or something. Tobit didn't tell me what they do which is bound to mean that they don't do very much. He was being considerate in front of Gloire. Oh God. Why did it have to happen so fast?'

'They told you. It was convenient because the DelMonicas were coming over anyway.'

'Well I didn't believe that for a moment, did you?'

'If they're so broke, how come their daughter went to Vassar and is now living in London, buying dresses off Tobit and studying medicine at Barts?'

'Oh darling, she probably got a scholarship. She's a very, very bright girl.'

'Brighter than Tobit anyway.'

'Don't say that.'

'Quick. Smile. Geoff Dixon's coming.'

'Oh God.'

'Leave God alone and have a Valium.'

'Shut up.' Lydia threw a smile at the school chaplain as he crossed the quadrangle. 'Hello, Geoff,' she called out.

Geoff Dixon had sideburns and his hair lay slightly over the top of his dog collar. He had a pretty wife, was tone deaf, quoted Bob Dylan in his sermons and encouraged the boys to call him Geoff to his face. Behind his back they called him the Ark, as in went out with. According to Clive, he had recently applied to work at a youth crisis centre in Liverpool and been turned down. If only Tobit had been content to wait and do the thing in style, Lydia might have been able to secure the services of Mr Gavin Tree.

'Clive. Lydia. Great to see you,' said Geoff and shook them warmly by the hand. 'Groom stood you up has he?'

'No,' said Clive, 'they're arriving together from London.'

'Oh right. Great. Nothing like breaking the old rules.'

'We're keeping an eye out for Gloire's parents actually,' explained Lydia. 'It's their first time in England and they may be a bit confused.' Lydia glanced down and saw that Geoff had brown suede shoes on under his cassock.

'So she's French?' Geoff asked.

'Half Martiniquaise,' Clive told him.

'Ah. And am I right in thinking Tobit wants the King James version?'

'That's right,' said Lydia. 'Beds and boards.'

'And with my body I thee worship,' rejoined Clive, mournfully grinding his cigarette stub into the historic masonry.

'Clive's done lovely flowers,' said Lydia, willing the chaplain to go away.

'Fantastic,' said Geoff obediently. 'Must go and check them out.' He hushpuppied his way into the chantry.

A horn blared out in Scholar Street and Tobit's little black Alfa Romeo sped through the gateway and across the cobbles of the quadrangle. The porter ran out of his lodge to stare. The scholars watched less openly, from the battered armchairs and sofas they had dragged into the open air. Gloire sat on the back of her seat and swung her caramel legs over the side of the car. They were bare and had white silk slippers on the end of them. Fully aware of the sensation she was causing, she stalked around to the other side and opened Tobit's door for him. Her white dress clung almost indecently low before throwing out a skirt that flew out at every turn of her hips. Lydia saw the artfully slashed panel in the back and recognized her son's handiwork. Clive looked aghast at Tobit's impeccable morning coat and wished that he had resisted rather more firmly Lydia's suggestion that he wear 'just an old suit' so as to put the DelMonicas at ease.

'Gloire you look enchanting,' said Lydia, banging cheeks with her new daughter. 'That must be a Tobit Hart you've got on.'

'Smile, Dad,' said Tobit and shook Clive's hand. 'Is Geoff in there already?'

'Yes,' said Clive.

'We'll drift in and say hello, then, 'cause I want him to meet Gloire. Why are you waiting out here?'

'Well your mother thought that . . .'

'I was worried that Gloire's parents might have trouble finding their way,' continued Lydia, with a twinkling smile at Gloire.

'Thank you, Lydia,' said Gloire. 'That's really thoughtful of you,' and, one hand wound under the tails of Tobit's coat, she was led to the altar.

'She smells of vanilla,' Clive remarked.

'Have a Valium.'

'Yes, please.'

Even as they popped pills, they saw the DelMonicas walk gracefully arm in arm under the arch. He was not in a morning coat, but the well-creased charcoal of his suit made Clive feel less *prêt-à-porter* than off the peg and on to the floor. She had not only the porter, but the porter's best friend, a clutch of gaping tourists and a slavering black labrador in her wake.

'Chicken sweetcorn patties,' murmured Lydia. 'Green bananas. Stuffed christophine. Royal Grenadan bloody icing.'

'What are you saying?'

'Help me.'

'What did you say they do?' asked Josephine, buttoning her gloves as they swung off Scholar Street under the arch.

'He's an English teacher in this place.'

'It's a school or what?'

'It's a sort of university for difficult children, I think. She's the local success story.'

'She runs a strip joint?'

'She writes cookery books and runs some faggoty delicatessen; snails in brine, wild boar pâté, stale German bread that kind of thing. Books, too.'

'Oh good. I was worried I might have overdressed.'

'That's them.'

'Where? No. *Doudou, tu me moques.*'

'No. It is. There by the cloisters.'

'*Mais . . . C'est pas possible!*'

'I bet you.'

'Sweet Jesus, now I feel gross. You could have told me they were hippies.'

'Wait till you see the whites of their eyes, Mammee, then smile.'

44

'Did you *have* to wear the red dress, *cariño*?' Mercy asked as Madeleine and she crossed the High Street to Labels, the new wine bar where her daughter was taking her for lunch.

'Naturally,' said Madeleine. 'I wear my dresses in strict rotation. I came with six, six days ago so it's time for the red one.' Her mother sighed heavily. 'I know it doesn't suit me now that I'm pregnant . . .'

'Ssh!'

'Now that everyone knows I'm pregnant, but it goes well with my hair and it makes me feel proud to be me.' She held open the swing doors and Mercy walked in past her. 'Would you rather we spoke Spanish?'

'Much.'

So they spoke Spanish.

Labels was a converted cellar. There were stools around a central bar for customers who wanted only to drink and tables tucked into whitewashed, up-lit vaults for those who wished to eat. Mercy chose a table and her daughter fetched a menu then joined her there.

'If this were in London,' said Madeleine, 'it would be the kind of place where married businessmen took their personal assistants after hours, but as it's in Barrowcester, it's patronized by mothers and daughters who want somewhere "naicer" than a pub. Who else ever comes here?'

'Boys and girls from Tatham's who want to smoke in

comfort and drink decent coffee.' Mercy gestured towards the bar behind her daughter. Madeleine turned and saw that most of the stools were taken up by Tathamites, round shouldered in their effort to pass unnoticed, heads lost in smoke. A small boy standing by one of the stools was lighting up. Madeleine caught his eye and grinned. Confused, he smiled, waved his lit match at her and turned back to his companions.

'Who's that?' asked Mercy.

'My latest conquest,' said Madeleine, shifting back to face her. 'I taught him how to smoke and where babies and puppies come from.'

'*Madoña*,' she muttered. She had thought that if they spoke Spanish, people might mistake them for tourists but already several were staring with amused recognition. Then an attractive, trousered waitress in a white shirt and black tie came to take their order and murmured that the manager said they could have whatever bottle they liked free. Madeleine chose a Montrachet, Mercy's favourite, and Mercy felt pleasure where she had harboured shame.

She had spent the forty-eight hours since her extraordinary experience in Deirdre's flat on Thursday in a state of raw nerves. Convinced that, while receiving her revelation about her unorthodox 'marriage', she had revealed too much to Deirdre's eager ears, she had been to Evensong on Thursday and to early Communion, Evensong and a quick lunchtime prayer on Friday. On each visit she had begged Barrowcester's God to visit discretion upon her friend. She had emerged from each bout of prayer searching the faces she greeted for the one that would find it hard to meet her eye, the one that turned aside in embarrassment, but found

only warm good wishes and congratulations on the sur-
vival of her 'ordeal'. Convinced as she was that her exposure
was imminent, each friendly glance came as a nerve-
twisting stay of execution. The terrific storm which had
struck during Friday's Evensong had made her yet more
tense and she had been grateful for the business of the rats
and poor Professor Kirby's manuscript as a brief alternative crisis to occupy her hands if not her mind. She had
tidied his room and made him up a clean bed. Then she
had gone to bed early, pleading exhaustion, and lain awake
half the night plotting her own doom. The telephone had
rung during her breakfast this morning and the Bishop had
told her of Deirdre's stroke. She had rushed to her friend's
bedside with a vast bouquet and found her deprived of all
but one, scarcely incriminating, word.

'Lovely.' Deirdre wept on seeing her. 'Lovely lovely
lovely.'

Holding Deirdre's hand and listening to her repetitive
sighs, she had shed a tear for the efficacy of prayer and
made a silent vow to devote herself in recompense to her
stricken friend's every future need.

Now the only question that remained was whether
to leave Madeleine in ignorance. The details of her parent-
age could be said to concern any daughter. It might also
be claimed that, when her father and grandfather were one
and the same, every girl had a right to know. Quite aside
from the dues owed her daughter, however, the contents
of Mercy's unblocked memory were extremely difficult to
keep bottled up. The mother's first impulse had been
to rush home and tell Madeleine all. It would be difficult to
explain to her how she had made her discoveries without

being sidetracked into an argument on the ethics and safety of spiritualism. That her discoveries were truthful, she had no doubt. She had tried in vain to explain her experience as a species of vivid daydream; the few brief images and sensations had laid bare a route back into her memory and already, as with childhood photographs too often scrutinized, she could no longer distinguish recollection from subsequent vision. Also, finding that she was now the girl's sister had made Mercy protective of her daughter's welfare in a way she never was as plain mother. Now they were allies against Man the Beast.

The wine arrived. Madeleine tasted it, even though it was on the house, then she raised a glass to Mercy.

'*Salud, pesetas* and rather less of *amor*,' she proposed. They drank, then ordered rare steaks *au poivre*.

'Well,' Mercy said. 'What are you going to do?'

'I'm keeping it, I'm afraid.'

'Why afraid?'

'Well, you can't want to be a granny yet, and I'm sure you'd rather you became one through the usual channels.'

'I'm not so sure.' Even as she imagined Marge Delaney-Siedentrop reacting in horror, Mercy found herself experimenting with a little liberal delight. 'I'm so *pleased, cariño*.'

'Really?'

'Really. And after all, it's not as though it's a secret any more. I think people would be far more scandalized after all the newspapers and things if they found you walking around baby-less.'

'And if it takes after you and Edmund it'll look so distinguished.'

327

'You say the sweetest things.' Mercy bit on a piece of bread from the basket before them and pictured a cross between poor, waistless Madeleine and Jésus' gross mother. 'Will you go back to work right away?' she asked.

'Fed up with me, already, eh?'

'Not a bit of it. Don't be silly. I just wondered. I mean, you're welcome to stay here as long as you like, but I thought perhaps your professors would be expecting you back.'

'No. I thought I might take an extended leave of absence and find myself a seaside hovel where I could be at peace.'

'Impractical as ever.'

'Well what would you suggest?'

'I think you should hang on to your flat. It could be so hard to find another one.'

'And where would you stay when you came down for the sales if baby and I were hiding away in a squalid lean-to in East Anglia?'

'I wasn't thinking of that at all,' said Mercy and wondered why they were being so untruthful with each other. More than anything she would like Madeleine to stay on in Barrowcester, her home, to have the baby. She could live in the granny flat and even pay her mother rent if she was worried about independence. It would be so nice. 'Here's our lunch,' she said.

Lunch passed quickly. As they ate their steak and salad, drank their wine and chatted amiably enough about baby-care and ways of giving up smoking, Mercy felt an encroaching sadness at Madeleine's departure. There was none of the normal relief that she was about to be left in peace again. Her daughter had been different on this visit.

Of course she was physically as hopeless as ever, blowsy and graceless as her paternal grandmother, but there was a new strength about her – one might waver before calling it poise – and Mercy realized that this had evoked something approaching respect. She wanted Madeleine to stay on. She wanted them to become friends. She did not want to be left alone with the awfully crippled Deirdre as sole companion.

After a token fuss, Madeleine insisted on paying the bill. She produced a credit card. Mercy stared at the dangerous piece of plastic and wondered how long her daughter could have been so rash. She was just standing for her coat when Madeleine tugged her suddenly by the cuff and sat her down again.

'Mum, there's something I haven't told you. I was going to run away without telling you and suddenly I know that would have made me feel a silly bitch. Sit.'

'How much more can there be?' thought Mercy. 'What is it?' she asked. That was it. She had *known* that there was something being held back. That was what had made her sad; not the departure but the secrecy.

'Evan Kirby's in love with me.'

Mercy felt first a stab of envy, then shock that she did so.

'*Cariño*, I could have told you that days ago,' she bluffed. 'Haven't you seen the way he's been following you around with those hangdog eyes? Too pathetic.'

'He's not pathetic. He's a very interesting man.'

'He's old enough to be your father.'

Mercy heard herself and was sickened.

'He's asked me to go away with him.'

'Where to?'

'I dunno. Somewhere where we can be quiet and safe.'

'Absurd. You don't even know him.'

'I think I know him quite well. We've had several long conversations.'

'And you think that's enough?'

'It's a start.'

'So you are leaving your flat?'

Madeleine seemed nervous suddenly. She reached up for their coats and started to play with her red dress.

'I don't know. Maybe. It's too early to say. Look, Mum, I've got to go and it's time you were back in the shop.'

'I go back to the shop when I please. It's my shop.' Mercy stood.

'Well I've got to go anyway, I said I'd meet Evan to talk before he sets off.'

'Well thank you for my lunch.'

'Oh don't be all cold and superior with me. It's been so nice just talking. And you've put up with so much this week, I feel awful. Will you come and stay?'

'Where?'

'Wherever I end up.'

Mercy laughed. The girl was still a child. A fat, foolish child. She kissed her cheek.

'Little Trouble,' she said. 'We'll see,' and they walked back up into the sunshine.

Unlocking the door of Boniface Crafts once more, she watched as Madeleine walked away then broke into an alarming run for home. As a child, Madeleine had never run if she could possibly walk. Mercy wondered at this revolution in her.

'Excuse me?'

He was a tall, Barrowcester blond youth with an orange rucksack on his back.

'Yes?'

'You are Mrs Merluza, yes?'

'That's right. Mercy Merluza. How can I help you?'

He wore shorts and his long legs were tanned and glistened with fine blond hairs.

'My name is Oskar, Oskar Svensson, yes? And the lady in the tourist information office said that you let out rooms.'

'Indeed I do. For how many nights would you be wanting one?'

'Five. Maybe six? I am here to make drawings of the tombs.'

'Lovely, Mr Svensson. Well, if you come to my house at eight Tracer Lane at say six o'clock, I'll have my daughter's room ready for you.'

'You are most kind. The address again, please?'

'Eight Tracer Lane.'

She was pleased with his ice-blue eyes and the delicacy with which he noted the address in a small green diary and refrained from asking about the rent. She would charge him a little less than she had the Professor.

'Good. I shall see you there at six o'clock precisely,' he said.

'Lovely.'

He left the shop, setting the bell tinkling over the door, and left her alone with her overpriced knitwear and ugly local pottery. She peered into her mirror to check the lie of her hair then put the kettle on for tea.

45

Lunch went quite well, possibly because they had never met and would in all probability never do so again. Emma had not gone to a great deal of trouble; she believed it kinder to strangers not to. She had bought a couple of tins of a superior brand of *vichyssoise* at Hart's along with a selection of interesting English cheeses an American would be unlikely to know, some fresh granary bread and a big bunch of grapes. She had also opened a bottle of white wine that Clive Hart had brought to supper once and which she therefore assumed was a few grades above plonk.

She had dreaded that he would go on and on about Jeremy, since her cousin was the obvious friend in common, but he had kept surprisingly quiet on that subject. At first. She had tried to lead him out on his work. She had not actually read the book on Hell but she had glanced at it in the library and read several lengthy reviews so she had done enough homework to pose a few convincing questions. They had sat eating at the kitchen table, chatting about the Last Judgement, Dante, modern Satanism and so on. He then began to relax with the wine (and the aspirins he had asked her for) and it turned out that he had been a great fan of her father's sermons and writings. He complained that religious discourse and history were such private forms that he knew only of her father's personality from what he could glean from the humanity of his observations and the quirkier of his footnotes. Nobody had asked her about her father in a long while. He was such a local figure that most Barrowers accepted him dumbly as a cultural *donnée*, like the Virgin Birth. She was hesitant at first then, once she had perceived that his interest was genuine, she found herself painting a wry, loving picture of the old man. She spoke of his manner of working, of the obsessive hours he would spend poring over seed catalogues or tracing the genealogy of a rose he was about to plant. She described his love of sandcastles and his dangerous habit of riding his bicycle abreast of one's own instead of behind or in front, so as to continue a conversation.

By the time she was loading the coffee things on to a tray to take through to the study, where the sun was just arriving, she too had relaxed completely. Evan Kirby was attractive for his age, not unlike Gary Cooper in fact. She had seen in newspapers in the choir school common room how he had become ensnared by Madeleine Merluza and was even rumoured to be paying for her abortion. She thought this a pity. She remembered Madeleine as a fat, spiteful little girl. There was a slight awkwardness when she asked in passing what he was working at now and he said,

'Finished. It's all finished,' in an unexpectedly belligerent fashion and drained a full glass of wine, but soon they were in the study and he was happily on the hunt for Dyce-Hamilton memorabilia. Coffee cup in hand, he stooped to peer at the photographs. He asked a few questions about Emma's adoptive mother, then picked up the beach photograph that had made poor Crispin cry.

'Is that you?' he asked, taking a closer look.

'Yes,' she said a little shyly.

'You haven't changed much. God in heaven! Is that Jeremy behind you all, with the seaweed on his head?'

'That's right. He was showing off as usual.'

'He hasn't changed much either.'

'How was he when you saw him last?' she asked.

'Oh. Same as ever. Still happily married,' he said, replacing the photograph with care and taking a seat opposite her.

'He's not married. Not any more,' she assured him. 'Are you sure we're thinking of the same Jeremy?'

'Oh God. Pardon me. I mean . . .' He was suddenly covered in confusion. Wild thoughts shot through Emma's mind of secret espousals, a Chinese beauty hidden away in Kilburn, a lovely but crippled poetess in Chiswick.

'What's the matter?' she asked.

'Oh God. I wasn't meant to tell you. At least, he didn't say anything, but I assumed Barrowcester being Barrowcester, that he hadn't told you. And now I've added insult to injury. But I guess . . .'

'What?'

'He's not married, exactly, but he does live very happily with a vet called James.'

'Ah. The lodger.'

It was as if she had just opened a door and found a whole roomful of people in garish party hats who jeered in unison and blew party poopers at her.

'Is that what he told you?' Evan Kirby's voice was full of avuncular concern and she wished him gone.

'Well no, not in so many words.' She grinned and put on

334

her brightest tone. 'It was just my naive assumption. I think Jeremy must have supposed that I knew and that I was being terribly civilized and unprurient. Do you think that was why Jill . . . er?'

'Yes. I reckon it's as good a reason for divorce as any.'

'How is Jill? I've heard nothing of her for ages. She sent a Christmas card the year after she left him and then nothing.'

'I'm not sure. I think she might have moved back to Exeter.'

'Back to the university?'

'Yeah.'

And somehow Emma managed to sustain her half of a conversation that was rapidly steered back to the unshadowed paths of banality. She forced herself to offer him a second and a third cup of coffee and even to show him around her late father's garden before he left at about three. She washed up as soon as he was gone and even dried everything meticulously and put it away in the cupboards.

Then she noticed that the cats were nowhere to be seen. She could not remember them having put in an appearance for several hours. Rubbing some cream into her hands, she set out through the house to look for them. They were nowhere downstairs, neither in the basement nor the potting shed. Starting to panic slightly, she hurried up the stairs. She was just emerging from her bedroom, where they sometimes lay on the bed, when she heard voices and froze. Two voices, one male, one female, were coming from behind the spare room door. Their tone was mocking, accusatory.

'So I told her . . . It's no use, I said . . .'

'Absurd. Quite absurd. But of course she never listens. Pathetic creature, really.'

'And now this.'

'*Mon cher*, I mean, *really!*'

There was a burst of mocking laughter. Panting with fear, Emma thrust open the door. No one was there but the cats who looked up, angry at the interruption, from the foot of one of the beds. Emma slammed the door to again, shutting them in. She ran to her room and threw herself face down on her bed, soothing her burning face in cool cotton.

'This is how it begins,' she said out loud. Faintly, because she was a floor up, she heard the glassy strains of Dr Feltram's harpsichord.

46

Dawn hung up her pinny under Clive's and Lydia's expectant gaze. She picked up her bag and a bottle of champagne.

'I think that's everything done, then,' she said. 'Thanks ever so much for the champagne, Mr Hart.'

'Nonsense,' said Clive. 'You did a wonderful job. Oh, and thanks for the paintwork on the porch!'

'Don't forget the rest of the turkey,' said Lydia. 'You can make a lovely soup with what's left.'

'Actually, I'm not going straight home now. Is it OK if I leave it and pick it up tomorrow?' asked Dawn.

'Of course' and 'Fine' said both Harts at once.

'Thanks. I'll . . . er . . . be off then,' said Dawn, looking at them with an amused air.

'Bye,' they both said. They watched her walk out of the kitchen and through the side door on to the street. As the door closed, Clive slipped a hand towards Lydia's waist but touched her buttocks instead.

'Don't you *dare* touch me!' she flashed at him. Using her left hand because her rings would make it more painful, she slapped him hard on the jaw, dived into the utility room and locked the door. 'Ohh you . . . ! Ohh!' she exclaimed, near speechless with rage, and burst into loud sobs. With the tears flowing she was more relaxed than she had been all day.

'Lydia?' queried Clive, a hand nursing his tender jaw. 'Oh don't be so childish,' he continued, raising his voice. 'Lydia!'

'Go away,' she barked, her voice clogged with tears. 'Go and . . . Oh God. Go and *do some marking* or something.'

'Come out and talk properly. I can explain.'

'No.' She blew her nose and coughed. 'Go away,' she said with a little less enthusiasm.

'I didn't touch Gloire, I swear.'

'Then why did I meet her backing on to the landing like that, telling you to "lay off of her"? Mmh?'

'I tell you she's a little minx. We were just talking in there then she heard you coming and put on that absurd charade.'

'Huh!'

'She was pissed off because I'd turned her down the other night.'

'What?' Lydia opened wide the door. She looked a wreck, but she had been through a great deal in the past few hours.

'Well not precisely that,' he qualified, 'but all through that supper with her and Tobit, she was pawing my leg like a highly sexed demon.'

'So when you stood up and her . . .'

'And her wine spilled, it was because she was half knotted round my knees, that's what.'

She walked past him into the sitting room, letting this explanation hang unanswered for a good forty seconds so that when she finally said,

'Doesn't sound very likely,' in her I-am-about-to-let-bygones-be-bygones tone, he was inclined to agree with her.

'No,' he said, 'it doesn't, but neither does Tobit's marriage to a medical black nympho with right-wing, nay, fascist parents with a dubious export empire and shares in South Africa.' She chuckled a little at this, in a tired way, so he pressed home his advantage. 'How about a drink?' he said.

'Yes please. No more champagne, though. I've got breath like old flower water.'

'A real drink, then.'

'That sounds like a really bad idea. Yes please.'

Kicking off his shoes – he had already tossed off jacket and loosened tie when their guests left – he padded through to the dining room sideboard. When he returned with two gin and diet tonics she too had kicked off her shoes and had drawn her feet up beside her on the sofa. He set the drinks on the coffee table.

'Hang on,' he said. 'I'll get some ice.'

'Oh don't bother,' she said, not reaching for her glass.

'No problem,' he assured her, already on his way to the kitchen.

'Bless you,' she murmured and half-heartedly plumped out a silk cushion to her left.

The service had gone without a major hitch. No dresses had been torn, no more than the honourable, small hankyful of tears had been shed and most of the food had been eaten. To this extent, Clive and Lydia could call the wedding a success. Rarely, however, had a day been so fraught with embarrassments. The first was when Geoff Dixon, albeit tone deaf, had spontaneously launched into 'Lord of the Dance' before the blessing and, since he showed no sign of letting up, they had all been compelled to join in, with much smiling and a little rocking from side to side, as if to show that this was all part of the plan. Their appalling underestimation of the DelMonicas' income and *savoir vivre* was so apparent to all present that no mention was made of it until Mr DelMonica took one look at the West Indian buffet laid out on the sideboard and said, in his best I-May-Be-Black-But-I-Sho-Am-Faithful accent,

'Why, Miz Hart, I ain't seen a spread like this 'un since I wuz lil' and Mammee'd celebrate harvest home on the plantation!'

That was embarrassment number two, luckily covered up by uproarious laughter from both Josephine DelMonica and her new son-in-law and the discovery that the food, if insulting, was delicious. Embarrassment the third had been when Josephine DelMonica was describing the delights of Martinique and let slip that her namesake, Napoleon's empress, had come from there. Her tongue loosened by champagne, Lydia had taken this for a joke and, while not finding it immensely funny, had giggled a good deal, thinking to set her guests at ease. After that they lost count. Josephine had taken Lydia on one side and confided that Dawn was a witch and that, being acquainted with such things from childhood, she *knew*. Therefore Lydia could not help noticing her making surreptitious signs to ward off the evil eye whenever Dawn came to top up her glass. Mr DelMonica attacked Clive for daring to be 'nothing but an English teacher' when his wife was being so much more 'go-ahead', and later Gloire was seen by Lydia apparently being attacked by Clive in the bathroom. Then, drawing fire rather too heroically for the embarrassment over the icing on the Trinidad Wedding Cake, which had misbehaved into Josephine's ample cleavage because it had failed to set properly, Clive had declared how surprised they had been at the announcement of the day's marriage.

'And why's that?' asked Josephine, from beneath the ministrations of Lydia and a hot, wet flannel. 'Because we're black?'

'No. Heavens no!' laughed Clive, puce. 'Because . . . well . . . Tobit . . . er.' And dried up under Mr DelMonica's and Lydia's withering stares.

'You mean to tell me that my daughter, our only child, has just thrown herself away on a snowflake faggot?'

'It's OK, Dad,' hushed Gloire.

'You mean you *knew*?' gasped her mother.

'Well yes. It was obvious. But it isn't any more, huh?' said Gloire, chucking her brand new husband under the chin then chasing him, laughing, from the room.

Flapping her flannel for emphasis, Lydia then found herself launching into an argument about whether her son was less of a 'man' for having experimented with members of the same sex. The other parents joined in. It was only during a lull after about ten minutes, that somebody thought to ask,

'Where are the children?'

and it was discovered that the newly-weds had pecked Dawn on the cheek and slipped away unobserved, for their working honeymoon in London. This had the effect of a total deflation and, after a few minutes of standing around like a pair of displaced souls, the DelMonicas had shaken hands all round and fled too. The terrible afternoon was rounded off by the indignant doorstep announcement by

their chauffeur that the Bentley had been attacked overnight by some local vandal with a key ring.

Clive returned with two fistfuls of ice for their gins.
Lydia murmured her thanks. He flopped into an armchair
by the fireplace. She made one of their secret animal noises,
wrinkling her nose and patting the sofa beside her. He
sighed, stood and flopped at her side instead, resting his
head on her shoulder. She was too tired to hold him, so she
draped her arm along the back of the sofa and simply gave
his head a brief rub with her cheek.

'I'm glad it's over,' she said.

'Glad they've gone.'

'Well. They were very nice, very . . . but.' She took a sip
of gin. 'No they weren't. They were horrid. I mean, not
because they were black, of course, just because . . .'

'Well, yes. You can't like people *simply* because they're
not white and you feel sorry for other white people giving
them a hard time.'

'Quite. I hate lots of white people too.'

'Some of my worst enemies are white.'

'You're laughing at me!'

'Yes.'

'Toad,' she said, almost laughing only she was too tired.
'You're glad they've gone, too.'

'Yes.'

'Especially Tobit.'

'No? Why do you say that?'

'You're jealous of him and me, that's why.'

'Well . . .'

'You're like a spoilt little boy,' she said and started to
tickle him.

'No! Ow! Please, Lydia. No!' he begged.

She snatched his glass out of his hand, placing it beside hers on the coffee table, and attacked him with both hands, interspersing the tickles with the occasional sincere pinch.

47

'I thought we were driving somewhere nice for tea,' said Dawn as Fergus turned off the High Street and headed for the Roman Bridge and Friary Hill.

'We are,' he said, 'but Marge Delaney-Siedentrop's friend Polly McCreery was in the Garden of Remembrance this morning and she said the roses didn't look well.'

'I thought you were looking a bit perkier,' Dawn said. 'Any news from Brooklea?'

'Yes. I rang them last night. She's being a devil, of course. It didn't take long.'

'What's she doing? Apart from the obvious.'

'They weren't being very specific, but the nurse I spoke with sounded as if she was having great difficulty being civil.'

'When are you allowed to make your first visit, then?'

'I agreed to go tomorrow. They were going to make me wait longer, but I think they've decided that seeing me might calm her down a bit.'

'Fat chance of that.'

He parked the car and together they walked into the gardens. The crematorium was tucked off to one side of the car park. It tried to look like a chapel in the Welsh tradition, but the horribly visible red-brick chimney emerging from the shrubbery at its rear and the queues of hearses and families on the busier days, accentuated its industrial purpose. When he and Dawn had come, with a modest gathering, to see what was left of Roger consigned to its flames, they had had to wait while one family filed out and another filed in. They had seen the sudden column of off-white smoke as the first family's beloved was consumed.

They had barely turned right from a little avenue of cypresses and passed a Friary Hill type who was leaving with a bunch of blue, suspiciously well-fed flowers tucked hastily under one arm, when Dawn asked, with quiet excitement,

'Do you see what I see?' She pointed along the leafy alley in which they were walking to where Roger's roses had been planted. For the first time in their acquaintance, Fergus ran. Caught up in the spirit of the moment and remembering that there was her bottle of champagne chilling nicely in his fridge for when they got back, Dawn ran after him.

Someone had pulled up the hideous pink roses, roots and all. A handful of leaves had fallen into the neat holes that remained. Dawn caught up with him and stood at his side, staring. He took her hand and squeezed it; another first.

'Oh Harpy, I'm so glad!' he said. 'Is that wrong of me?'

'Don't be a wally,' she said, squeezing his hand back then letting it go because the difference in their heights made the posture a difficult one to maintain. 'Who do you think did it?'

'Someone very, very kind, with absolutely no taste,' he said then caught her eye and grinned. 'Harpy, you *didn't* . . . ?'

'Don't look at me,' she said. 'I flatter myself that some of your taste has rubbed off.' He laughed, turning to go and patting her on the back as she turned to walk beside him. 'The nursery's open on Sundays,' she said. 'You could go after breakfast and have something new in here by lunchtime.'

'Yes,' he said. 'Something snow white and very old-fashioned with thorns all over.'

'Be a devil and have some pink.'

'More pink?'

'Tasteful ones like that Thomas Hardy you've got at home.'

'Mme Hardy. But she's white. You're thinking of Zephirine Drouhin.'

'Whatever. Pink's more romantic.'

He laughed at her so she winded him with a flap of her hand.

'Sorry,' he said. 'But it's got to be white. Frau Karl Druschki perhaps or Alba Maxima.'

'Alba who?'

'Great white. Like the shark.'

48

Considering his infernal hangover, Emma Dyce-Hamilton had cheered Evan up slightly. The surprise of finding a pretty, young woman where he had expected a sadder, stuffier one buoyed him up. He had flirted a little and proved to himself that he was not going to lose control every time anyone asked him about work. The gaffe about her cousin's love life was rather awkward, but if he told Jeremy at once he was sure that oil could be poured on troubled maidenly waters and no harm done. The gardens he passed had an anthracite brightness after their recent soaking and he felt slightly drunk. The air was suddenly rent with a tooting horn and the young couple he had seen in Dimity Street the other night, rounded a nearby corner in their open-topped Alfa Romeo. In daylight he was almost as decorative as she. He was dressed for a wedding, his black girlfriend for a cabaret. She was throwing back her head and laughing as if she were high on something.

'Yeah,' she whooped. 'Fast fast fast!'

Evan stood to watch them disappear honking around another corner, caught himself smiling from ear to ear, then remembered his head and stopped.

As soon as he got in, he telephoned the agency and told Jeremy all. He started merely by telling him of lunch with Emma but the sane, non-Barrower sympathy on the other end of the line was such that the horror story of the manuscript came spilling out.

'Well the first thing you can do,' said Jeremy, when he had finished oh-my-Godding, 'is to sketch down a synopsis of how it would have been.'

'Why bother?'

'It looks as though we've got Queenie Dawson at the Beeb interested in buying *Visions of Hell* for a big documentary or even a little series. If we can show her there's going to be another, that would clinch it. Who knows, if you really couldn't face re-writing it all in book form, you could always cobble up a TV script out of what you can remember and the notes that are left.'

'There aren't any notes.'

'Liar.'

'Well . . .'

'God, Evan, you know you could do it standing on your head.'

'I can't stand on my head. Never could.'

'See? You're cheering up already. Now are you coming back to London?'

'I suppose so.'

'Or would you rather run away?'

'Run away.'

'Take the cottage, then.'

'Which?'

'Ours. Well, it's James's really but what's his is mine et cetera. Do you know Pembrokeshire?'

'No.'

'It's very *Tristan* like north Cornwall, only without the beaches and brats.'

'Fantastic. But don't you ever go there?'

'My dear boy, we've been every summer since we met and poor J's been there every summer since he was about eleven so we've more than had enough. We can't be bothered to let it as it's full of "family" stuff that we'd have to lock up and so on. Keys are with ... Have you got a pencil?'

'Yup,' said Evan, snatching one.

'Keys are with Mrs Rees in the post office. Her daughter can drive you up there and show you how to turn on the water and gas and so on. Now I'd better tell you about trains and things. You'll have to change at Haverfordwest which is always dreary but it's better than Welwyn Garden City. So take a book. Now ... '

Evan rang up the station next, to find out about train times. He could catch a Cardiff train in just under an hour. Packing would not take long, he thought sourly. He rang for a taxi to pick him up in thirty minutes. He tore off the page of Jeremy's directions then performed a quick sum to work out his board and lodging. In the kitchenette he wrote out a cheque to Mrs Merluza, adding a fiver for telephone calls and cooking brandy. Then he hurried around picking up his things. He was just slinging *Towards a New Mythology* on top of his quickly filled case when he caught sight of a hand just outside the French windows. It was not a normal hand, being caked with mud and having nails as long and thick as dog's claws. Still clutching the soap he had been about to wrap in a plastic bag, he hurried to open the window.

He found what must once have been a child, lying on its front with one arm thrown forward. It had a great mass of red hair matted up with twigs and leaves. The skin was so grimy that it took a few seconds to see that the child was naked. He slipped the soap into a jacket pocket, crouched and lifted the body a little by its shoulders. It had one of the bowls of poisoned nuts in its grasp. Half had been eaten but it – actually, now that he looked, it was a she – she was not quite dead. She let out a quiet moan as he tried to turn her over. He set her gently down again then raced for the telephone and began to dial nine nine nine. Then a devil in him slammed back the receiver.

What could he tell them? That there was an animal that might once have been a kid in his landlady's back garden and that he had just poisoned it? Not plausible, certainly, but true. His better nature was just reaching out for the phone again when he thought of the appalling backlash of publicity he might be bringing on to Madeleine. Then the doorbell rang. Evan opened the door a crack like an interrupted murderer, found it was the taxi driver and asked him to wait. Shutting the door he heard a clatter from the garden. He ran back through the granny flat to the French windows and came to a panting halt. She had gone. There was nothing but the poison bowl – now empty, and a little to one side – and a scooped-out trail where she had dragged herself through a flower bed. He checked everywhere, even looking over the fences on each side and checking the little alley at the end of the garden. Nothing. Petra Dixon had explained that the hill was full of tunnels and holes. He was startled by the doorbell, glanced at his watch and saw that he would have to rush for his train. Diary, suitcase and last banana were snatched and soon he was in the taxi.

As they drove down the street towards the Close, he saw

someone jumping up and down waving her arms. It was Madeleine. He tried to open the dividing window to ask the driver to stop but it was stiff and by the time he had, they had left her far behind. As the taxi sailed him past the Cathedral for the last time and began the descent down the hill to the station he remembered a girl in a pink dressing gown with a blue swallow on the pocket. Deeply disturbed he toyed once more with the idea of calling the police but the train was already waiting at the platform and it was all he could do to buy a ticket in time. He would come forward if there were anything in the papers.

49

Claire Telcott confronted Lilias in the middle of the day room.

'I think we had better go to our room and have a little lie-down, Mrs Gibson, don't you?' Her tone was icy and *It's a Wonderful Life* went unwatched for a minute as twelve pairs of rheumy eyes watched her frogmarch the new resident out of the room and up the stairs.

'I hate you,' Lilias said as they climbed in the sub-tropical heat.

'Now there's no need to talk like that,' said Claire Telcott.

'I hate you and I hate you and I hate you. You are a deeply evil person.'

'You're not so likeable yourself, dear,' the Matron hissed.

'I heard that,' quavered Lilias.

She had heard a lot of things since Fergus abandoned her. Lying in bed she had heard this evil Telcott woman plotting to poison them all. She had tried to warn her fellow prisoners.

'There aren't any minerals in this spa,' she told them, 'only cyanide and they're putting it in in tiny quantities so that the coroner won't know there's been foul play. We absorb it through our skin like plants.'

Nobody had paid her the least attention, however. She

suspected that their passivity was the result of a longer exposure to the 'treatment' than she had yet suffered.

There had been a quieter moment this afternoon, after they had drunk their vile, milky tea, so she had slipped off to pursue her private investigation. All her life, it seemed to Lilias, she had been deceived on a crucial matter. It was all her mother's fault. Her mother had been a tight-lipped, dark-humoured woman who used to put salt on slugs to watch them fry in the sun. For a practical joke she had taken Lilias from her potty and trained her to sit on the lavatory facing the door. All her life Lilias had harboured a sneaking suspicion that this was somehow wrong. She could see it in the eyes of prim women as they dabbed on fresh lipstick in the ladies' room at the Theatre Royal, and in the way people peered at her from the side of their faces as she emerged. They all faced the tank and she alone faced the door. For years she had kept her dark secret, snatching glances at bathroom catalogues in a vain search for the truth. Of course she could ask no one outright, although just lately she had been taking advantage of her seniority to be a little bolder. She had long given up any attempt at conforming and facing the tank herself; the firm instructions of one's childhood are far too hard to unlearn. She was left to face the door knowing in her heart that, used as they were to it, the other way round was perfectly comfortable for everyone else. Fergus had been potty trained by her interfering mother-in-law so even he was in on the conspiracy. The sole respite she had found had been after her husband's death when the spirit had moved her to leave her son with his grandmother and follow Saint Paul on a mission to the unconverted; the African bush offered a refreshing lack of organized sanitation.

'I don't care if you did hear it, frankly, Mrs Gibson,' Claire Telcott continued. 'I make no secret of the fact that you've been very difficult. I'm sure an impartial observer would agree with me.' She changed her tone, fancying that she saw a softening in the lie of Lilias' mouth. 'We so want you to be happy here. All it takes is a teensy bit of cooperation.'

They had finally reached the landing. Lilias was panting from the effort of the climb and her irritation at this insufferable woman's tone, and was beginning to agree that what she really needed was a little 'lie-down'. Then she saw the chance of a lifetime. Someone had just slipped into the landing lavatory and not closed the door behind them. If she rushed she would see. Quick as she could – she always kept a little speed in reserve so as to take her warders by surprise – she broke free of the matron's guiding grasp and staggered over to the lavatory door. Claire Telcott's cries confused her, however, and she found herself pulling the door to behind her and locking it.

'Mrs Gibson! Mrs Gibson!' the Matron called.

Lilias made no reply, enchanted by what she had found. There was a tall young man with a quantity of blond hair, and he was facing the tank. He was also fully dressed and had both hands firmly clutched around the pipe that led down the wall from the tank to basin. He did not seem at all perturbed to find her in there with him, but turned half round, smiled and beckoned her with his head. Eager for a full vindication of her cherished beliefs, she came forward and sat down behind him riding pillion as it were.

'Mrs Gibson? I insist you come out at once. It's no use waiting for me to go away. I've got a key so I can come in and get you out if you won't come quietly. I'll count to three. One.' The little room filled with a warm breeze and a delicious smell like new-baked bread and honey. 'Two.'

'Hold tight!' the man seemed to shout over the sound of rushing waters.

'We're off!' whooped Lilias and the wall before them started to melt in the brilliant sun.

'Three! Right. Ready or not, I'm coming in.'

There was a loud rattling as Claire Telcott thrust her key in from the other side and unlocked the door, but Lilias was beyond hearing.

50

It was already dark when Dawn walked back to Bross Gardens. She had broken her iron principle of never becoming drunk. She and Fergus had polished off her bottle of champagne in no time, listening to one after the other of his eclectic collection of old singles. Then he had disappeared to the kitchen and returned with a rack of toast, butter, smoked salmon, lemon juice, pepper mill and a bottle of Veuve Cliquot that he had been keeping in the fridge. They had wolfed the salmon and toast but it was not enough blotting paper for such a quantity of wine and, after a slightly fervent goodbye hug, she found herself home in record time. She wondered if perhaps she had been running or skipping unconsciously and hoped that someone she knew had seen her and been alarmed. Suppressing an impulse to jangle Mrs Parry's doorbell then hide, she let herself in and walked through the dark to the kitchen.

Hoping to ward off the acid stomach she feared she might be getting, she splashed some milk into a saucepan to make cocoa. She was looking for a teaspoon with which to prise open the tin when she heard scratching and saw a tiny, long-nailed hand at the bottom window of the garden door.

'Sasha!'

She almost shouted her daughter's name. It was hard to open the door properly as the body was so close. Whining with frustration, Dawn raced back through the cottage, out of the front door and round to the back by the side passage. Sasha – she knew it was her – was lying on her river-soaked side, clutching at her stomach. Dawn hesitated, then, seeing the child was not going to flee, stepped out of the shadow and dropped beside her.

'My baby,' she whispered. As she reached out and ran a hand across the muddy forehead a wild trembling went through her daughter's body and the light from the kitchen picked out the whites of the eyes as they twisted to look up at her. 'Christ,' said Dawn, 'it's you,' and sitting with her back against the door, gently drew Sasha over so that her shoulders were resting on her lap. The shuddering continued and the smell of river weed was joined with a pungent animal scent, a smell of pain, of death. Dawn could feel the sweat breaking out on the crusted skin in her embrace. Pulling her sleeve over her hand, she wiped some weed off Sasha's wet face. Sasha gave a wild jerk and clutched at her stomach again. 'Ssh,' Dawn soothed. 'Ssh, baby. Ssh.' With a soft, pained growl, the child twisted her head and bit hard on her mother's forearm. Dawn winced at the needle-sharp teeth but left her arm in their grip, continuing to stroke with her free hand. 'Ssh,' she said. 'Ssh.' There was another strong smell and she felt Sasha's urine soak her dress. 'Poor baby,' she said. 'Sashasashasasha.' She rocked the clenching child. There was a last spasm and the biting stopped. After the growling and the hard, agonized pants, the final outlet of breath was quite, quite human.

Now Dawn could cry. Curled in a corner, lit but safe from sleeping, neighbourly eyes, she gave herself up to grief. She rocked. She sighed. She was torn by spasms of voiceless sobbing and her drenched face glinted in the kitchen light.

How long she stayed there she was unsure; an hour, possibly two. Occasionally she would pause and look up, distracted by the sudden whistle of some night flier over the Bross, then her gaze would drop down to her own, childish face which stared sightlessly up from her lap and she would slide once again into her important sorrow.

When there were no tears left, she laid Sasha to one side, unhooked her spade from the side wall, turned out the kitchen light to give her privacy and went to dig in darkness. She dug the grave near the river, where the soil was softest, but not so near that it might be reached by the waters in winter. She dug in a flower bed so that there would be no trace of disturbed earth. She wrecked her only good shoes in the mud and grazed her legs. Her dress would be filthy. She continued in numb endeavour. By the time she was up to her waist, her body was streaming sweat which the breeze chilled on her skin although she was boiling within. Her palms felt raw. There was a faint pallor in the sky; sunrise was not far off. She carried Sasha into the pit aware, after a last embrace, that her skin now carried the musky scent of her child. She began to shovel soil quickly then stopped, dropping the spade to one side and fetched the black candles from the kitchen. These she buried too. Crazed with exhaustion to the point where she did not care if all the Mrs Parrys in the world were watching her, she stripped off her dress and hurled it with all her might into the darkly shining Bross. The shoes she tossed one two after it. Then she trailed the spade back to its place on the wall. The dew-soaked grass felt good on her hot feet. Upstairs she bathed rapidly, so tired that she was unable to tell whether the water was scalding or icy, then fell into bed and the sleep of the just.

51

The late-morning sunlight was broken up by the countless little white and green glass lozenges that made up the windows of the Lady chapel, and chequered the heads and shoulders of those assembled much as if they had been gathered on a forest floor. As they rose from the last prayer for the soul of their dead sister, the little portable organ stationed near the door played an introduction and they launched somewhat gingerly into 'God Moves in a Mysterious Way' aided by the Scottish Masons who had politely downed tools in the Patron's chapel and come to listen.

'He plants his footsteps in the sea/And rides upon the storm.

'Deep in unfathomable mines/Of never-failing skill . . .'

Although Lilias Gibson had no relatives at hand beyond her son and was known only by repute to his neighbours, Lydia was happy to see that there was a much better turn-out than poor Roger Drinkwater's funeral had occasioned. She was also happy to see that her cleaning woman and Fergus were not so very close that Dawn could leave her sickbed for his mother's funeral. She was also glad that she had come early enough to do a little extra zealous 'holy dusting'. There were a lot of people here to whom she had never spoken and several, presumably clients of Fergus, whom she had never seen. She sang along in her thin, sharp voice, found her eyes filled with a few tears and was glad.

'Ye fearful saints, fresh courage take:/The clouds ye so much dread . . .'

The six bearers carried out the tiny coffin with Fergus walking a few paces behind them. The coffin was a most peculiar shape. It had eight sides, as usual, and was of a suitably diminished length for a little old woman, but seemed unnecessarily deep. Grotesquely so, almost. Perhaps this was a new fashion; it would be like Fergus to be style-conscious, even in grief.

Lydia arranged her face into what felt like a sympathetic glow in case Fergus looked to one side and saw her, but his eyes kept firmly ahead. She liked to think he would be happier now. They all knew it had been a merciful release for son as much as mother. When Dawn was up and about again she would sit her down for a long elevenses and ask how he was coping.

'Are big with mercy, and shall break/In blessings on your head.'

As she started to drift out with the little crowd she saw Mrs Merluza pushing poor Mrs Chattock in her wheelchair. If possible, the Bishop's mother looked more unworldly than ever; perhaps, thought Lydia, she was on some kind of painkiller.

'Hello,' she said.

'Hello,' said Mercy. 'Lovely service, wasn't it? So peaceful, I thought.'

'Yes. Lovely,' said Lydia and bent down to greet Mrs Chattock. 'Morning,' she said loudly. 'I think it's marvellous the way you're up and about so quickly!'

'Lovely,' said Mrs Chattock sleepily, looking first to one side then the other. 'Lovely.'

Lydia sighed as she stood upright once more and caught Mercy Merluza's eye. Mercy shook her head sadly.

'So frustrating,' she said quietly then mouthed the words 'Borrowed time' and shook her head again. 'I say . . .' she went on.

'What?'

'Did you notice something a little . . . well . . . odd about Lilias Gibson's . . . er?'

'Well yes. I did rather. Do you have any idea why . . . ?'

'Well I know Claire Telcott vaguely,' said Mercy eagerly. 'You know, she's the Matron up at Brooklea, where poor Mrs Gibson had just been sent to rest herself.'

'Yes.'

'Well I met her in the town this morning, looking in the window of Daniella's, and she said that they'd had a terrible time.'

'How do you mean?' Lydia stood on one side to let some more people pass, and Mercy wheeled Mrs Chattock out of the way too.

'Apparently she had some kind of fit when her, you know, her attack started.'

'How awful!'

'Yes and it was in . . . in the Little Girl's Room and when they finally got in there to rescue her, there was water everywhere – coming under the door, even, Claire said – and she had actually tugged the pipe off the wall and out of the bottom of the tank. There was a hole in the masonry. Right through to the sunshine!'

'No!'

'Yes. And of course that's why the, you know, why it was such an odd shape.'

'Sorry,' Lydia said. 'I don't quite see why.'

'Well, they couldn't get her hands off the pipe,' Mercy enthused. 'They had to get a mason to trim it as best as he could and then leave a great piece of it in her clutches.'

'Lovely,' said Mrs Chattock suddenly, then much more loudly, '*Lovely!*'

'Oh dear,' said Mrs Merluza. 'I think she wants a cigarette. I must get her outside quickly or she'll start to cough. I have to put them in my mouth to light them for her; makes me feel quite sick but what else can one do?'

Alone once more, Lydia walked slowly along the outside of the quire. Through some of the arches she could see a mountainous flower arrangement hung with white toy birds where Saint Boniface of Barrow had his makeshift habitation. Mrs Merluza and the wheelchair receded into the milling throng of tourists. The Scottish Masons, who had been so tactfully unemployed during the service, returned to their noisy work in the Patron's chapel. Lydia paused in the south transept then decided that, rather than leave by the Glurry as usual, she would walk out along the great nave and through the west end like everybody else. She passed Mrs Moore and Sam the verger carrying a long bench between them and said good morning. She stopped to smile at a crowd of enchanting black children who were being guided round by Canon Wedlake and several of whom beamed back at her instead of attending to him. She had a brief chat with Emma Dyce-Hamilton, who was over to talk to the Dean about arrangements for the choir school's confirmation service. Emma did not look at all well. They did say she was a little absent-minded. The poor, neglected thing had forgotten to brush her hair. Then

Canon de Lisle's voice came over the loudspeaker system to remind the tourists that this was a house of God and to ask them to join him in a brief prayer. Lydia hurried out. She was no good at praying standing up. Besides, having in her small secret way saved the Cathedral's reputation, she felt she could grant herself a few days' special dispensation.

52

Dawn was in the open air for the first time in four days. The morning after Sasha's death she had been woken by the telephone. Presumably this was Fergus ringing to ask her to come to admire his new roses. She did not answer it and she lay motionless when it rang again in the afternoon. She lay in bed all day, venturing out only to use the bathroom and to make cups of tea. She did not get up on Monday either, but lay there checking off a missed work appointment in her head at each neglected sounding of the telephone bell. On Tuesday she rang Mrs Merluza and Fergus's answering machine to explain that she had been forced to rush to the aid of a sick aunt. For Lydia Hart she had summoned up a throaty choke and muttered about highly infectious gastric flu. With a certain irony she decided that the aunt was the same one she had been meant to be visiting during her pregnancy; 'Auntie June in Leeds'. She was not prostrate with sorrow all this time; she simply felt the need to be alone, undressed, to think things through.

She had lain staring at the bedroom ceiling on the first morning and perceived, with the clarity of one not given to self analysis, that she was utterly at peace. As a child she had played a game where a friend pressed hard on the top of her head for the count of thirty then released her, so inducing the sensation that her skull weighed nothing and that her neck was growing as long as a swan's. The feeling now was like that. She felt different, new, because something had stopped. It was now that she could say to herself,

'I had a daughter, but now she is dead', that she could see how much the worry of Sasha's welfare and whereabouts had been pressing in on her thoughts. And for how long. Sasha was dead but Dawn had done her grieving. Her daughter had quite clearly been in no state to take a place in Barrowcester society and trying to keep her presence a secret would have proved a crippling strain. Sasha had been more an idea for her than a person and it was difficult to grieve long over so unknown and unknowable a daughter. Dawn was left with an obligation to live in the cottage and to guard its garden from curious shovels until her dying day. She also found herself tending the small but long-rooted satisfaction of having been recognized as a mother, if only on a brief, bestial level.

This morning she had telephoned Fergus from her bed to say that she was back and to ask about the roses and he had told her that in her absence his mother had died.

'You missed the funeral.'

'I'm sorry, Fergus.' Rare for her, she felt a twinge of remorse. Mrs Gibson had been in her wild way curiously likeable. 'Was it bad?'

'No. Not really. She had a massive coronary – very quick – and the woman at Brooklea handled everything for me.'

'She hadn't been there long.'

'No. I think they felt they ought to deal with the funeral directors and everything for me to earn the fat profit they'll have made. I'd paid a non-returnable month's rent.'

'Had she started playing up?'

'Well they were very discreet but I think she might have. She . . .' He broke off to laugh.

'What's so funny?'

'She was vandalizing a loo when she went.'

'Good for her.'

'How's your aunt?'

'Auntie June? Oh fine. Faking as usual, I think, but she looked pretty ropey. I've got a neighbour of hers to keep an eye on her.'

'Oh, Harpy, I'd love to see you. Are you busy this morning?'

'Well I'm meant to be doing for Lydia Hart but I haven't let her know I'm back yet. She thinks I've got gastric flu.'

'So I gather. Why didn't you tell her the truth?'

'I felt like lying.'

'Be a devil and skip her.'

'See you in an hour.'

As she hung up, her eye fell on the copy of *Visions of Hell* that lay on her bedside table and she remembered her resolution of the night before. When she had dressed, she opened the kitchen drawer and took out the thin, old book Evan Kirby had let her borrow, and a piece of paper.

'Dear Mr Kirby,' she wrote. 'I return the book you lent me. It was very trusting of you and I want to thank you because I got the thing I wanted and no longer need the book. I know you thought I was after a man or money or something but you were wrong. It was a little red-haired girl; my daughter. I can only write this because you aren't from here. I used the fifth incantation (page 9). Yours sincerely, Dawn Harper.' Then she wrapped book and letter

in brown paper, ready for posting. She would steal the
address off Old Merloozy when she went there to clean
tomorrow or, failing that, post it to his publishers for
forwarding.

Dawn had climbed half way up the High Street when
she noticed a small commotion coming her way. At first all
she saw were several children rushing headlong down the
hill cheering and being pursued by a couple of barking
dogs, then she saw that they were chasing a thin stream of
water. (Drains were scarce on the hill, the slopes rendering
them largely unnecessary, or so some tight-pursed counsel-
lors must once have thought. When it rained heavily the
lower parts of town, like Bross Gardens, were awash.) The
children hurtled past her, chasing the water and chased by
the dogs. Dawn continued upwards, noticing with some
amusement the way in which shoppers were pausing on the
pavement to watch the dusty flood as intently as if it had
been a bicycle rally. She slipped into a cake shop – not
Hart's because she disliked adding to Lydia's considerable
wealth – and bought some doughnuts to share with Fergus.
When she emerged she found that people were heading
towards the Close. She had to walk the same way before
turning off. There was a curiously excited atmosphere.
People were laughing and craning their necks. There
seemed to be dogs everywhere – none of them on leads and
all of them in a near-frenzy. Incurably inquisitive, she
decided to approach Tracer Lane by Tower Place and the
Close and so catch a glimpse of whatever was causing all
the fuss.

Dawn only ever entered the Close to take the short cut
to the Bishop's Palace, and she would not be going *there*

again. In her Christian phase she used to come every day. She looked over the heads at the birds wheeling around the sunlit towers and wondered whether she might not slip into Evensong tonight or tomorrow maybe; for old times' sake. She pushed to the other side of the pavement and saw that there was even more water here. It was running fast and lay so deep all over the road that the gutters could not drain it all away. There was a woman with a little girl on her shoulders and the girl and Dawn both gasped with surprise at the same time.

The great lime tree, centuries old, that stood yards from the west end, had sunk. The ground seemed to have melted beneath it and the whole trunk had been swallowed. The lowest branches now rested on the grass. There were leaves and twigs scattered everywhere. Four or so policemen were trying in vain to put up a rope to keep the crowds away. Several children and one or two youths who had forgotten to be mature had slipped easily past them and were climbing among the foliage and rudely displaced birds' nests. One girl who could not have been more than nine had reached the topmost branch, which at dawn had been up near the Cathedral roof, and was excitedly waving what looked like a pair of knickers. The trunk had evidently interrupted the course of one of the underground streams for the water Dawn had seen on the way was gushing up from beneath the incongruous mass of earth-bound boughs. The water was brown with clay but the sun was hot and it looked so inviting that Dawn took her shoes in her hands and jumped into it to paddle. All around her people were doing the same and the ubiquitous dogs were running riot, splashing innocent passers-by and pawing awestruck, mud-dabbling infants. A policeman had taken out an electric loudhailer and was trying to drive people back with threats of further subsidence but his words were lost in the holiday din.

'Harpy! What the hell are you doing?'

Dawn turned slowly to scan the crowd. She had moved to where the water was deeper and was peacefully rubbing one bare foot against the other and splashing the insides of her calves. She saw Fergus, who was staring at her from the safety of the pavement a few yards away. Dreamily she beckoned him with the hand that was holding her shoes.

'Come,' she called and smiled.

Over pre-Evensong tea and banana loaf later that day, Marge Delaney-Siedentrop told Mercy Merluza that she and her husband had seen the newly motherless bachelor sharing a bag of doughnuts with his and her cleaning lady.

'Both of them up to their knees in that filthy water,' she said. 'He's quite clearly taking the sad loss of his mother very hard, poor man. Of course, St John and I just happened to be passing.'

53

Evan was sitting in the sunshine working. It had not rained for a fortnight. According to Mrs Rees, the postmistress, this would shortly be recognized as a drought and they would be forbidden to wash cars or water gardens. Every morning, after his coffee and the first cigarette, he took a shower to wake himself then dragged the little kitchen table out on to the grass to start work. The cottage was at the end of half a mile of dirt track and there were fifteen good strides between front door and cliff-top. Being a holiday house, it had no real garden and the salt would have discouraged any but the hardiest plants, but there were tough old lavender and rosemary bushes in heavily fertilized soil under all the landward windows. In the warm evenings, they sat with all the windows and doors open and the air was full, now of sea and peppery gorse, now of sun-baked herb. The cottage was whitewashed on both sides of its thirty-inch walls. The old broad slates had been lovingly reset and the fireplaces in kitchen and bedroom perhaps a little too lovingly reopened. A bathroom had been cleverly tucked into an ex-coal bunker. Hot water and, when necessary, heating was provided by an Aga so that the picturesque old bread oven could be filled with books and covered with cushions to make a kind of snug. A ladder on one side of the kitchen/living room led to a sky-lit hayloft. Madeleine had insisted on sleeping on this

as soon as she saw it so Evan was left with the more ortho-
paedic comforts of the main bed next door.

She was a few yards away from the table now, slouching
in a deck chair. She was working on the first baby bootee,
which she had unpicked once a day for the last week. She
had sworn on emerging from the bathroom two hours ago
that she was swelling in the girth but Evan could still see
nothing.

A coastal path ran from one end of the twisting Pembrokeshire seaboard to the other and seemed to be very
popular with bearded hikers and women like nuns in mufti,
fat crosses bouncing unabashed on their energetic breasts.
Officially it ran straight through the point where Evan
always pulled the table and on through where Madeleine
liked to set up her deck chair. The two of them seemed to
exude such a scent of virtuous toil, however, that every
walker turned off into the field about a hundred yards away
and took a long cut around the back of the cottage so as to
leave them in peace. Mrs Penfarren had intimated to Evan
yesterday that the villagers knew who Madeleine was and
were 'very proud'. He had passed this news on and she still
chuckled to herself about it at intervals.

'Innocent Victim of Papist Beast Clutched to Bosom of
Chapel-goers', she had mocked.

He glanced across at her briefly as she frowned at her
needles. He hoped she was happy. She seemed so. At least,
she seemed as happy as any chain-smoker might who had
forced herself to give up. When she made this rash but noble
decision as she was finishing her last packet on Haverfordwest station, Evan had offered to give up too to keep her
company, but she had said that the least he could do was to

keep going and to blow a bit of smoke around so as to give her a nostalgic sniff from time to time. His surprise at her sudden appearance on his train out of Barrowcester had seemed to be slightly less than hers at finding herself on it.

'Oh God. I feel such a fool,' she had panted, pink, sweat gleaming on her nose and cheeks after her rush.

'Why? It's . . . It's lovely to see you. I was sorry not to have a chance to say goodbye.'

'Where are you going?'

'St Merrots.'

'Where's that?'

'Pembrokeshire. I've been lent a cottage on the cliffs for as long as I like. Where are *you* going?'

'Well . . . Oh *hell*.' She slung down her bag. 'Thought you were going to London.' She lit a cigarette. 'Well, look Evan. Can I come too?'

'Why ever not?' he had started but she had gabbled on.

'It's just that . . . Oh I dunno. Don't worry. I'm not eloping with you or anything but I'd like to go somewhere peaceful to have the baby. Anywhere but smelly old London or the Earthly Paradise.'

'You're going to have it?'

'Of *course* I am. I was going to tell you yesterday but then I lost my temper and then . . . Mum told me about your manuscript. I started to write you a letter but I threw it away. You probably want to escape to peace and solitude. We'll just chat a bit and I'll get out at the next stop.'

'Don't be silly.'

'I have been silly.'

'Well be silly some more. Shall I go to the bar and get something to celebrate with?'

'No,' she said. 'Yes.'

'Gin and tonic?'

'I'd rather have a Newcastle Brown. Or maybe I should be drinking Guinness now. Oh bugger. Evan, do I want to be a mother?'

'Yes.'

'Any chance of a pork pie?'

Either she had read the diary or she was extremely intuitive. In the past weeks, as they had made tentative excursions into the village, as they had hollowed out a shamelessly comfortable routine for themselves, she had seemed fully aware of his feelings and of the slightly unresolved nature of their impromptu ménage. She did not discuss but she patted him on the shoulder from time to time or kissed him on the top of his head while he was working. Last night she had muttered something about 'waiting a little bit to see'. She was proving wonderful company, mainly through her shared love of silence in the right places. She too was working on a book but she refused to let him see it yet. She worked on it in the afternoons while he was taking constitutional walks along the cliff paths and she worked on it far into the night. He could lie in bed watching the glow of light from her bedshelf across his open doorway and hear her sigh and turn pages. A lot of brown paper parcels had been arriving for her at the post office and seemed to be full of photocopies of erotic or downright disgusting drawings.

When Evan telephoned Jeremy to say that he had arrived safely and why and how he was not alone, his agent could hardly believe his luck. Apparently she had become a potent fantasy figure on the literary agency lunch circuit and all the Jeremies had been praying that she would wander into their offices and ask to be represented. Watching her lying on her back on the grass outside to watch the sunset, Evan had told his agent that she seemed to be working on something faintly scandalous and that he'd let him know when she'd finished whatever it was so that he could pounce.

He threw down his pen and stretched, tipping back his chair on the daisy-flecked turf. Madeleine let her busy hands sink to her lap and looked across to him. She smiled, the sun in her unbrushed hair.

'How's it coming on?' she asked.

'Great. I think. A bit odd but it's bound to be as it's new. How's the bootee?'

'Sod off. The wool's gone all grey. I think, when the Thing arrives, I shall dress it all in black with maybe some rubber accessories.'

'I'm sure if you let slip to Mrs Rees, she'd have all the charitable women of St Merrots knitting for you.'

'I'm not a charity. Anyway I enjoy knitting; it's just a long time since I last had a go.'

'You never give up, do you?'

'No. The meddlesome priest said it was part of my "bulldog charm".'

Evan flipped his exercise book shut and watched a distant fishing boat drift.

'How does a spot of cold ravioli grab you?' he asked.

'I thought we were going to start being healthy for the Thing's sake.'

'We are. Eventually. Do *you* feel like chopping up vegetables?'

'Not a lot,' she confessed.

'I'll get the tin opener.'

'No. My turn,' she said, lurching upright with a grunt and tossing the knitting disgustedly into the chair behind her. As she passed him she stopped to rest a hand on his shoulder. 'Present for you,' she said and solemnly laid a handkerchief before him. It was neatly ironed and white with a little F and a soldier embroidered in one corner.

'Why thank you,' he said, nonplussed but charmed. He turned round. 'What's the F stand for? Fitzpatrick?'

'No,' she said quietly and walked into the cottage.

'Fornicators?' he shouted.

'No,' she called back, clinking plates.

'Friends?' he asked, too quietly for her to hear. He sighed and opened his exercise book again. He scanned the paragraph he had just finished and made a rapid improvement. *Towards a New Mythology* had been donated to the waiting room on Haverfordwest Station and Evan had asked Jeremy to find him no more reviewing work until further notice. In his late forties and to Jeremy's thinly-veiled alarm, he had embarked on his first novel. Despite the letter that had come from Dawn Harper his present idyll was overshadowed by dreams that crept up on him nightly; dreams in which the corpse of a wild-haired child rose up through bubbling soil in a rain-churned flower bed. He had never told, would never speak of what he had seen in Mercy Merluza's garden, but he hoped that by writing a narrative that offered an explanation for it he might rid his nights of the child. Sometimes, when there was a wind to lift a spray off the waves, salt splashes landed on the paper and made the ink run.

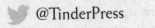